About the Author

Ste Sharp studied Evolutionary Biology at Sheffield University and is the lead singer/guitarist of indie-band Atlas, so considers himself a rock'n'roll scientist at heart. When he's not writing fantastical adventures, Ste wrestles computers and lives in Suffolk with his wife and two sons.

DARWIN'S SOLDIERS

DARWIN'S SOLDIERS

BOOK ONE OF THE ORIGIN TRILOGY

STE SHARP

Unbound Digital

This edition first published in 2018

Unbound

6th Floor Mutual House, 70 Conduit Street, London W1S 2GF

www.unbound.com

ISBN (eBook): 978-1-912618-11-8
ISBN (Paperback): 978-1-912618-10-1

Design by Mecob

Cover images:

Printed and bound in Great Britain by Clays Ltd, Elcograf S.p.A.

For Christine and David Knowles, for raising the most beautiful woman in the world.
And to Mum and Dad, for your endless support.

Dear Reader,

The book you are holding came about in a rather different way to most others. It was funded directly by readers through a new website: Unbound.

Unbound is the creation of three writers. We started the company because we believed there had to be a better deal for both writers and readers. On the Unbound website, authors share the ideas for the books they want to write directly with readers. If enough of you support the book by pledging for it in advance, we produce a beautifully bound special subscribers' edition and distribute a regular edition and e-book wherever books are sold, in shops and online.

This new way of publishing is actually a very old idea (Samuel Johnson funded his dictionary this way). We're just using the internet to build each writer a network of patrons. Here, at the back of this book, you'll find the names of all the people who made it happen.

Publishing in this way means readers are no longer just passive consumers of the books they buy, and authors are free to write the books they really want. They get a much fairer return too – half the profits their books generate, rather than a tiny percentage of the cover price.

If you're not yet a subscriber, we hope that you'll want to join our publishing revolution and have your name listed in one of our books in the future. To get you started, here is a £5 discount on your first pledge. Just visit unbound.com, make your pledge and type JOHNGREENE18 in the promo code box when you check out.

Thank you for your support,

Dan, Justin and John
Founders, Unbound

Super Patrons

Joanne Aguilar-Millan
David Allington
Lynette Allison
Joe Bailey
Ian Baker
Martin Banham
Matthew Barnard
Samantha Blackwell-Heard
Colin Bottle
Peter Breeden
Kate Bulpitt
Andy Checker
Eddie Cook
Dave Cottrell
Anna Crickmore
Tanya Daniels
Simon Darnell
Steve Davis
Simon Deacon
James Dee
Sarab Dogra
Jason Edmonds
Matt & Em & Luc & Erin
Ian Farrell
Adam Ferjani
Martin Gay
William Goodey
Angus Gormley
Mike Griffiths
Steve Harris
Purdie N Harris
Mark Hendle

Matt Holmes
Stephen Hoppé
Michael Hunt
Deborah Hutchings
Jean-Michel Jack
Colin James
Kerensa Jennings
Mark Kemp
Dan Kieran
Chris Knowles
David & Chris Knowles
Kerry Leatherdale
Claire Longhurst
Wayne Longhurst
Eric Mason
Tim May
John Mitchinson
Chandra Mukherjee
Sonya O'Reilly
Mark Oakes
shenaz Oreeawon
Sheryll Osbiston
Casey Pearce
Marnie & Phill
Andrew Pirie
Justin Pollard
Tracy Potter
Andrew Pound
Donald Proud
Claire Pulford
Darwin Rain O'Donnell
Paul Riley
Simon Roper
Jasmine Rowe
Donna Rustage
Cath Sharp

Ste Sharp
Roger Sidwell
Smudge
Roy Stordy
Paul Swales
Richard Taylor
Vanessa Ward
Jay & Danny Ward
Trevor Warren
Paul Weekes
Maureen Weekes
Tom Weldon
James Wells
Carol Willis
Lee Wilson
Amanda Witham
Nick Wray
Drew Wright
Richard Wright

Chapter 1

Private John Greene of the Royal Fusiliers stumbled through the dim forest with the Lewis light machine gun held tight across his chest and his khaki bags strapped across both shoulders. He shifted his gun, wondering why it was called 'light' when it was three times the weight of his old Lee Enfield rifle.

The trees grew less dense the higher he got, giving him a view of the sky but little else, so he pushed on, determined to find a viewpoint to look for buildings or landmarks he recognised. This didn't look like Flanders though, he thought. It smelt different too, like a wet dog's blanket.

Last thing he could remember was defending his trench, manning his gun with its bipod propped on sand bags, spraying bullets at the line of Germans crossing no-man's-land – then a blinding flash of light, and he was here. Was he behind enemy lines? Or maybe he'd been gassed? Gas would explain why the clouds were green, he thought.

He jumped on a rock to scout ahead.

Nothing.

As he turned to get down, he slipped.

'Bugger it!' His bags clattered against the rock and images flashed before his eyes: explosions ripping up the ground; bodies in the mud; a pile of bloody sheets. He tried to force the images out of his head by focusing on his son, Joe. Joe singing nursery rhymes.

Lying on the ground, John pulled a worn photo from his pocket – Rosie – wrinkled his nose and whispered, almost in prayer, 'I must be strong.' He pictured little Joe running up to greet him, let out a sigh, got back up. Come on, he told himself, you can walk back. Done it before, eh?

It had taken John weeks to get used to life on the front line. At first he'd welcomed the distraction of digging latrines and laying wire – it took his mind off Joe and the loss of Rosie. Every job drained him so when he rested, whether it was on a pallet or against a mud wall, he always found sleep.

Then the artillery had started. The attacks and counter-attacks. Men died, horses died. Charges were made over the top and whole platoons didn't come back. When John saw the damage a sniper's bullet or mortar shell could do, the fear set in. The charges, retreats and the switch from the front line to the reserve trenches became routine, but every time he rotated back to the front line, every explosion and rifle shot picked and gnawed at John's nerves. He knew it was the fear that would kill him in the end, just like it had Johnson.

None of it compared to his night in the crater though.

He stopped walking. Was that someone shouting?

'Miks?' the voice shouted again, clearer this time.

John lowered his gun, checked the disc-like magazine was clipped in.

'Miks nuud?' the man called out.

After months in the Belgian trenches and villages, John had learnt a bit of French and German – even Flemish – but he didn't recognise this language.

John backed away further then heard a new voice. He crouched and froze. Another voice rang out from further away… and another. They multiplied, coming from every direction: new languages; odd-sounding languages; some desperate; others angry. John shook his head and breathed in deeply to control his panic. He had to stay strong.

The shouts and calls were merging into one sound, reminding him of the noisy rookery next to the farm where he'd been stationed. Focus on Joe, he told himself. He pictured his son playing with a wooden train. Joe had just turned two when he'd left for the war. He remembered the day he caught the bus to East Ham to sign up for Kitchener's army. Pictured his parents holding Joe, standing proudly outside their greengrocer's shop in Whitechapel, alongside John's grandfather. John flinched. He didn't miss his grandfather: sitting in his fireside armchair, barking orders like he was still in the army.

John's hand clasped the tin soldier on the cord around his neck, and he closed his eyes to picture the *Greene's Fruiterer and Grocer* sign above the family shop, the pyramids of fruit and veg. The place had been a sight for sore eyes after a day of deliveries with the old horse, Jess, and her cart. What he wouldn't give to see it now!

'If you're not sure what you need to do, lad,' John's father often said, 'take the time to think it through. And if you're going to do anything important, make sure you've been to the lavvy first.'

John laughed. Alright then. He put his gun on the floor, found a tree and unbuttoned his flies.

As he relieved himself, he tried to make sense of where he was. He hadn't seen any other soldiers, just heard foreign shouting, so... had he somehow strayed behind enemy lines?

He stared up at the green-tinged sky and wondered if he would ever make it back home. What would happen to Joe if he never made it back? John's parents would look after him, of course, but the boy needed his father, especially without a mother. And what about home? Would he ever see Woolwich Arsenal get back into the First Division? Or have another lock-in at the King's Head?

John shook his head. He'd just been knocked out and left behind, that was all. I'll get my bearings, he thought, be back with the lads in time for tea. He ignored the shouts echoing through the forest and made his way along a dry stream bed.

He shifted the position of his gun to give his arms a rest, but he'd never carried it this far before and soon had to stop for a rest. The Lewis gun wasn't like the Vickers machine guns they had built into the trenches – this new American automatic rifle was just a few inches longer than the Lee Enfield rifle he'd been issued with during training but weighed a damn sight more. He stretched his back. If he wasn't... *wherever* he was, he could unclip the magazine fixed to the top or strip off the barrel shroud – thick as the pipe on the back of his mother's kitchen stove, he thought. Right now, that didn't seem wise.

John picked his gun up but had only made a few steps when a noise in the branches above stopped him.

'Who's there?' he shouted, spotting a shape in the tree and following it as it jumped down through the branches.

'Name yourself!' John shouted. He checked his magazine again and pulled the gun up to aim as a man dropped to the ground, half naked and covered in paint, yelling as he landed.

'Prohiba!'

John stood his ground.

'Prohiba homusionem!' The man's wild eyes widened as he jabbed a three-pronged spear at John.

John was too confused to be scared. Who was this nutter? He smiled.

'Ego ridiculam?' the man barked.

John thought he recognised some of the words… was that Italian the man was babbling in?

'Sorry, mate, I don't understand you.' John lowered his machine gun and tried some French. 'Je ne comprend pas.'

'Quid agis homusionem?' the man barked, hopping from foot to foot in his sandals.

'Listen, I don't understand you. I'm just trying to get back… home.' John's shoulders dropped: he'd had enough of this war.

The painted man stared at John and twisted his head in a manner that unnerved him. He'd seen it before: a lad in his battalion, Johnson, had lost all emotion: no smile; no fear. The next day he bayonetted his commanding officer, and was shot running across no-man's-land in his underpants.

'Tim-entes?' the man growled and took a step forward.

'Oi, don't you try nothing!' John said and took a step back.

He could see now it wasn't paint the man was covered in but tattoos. Maybe he was lost as well, John thought.

The man growled and jabbed at John's head with his trident.

'Bollocks to this.' John slipped the safety off and fired a burst of bullets into the dirt, showering the painted man with earth.

John was used to firing the gun on its built-in bipod, not holding it loose, so the power of the shots sent him stumbling backwards over a branch. The noise of the gun reverberated around the forest, silencing the nearest shouts, but John didn't care, he'd heard it a thousand times before and by the time he was back on his feet, the man had gone.

'Yeah, fuck off, you nutter!' John shouted, feeling a surge of energy rush through him.

He took a second to calm his breathing and realised, now it was quiet again, that he could hear bells ringing in the distance. He resumed his walk, aiming for the bells, and soon spotted a black object on the grassy crown of the hill. John stood on the forest edge watching people coming out of the woods, heading for the hill's crown. Who were they?

Tentatively, John stepped into the open to join what looked like other soldiers. They were all armed. Some carried guns, others held swords or spears and most wore armour. He recognised one man's blue coat with red collars and cuffs from a book his grandfather kept by his armchair – a Russian infantryman from the Crimean war. He's long dead, John thought. So did that mean he had died as well? Was this... some kind of soldier heaven?

John felt dizzy, leant on his gun. I have to get out of here, he thought. Somewhere safe. He was turning to go back into the forest when the thought came to him: but if I'm dead... maybe Rosie's here too? But where were his mates from the Thirty-second and the soldiers who had died at Transloy? Where were all the Huns he'd shot from the crater? John hadn't seen one uniform from Flanders yet – friend or foe.

A bemused look crept across his face as new warriors came into view, some he recognised from his grandfather's old books – a Roman centurion with a rectangular shield and a Mongol archer – and others he didn't – a bronze-armoured spearman and a tall African warrior holding an incredibly long spear.

Has the gas sent me doolally? John wondered.

Scores of soldiers weighed up their nearest neighbours with scorn or derision. Some fought and some talked. The warriors from ancient times inspected their neighbour's weapons with confusion, while modern soldiers eyed their ancestors with suspicion, fearing a practical joke. They were all heading to the summit, towards the black tip, which wasn't a building after all, John realised, but an obelisk, like Cleopatra's Needle back home by the Thames, only this one looked to be covered in white markings of some sort. Was that writing?

John stopped, turned his head like a deer sensing a predator. He'd heard someone speaking English.

'Hello?' He turned to locate the voice, staring at the people around him, but the voice came and went.

'Station command... Delta... read me?'

John stepped through the crowd.

'Can you read me?' the American voice was clear now.

John saw movement inside a grove of blue-leaved trees and pulled the branches back to see a crouching man speaking to his wrist.

'Do you copy?' the man sounded anxious.

John studied him before venturing any nearer. He wore a skin-tight grey suit, a shiny helmet and a small backpack. No weapon? John relaxed: this man was the least dangerous person he'd seen yet – maybe he was a communication officer?

'Station command, this is Delta-Six. I repeat: the enemy have transported me to an unknown location. Positioning systems down. No satellites or orbit stations located. I may be under sedation or captured in a virtual world. I will make contact on the hour, every hour. Delta-Six, out.'

'I was starting to think I was the only English speaker around here!' John's throat felt dry.

Delta-Six jumped to his feet and strode over, pointing his clenched fist at John. 'Stay there,' he demanded.

'Oh... I guess I can't look too friendly walking round with a machine gun, can I?' John froze as Delta-Six turned a blue torch on him.

'Where are you from?' the American snapped mechanically.

'Whitechapel, London but...'

'No. Where *exactly* have you come from?'

Delta-Six loomed over John, but he was used to people being taller than him.

'Well, Belgium – Flanders.'

'When?'

'Nineteen Seventeen, April the...'

Delta-Six sniffed and walked out of the trees.

'Wait! Where are you going?' John shouted, fumbling through the branches and back into the open. 'Stop! Oi – just tell me where we are... you're the only bloody one who speaks English...' Swinging his gun under his arm, John chased the American. 'Wait!' He reached out but as he touched the man's shoulder an electric shock blasted through his hand and everything went dark.

Delta-Six's face came into focus. 'At least my auto-defence still works.'

John rubbed his eyes and blinked, then looked at the red patch on his palm where he'd been shocked.

'All I want to know is why I'm here,' he said.

Delta-Six spoke slowly – 'I can't trust you. You may be my enemy' – and walked away.

'Great,' John said.

Keeping his distance, John cradled his gun and sighed when he pressed his burnt hand on the cool metal to soothe it. He followed Delta-Six to the black obelisk and watched him circle the stone, side-stepping the ever-growing crowd of warriors who gazed up at the brilliant-white carvings.

'Some kind of archaic script,' John heard Delta-Six mutter as he passed.

'What does it say?' John asked, but was ignored.

An inquisitive Arab, dressed in scarlet robes and a maroon turban, tried talking to John, apparently mesmerised by his machine gun. 'Get off!' John pulled it back. The Arab turned to Delta-Six and shouted, as though giving him an order, but was ignored by him too. John studied him: a lethal-looking curved sword swayed within his robes and his furrowed brow reminded him of the old, fierce French teacher at his school – Monsieur Boivin. How had he managed to dye his beard red? he wondered.

In the distance, a clash of steel rang out and the cry of a dying soldier signalled the end of another feud.

John could feel the pressure building. 'Delta-Six!' he shouted. 'What does it say?' He stood in the tall man's path, careful not to touch him this time.

Delta-Six frowned and looked down. 'My systems don't recognise the code.'

John squinted. 'But you must know something. I mean, why are we here?'

'No, I–'

'Humans,' a resonant voice silenced him. 'You are the chosen. You are the supreme warriors of your species.'

Heads turned. Everyone appeared to understand the voice, which was odd, John thought, because it was speaking plain English.

'Those who stand against you fall in great numbers and those who fight alongside you pale into insignificance.'

The crowd parted and the speaker appeared: his eyes fixed on the obelisk as he walked. He was short, like John, and wore layers of rough, brown material with his face hidden beneath a hood.

'You are challenged to reach the silver gates within the next fourteen days.'

Delta-Six scanned the man as he passed.

'Follow the path which leads to growth, strength and endurance and you will achieve victory.' The newcomer pulled his hood back to reveal a bearded face. Although his red hair was free of grey streaks, the wrinkles around his eyes suggested he was older than fifty. 'This is what the inscription states,' he said and pointed at the obelisk.

The Red Arab moved forward and asked the newcomer a question, to which he replied, 'I am Althorn and, like you, I have been taken by the gods and deposited here on this wild hillside.'

The Red Arab nodded.

'You speak English?' John's question was lost in a cacophony of other questions.

Althorn raised his hands and tried to answer each question, but no matter the language of the question, his reply was always in English.

A warrior with a long spear and red cloak asked a question.

'The writing says we are challenged to reach the silver gates,' Althorn answered.

A man with a silver helmet and short sword shouted another question.

'I haven't brought you here. I heard your questions and read the script for you.'

The crowd grew aggressive as, like John, they only understood the answers, not the original questions.

'A Bronze Age warrior,' John heard Delta-Six say, 'but able to communicate with everyone. How can you read the script, if nobody else can?' Delta-Six asked.

Althorn shrugged. 'I have been taken from my land and brought here. I know nothing else.'

A man in a black uniform with a red armband pushed forward, shouting what John recognised as German.

'As I said, the writing–' Althorn began to reply but Delta-Six moved in and touched the German on the shoulder, where a tiny spark flashed and the man collapsed into a pile of fine powder.

Those nearest stepped back and gripped their weapons a little tighter.

'The laws of physics must be distorted,' Delta-Six whispered. He turned to Althorn. 'Where are you from?'

'I am Althorn of the Careni people, south of the mountains. I am a… soldier for hire.'

'Hey buddy! What the hell's going on here?' A short, butch man in a dark-green uniform pushed his way through the crowd.

John smiled. 'Another American? I'm John.'

'Hey, a Limey! Christ, who isn't here? I'm Crossley – what's going on?' He puffed on a cigarette as he spoke.

Delta-Six shook his head. 'A Second World War marine? It's just too perfect to be real.' He asked Althorn, 'How can you understand all these languages?'

'I don't know,' Althorn frowned.

'What language do you speak?' Delta-Six asked.

'Careni,' Althorn replied. 'But I know a few words of–'

'Have you consumed anything since arriving here?' Delta-Six asked.

'I have eaten these.' Althorn pulled a few mushrooms from a bag. 'From down by the tree line.' Althorn pointed to the purple-leaved trees fringing the hilltop. 'Would you like one?'

Delta-Six declined.

A tall man, with a broadsword swinging by his side, pushed through the crowd. Although he wore no armour, John assumed by the emblem on his tunic he was a knight. The handsome man picked a mushroom from Althorn, chewed and swallowed. He stared at the crowd with a look of annoyance. 'Well? How am I to know if the bloody thing has worked if nobody speaks to me?'

The soldiers erupted into a volley of cheerful shouts as they clearly understood every word the knight had spoken.

'God be praised – it worked,' he laughed.

Althorn looked relieved. 'And now we have another translator.'

John saw men run off to find mushrooms of their own, but stayed put as the knight handed out Althorn's mushrooms. He smiled as a tall archer with an athletic figure strode up to the knight.

'It is my pleasure to serve such a beautiful lady, ma'am.' The knight bowed and offered her a mushroom.

John couldn't help but stare at her curved body.

'Pretty fine lady, eh?' Crossley said. He was probably the only person short enough for John to talk to eye to eye. 'I wouldn't try anything with her though.'

'What? Why?' John felt himself blushing.

'That Amazon's more tiger than princess, believe me.'

'Really?'

'I saw some Frenchy trying to get his way with her,' Crossley said. 'She had a knife at his balls quicker than you could blink.' He nodded at three men. 'See?'

John caught a glimpse of a soldier in a blue tunic, limping and sporting a black eye. 'I–'

A distant explosion made them turn and John saw a leg fall from the sky, shortly followed by another explosion and an acrid smell John recognised as burnt flesh. He felt the urge to fall to the floor and had one hand on his gas bag. The men and women around him had raised their shields or stared at the forest, while others were running away.

'There are some orange toadstools in the woods,' Althorn said and rolled up his sleeve to reveal a nasty rash on his forearm, 'but these men do know how to check their food, don't they?'

John squinted at the rash. He knew of poisonous toadstools but how could one explode?

'I gotta get my hands on some of those!' Crossley said, then asked, 'But are these 'shrooms worth all this? I mean, why can't us English-speaking boys just stick together, right?'

'Communication can be more important than any weapon you wield,' the tall archer said.

'Hah!' Crossley shook his head, then did a double take. 'Those things really work?' He took a mushroom and looked at John.

'I guess things can't get much worse,' John said and popped a piece into his mouth. He waited a few anxious seconds before what sounded like a distant biplane crossed behind him and the murmur of voices transformed into a muddle of English. He clasped his hands over his ears. It sounded like everyone was talking to him. He looked at Crossley, who was smiling.

'Amazing!'

Tensions eased as the warriors talked to one another.

John spotted Delta-Six on the edge of the crowd and joined him. 'What are you doing?'

'I'm getting out of here.' Delta-Six pointed to a range of golden-coloured hills. 'To the silver gates and back to my war where I'm needed.'

John frowned. 'You *want* to go back to your war?'

Delta-Six connected a yellow tube to his streamlined backpack. 'I'm sure I could help, but my protocol dictates I leave. I have no choice.' He stepped away. 'So long.'

Hot vapour streamed out of the backpack, pushing Delta-Six into the air and away from the hill, painting a white trail behind him.

'But we need your help!' John shouted, as he and hundreds of pairs of eyes watched their best hope of survival disappear.

John looked at the obelisk. 'Well I'll be damned!'

The script which snaked up the black stone was in English now. At least it was to his eyes:

Humans. You are the chosen ones. You are the supreme warriors of your species. Those who stand against you fall in great numbers and those who fight alongside you pale into insignificance. You are challenged to reach the silver gates within the next fourteen days. Follow the path which leads to growth, strength and endurance and you will achieve victory.

John stroked the letters but flinched: he had white sores on his palm and fingers where he'd been shocked by Delta-Six. He found a rock to sit on and leant his gun against his leg so he could soothe his hand on its cold metal.

'So what do we do now?' a swordsman in chainmail asked. 'And do we get paid when we get to the gates?'

Althorn shrugged, pulled up his hood and stepped away.

'Who's in charge?' someone asked.

The calm created by the effects of the mushrooms began to erode as each person's anxieties and frustrations crept back.

The Arab with the red beard was questioning a rifleman. 'Where are these silver gates?'

'Delta-Six knew where the gates are,' John said quietly.

'We've only got fourteen days!' a Roman said. 'What happens after that?'

John tried again. 'Delta-Six knew the way to the silver gates.' But nobody heard him. He thought about giving a burst from his gun to get some attention, but it was a bit risky with the swords, axes and other deadly implements around.

His grandfather's face popped into his head. 'Stop being an imbecile and speak up, boy!'

'I know where the gates are!' John shouted and everyone turned to him.

'Do you?' Althorn asked.

John swallowed. 'Yes. Well, Delta-Six said he was heading for them – past the golden hills.' He pointed.

Althorn smiled. 'So we know our direction.'

'So we just start walking?' the Red Arab asked. 'What about supplies?'

And the arguments grew again.

'That Delta-Six was probably a decoy anyway. Set up by whoever put us here,' Crossley said.

'Should we wait for nightfall to see the stars?' the tall knight said.

'Then we could just find our way home, couldn't we?' said a rough voice, and John pictured the tattooed man with the trident. He daren't turn around in case the man recognised him.

'You can try walking back to where you came from,' Crossley said with a snigger.

'My home was destroyed by the Romans,' the man sounded as menacing as John remembered, 'they sowed salt in our fields, killed our elderly and took us into slavery… they made me fight for their entertainment.'

'Sounds shitty,' Crossley said. 'Really… but I don't give a damn. Walk wherever you want to.'

John took a peek: it was the same man, standing ten paces from Crossley with his trident lowered.

'Do not poke fun at me, little man. I am Sakarbaal of Carthage.'

'I'm not poking fun, I just–' Crossley stood with hands on hips. 'Hey, if I wanted to poke fun at you, I'd ask about your tattoos. I mean, seriously? What's with all those?'

'I will skewer you, little man,' the gladiator stepped closer.

Crossley stood his ground. 'You want to kill me with your oversized fork just because I don't like your body paint?'

'This fork will tear a hole from your arse to your mouth, you little–'

'Okay, now you're being offensive.' Crossley pulled a shiny revolver from his holster and cocked it. 'I'm only two inches shorter than average.' He aimed the gun at the gladiator's head. 'One more step and I'll put a hole through your head.'

Sakarbaal of Carthage paused.

'Oh, you've seen a gun before, eh?' Crossley was smiling.

A crowd was building around them.

John stepped forward and the man's wild eyes flicked to him. He sneered as he recognised John. 'You little men with your pissy weapons are like children. When you fight like real men, I will have respect for you.' He spat on the ground and walked off.

Crossley turned to John and tucked his gun away. 'You and him had previous?' he asked.

'You could say that,' John tapped his machine gun.

'I've got a feeling this whole hill's full of muscleheads like that – we'd better watch our backs.' Crossley held his hand out. 'You're John, right?'

'John Greene.' John shook the American's hand but winced and pulled away. 'Shit,' he said and looked at his burnt palm.

'Sorry, buddy!' Crossley looked at the burn. 'Jeez, you need to get something on that.'

'No, it'll be alright,' John replied and pressed on his cool gun, sure it would heal in its own time.

'Why *should* we go to the silver gates?' a Spartan with long hair asked as John joined the circle that had formed around the obelisk to become the soldiers' forum.

'I don't think we have a choice,' the knight replied.

'I don't see much point staying on this hill,' a spearman added.

'Maybe we should stop thinking about where we want to go,' all eyes turned to a bronze-armoured warrior, 'and decide *how* we will get to these silver gates.'

'What do you mean, Persian?' asked the knight.

The man paused before answering. 'My name is Samas and I am from Babylon – I fight for the Persian Empire, but I am not Persian.'

'Very well, Babylonian – but why do you ask *how* we should travel?'

Samas straightened his back. 'This is a strange land. There are dangers here.' He pointed his spear at the dark woodland. 'Look at what happened with the toadstools. We must decide whether to travel as one or to journey in smaller groups – ensuring some will make it through.'

'If we split up and travel in the same direction we will get in each other's way.' The Red Arab spoke with a deep voice. 'Resources might be scarce… food, water and so on.'

'So we go at different times,' Crossley said. 'Personally I'd rather go now and get a camp set up before whatever comes out at night finds us unprepared!'

'No,' the Red Arab replied. 'We would travel faster in the cool of the night.'

Arguments broke out throughout the group and John looked around, bemused by the sight of so many diverse people arguing fluently in the same tongue. A huge Maori with a tattooed face argued with an Asian spearman adorned in jewelled armour, while a Roman soldier was having none of a medieval lancer's suggestions.

'Quiet, quiet! People! Let's have some order!' A commanding voice drew everyone's attention. 'Thank you!'

A tall, slim soldier stepped onto a rock, wearing a suit of armour marked with what John recognised as Chinese symbols. This had to be another soldier from the future like Delta-Six, John thought. A headpiece covered the soldier's face but the voice was louder than John had expected and distorted like when his officers used megaphones to shout along their trench during bombardments. 'We must keep order if we are going to succeed in our mission. I suggest everyone who wishes to travel at night moves to this side,' an arm gestured to the right, 'and by day to this side.'

After a few mumbles, the rabble steadily split in two with an equal split of eighty warriors moving to each side, leaving a scattering of unsure warriors in the middle – including John – and one Japanese samurai who simply walked away, choosing to go it alone into the forest, it seemed.

Crossley caught John's eye. 'What's the point in choosing a group anyway?'

John shrugged. 'Safety in numbers?'

'Maybe.' Crossley tilted his head. 'But I'm outta here the first chance I get.'

'How will you get home?' John asked and shook his head when Crossley offered him a cigarette. He'd tried a few with the lads in the trenches but they just made him cough.

Crossley shrugged and lit his. 'Who knows? The whole thing's screwy if you ask me.' He gestured at the men and women surrounding them. 'They can't be real, right?'

John answered truthfully, 'I don't know.' He'd accepted what was going on just like when Rosie died and when he'd been stationed in the trenches: he felt numb and just got on with it.

'So, you got a home to get back to?' Crossley asked.

'Yes.' John thought of Joe's cheeky face and smiled. 'I've got a son.' He pictured Joe tearing about the family shop, weaving in and out of the piles of veg or jumping up for a cuddle when he came back from his deliveries.

John pulled out the tin soldier around his neck. 'I bought him this in a Calais market. When I get back to London I'll give it to him.'

'London? Jeez...' Crossley exhaled a puff of smoke. 'That place took a helluva pasting from the Luftwaffe. I met a Limey who told me his whole neighbourhood got flattened in one raid. One raid! Some ammunitions factory.'

'Really?' John frowned. 'I didn't hear about it. I heard some Zeppelins had gone over but–'

'Zeppelins?' Crossley laughed. 'Hell, no! Bombers – you know, Junkers and Dorniers? Five-hundred-pound bombs – thousand-pound bombs.' He stopped and looked John up and down. 'I thought your kit was old but...' he pointed to one of John's bags, '...gas mask, right?'

John pulled out the cloth head sack with two glass discs and mouthpiece. 'Only used it twice.'

Crossley nodded and took a drag on his cigarette. 'So you're fighting the Great War, right?'

'Yes,' John replied.

'Well I'm fighting in the Great War's bastard son. The Second World War we call it... for now anyways. About twenty years after your war, it all flared up again.' Crossley raised his eyebrows. 'Germans.'

'But... our war was the war to end all wars.' John's voice trailed off and he took a sip from his canteen. 'Did we lose?'

'Oh no, we won alright – just didn't do a good enough job of it.' Crossley shook his head. 'Plus this time the Italians joined in, and the Japanese.'

John took a deep breath. It had all been for nothing then: his friends blown to pieces; the civilians killed in their homes; the men he'd killed from the crater.

'So your wife'll be waiting back in London with your son?' Crossley asked.

'Joe's there, but Rosie... er, no.' John felt the familiar chill run through his stomach as he pictured Rosie's dead body. 'She died.' He pictured Rosie's face, the way she smiled every time he took her back to the Chapel music hall where they first met; the white lace in her hair on their wedding day; the way she had rested her hand on her pregnant belly. He remembered Joe as a helpless newborn and the days and nights John had spent desperately trying to feed him with one of the new bottles with rubber teats his father had managed to get hold of.

'Shit, I'm sorry,' Crossley said and patted John on the shoulder.

The affection nearly made John cry but he turned a sniff into a cough.

'April the Fifteenth, 1912,' John said.

Saying the exact date made it feel less real for some reason, like it was part of history now.

'Hey, I know that date – Titanic, right?' Crossley said. 'Shit. Must have been awful.'

'No, I...' John looked at Crossley to tell him the truth but the Chinese soldier was speaking again.

'Quiet! Thank you. Now we need a spokesman to talk to these abstainers.'

John and Crossley were in the minority: just twenty soldiers waited to choose their side.

For those wanting to travel by night, the Red Arab stepped forward, while the handsome knight, who introduced himself as Sir William Lavalle, stepped forward for the day travellers.

'Just like being at school waiting to be picked for footy,' John joked.

'Yeah, only this time we're the ones choosing,' Crossley whispered back.

The Arab spoke first. 'I am Mihran ibn al-Hassan.' He paused and John wondered if he should know his name. 'Under the cover of darkness, we will be hidden from our enemy's eyes and we will travel faster when the temperature is coolest.' He spoke calmly. 'Travelling at night is the obvious choice.'

Nods and jeers behind him showed his group's approval.

Next came Sir William. 'We should not challenge the natural order of things – we work in the day and sleep at night. If we travel in daylight we will see our enemy and defend ourselves better.' The day group chanted their support. 'And it would be easier to lose our way when travelling at night.'

John still didn't know which group to choose.

'Who do *you* choose?' a tin-helmeted soldier asked the Chinese soldier.

'I choose night.' The future soldier jumped off the rock and walked to Mihran, the Red Arab.

For some, that was enough.

John looked at both sides, weighing them up: Night had Samas, the Chinese soldier and Mihran, while Day had Sir William, the huge Maori and Althorn in its ranks.

A shudder ran through John as an image of the war he'd left behind appeared in his mind: explosions lighting up the night sky and screams in the dark. His worst times had come during the night. He caught a glimpse of Sakarbaal, the tattooed warrior, in the night group, who fixed his eyes on John and drew a line across his neck.

'Day Watch, definitely Day Watch,' John said and stepped over to Sir William's side.

'We need a leader.' Sir William Lavalle towered over John and Crossley as he addressed the newly formed group of nearly ninety soldiers.

'Althorn is the best choice,' the tattooed Maori said.

'He should have the final say in any decision,' agreed a blue-turbaned fighter who cleaned a long curved sword.

Althorn shook his head. 'I'm not a leader – I can't make decisions for us all.'

'What about Sir William?' the Amazon archer said. 'He has shown the courage of a chief.'

The handsome knight shook his head. 'No, we are all equals here, in this unknown territory.'

'Yeah,' Crossley joined in. 'We should all have our say.'

Many in the group nodded.

'So how do we decide?' John asked.

'We wait for the right leader to emerge,' Sir William said. 'The Lord will show us who should lead.'

'Or we cast votes when we need a decision?' the Maori suggested.

'And we go with the most votes?' Sir William asked.

'That's democracy…' Crossley quipped.

'I'm happy with that,' Althorn said.

'I'm not sure,' the Amazon shook her head.

'It will work for now, sweetheart,' Crossley said. 'So shouldn't we get a move on?'

'Not before we have our rules.' Sir William looked stern. 'We need guidelines on how our group should behave in combat and how we vote to make our decisions...'

As the conversation drifted off, so did John. He rubbed his palm, which still ached, and watched the Night Watch, who had set up camp and now talked in a huddle.

'What happened to your hand?'

John turned to see Althorn.

'I burnt it,' John said, and showed him the white blisters on his palm.

Althorn studied it and said, 'Keep it cool and it should heal itself.'

'I can try,' John said and placed his palm on the metal of his gun.

Someone was shouting in their direction and John turned.

'You! With the...'

'Gun.'

'Yes, you with the gun!' Sir William pointed at John. 'How do you vote – quick march, steady or alternating?'

John felt the weight of his gun and bags. 'Steady,' he answered.

'Alternating,' a blue-suited rifleman said.

'Steady,' Althorn said.

'Steady march it is then,' Sir William concluded. 'Best to be wary at this stage, I agree.'

'So, can we go now?' Crossley asked with raised eyebrows. 'Or do we have to vote on which foot we step with first?' He laughed and walked down the hill into the forest.

Chapter 2

As the Day Watch left the obelisk hill, Mihran ibn al-Hassan studied his companions – the Night Watch – as they set up camp around the obelisk. It was clear there would be a power struggle here. Everyone would want power, or so he'd thought.

'I am Field Officer Li, and I cannot assume the role of leader.' The Eastern soldier had been a popular choice. 'I have no experience of coordinating such a large group.'

'But you are from an advanced age,' a leather-clad archer said. 'You have more knowledge than any of us here.'

'That is true,' Li replied. 'I know how each of your empires flourished and died, I know the history of your nations and the battles your people won and lost – but I have never led soldiers.' The shiny face shield remained down, which distorted Li's voice. 'Personally, I would never choose an inexperienced chief over a battle-hardened captain.'

Several men nodded and Mihran held back the questions he longed to ask about the empire his army had been building.

'How about the white-haired one?' A warrior with an obsidian club pointed to the tallest man in the group.

All eyes turned to the blond man, who puffed his chest out and tried to look serious.

'Why?' a man with an incredibly long bow asked. 'He looks like a thug if you ask me.'

'He is the only race here I recognise,' he shrugged. 'I trust him.'

The big man looked confused and asked, 'How does he recognise me?'

'Vikings from the settlement of Vinland made contact with the late Mayan Empire,' Li said, 'and early Aztec culture – two rotted boat hulls and at least one gene can be traced through the –' Li paused, then said, 'Your ancestors may have met.'

Mihran nodded. After the discussion he intended to have a long talk with Li to understand who these people were and what a gene was.

'So who *wants* to be leader then?' the bowman asked. 'Surely it would be easier to sort things out that way?'

Samas, the Babylonian, stepped forward in his shining bronze armour. 'I am a captain – I can lead us.'

Mihran sneered at the foot soldier but could tell by the faces around him this was a man they would follow.

'I have led men into battle and fought side by side with them,' Samas continued. 'I would gladly assume the position of leader of this fine group of soldiers.'

Applause broke out amongst the group and Mihran could bear it no longer.

'What do you know of navigation?' Mihran asked. 'How will you lead us to the silver gates if you don't know their location?' He stepped forward. 'What shall we eat and how shall we travel without horses?'

Mihran held Samas' stare and his cloak flapped open to reveal armour equally impressive as the Babylonian's.

'You wish to lead these men?' Samas asked.

'Yes,' Mihran raised his head. 'My people were chosen to lead and I, Mihran ibn al-Hassan, will be your leader.'

A few warriors shook their heads, while others nodded in agreement. Maybe they had heard of his achievements on the battlefield?

'And you have answers to your questions?' Samas asked.

'Not all,' Mihran replied honestly. 'But we will struggle without provisions.' He pointed to the forest. 'And we need to get clear of this woodland to maintain our direction.'

'One man cannot be the expert on everything,' Samas retorted.

'Without one clear voice, nobody will listen and the army will fall apart,' Mihran replied.

A dark-skinned soldier with a short spear stepped forward to speak. 'I vote for Mihran.'

The bowman said, 'Well, I vote for Samas, because if we have to fight we need him to direct us.'

Mihran could see the problem here. Many of these soldiers were infantry who looked for a strong fighter to stand with them in battle – they despised the generals who made decisions for them – but Mihran knew an army was more than its muscles and weapons.

Discussions were breaking out throughout the group.

'Wait. Be quiet!' Li took the floor once more. 'We don't need any more divisions – our group has already split in two.' The soldiers quietened down. 'Both Samas and Mihran can lead us. One to lead our journey,' Li looked at Mihran, 'and the other to lead in battle,' with a nod to Samas.

A rumble of agreements ran around the group and Mihran gave Li a nod of approval. It was good to find a soldier of a similar mind.

The Day Watch developed a natural rhythm, walking in single file and alternating the lead and rear every ten minutes. They pounded a rhythm on the woodland floor, keeping their thoughts to themselves as they wound through a forest of golden-barked trees which formed a light canopy overhead. As the descent became less steep, larger trees became visible, along with clutches of giant bamboo. It was unsettling for Althorn not being in the mountain lakes and snowy peaks of his homeland and he felt something was wrong here: his hand instinctively felt for his bone-handled dagger and the touch brought back his memories from the previous night.

Althorn had been waiting for hours tucked behind a hummock of wild grass a hundred paces from the village as the stubborn sun set. I'm getting too old for this, he'd thought, and resisted the urge to urinate, worried the smell would betray his position.

He ran questions through his mind to pass the time and keep alert.

What was that bird calling? A lapwing.

What was his earliest memory? Shooting an arrow from his father's bow.

How many men had he killed? Fifty? No, it had to be more – there was the grassland tribe who wanted their rival clan's sons murdered. Had it been a mistake to let those young boys live? Killing children was something he refused to have on his conscience. Either way, the grassland tribe had accepted the burnt bodies and paid him well. If they'd discovered the truth, it had been long after he'd made it back to the mountains.

He preferred the mountains – more places to hide.

Now he had one more king to slay. They were getting younger

and he was getting older, he remembered thinking. In his youth, Althorn had stood in the front line of many great battles, slaying men in their prime. Fighting men. But that was long before the defeat at High Ridge when his clan had been destroyed and taken into slavery.

Movement by one of the buildings signalled the change of guard. He had to move fast before the new man's eyes acclimatised to the light.

Through steady, workmanlike killing, Althorn had made it to the main hall of the enemy village, leaving a trail of dead bodies from his grassy hiding place to the hall's door. His garrotte had dripped with maroon blood by the time he was done.

Althorn tensed as he hid in the darkness of the great wooden building, to stay focused. The hall was only twenty paces long, but his vision was impeded by smoke from a fire. With the toes of a thief, he made his way across the earthen floor, creeping around sleeping dogs. The curtained door at the other end was his goal – the king's chamber. Guards slept on either side of the doorway but their open mouths and empty beer horns suggested it would take thunder to wake them. Taking his time, Althorn parted the embroidered curtain and squinted to see two shapes in the straw bed and paused to listen. Two sets of breath. One deep and one shallow.

This was the place.

'Mother?' a child called out.

Althorn froze. He hadn't seen the children in the hall. Speed was vital, so Althorn stepped to the far side of the bed, took out his knife and aimed for the larger shape's neck.

All hell had broken loose. Vicious fists flew at Althorn, who stabbed again, aiming for the chest: his blade scraping against bone as it twisted between ribs. Screams from the woman beside the dying king were joined by barking from the hall. The king fought back in the dark, gurgling on blood, and the woman leapt at Althorn. A fist caught him in the eye, so Althorn swiped back with his knife hand. The curtain swept back and firelight was cast on the bloody scene.

Everything fell silent.

Beneath Althorn, the king had breathed his last in a twisted shape of agony. Beside him the woman swayed and fell back, clawing at a red line across her throat. She squinted, looking Althorn directly in the eye.

'Althorn?' she'd whispered, and breathed her last.

A child's screams were cut off as Althorn fell deaf, staring at the woman in horror. What was she doing here? And why was she bathed in silver light? He turned to the warriors in the doorway. Why hadn't they attacked? They were shielding their eyes. Althorn looked down to see the light was coming from him.

Then, in a flash, everything had disappeared.

Now, Althorn took in the soldiers who walked with him: they were too well fed to be foragers or wanderers like him. They must have had every meal prepared for them while they spent their days training for war, he thought with a tang of jealousy.

'We must find water.' A spearman, wearing sparkling armour, broke the silence.

'There must be a stream flowing down this hill,' the tall female archer answered.

A murmur flowed through the line and, listening in, Althorn could tell the group were realising what he already knew – they were totally unprepared for this journey.

'We will come across a water source soon,' Althorn reassured the group, wondering whether his age played a part in the father-like role he seemed to have acquired. 'The land is levelling out.'

Althorn was probably not much older than the Arab in the Night Watch – Mihran, wasn't it? – but his years as an assassin, tracking targets across mountains and nights spent in the elements, had taken their toll. The thought of his last kill made him shudder. This was his penance – the gods had brought him here to pay.

'When we find a stream, we set up camp,' Sir William bellowed from the rear of the file. 'Night is drawing in.'

'Maybe we should spread out to find water?' John suggested.

'We could walk in groups, within sight of each other,' the turbaned swordsman added.

'Do we have to vote on it?' Crossley said, showing his neighbour a smile.

'No, we do not have to vote,' Sir William shouted from the back.

'Anyone against the idea can speak up now. We won't have long until nightfall.'

Split into smaller groups, they covered a width of a hundred paces, and the plan soon paid off when a call from the left flank redirected them to the sound of running water.

'Thank God for that. My tongue's as dry as a bone.' Crossley knelt at the stream, ready to fill his canteen next to the soldiers scooping water with their hands.

'Wait!' Althorn shouted. 'Remember the mushrooms?' Althorn looked at the blank faces with dismay. 'We have to test everything we eat and drink. Who knows what effect the water will have on us?'

'So, how do we test it?' asked Crossley.

'Smell… touch. Test some on your skin.' Althorn ran a few checks to show them how: his elbow, wrist and lips showed no reaction. 'This is good water.'

The waiting soldiers leapt into the stream, ladling handfuls of icy water into their mouths.

'We should camp over there,' Althorn nodded towards a raised plateau. 'And look for roots and berries before it gets too dark.'

'How about meat?' asked the muscular man with the tattooed face.

'Have you seen anything here to hunt?' the tall female archer asked.

A silence descended. It was true – no mammal, insect or bird had been seen or heard during their journey. That's what was wrong, Althorn realised. This forest was too quiet.

John was finding it difficult to fall asleep. He was as comfortable as he'd been in any trench, using his bags as a pillow, and he felt safe because scouts had been positioned in a wide ring around the Day Watch. It was the soldiers by the fire, and their conversations about their last memories, that kept John awake.

'…the thick of battle,' one voice held the stage, 'and the field was pure mud. I led my men into the enemy and broke their shield wall. It was wild!' John could tell the man was smiling.

'Sounds like a glorious battle!' someone agreed.

Why did these men love war so much? John wondered as he drifted in and out of sleep. His grandfather had been the same, telling his big stories from his worn-out armchair by the fire: battles past and present – how they should have been won or won quicker – cannons; horses; comrades; and scars. As a young boy, John had been enthralled, listening to the stories of cavalry charges, sieges and riflemen.

'Balaclava!' His grandfather announced the start of a new story with a shout.

'Hush, father.' John's mother tried to quieten him but told John she secretly loved his stories.

'It was an incredible victory,' his grandfather said in his thick accent, sticking out his defiant chin.

'You live in England now,' John's father often berated his father-in-law, 'and I don't want you giving my customers any reason to shop elsewhere.'

'Shop is shut,' John's grandfather would reply before continuing with his story.

John's grandparents and his mother had emigrated to London in the 1880s along with thousands of Jews fleeing the anti-Semitic pogrom in Russia after King Alexander II's assassination. John could remember his grandmother's sweet smile and hot soups, but little else. His mother told him how she'd often taken him to the art galleries, to see the great works of Russian art, but his grandfather only had time for the military museums and libraries, where he would read the Russian newspapers and complain about the state of his homeland.

John wondered how many times he'd heard his grandfather's stories. When he'd reached his teenage years, the stories had grown repetitive and tiresome, his grandfather louder and grumpier. He was bitter, and wouldn't listen when John argued back.

'The Russians won at Balaclava,' John told his grandfather more than once, 'but Britain and her allies won the next battle and won the war.'

'This,' his grandfather held up his medal from Balaclava, 'is victory.'

John's father told him there was no arguing with a man proud of the country that had driven him out, but still John tried to talk sense into him. So of course it was John who bore the brunt of the old man's lecturing, until he started to resent it, and to even feel ashamed of his grandfather's nationality. Then the Great War broke out and, when Russia became an ally, every conversation led to the same conclusion.

'You must fight for your country, John!' His grandfather would stare at him. 'Defend your land!'

John stared into the tree canopy above and tried to push the memories away. The palm of his burnt hand pulsed with dull pain, so he cooled it on his gun again. He listened to the talking around the fireside again, as someone asked Althorn about his last memory.

'I have fought in many battles.' John could hear sadness in Althorn's voice. 'But my last kill was... nothing heroic.'

'Remember what the obelisk said, Althorn.' John recognised the tall archer's voice and was sure Crossley had called her an Amazon. 'We are the chosen – you are a great warrior or you wouldn't be here.'

'But why was *he* here?' John thought. He wasn't a great warrior. He'd been practically forced to sign up for Kitchener's Army and had hated his war. He never wanted to fight and didn't want to do it again... he was a coward compared to these brave fighters. *You are a great warrior or you wouldn't be here.* With her words circling his mind, John had finally slipped off to sleep.

Samas led the left flank of the Night Watch through the dark forest, while Mihran led the right alongside Li, whose green visor had become their focal point. Samas cast a look back at the scores of silhouettes of soldiers he now commanded: each carried a different weapon – some of which he'd never seen before – and they fought with differing styles. He wondered how he would command such a unit and thought of the variety of men he had led into battle. They were from across the vast Persian Empire and many didn't speak the same language, yet all had fought well once they had been drilled and knew the commands Samas shouted.

Samas found it hard to believe that it was only that morning he had walked through the army encampment on the dry Cilician plain between mountain and sea, with children in the camp stopping their games to watch him.

'He's one of them,' he'd heard one wide-eyed boy whisper, eyeing the crest on his breastplate which told of his elite status.

Samas gave them a mock salute and smiled to himself when he had passed. At their age, he had been practising sword fights just like them, while the real battles took place within earshot.

He pushed his helmet on and walked with head held high through the rear ranks. When he reached his men at the front, who stood on the banks of the river Pinarus, he could see the Greek army, led by their new Macedonian king, Alexander, swarming across the grassland beyond.

Samas gave individual men words of encouragement then turned to address them all, seeing the colossal bulk of the Persian army behind: a monstrous crowd of tense muscle and glinting metal.

'Who are these newcomers who come to test our blades?' Samas shouted and gave a mock laugh. His men were well trained and ready to die for their Persian king but he saw nervous eyes. 'Today we show the gods what men we are!' He yelled and raised his sword. 'Today we show them,' he pointed his sword at the advancing Greeks, 'what defeat tastes like.'

Samas gave a drill call and, in a well-rehearsed move, the entire unit moved one step forward and released a deafening yell.

The Persian war machine was soon brought into action as the Greeks arrived. Cries filled the air and a cloud of Persian arrows flew over Samas, darkening the sky before diving viciously, thirsting for Greek blood. Engagements flared on the flanks while Samas' men held the river bank as the opposing infantry thrust their long spears over the shallow water.

'Hold!' Samas shouted and his men waited out the tense, hour-long minutes.

Through the din, Samas heard distant calls for changes in formation. Something was wrong, he thought. A charge of Greek horsemen appeared at the ford to his left, triggering a volley of Persian javelins. Samas knew the infantry to his left would move to protect the ford, pulling his men in too. To the right, the Greek cavalry were cutting off the Persian horsemen, so Samas had to defend the ford or the cavalry would have a clear line through to Darius himself.

With a rousing call, Samas turned his men away from the riverbank. 'Time to do some real fighting!' He raised his spear. 'Turn and march.'

The unit walked, sped to a jog, then sprinted with each call from Samas. He was right – the Greek cavalry were already cutting through the infantry line.

'Attack!' Samas yelled from the front as they ran full speed into a wave of horsemen. 'Strong arms and strong legs!'

The weight of the men crashed into the cavalry, with spearheads stabbing the Greek riders and shields knocking the horses to the ground. Samas dodged lances and lunged with his spear to dismount a rider. With a deft sidestep, Samas thrust his short sword up through the rider's chin, killing him instantly.

And it continued: blood; slicing; gore; and death. After five bloody minutes, the Greek cavalry retreated and Samas caught his breath as he called his men to order, creating a defensive wall of shields and spears.

'Here they come again. Hold!' Samas ordered without thinking – he was a machine now: reacting; fighting; defending; leading.

The enemy cavalry wheeled around to smash into the left flank and, as they slowed, Samas leapt at the nearest horseman, parrying and lunging like a man possessed. Now in his element, fighting hand to hand, he swept his way through his opponents and into the Greek infantry. Samas was as one with his weapons: turning gracefully to meet each new foe and attacking with animal speed and ferocity. Spear and sword felt like extensions of his arms as, with a burst of power, he lunged forward to cut down two Greek hoplites. He felt the sound of battle fade away but kept fighting and, as he pulled his spear and sword out of each hoplite, saw a light grow around him. A cool breeze washed over him as the nearest soldiers stepped back.

Then, in a flash of white light, everything had gone.

Now, in the forest, Samas listened to the footsteps behind him and the snapping branches as the army progressed. He hadn't spent much time in woodland but had expected to see more wildlife. In fact, he was yet to see a single creature in this new land.

'It's very quiet,' Samas whispered to the man with the longbow.

'No birds or mammals,' the archer agreed. 'Just that deep noise.'

'What deep noise?' Samas slowed down.

'Can't you hear it? A low rumbling sound, like a waterfall? It started a few minutes ago.'

Samas shook his head and sped up to join Mihran. 'The English archer can hear rumbling.'

Mihran seemed more annoyed with Samas for breaking the silence than for his warning. 'And?' he asked without turning to look at him.

Li had taken him seriously, stopped walking and was pressing buttons on a wrist strap now.

'I need to run through the wavelengths,' Li whispered, 'infrared is picking up something... spread out quickly!' Li's voice amplified. 'As fast as possible! Seriously, spread out! Run that way or that way.' Li backed away. 'Just run!'

'What is it?' Samas asked.

He got no response, but heard a whisper. 'They're extinct...'

Samas ran through the forest, keeping up with Li and Mihran.

'What is it you see?' Mihran asked.

Samas turned his head and heard distant rumbling. 'I hear it now.'

The ground trembled beneath their feet.

'Shit! They're heading straight for us,' Li shouted, 'RUN!'

As the forest exploded behind them, Samas threw himself behind a log with Mihran and Li. Crouched, Samas dusted himself off and peered into the darkness. Several large shapes came crashing through the trees, scattering the warriors into the darkness.

'What was that?' Samas asked after the shapes had passed.

'An elephant,' Li replied.

'Then we must be in India,' Samas said.

'Nothing to indicate we're on the Indian sub-continent,' Li said. 'The other animals give us no clue... rhino, mastodon. My night vision gave me a good look at the elephant when he passed – a war elephant, circa AD100.'

'What is AD?' Samas asked.

'I'll explain later,' Li replied. 'First we need to regroup.'

Samas shook his head. 'And what is *night vision*?'

'This visor,' the cover slipped back with a touch of a button, disappearing into the slim helmet, 'allows me to see in the dark.' The visor slipped down again without a sound.

The idea of seeing in the dark was easy to accept, many desert creatures did it, but what Samas had seen beneath the visor shocked him.

'So you can see in the dark!' Mihran had overheard.

'Sure,' Li replied, 'and they're coming back!'

'Over to you.' Mihran patted Samas on the shoulder with a grin. 'Now I will see how good you really are.'

Samas tried to ignore the taunt as he ordered. 'Regroup. Injured men can wait.'

He thought back to his training. Although the Persian army had elephants, they had yet to use them against Alexander. Samas had simply been told to get out of an elephant's way if he ever saw one and let the archers pick off the riders.

'Regroup! Regroup!' Mihran shouted out across the forest.

He's doing that just to get the elephant's attention, Samas thought, and tried to control his emotions.

'Okay,' Li said. 'It's coming straight for us – we have fifty seconds max!'

Samas thought quickly, weighing up his troops, and then called out orders. 'Archers, behind this fallen tree. Spearman, take the left flank. After my call, count to five then attack. Everyone else with me on the right flank. And Li?'

'Yes.'

'I need it to run straight through here.' Samas gestured to the long clearing, and noticed Mihran was watching him closely.

'Sure,' Li replied as a beat of immense angry feet pounded towards them. Li stood at the centre of the trail of destruction, visor glowing green, weapon poised.

The rumble grew, a wild shriek ripped through the air and the enormous silhouette burst into the light of a flare set off by Li.

The elephant was covered in metal armour and drapes, with gore and blood dripping off its spiked tusks.

'Ready.' Samas felt the ground shake beneath him. 'NOW!'

The soldiers with him on the right flank leapt into action, yelling, throwing whatever was to hand: spear, rock or helmet. The elephant stumbled, whipping its tusks. Seconds later, the left flank burst into life, stabbing the charging elephant with long spears and pikes. The elephant's red eyes streamed as it swung its tusks wildly and stumbled. Li fired a series of pulses into the forest ahead, setting the leaf litter alight, and the archers stepped forward, dropping a fallen branch in the elephant's path, tripping it up with an almighty crash.

Samas grabbed a pike and ran to finish the elephant off, but a flash of yellow light dazzled him and he stumbled to a halt and clasped his hands over his eyes. Through his fingers he saw a jet of pure sunlight burning deep behind the elephant's eye, leaving a steaming hole in the corpse's head.

Everyone stared at Li.

'Why didn't you let us kill it?' Mihran barked.

'I don't agree with cruelty to animals,' Li replied.

Samas looked at the dead elephant and shook his head, wondering how that didn't count as cruel. 'Why didn't you just use your...' he gestured at the rifle, '...weapon in the first place?'

'Too risky,' Li replied. 'I wasn't sure how my rifle would work here.'

'You will give us a warning next time,' Mihran bellowed.

Samas caught his breath and turned a 360-degree circle listening for other sounds. He spotted the archer who had been first to hear the stampede. 'What do you hear?' he asked.

'They're far away now,' the archer replied. 'Listen: you don't mind us eating it, do you? I'm bloody starving!'

An hour after making camp around the dead elephant, the Night Watch were eating thick slices of charred elephant steak. Samas sat with Li, who had explained where many of the soldiers had come from. Mihran shared a fire in silence with Olan the Viking and the chatty, tattooed Carthaginian was laughing with an Egyptian warrior.

Samas looked at Li. 'Tell me about the great Achaemenid Persian Empire,' he said. 'Did it grow to encompass the world?'

'Do you really want to know?' Li asked.

'Of course,' Samas replied without thinking. Why wouldn't he want to know?

'Well.' Li's visor remained down. 'After Alexander the Great conquered–'

'Alexander the *who*?' Samas asked. 'You don't mean... the Macedonian? The *Great*? You must be joking.'

'No. Which battle did you say you were taken from?'

'We were fighting near Issus,' Samas replied.

'Ah...'

Samas felt his heart speed up. He knew the battle was shifting in the Greeks' favour, but surely they didn't win?

'I'd better start from the beginning,' Li said and talked of Samas' battle at Issus. Of how Alexander's cavalry had broken through the line and Darius had fled the battlefield.

Samas stopped eating and stared into the fire.

Alexander, Li explained, was possibly the greatest general of all time and had gone on to take the city of Tyre, Gaza and the Egyptian region. 'Do you want to know more?' Li asked.

Samas nodded. 'Everything.'

A sense of guilt was rising in his stomach. Surely, if he had been there, this wouldn't have happened. He needed to know it all.

Li continued with Alexander's short but epic life and the end of the Persian Empire as Samas had known it. The scale of events overwhelmed him and his guilt slowly ebbed away. What could he, one man, have done against such a war machine? He had been just one spear in a sea of blades.

'So, all this happened before you were born?' he asked.

Li nodded.

'But you lived in a different world – a different time.' He paused as a thought came to him. 'When the beasts attacked, you said they were extinct. Which ones were you talking about?'

Li's head dropped. 'All of them.'

'Even the elephants?'

'Yes.'

'And yet you killed it,' Samas said.

Li took a second to respond. 'The soldiers are more important.'

Samas sighed and looked at the people around them, new weapons and strange faces, and struggled to accept they were from different times. He sighed, remembering his father's old stories of great battles. From what Li had said, Samas' battles were just old stories now too.

Samas thought of mushrooms, obelisks and elephants, unsure of what they would encounter next, and looked up through the canopy to see early dawn was giving the branches shape.

'There's something else I want to ask you,' Samas said. 'About your face, I...'

Li pretended not to hear and yawned. 'Oh, I'm tired. Best get some sleep.'

Samas nodded back. 'Yes, of course.'

A secret it is then, he thought.

When John woke he knew something was wrong.

He saw leaves above him and remembered he was lost in a forest with a group of strangers – but something had changed overnight. Staring through the yellow leaves at the faint sky above, he stretched to ease his aching joints but his arm felt numb and heavy. He pulled back the coat he'd been using as a blanket and gasped: his palm was stuck flat to the side of the black metal body of his machine gun, near the trigger. He tried to prise his fingers off the metal but they were stuck fast, and if he pulled harder he would tear off his skin. How did it get stuck? He hauled the gun onto his lap and stared at his fingers and palm – which were embedded a quarter of an inch *into* the metal. He had to hide it. John looked around: everyone was asleep. He pulled his numb arm and gun up to his chest, stood up and walked away, only to stumble over a foot, slip and crash on his back.

In a flash, the tattooed face of the Maori loomed over him.

'Sorry.' John's voice came out higher than he'd intended.

The Maori's wide eyes narrowed and he spoke in a hoarse whisper. 'Why wake me?'

'It was an accident, I...' John looked at his arm.

The Maori tilted his head and stared.

'I just woke up and it was stuck,' John said.

Movement behind the Maori caught John's eye, so he sat up and covered the gun with his coat.

'What is happening?' John recognised the Amazon's whispered voice and curved silhouette.

'His hand is stuck to his weapon,' the Maori whispered.

John let her study his hand. 'They've become one.' She moved close to feel John's brow. 'What is your name?'

John swallowed. He hadn't been this close to a woman for months. 'John,' he replied.

'I am Euryleia. Do you have a fever, John?'

'No I'm fine, really. I burnt my hand yesterday when Delta-Six shocked me.'

'The flying man?'

John nodded. 'I cooled it on my gun.'

'But how could such a thing happen?' the Maori said.

'This land is strange.' Euryleia removed a leather canteen from her belt and poured a trickle of water on John's hand. 'Does this help?'

John frowned. The water made his hand tingle, and it felt like his hand was being drawn into the metal. He pulled but his hand wouldn't budge.

'No, sorry.'

At this rate his hand would be inside the gun in a few hours.

'How am I supposed to walk with my arm like this?' John looked at the rest of the group who were waking. 'I don't want to slow us down.'

'Is it heavy?' Euryleia asked.

'Yes,' John said. 'If you give me a hand we can strip some parts off it – make it lighter,' he said, thinking how he could unclip the magazine, bipod and butt and maybe remove the cooling shroud from the barrel. But he'd have to carry the stripped-off parts in his bags.

Euryleia smiled but her eyes were full of concern. 'Maybe I can fashion a sling from your belts and bag?'

John pictured the soldiers he'd seen at the Belgian field hospital with lost limbs or blinded by gas: they'd been told they could adapt, but few had lived a life they could call normal. What if his hand didn't come off? Would his arm have to be cut off? Or would it be stuck forever?

'That would be great.' John looked up. 'But don't tell anyone. I'm sure it'll get better.'

Several hours later, and well into a full day of hard walking, the monotony of the woodland and the rhythm of the pounding feet took hold of the Day Watch and questions drifted along the line.

'Why are we here?' a Roman soldier asked.

'It's a challenge,' Sir William answered, striding ahead at point.

'But why us?' John asked.

Althorn answered. 'Maybe we are being punished?'

'What?' Crossley stared at the Celt. 'Why are we being punished, exactly?'

'For the lives we have taken,' Althorn replied, his expression hidden by his hood.

'Now listen to me.' Crossley slowed Althorn and the leaders down. 'Every life I took was an enemy soldier – Nazi, SS, Italian, you name it – *all* enemy soldiers.'

'But every death is still a life taken,' Althorn replied.

'And countless lives saved. Jeez!' Crossley threw his arms out.

'Why do *you* think we are here?' Euryleia asked Crossley, but he stayed silent.

'All we know,' Sir William said, 'is we must get to the silver gates.'

'And what happens when we get there?' the Maori asked.

'Who gives a crap?' Crossley shook his head and stormed off in a cloud of cigarette smoke. 'We'll find out when we get there.'

'What race did he say he was from?' Sir William asked, with a look of irritation and confusion.

'American,' John answered with a smile.

During a rest break, John eyed up Crossley's brown lace-ups with a pang of jealousy. What he would give to replace his cracked, hob-nailed boots? They creaked like iron gates and carried the stench of the last latrine he'd waded through.

John took in the rest of the soldiers too: nearly a hundred of them, and so different from one another. They were nothing like the men in his battalion. When they'd first met, they'd been boys and knew nothing about war. They'd seen pictures and read enough stories to make war seem glamorous – they would be heroes! How little they knew. These soldiers around John now were older, and something in their eyes told John they'd seen death, had killed to stay alive and lost friends. That was all war was to John.

'Are you tired?' the Maori asked.

'I'm fine – just getting used to the weight,' John replied and stretched his back, which had been twisted by the awkward position of the gun.

'Let me carry a bag,' he offered.

John thought about declining but didn't want to be rude. 'Thanks.' He passed his bag of gun parts over. 'I'm John, by the way, John Greene.' He stretched out his left hand.

'I am Mata.' He accepted John's extended hand with a look of confusion.

When they resumed their walk, John and Mata's conversation flowed and naturally came back to their wars.

'And you fight in lines cut into the ground?' Mata asked.

'Yes,' John answered. 'Sometimes we take over Fritz's trench, but sooner or later we end up back in the first one we dug.'

'And you have shelter?' Mata asked.

'Some, for officers and stores,' John replied.

'Sounds like a pā, but we build ours on hilltops.'

'Good idea.' John pictured water flowing downhill, carrying turds and dead rats with it.

As he and Mata walked on in silence, the talk of muddy trenches reminded John of his night in the crater. It felt like a story John would tell about someone else, not himself. They'd called him a hero when they found him tucked up in the bomb crater with a puddle full of empty shells and the shards of the tree stump that had saved his head a dozen times.

'You're a living miracle,' Edmonds had said.

'No, no,' John had protested: he'd just been cut off from the unit.

His platoon had advanced across the narrow strip of land towards the enemy line, hidden by smoke from the earlier bombardment, and John's job was to carry the Lewis gun to the right flank where he and Jones would cover the infantry from flanking fire. Wire-cutters had been at work throughout the night, clearing a path for the main body of soldiers, and they had a couple more Lewis gunners with them to pick off the German machine guns fixed in the trench.

The artillery sounded far away but then all hell broke loose. Shells exploded around them, sending the soldiers running for cover, and their shouts were heard by the enemy, who opened fire with their machine guns. A shell exploded near John, throwing him clear of Jones. He'd panicked, he admitted that now, but his panic had saved him. He'd grabbed cartridges off the ground and scrambled into the nearest hole with his gun. He flipped the bipod out, pointed the gun at the enemy and waited. He could hear men dying and put his gas mask on when the acrid stench of burnt flesh and cordite wafted his way.

When the shouting stopped, he knew he was alone, but was given no time to think about what to do. Out of the smoke came the enemy, and John defended himself. Over and over again. He would release a burst of fire, then reposition his gun a foot to the left, then fire at the next shadow, and so on. Time became irrelevant as his world turned into an endless grey storm of lightning and death, with wave after wave of Huns attacking and falling before him. Cold night and wet day crept past with John in constant fear, warmed only by the heat of his machine gun, which steamed and fizzed in the rain.

'We only found you 'cos we saw the whites of your eyes, Johnny!' Taylor said the next day.

John hated being called Johnny.

The rest of the boys had been grateful.

'Well done, mate. Saved our bacon, that's for sure.'

'Yeah, we'd have been gonners if Fritz had got through.'

The lads acted strangely after that and reckoned he would get a medal. They looked up to him in a way which made him feel uncomfortable, like they expected more from him.

'Looks like you had enough ammo, eh?' Smithy had grinned. 'Nolan reckons you must have shot a hundred Huns – a whole bloody pile of 'em!'

He was just doing his job, John had told the officers: he'd fixed his gun and held the line. He didn't know which way to run, but he couldn't tell them that. John pictured his grandfather shouting and scowling: fighting was a soldier's duty! Never run!

John looked at Mata and wondered what his battles had been like. Eventually, he built up the courage to ask what he'd been dying to ask. 'Mata, why do you have those markings on your face?'

'My moko?' Mata ran a finger over the intricate black lines across his forehead and down his cheeks.

John nodded. 'And the ones on your arms.'

'They're marks from important times in my life: battles; children; my wife.' Mata grew in size as he spoke of his people. 'Special designs from my tribe. They show other warriors how strong I am.'

'I see.' John smiled and wondered what tattoos he would have if he were a Maori. One when he married Rosie and another the day Joe was born. One for signing up for Kitchener's Army, one for his first kill and another for the night in the crater. But would he want those reminders on his body? He was already scarred by Rosie's death, and the tin soldier around his neck reminded him of Joe – he didn't want any reminders of war. He just wanted to be home.

Chapter 3

'How far to the golden hills, Althorn?' Sir William asked as they walked through the forest.

Althorn sighed, not wanting to be labelled as the group's guide when he knew as little about this land as everyone else. On the positive side, he'd learnt a lot about his companions thanks to their desire to talk to him.

'We should reach them tomorrow evening,' he said and pulled up his hood.

'If we had horses, we'd be at the gates in no time,' the knight replied.

'You're not used to all this walking then?' Crossley called over.

Sir William lifted his head as though considering a response, but remained silent.

'I suppose, being high-born,' Crossley continued, 'you're used to having servants and a squire and–'

Sir William rushed at Crossley, too fast for him to react, and pinned him against a tree trunk with a knife at his ear.

'You know nothing of the hardships I have endured, A-merry-can,' Sir William growled.

Althorn held back, not wanting to get involved. He noticed John was nervously shifting from foot to foot as Crossley fought for breath, wide-eyed and grasping at the knight's arm.

'Taunt me again and I will tear out your tongue,' Sir William whispered clearly.

'Enough!' Euryleia shouted.

Sir William blinked and let Crossley fall to the ground, choking. Euryleia helped Crossley up and gave him a sip of water.

'We must keep moving!' Sir William shouted and stomped off with his determined, long stride.

Althorn gave a wry smile. He didn't like bullies and felt sorry for Crossley, but for some reason his respect for Sir William had just gone up a notch.

Crossley remained silent afterwards, clearly nursing a bruised ego, while Althorn's thoughts returned to finding food. He had found edible roots, leaves and nuts, but a group this size needed more – and they needed meat. Creatures had been seen scuttling through the undergrowth and small animals attracted larger beasts, so Althorn scanned the patches of bare earth for paw prints or marks.

Further on, the forest opened to reveal a glade with ankle-high yellow grass with a small pond at its centre where a cloud of brightly coloured butterflies – sunset red and lemon yellow – flittered and swarmed around a broad tree covered in tiny black flowers.

'Wait!' Althorn whispered.

He had seen movement by a cluster of brown rocks some thirty paces away, so stepped to one side to see a wild boar rooting through the earth.

A figure moved on Althorn's left: Mata, who stealthily ran into the pig's blind spot. Althorn watched the Maori creep forward, holding his club high, closing in without a sound. Fifteen paces. Ten. He stopped and crouched low. The boar tentatively raised his head and Mata froze. A second later, a black-maned lion leapt out of a bush and pounced on the boar with a flurry of fur and incisors, mauling it to the ground.

Mata stood motionless, staring at the predator. Blood dripped from the lion's mouth as it looked up from its kill. Its eyes fixed on Mata and it dropped the dead boar, stretched to its full height and, with a muscular judder, released a deep, wild roar.

'Tane-Mahuta!' Mata's shout could be heard across the glade.

Silence fell across the forest like a blanket, and time seemed to slow down as Althorn watched the lion tense its muscular back and legs. A snarl wrinkled its nose and it released another threatening roar. Althorn wanted to rush in and help, but what could they do against such a beast? Beside him, John fiddled with his gun and let out a whimper. Then Althorn saw the bejewelled Thai spearman and the Sikh swordsman creeping through the grass. An archer to Althorn's right fitted an arrow to his bow, and spearmen were raising their weapons.

With another roar and a flash of claws, the lion shot forward at Mata. The Maori twisted away from the beast and cracked it on the shoulder with his patu club, deflecting the lion's charge, but was hit by a wild paw and crashed to the ground. Full of momentum, the lion turned and leapt at the next threat – the Thai spearman. An arrow thumped into the lion's flank, but it barely flinched as it swiped away the Thai's pike and grabbed him in his strong jaws. More arrows thumped into the beast's side as the near-dead Thai desperately lashed out with his knife. In response, the lion gave him a violent, neck-breaking shake and nonchalantly disembowelled him with a swipe of a clawed paw, sending jewels and guts across the forest floor.

The turbaned, Sikh swordsman – who Althorn assumed had been holding back for fear of catching the Thai – jumped in and hacked into the lion's neck, paralysing him instantly. With a second stroke he cleaved the lion's head from its body.

The whole incident had lasted less than thirty seconds, leaving Althorn's heart pounding. He ran to Mata, past the Sikh who stood motionless, as dark blood ran and dripped down his sword.

'My God – what happened?' Sir William had returned with the soldiers in the vanguard.

'I was tracking a pig when that appeared.' Mata pointed at the lion's body.

Sir William stared at the slashes across Mata's chest. 'You were lucky.'

Mata clenched his teeth. 'What if there are more demons like that out there?'

'That was no demon, it was a lion,' Althorn said.

Mata's face looked blank.

'Where on Earth are you from? Never seen a lion?' Sir William asked with a chuckle.

Mata gave Sir William a stare that could de-feather a chicken. 'No, I have never seen a lion before.' He grimaced, controlling his pain.

Euryleia joined them. 'Can I help?' She squinted at the cuts. 'We must stop the bleeding.'

'You need to clean the wounds first.' Sir William turned. 'I'll leave you to it...'

Euryleia poured water over Mata's chest, who could do little to resist.

'I found this plant.' She held a segment of flat, red root in her palm. 'It's similar to one we use in my land to draw poisons. I could make a poultice for the cuts.'

Mata nodded and stared into the branches above.

Althorn stepped away to look at the headless lion and the remains of the Thai spearman. The Sikh swordsman was explaining what had happened to those who hadn't seen: '...threw him to the ground and I made my move.'

'Don't worry, it's over now,' Althorn said.

The swordsman shook his head. 'I have fought man-killers before... but the spearman. His death was avoidable.'

'His armour probably helped him survive longer than I would have done,' Crossley said, fingering the debris of precious jewels scattered around the dead man.

'For all the good it did him,' John said.

Even after witnessing countless deaths, Althorn still found it a numbing experience. 'There was nothing you could have done,' Althorn told John, who cradled his gun against his chest. 'Strange things are happening here which are beyond our understanding.'

John nodded.

'You with the, err... gun?' Euryleia called out to John. 'He's asking for you!'

Althorn followed John to Mata, who was lying at the base of a tree with an improvised bandage across his chest.

'Mata – I'm so sorry I couldn't help.' John crouched beside the Maori.

Mata smiled. 'Next time I'll set a trap instead, eh?'

Althorn cast a glance at the lifeless boar. 'Looks like you had to earn your meat.'

'Maybe I'll take a slice of lion too. To give me extra strength.'

Althorn smiled and remembered how Mata had deflected the lion's charge. 'I don't think you have to worry about that, Mata.'

'You know this man's name?' The Sikh joined them.

'Yes,' John said.

'Did you know his name?' He pointed at the torn body of the Thai spearman.

'No. Why?'

'Why?' The swordsman frowned. 'We have lost men and we didn't know their names. If I die in this land, I want you to know my name, my traditions… and burn my body on a pyre.'

'I don't know what this man's rites would be,' Althorn replied. 'But we should bury him to keep his body from scavengers.'

'Agreed.'

'But what about names?' The Sikh looked from soldier to soldier. 'We must introduce ourselves properly. I will start… my name is Randeep Bhangu.'

'Right then,' Althorn said. 'You all know I am Althorn.'

'Yes.' Randeep turned to Sir William.

'Yes, well, I am Sir William Lavalle.' The knight looked at Crossley. 'But seeing as titles are of little use in this country, you may call me Lavalle.'

Each person took their turn, throwing their name to the wind, in what looked like some bizarre ritual for the dead Thai spearman.

'Euryleia of Scythia…'

'I thought you were an Amazon?' Lavalle looked perplexed.

'Amazon?'

'The Greeks' name for your people.' Crossley helped out. 'You know, those guys your ancestors fought with at Ilium?'

Euryleia squinted a little and raised her chin, suggesting she thought Crossley was making a joke.

'Anyways… I'm David Michael Crossley. US Marine Corps. Sapper. Just call me Crossley.'

'Sapper?'

'An engineer. Construction, tunnels and… I blow things up.'

The Day Watch continued to name themselves, giving their rank and the name of their country or tribe.

'I am Tobar Secundius, centurion of the glorious Roman army of Emperor Septimius Severus.'

'I am Mata Tiri Nui of the Ngati Rahiri tribe of Aotearoa.' The Maori was sitting up now.

John stepped forward sheepishly. 'My name's John Greene – Royal Fusiliers, Thirty-second Battalion. Machine gunner.'

After burying the Thai warrior in the glade, the Day Watch abandoned the lion's body and used the Thai's pike to spear and carry the dead hog. They travelled without speaking, which John soon realised was because these great warriors were afraid: afraid of what other horrors this land had in store for them. Back in Flanders, John knew who the enemy was and what weapons they used, but this land was as unsettling as it was dangerous.

A couple of hours after the glade, Tobar, the Roman, shouted down the line, 'Whose turn is it to carry the pig?'

No one replied.

'How about you?' the centurion bellowed at John. 'The short man with the gun.'

John looked up at Mata beside him, then back at Tobar. 'I...'

'You're what?' The Roman laid the boar down, blocking the path. 'We should share the burden... unless you don't want to eat tonight?'

'No, it's not that, I...'

Mata stepped forward, eyes glaring.

John winced. 'Look, we don't need any trouble, it's just...'

'He's injured,' Euryleia stepped in.

'He doesn't look injured to me,' Randeep said, 'and if he can carry that gun he can carry the pig.'

'Show him,' Mata said, without taking his eyes off the Roman.

Euryleia laid a hand on his arm, 'You don't have to, John.'

John shivered and held his arm tight, fearing he would be rejected if they saw what had happened to him.

'Show him,' Mata repeated and turned to him. 'There is no shame.'

With a sigh, John unhooked the straps of his webbing and lowered his gun to reveal his merged hand and gun.

The warriors grouped around gasped.

'Step back!' Mata shouted.

'He's cursed!' Tobar said.

'His hand is stuck, that's all,' Euryleia said.

'It's more than stuck,' the Roman said, 'it's being eaten by the metal!'

John recognised the sympathetic looks he'd seen when visiting friends in field hospitals: the looks of pity. He pulled his arm back.

'Well, whatever's happened I can't go bloody lifting any pigs now, can I?'

The Roman shrugged. 'No, but we all have to earn our place in the group,' he said and walked off, leaving the boar on the ground.

John unstrapped his arm and checked his hand in the light of their evening fire. His fingers had sunk deeper into the black metal body of the gun, which was now moulding over his tingling fingertips. God knows what will happen when my hand gets inside, he thought.

It was strange how detached he'd become about it, but John knew war had a power to disconnect soldiers from aspects of life. The noise, death and destruction gave you a different perspective on what was important and, as far as John was concerned, he was alive and wasn't in pain, so he'd nothing to complain about.

He cast an eye around the camp. The surreal grouping of soldiers and warriors was still a sight to behold. Relaxing around the main fire, Lavalle reclined beside Euryleia, while the intimidating, tattooed face of John's friend Mata glimmered in the firelight near the hooded figure of Althorn and the blue turban of Randeep, who was walking over to join him. John could see how, in ages past, these warriors were worshipped for their prowess and skill. War was an art to them and death was glorious. So, if he was surrounded by great – if not the greatest – warriors on Earth, why was he among them? He was no skilled swordsman like the Sikh or veteran of countless battles and sieges like Lavalle. The only thing that connected John to everyone else was the number of men he'd killed. Was that all it came down to?

Althorn turned the boar on its spit and clear fat bubbled and dripped out of the cooking flesh, exploding on the hot logs below. It was the best food John had smelt for months.

'I can take over for a bit, Althorn,' John said.

'No, you rest.' Althorn glanced at John's arm and gave a fatherly smile.

John blinked and turned from the fire to Mata. Even though he was injured, Mata had stood up for him against Tobar. John smiled: a proper warrior was on his side! He had to return the favour.

Crossley returned from the perimeter, grinning. 'I've set a few traps… for food, not enemies.'

'Sounds like an easier way to get food,' Mata said.

'The lion could have been a one-off, you know.' Crossley tried to lighten the mood. 'An escapee from a zoo or an old pet someone had forgotten about.'

'He looked wild enough to me.' Randeep's eyes stayed transfixed on the fire.

Crossley shrugged.

There was no point in hiding his gun now, so John looked at his fused hand again. A small nodule of metal had appeared where the tip of his little finger had been absorbed, and the gun had changed elsewhere: the barrel was shorter and the trigger had moved. He nonchalantly poked the logs with the muzzle and stared into the hypnotic flames while he watched Euryleia preserving morsels of food in the wood smoke as she talked to Lavalle.

'I was on my horse. We'd been tracking a group of bandits who had attacked an outlying village some days before.'

Lavalle was silent, staring into the flames.

'They had burnt the houses, taken women, children and food,' Euryleia paused, 'so when we found them crossing the plain, we ambushed them. I fired three, maybe four arrows – two kills, one maimed – then they started firing back. But we had them surrounded. We started picking them off one by one. I hit one in the chest and the sound of my horse's hooves faded away… like I was riding on sand.'

'And the light changed?' Lavalle asked.

'Yes,' Euryleia turned to Lavalle but he looked away.

'The last thing I saw were the children taking off their bonds.' Euryleia looked at Lavalle and waited.

Euryleia wanted to hear about Lavalle's last battle, but the knight remained silent. John felt ashamed for listening and looked away.

'Strange Lavalle doesn't share his story, hey?' Crossley whispered, having listened in too.

John shrugged.

'He's odd.' Crossley shook his head. 'I mean, he's a Knight Hospitaller right? So why didn't he see to Mata's wounds? And where's his armour?'

'I don't know.' John looked back at Lavalle, wondering what his story was. His arm twitched. 'This whole place is messed up.'

'True,' Crossley said. 'It wasn't chance those mushrooms were growing by the obelisk.'

'So who put them there then?' Randeep asked.

'Whoever brought us here I guess.'

'What do you think, Lavalle?' Randeep asked. 'Who has brought us here?'

Lavalle tensed before answering. 'A greater mind is at work here. Surely only God would be so great?'

'Wait a minute,' Crossley said. 'You aren't saying God has brought us here?'

'Who else would have that power?' Lavalle stood up, wearing the same annoyed look as before, and Crossley shifted to keep the fire between him and the tall knight.

'Listen.' Crossley held out a hand. 'I may have been wrong about what sort of life you've had, okay, but you can't go saying stuff about God as if you own him.'

John felt his cheeks warm and looked around for Althorn, but he couldn't be seen. He was usually the one to calm things down.

Lavalle didn't move, but his furrowed brow showed his mind was racing. 'I would never presume to... *own* God, but no other power is strong enough to bring us here.'

His tone was reserved, thought John. Did he feel bad about threatening Crossley earlier?

Lavalle continued, 'God has taken me to some inhospitable places. Who am I to know his plan?'

Crossley was about to reply when John let out a yell. He leapt up with his gun-arm in the air.

'My arm's on bloody fire!' he shouted.

Everyone stared, open-mouthed. John grabbed the nearest canteen and poured it over the hot muzzle, sending a thin trail of steam into the canopy. Then he looked at the firelit faces. A smile appeared on one, then another, followed by sniggers of laughter which grew contagious until someone burst out laughing.

'You're supposed to look after your weapon, remember?' Crossley's laugh was the loudest.

'And your weapon will look after you!' someone shouted back.

John hung his head sheepishly.

'Alright, alright… stop laughing,' he said, but couldn't help but join in.

Mihran was up before dusk, using the last hour of daylight to check on those injured by the raging elephant. He was desperate to make up ground and worried they would slow them down.

Two days gone, twelve left.

Silently stepping over bodies, he checked those with broken bones, hoping their makeshift splints would allow them to travel, and listened to those with internal injuries. Two soldiers had died in their sleep: a Hebrew swordsman and a French rifleman.

He was barely conscious of it, but Mihran had created a collage of the group in the back of his mind. It was a subtle mesh of each soldier's abilities and prowesses: how they balanced and complemented one another, both as a travelling group and as a fighting unit. With the dead men removed from the collage, it reshaped accordingly.

A silhouette and a faint green light caught his attention.

'Good evening,' Li whispered, scanning the dead bodies.

'These two are–'

'Yes. A shame. I've scanned everyone else and nobody should slow us down.'

Mihran smiled. 'Wounds heal quick here,' he said.

'Yes,' Li agreed and looked up at the dwindling light. 'We should wake everyone and pack before sundown.'

Samas stepped forward and gestured at the strips of elephant meat they had left smoking during the day. 'And pack the rest of the meat.'

It seems I'm not the only one who can't sleep, Mihran thought and turned to Samas. 'My children often had trouble sleeping after a nightmare.'

Samas sniffed sharply.

'How shall we carry such a quantity of meat?' Mihran goaded him again.

Samas stared at him. 'We'll wrap it,' he looked around, 'in leaves or in the clothes of the dead, for all I care.'

'You would show disrespect for our fallen allies?' Mihran was enjoying this. It felt good to taunt him and get such a quick response.

'No.' Samas was squirming. 'But food is scarce.'

Mihran took a step forward. 'You risk our safety by weighing us down and–'

'Stop!' Li stepped between the men.

Samas raised a finger. 'Do not tell me to–'

'Or what?' Li cut the Babylonian off. 'And you?' Li faced Mihran. 'You're both wise enough to know I could cut you down in a second.'

The argument woke the rest of the group, who stirred.

'You are both from the same land for God's sake… Damascus, Herat and Byzantium… same cities – different names maybe, but you both fought for the same land.' Li looked at each one in turn. 'Surely you can find some common ground?'

'Yes.' Mihran looked down his nose at Samas, remembering his history lessons. 'I am fully aware of how the Persian Empire crumbled under Alexander's heel.'

Samas narrowed his eyes. 'It would have been a different story if I hadn't been taken from my battle, believe me!'

'Ha!' Mihran turned and walked off.

An hour later, as the Night Watch moved through the forest at a fast pace, Mihran remained silent, preoccupied by Li's words. The cities had just been dots on a map to him: trophies to be fought and won; nothing more than a list of victories; weak armies and soft citizens lucky to be taken under the wing of the Arab expansion. Mihran pictured the cities and the sieges, and his last battle came back to him as he walked.

General Khalid ibn al-Walid's outnumbered army had been fighting the Byzantine army for six solid days in the August heat of Yarmouk, east of the Sea of Galilee. The Arab army had been wearing the enemy down with day after day of infantry manoeuvres and hammer-and-anvil tactics, raiding the enemy flanks with light cavalry. On this last day, General Khalid had victory in his sights.

Days of fighting on horseback had taken their toll on Mihran, yet he daren't show it. He was high-born, from the Quraish tribe, with the honour of becoming a great warrior bestowed upon him from birth. He had been trained in martial arts, on horseback and on foot, and was a master of them all. He excelled with the lance, sword or bow and had switched between all three as he and his team of horsemen had repeatedly wheeled from one section of the battle to another, crashing into enemy lines with sharp blades swinging.

It was on a raid, as his unit of armoured horses smashed into the exposed flank of Byzantine centurions and Mihran's lance sheared through shield and breastplate at a terrifying speed, that he sensed the noise of battle slip away, replaced by an echoing ticking sound, and then a surge of energy radiating from his body until – flash – the blood, the dust and the sun had disappeared.

Mihran looked back at the silhouettes of the gaggle of soldiers he now commanded and wrinkled his nose. These were just low-born fighters pretending to be soldiers. Poor imitations of himself, they faked the virtues of a great hero: honesty, strength and courage.

'Your battle speed is impressive.' He heard Li speaking to the tall Zulu warrior.

'I am battle-ready in seconds,' the Zulu explained. 'In my land there are many night raids on villages.'

'I see,' Li replied. 'You are one of Shaka's men?'

'Yes.' The Zulu sounded surprised. 'Ndleleni is my given name.'

'On the road,' Li replied, seemingly translating. 'You use the assegai?'

'Yes.' Mihran heard a blade slip free. 'Our greatest weapon. It lets us get close for the kill.'

Mihran added the mental image of the blade and attack manoeuvre to the picture of Ndleleni in his mind.

The Assyrian archer and the Aztec warrior could be heard too. 'I wear it for protection.'

Mihran assumed the Aztec was talking about his jaguar-skin coat and headpiece.

'I only need my bow for protection,' Marodeen, the Assyrian archer, replied. 'I heard some birds earlier – we could shoot a few?'

'We don't need any more meat,' the Aztec replied. 'The feast last night gave me my strength back!'

'It couldn't harm to practise though. Come on!' Marodeen said.

'I guess.'

'We're heading off for a detour!' Marodeen shouted.

'Don't stray far,' Samas shouted back.

'Where in the heavens are they?' Mihran asked as the Night Watch took a water break and sat around a large fruiting tree.

'I swear I can smell roast pig.' Sakarbaal stood up for a sniff.

Mihran ignored him, pacing on the edge of the circle. 'We don't have time for this. I don't know why you let them go.' Mihran taunted Samas again. 'We may have lost another two men.'

'There's one of them!' Sakarbaal called out.

'Where?' Olan asked. 'Oh, the bearded archer. What's his name?'

'Marodeen,' Li replied.

'Marodeen!' Samas called out. 'What's wrong? Where's–'

'Dead,' the Assyrian shouted. 'We need to leave!' He was clearly panicked.

Mihran was already up and walking away. 'Tell me what you saw.' He beckoned Marodeen.

Marodeen's eyes were wide with fright. 'Killed by some…' he fought for breath, '…huge… monster from Gilgamesh!'

'Did it follow you?' Mihran asked.

'No, I don't think so.'

Mihran didn't wait to hear any more. 'Fast pace!'

As he ran, he felt the mental image of his men becoming clearer as he sensed their vulnerabilities along with their skills. Although he wouldn't admit it, he now knew they shouldn't be travelling at night, and if they were to survive they needed to find the Day Watch.

John woke. The fires had died to glowing coals, peeping through blackened logs like demon eyes, while the grey haze through the leaves above whispered dawn.

'I dreamt of drums,' he told Randeep, who stood over him after waking him for guard duty.

'Crossley said there was a commotion earlier,' Randeep replied. 'Distant rumbles, like thunder, he said.'

'That could have been it,' John said.

He sat up and checked his gun. His hand was deeper in the metal now and the gun had changed: the barrel was shorter and the wooden sections had fallen out, so he shoved them in his satchel. He strapped the gun to his chest and walked to the camp barrier of broken branches and scanned the undergrowth as he walked the perimeter. The forest was coming to life. A distant whistle sounded like no bird he'd ever heard, then he saw a family of rabbit-eared hedgehogs walking in line and he smiled. Keeping his eyes on the uneven forest floor, John noticed a line of large red ants scurrying through the dried leaves.

'Hello…' he bent down for a closer look.

Every other ant was carrying an object: a red berry, a blue flower or a white stone. Vibrant colours – no browns or greys.

John made a quick 360-degree check for danger then followed the line, careful not to stand on the busy creatures. The line converged with another then another, until the streams of ants became rivers, five-thick, flowing with brightly coloured objects, which John followed around an enormous, white-barked tree.

'Wow!' He stood, hands on hips, watching thousands of ants carrying their loads to a giant ant structure.

On its back sat a large queen ant surrounded by guards. For some reason, the ants bringing tributes reminded John of Christmas – of presents and the Three Wise Men.

Have they found religion? he wondered.

When he strolled back to camp, the group were rousing themselves and John heard Althorn and Lavalle as they kicked dirt onto the main fire.

'I should scout ahead,' Althorn told Lavalle. 'Check our route and make sure we're heading in the right direction.'

Lavalle frowned. 'You should take someone with you.'

'No, I'll be faster on my own.' Althorn's hand touched his stomach.

'How will you find us if we change direction?' Lavalle asked.

'Don't worry.' Althorn smiled and looked at John and the rest of the group. 'I'll be able to track you.'

Lavalle nodded. 'Godspeed.'

The rest of the group breakfasted on wild pork and the roots Euryleia had foraged, and any spare meat smoked overnight was wrapped in leaves and distributed evenly.

Mata stood up with a groan. 'I can't wait to get out of this forest,' he grimaced, 'and get some sun on my skin!'

'Sure is gloomy under these trees,' Crossley agreed.

Two hours later, bird song filled the forest they walked through. Crossley pointed at a conifer-like tree with black, flat needles that snapped shut with a clap when the wind tickled it.

'I've never seen anything like it.' John shook his head and smiled. 'Whatever next?'

'How about a tree covered in lollipops?' Crossley said. 'Any chance of that?'

'Well it looks like the golden hills are near,' John said, pointing to where the woodland thinned out.

'Wait!' Randeep shouted and the line stopped. 'Did you hear that?'

John held his breath.

'A rustling sound… listen.'

'It's just the wind!' Crossley replied.

'No, I heard it too,' Lavalle said, 'a brushing sound, like sand on wood.'

The warriors started to bunch up, with the twenty or so with spears keeping to the outside, next to those with shields. Apart from the rush of blood in his head, John couldn't hear a thing.

'There!' Mata pointed into the canopy of a stand of trees. 'Something grey up there.'

More shouts came, and John could see they were being circled by a beast nobody could describe. Black eyes, white teeth, grey tail. John heard swords being unsheathed and cradled his gun-arm, feeling useless.

A clap sounded behind them and all eyes shifted to a black-needled conifer where a dark shadow pulled itself from the depths of the forest. The shadow lengthened and swayed like a fish through water. All eyes fixed on the shape as it revealed itself: a seven-metre-long great white shark. With frightening speed, the shark flew at them. Lances and swords glanced off its tough skin as it sped past and a Cossack soldier fell to the ground as a fin sliced through his leg muscles. Then the shark darted off with an Incan warrior in its jaws.

'Regroup! Regroup!' Lavalle yelled.

'Form a circle!' Mata shouted.

'Shields in the centre above our heads, spears on the edge,' Euryleia added.

Weapons and shields clashed then, when they reached formation, a cold silence fell.

'It swam through the air.' John heard Crossley talking to himself.

'Give the javelin throwers room to manoeuvre,' Lavalle said calmly. 'And then–'

The sight of the shark cut him off. The beast dashed in, as if it were in the thick atmosphere of the ocean. A sword jabbed out to nick a fin and a spear lodged itself in the shark's flank, but nothing slowed it down. In a flash it had snapped its jaws around Tobar, the Roman.

'Help!' the centurion screamed as the giant jaws crushed his rectangular shield around him and dragged him away, leaving a trail of armour and blood behind.

'There's nothing we can do!' John shouted above the yells, as Lavalle tried to organise the group.

'We can't defend against that!' Crossley shouted.

'Of course we can.' Lavalle was defiant.

'Lavalle, we've lost two men already.' Euryleia looked panicked. 'We should go before we lose more!'

'We have to decide quick!' Lavalle said and, before he could ask for a show of hands, the group scattered out of the forest and up the open hillside of orange and yellow cacti.

John joined the rush and only looked back to stop to catch his breath halfway up the hill. Trees were shaking on the edge of the forest, giving the shark's position away. Then it burst out, charging at the soldiers at the rear, who defended in vain against the large predator. Archers attacked from all sides but no arrow stuck.

John spotted a blur of movement rushing through the trees from the right. It cut in between the shark and the soldiers and was followed by a series of small explosions. Shocked and showered with dirt, the shark swerved and dodged, snapping its enormous mouth at the air.

'Woo-hoo!' Crossley shouted.

Confused by the attack, the shark flicked its powerful tail and flew back into the trees, followed by more explosions. The warriors on the hillside stood in silence as the blur slowed to form the figure of a laughing Celt holding a catapult.

'Althorn!' John shouted and the crowd erupted with a cheer.

'I really need to get some of those toadstools,' Crossley said.

But their joy was short-lived.

'What's that noise?' Mata asked.

John could hear a low rumbling sound.

Mata looked up. 'It's coming from over there.' He pointed across the forest, back to the obelisk hill from where they had started their journey.

John ran uphill to Lavalle and Euryleia to get a better view.

'Is it an earthquake?' Euryleia asked.

Crossley shook his head. 'Not if we can't feel it here.'

'Then what is happening?' Lavalle squinted.

The rumbling stopped and, in the distance, the entire obelisk hill dropped from view as though falling into a huge hole, leaving nothing behind but a cloud of dust.

Chapter 4

'Another typical Sorean,' Panzicosta said.

The cat-like creature, which had been covered in a thick coat of brown fur, breathed heavily through its broken muzzle. Four foot tall when standing on its hind legs, it now hung limp on hooks in the corner of the dark cave of a room. The sight sent a warm shiver through General Panzicosta and his scales rippled in delight with each slice of the knife. Casually, he snipped off a section of digit and punctured an exposed organ with one of his many spiked and bladed appendages. A gurgle came in response from the dying creature's torn throat and, in the opposite corner of the room, a small red-skinned reptile made clicking noises as it recorded Panzicosta's comments.

'No adaptations of any worth, alas. Nothing we could use.' Panzicosta sighed. 'And I do get terribly bored when they run out of energy.'

He nonchalantly snipped another length off the Sorean's tail, ignoring the whimpers, and stared out of the solitary, tiny window in the mud-brick wall, watching as a blue-shelled sentinel scuttled into the camp, straight for a water pit, where it flicked muddy liquid onto its protective carapace, which hissed with steam. The sight raised Panzicosta's spirits. The sentinel eggs had been positioned along the desert border, designed by Doctor Cynigar to hatch when disturbed by foreign army activity, so this arrival meant good news.

Panzicosta watched the other Brakari as they busied themselves, the giant arthropods with shells of midnight blue like his own whipping and zapping creatures carrying loads or constructing rude shelters. The camp buzzed with furred bipeds and limbless pyramids, reptilian worms working alongside twelve-foot-tall robots that lurched and jolted as the controlling braces around their necks and limbs shocked them into action.

The smell of the dying creature pulled Panzicosta back to his work, and he turned to face it.

'One last time,' he growled, 'why do you not fight us?'

The Sorean coughed, sending a spray of bubbled blood down its sliced chest.

'Why do you hide away?' Panzicosta asked. 'You are a martial race – you must fight!'

The Sorean's eyes widened with something Panzicosta had seen many times before – the final burst of defiant energy.

'We will…' the Sorean struggled with each word, but Panzicosta drew strength from its pain, knowing its end was near, '…never be defeated.'

Panzicosta had heard it before and glanced through the window again. The sentinel was talking to a guard who gestured in Panzicosta's direction. It had better be good news, he thought, and faced the Sorean again.

'You will never be defeated if you don't fight, you cowardly piece of shit,' he said as a shadow darkened the room's doorway.

'General Panzicosta,' the stout guard growled.

'What?' Panzicosta snarled and snapped his scales.

'A sentinel has returned.'

'Bring it to me.' Panzicosta paused a second, then punched a claw into the bloodied Sorean's neck, beheading it instantly. He felt a warm shiver run through his body as he strode past the guard.

Outside, on the muddy ground, the blue sentinel cowered before Panzicosta.

'Report,' Panzicosta said with feigned lack of interest.

'Victorio Brakarius, General,' the sentinel replied. 'I am the first awakened. Newcomers have arrived. Beyond the lake.'

'Details?' Panzicosta barked.

'The Draytor left the central lake to intercept them. It reports they are bipeds with internal skeletons.'

'Like these bloody Sorean. Soft-bellied shitbags,' Panzicosta replied and turned a circle as new thoughts came to him: soft creatures would mean victory… soft creatures were fun to pull apart. 'What else from our shape-shifter?' Panzicosta asked.

'The Draytor has intercepted the group. It killed one soldier and has taken its place.'

'Good.' Panzicosta raised himself up on his stout legs. It was always pleasing when his soldiers worked for his glory without any effort from him. 'Eat to replenish,' he told the sentinel and gestured to a wooden cage of mangy rat-like creatures.

'The Draytor reported one soldier was seen flying, General,' the sentinel continued.

'Interesting.' Panzicosta scraped two forearm blades together. 'What became of it? Is it heading our way?'

'No, General. It crashed soon after take off.'

'Start log.' Delta-Six recorded his journal as he strode purposefully through the forest. 'Day two in unknown country. No link with recon sats. Net link down. Resources sixty percent, energy levels seventy-six percent. Mental state below optimal. No injuries from crash. Unsure of cause. Possible lightning strike.'

He paused to peer up through the tree canopy at the green-tinged clouds above.

'No word from my team,' he continued. His training dictated he must record all thoughts so that, even if he was killed in action, his observations could be downloaded later and used by intell. 'Coded messages have been sent on emergency broad-widths, but no response from base. I assume I'm in enemy territory or captured. It's possible the Guevarians slipped me hallucinogens or hooked me up to a VR prison. End log,' he commanded and a quiet beep responded.

Delta-Six resumed his walk, keeping to the high ground where possible.

If he remembered correctly from the briefings, his computer system was an array of processors, databases and analytical cores distributed throughout his shield suit and linked to his body through several neural inputs. He hoped none of it had been damaged by his crash.

'Replay recent events,' he ordered and scanned back to his last memories before the hill.

A box appeared in the top-right corner of his vision and, as he ducked branches and avoided trees, he watched the playback from his hip camera: shapes appeared through a grey mist as he descended in formation with his squad, closing in on a Guevarian cloud base. The fire teams separated, the Guevarian fortress appeared from the clouds and then lines of light cut across the screen as Delta-Six opened fire, followed by a blinding flash.

The next image was of grass.

'Away,' Delta-Six said and the replay box vanished.

The flash of light must have been an anti-air missile, he thought, which suggested he had been captured and the virtual environment hypothesis was most likely.

But it felt so real.

A warning light flashed on Delta-Six's screen.

'Start log,' he said. 'My power cells are being sapped. Searching for solar input.' He looked up and remembered the mini-sat he had sent up on arrival. 'No message from Copan-One since initiation.'

A new warning light appeared on the screen, followed by the message *filters disabled.*

What filters? Delta-Six thought. Filters had never been mentioned in any briefing.

He stopped and, as per training, allowed his mind to clear, allowing him to sense any cyber-attack or degradation of his systems. He let his mind wander across his body, from his feet upwards. It felt different. It felt... open. But if his systems had filters, what was being filtered out?

He scanned through his memory videos – nothing new there. The guys from his fire team – all their files looked the same as his had before – but his file was larger. Delta-Six opened it up and found a range of new biometric data files dating back to his initial cloning.

Delta-Six woke with a start and reached out to grab the nearest thing... a branch? He steadied himself, let the remnants of his nightmare fade and took in his surroundings. Three nights he had spent like this, sleeping in trees, listening to the night creatures and wary of any attack.

He unhooked his night hammock, stuffed it back in its pocket and clambered down to the forest floor, where he gave his suit a quick check: feeling with his hands while his diagnostic systems ran tests through the circuits. Then he checked his night traps... all empty.

With a sigh, he realigned his geographic pointers and resumed his journey.

'Start log,' he spoke as he walked, not wanting to waste time. 'My suit has degraded overnight with three sections reduced in size. It could be a default mode to conserve energy we weren't briefed on.'

Lights flashed on his screen as various sensors picked up life in the forest outside his peripheral vision. The night settings were still on, so the movement and sound detectors were set to maximum.

'My biodata suggest I'm lacking minerals despite my daily pills and... odd to say, but I have the urge to eat soil. I can't say wh–'

A red circle appeared on Delta-Six's screen and he turned to where his sensors showed a life presence nearby. Nothing was visible through the undergrowth, so he closed in, walking softly across the leafy ground. Sounds were coming through now – voices magnified by his sensors.

'...the Night Watch would be doing.' A voice came through, interspersed with clicks which Delta-Six recognised as a sign of the translation processors working.

'Sleeping?' someone replied.

'You wouldn't get me travelling at night,' someone else said and a name popped up on Delta-Six's screen: John Greene.

Delta-Six stopped behind a stand of bracken, used his visual filters and magnifiers to focus in on the group of soldiers, his systems recognising various faces from three days earlier on the hill, flashing images on his screens where names were unknown. Behind John, who had his gun and arm tied to his body in a sling, the Scythian archer was tending to an injured Maori.

'Your wounds are healing well,' she said.

'And this?'

The Maori pointed to his abdomen.

'Green... but not an infection,' she replied. 'From the red root perhaps? How do you feel?'

'I could use some sun but–'

A shadow appeared to Delta-Six's left, and he reacted swiftly: rolling back to a defensive position with his arm laser pointed at the shape. 'Hold!' he shouted as the word 'Althorn' appeared on one side of his view.

Althorn pulled his hood back and held out a hand. 'I didn't mean to surprise you,' he said. 'Why don't you join us?'

Delta-Six cursed his alarm system for not picking Althorn up and triggered a hormone jab to counteract his adrenaline spike.

'You could be enemy agents,' Delta-Six replied, holding his arm steady.

As he said the words, he didn't feel any corresponding emotion. He couldn't explain why, but it unsettled him.

Althorn shrugged and said, 'We are not your enemy.' He pointed at Delta-Six's suit. 'You are changing too, I see.'

'The laws seem different here,' Delta-Six replied, realising how desperate he was for human contact.

Althorn nodded. 'This is a strange country.' He looked to the group, then back. 'When you need us, you can join us.'

'Yes,' Delta-Six replied and lowered his arm. 'But my training dictates…'

'We could use your help,' Althorn said. 'To guide us.'

Delta-Six felt the urge to join them, to be part of a team again. But his survival instincts were overpowering his logic with reasons not to join them: it could be a trap; they could be Guevarians; he was better on his own; trust nobody.

'Good luck,' Delta-Six muttered and walked away.

Isao Yakamori dropped into a mellow state of meditation, internalising and clarifying his thoughts. His mind slipped back to some days earlier when he'd first arrived on the grassy hill, fresh from war. One minute he'd been slicing through a troop of enemy soldiers with his long, flawless sword, about to duel a fellow samurai fighting under his enemy's banner, the next he was on a grassy hillside, surrounded by strange-looking soldiers. The men had walked towards a ringing bell, but Isao had seen a vivid streak of white, painted by an unseen hand in the green sky, and set off straight away, unaware of where he was headed. He'd raised an eyebrow when he heard distant explosions and a roar of voices, but by then he was well into the forest.

Now, Isao brought himself back to the present, climbed down from his sleeping place and straightened his undergarments. He attached his sword to his belt and set off once more, pondering his task. He travelled light and covered ground quickly, admiring the change in landscape as he progressed.

He had left his mind blank and suppressed his questions so they would resurface answered in his dreams, but one thought kept returning: the flash of light. He knew it was important but, like a cup of water forever out of reach, he remained thirsty.

Then it came to him – Master Takahashi's tales. The flash! A memory returned from his disciple days, sitting on the monastery floor. If he remembered correctly, there was an ancient tale where a great warrior had been taken from the battlefield by a lightning bolt. Isao had not given the stories the slightest credibility, but now…

A noise in the forest attracted him: a commotion forty paces away. The swish of feet dancing across the leaf litter was common enough, but a peculiar wild growling intrigued him, so Isao skirted round under the cover of scrub, to get a good view. As he neared he could hear the familiar, liquid sound of steel slicing through flesh and a deep-throated scream from the beast. The pounding feet of the large creature sounded frantic.

Isao edged forward, peeking through the undergrowth to see silhouettes circling a large striped beast. A piercing shriek, hauntingly cut off mid-note, sent a shiver through Isao's body and signalled the end of the fight, followed by the heavy thud of the dead animal. Isao quietly bent a branch back to see the blood-soaked body of a tiger, flanked by two samurai warriors.

'Start log,' Delta-Six whispered as he crouched behind a bush, focusing on the three men his sensors had picked up.

Each spoke a different dialect of Japanese, which his systems translated for him. One was armed with a bow and quiver of arrows, while a second carried a sword and a bow. The archer's clothing was more suitable for riding horses than for infantry warfare. Accessing his database, Delta-Six matched the language and style of armour for each soldier: the earliest samurai was from the Kamakura period, the second from the northern island of Kyushu, from the time of the Mongol nautical attacks, and the third from the later Muromachi period.

They stood around the body of a tiger.

'Where did this Western beast come from?' asked the Kyushu samurai.

'I do not know,' the Kamakura swordsman answered, while the third shrugged.

They kept their distance from each other, Delta-Six thought.

'You have come from battle?' the eldest samurai asked.

'Yes. You?'

'We all have.'

'What about those other soldiers? The foreign ones?'

The tallest samurai shook his head. 'An invasion?'

'No.' The Kyushu samurai looked stern.

'Then what is to be done?'

'We are deserters.'

'Yes.' The eldest nodded. 'We have abandoned our allies.'

'Disgraced our daimyo.'

'Broken our vows.'

'The shame will be too much to bear.'

They chimed in unison. 'Seppuku.'

What happened next shocked Delta-Six. He had witnessed the aftermath of some horrific events during his war but this shook him emotionally. His systems suggested the samurai's act was part of a ritualistic code of honour – bushido, or the way of the warrior – but he found it senseless.

He watched the playback on his vid-cam. The three samurai knelt and each drew a short dagger. Without a glance to his neighbour, each man plunged the blade in his belly, dragged it across in a sharp disembowelling movement, pulled it out and stabbed himself in the throat. Each man bled to death with low groans and gargled breaths.

There was little Delta-Six could have done even if he'd wanted to, but that wasn't why he re-watched the video. Something strange happened after their deaths. He focused the recording in as a faint mist gathered around the bodies, moving like a serpent, nestling between limbs and in the folds of their cloaks before forming a distinct cloud over each body. The three patches then rose to form humanoid shapes, which circled once before wafting away together. All that was left behind were three piles of clothes and three evaporating trails.

'Start log,' Delta-Six spoke as he fixed a skinned rodent on a skewer over a fire of glowing coals. 'Now I'm past the golden hills, this new forest must be a short distance from the expanse of water I saw during my brief flight.'

He adjusted the skewer, then unfolded a cup from his pack and mixed powders and liquids.

'Systems are low on power,' he continued, 'with no direct sunlight to recharge, and my upper back is bruised where the jetpack sits on my spine.' He paused, wondering whether he should continue with his trail of thought. 'This journey… I've never had so much time. Time to think. To think freely. I have to conclude some of the removed filters were a safety net restricting my thought processes. It would explain the mental freedom I've experienced these past few days. But why would the generals control our thoughts? They may want us to fight like robots but until they get the glitches fixed in the new fighting units they'll have to put up with us humans, warts and all.'

Delta-Six twisted the skewer and stared up at the tree canopy. His thoughts drifted back to the Himalayan training camp after his final growth-boost session in the Mariana labs where he and the other clones were briefed. Delta-Six's Alpha, Beta and Charlie were grouped there. All sixes like him, so there was no pressure to be the first. They completed the physical tests and stress analysis soon enough, so moved on to marksmanship, where they met Colonel Johnson.

'Right you freaks, line up!' The Colonel looked a pure military man. 'Produce your weapons and give me five shots on each target.' They assumed their positions and Delta-Six heard the Colonel mumble, 'I don't know why we bother with this.'

'Sir?' Delta-Six asked.

'This whole thing's a joke.' He shook his head and straightened up.

Was he depressed? Why hadn't the emo tests picked that up? Maybe his posting was a punishment?

'Delta-Six. Your score will be the same as your… brothers'. Identical,' the Colonel said with a sneer.

There was hatred in his eyes. It wasn't the first time Delta-Six had seen it – the regular soldiers despised him, but Earth's manpower had been severely reduced since the exodus. Anyone who had fought in the colonies wouldn't hack Earth's gravity again even if they did want to come back.

'You're all the same,' the Colonel walked the line. 'Alpha, you'll get seventy-one percent, Beta sixty-eight percent, Charlie sixty-three percent and Delta fifty-eight percent.' He sighed again. 'Just get on with it.'

Delta-Six pulled the skewer out of the ground and bit into the tough, charred rodent meat. Not tasty, but it would do, he thought.

He remembered the look on the Colonel's face when his score came back: a mix of confusion and fear. Delta-Six had scored eighty-three percent.

General Panzicosta strode out of the low, domed building, happy to have room to stretch his six broad legs.

'If it's not completed on my return I will feed you to a pack of Skrift.'

'Yes, General!' a shrill voice replied from inside the hut.

The collection of Brakari officers waiting in the mud stopped their chatter. Dawn was breathing light into the hazy sky and gave shape to the scattered buildings of their outpost.

'Is my Lutamek prepared?' Panzicosta demanded, opening the spiracle holes across his body to sniff the morning air.

'Yes, General. Oiled and charged,' replied a broad Brakari with barbed spines lining his shell.

'And braces? Does it have braces?' Panzicosta bristled. 'Two days ago a Lutamek ran amok and killed three officers.' His mouth-pieces twitched as he loomed over the officer. 'We don't need to lose any more, do we?'

'No, sir.'

'Good. We must find a more suitable restraint for these leviathans.'

A smaller officer stepped forward. 'General, I triple-braced the mechanoid myself.'

The grey, long-tailed Brakari's body was sleek as though designed for speed.

'Good,' Panzicosta replied and strode to the Lutamek: a five-metre-long metallic box that sparked and shook, revealing its true nature. He gave it a casual flick with a spiked claw and turned back to the officer. 'What are your tasks here, Bitet?'

'Sir, I am now known as Millok… after my transformation.'

Panzicosta's scales flexed and Millok took a step back. Slowly the scales lowered.

'Yes, Millok.' Panzicosta wasn't keen on female soldiers in his army – they only had one use as far as he was concerned. 'Your tasks?'

Millok's grey body swayed a little. 'Guard duties, feeding, Lutamek-bracing…'

'Are you bored here, Millok?' Panzicosta asked.

Millok stretched to her full height, still only reaching two-thirds of Panzicosta's frame. 'I am a proud Brakari warrior, General. As you know, my clan defended the Gulm Islands for…'

'Yes. I know Brakari history.'

This was growing tiresome. Panzicosta considered killing the officers around him and taking the female to one of his torture rooms but he remembered his orders. 'Are you bored here?'

'Yes, sir.'

'Then it is decided,' Panzicosta leapt onto the back of the Lutamek. 'Doctor Cynigar wishes to further his experiments when we reach Abzicrutia.'

'Again, General?' Millok asked.

'Yes. You will accompany me.' He moved his rump to a depression and looked down at the officer. 'And if you cease questioning me, you may make it to Abzicrutia alive.'

Millok made a twisting movement with her head then leapt onto the front of the large machine, whose grey and black sections were punctured with crude service panels. Tank tracks had been bolted to each side, transforming the fighting machine into a transporter.

'You can drive, Millok, and be assured, if it misbehaves I will be picking the remains of your guts from my mandibles with your tail.'

'Yes, sir.' Millok tapped a panel in the Lutamek to reveal a set of buttons. 'Are you ready, General?'

'Of course I'm ready,' he snarled. 'I have been waiting an eternity for this moment. It's time to prepare for war!'

'Come on short-ass – wake up!'

John stretched a leg and wrinkled his nose.

Crossley was standing over him.

'Ten days and counting, Limey – we need to get a move on!'

'Right,' John said and raised his good hand.

He sat up and rubbed his eyes. Images of a dream came back to him… no, it was a memory. He'd been nine, and his parents and grandfather had taken him to Margate for the day: a stick of rock; a donkey ride; Punch and Judy; a race along the sand. John had been in the lead but slipped a few steps from the tape.

'Stupid boy!' his grandfather had shouted. 'Why did you fall over? Stupid boy!'

John breathed deeply and stared at the cave walls of their temporary haven. The sound of water crashing some hundred feet below was dulled by the curtain of water that hid the cave. He strapped his gun-arm across his chest and stood up. 'I need a wash.'

'Sure,' Crossley said and returned to his conversation with a Russian soldier. 'So the Germans never learnt, seriously, we just walked up and…'

'We'll leave as soon as Althorn returns,' Lavalle called out as John passed.

A Thracian spearman played a game of stones with a Polish swordsman near the mouth of the cave.

'And I win again! Shall we play another?'

'I think you may be too good for this game. How about a new game? Let's play for money,' the Polish man said.

'Money? What use is money here? How about that gold ring of yours?'

John stepped onto a ledge that zigzagged down the cliff face. Randeep was further down, practising with his long, curved sword, sending sprays of water across the rocks. Further down, John caught a glimpse of Mata, who had been complaining about the dark cave and stood now in ankle-deep water, basking in the hazy rays of light. His wounds had healed, leaving three parallel scars to accompany his tattoos.

Eventually, John found a secluded shallow pool set into the rock wall and started the laborious process of getting undressed. He let his gun-arm hang loose by his side and slipped his left arm out of his jacket but it snagged when he pulled the right sleeve off, tearing on the metal of his gun.

'Damn it!' John cursed and crouched down.

He closed his eyes to summon more energy. He'd have to rip his shirt sleeve too and somehow wash without getting this hand wet – the last time he did that it sunk further into the metal.

After some puffing and panting, John got the rest of his clothes off and slid naked into the cool water with a sharp intake of breath. He held his gun-arm high and studied it: the barrel had shrunk to half its original length, his hand had been completely absorbed into the stock of the gun and a black sheen on his wrist suggested metal was seeping up his arm.

With a sigh, John closed his eyes and allowed the journey of the past few days to wash over him. Two days crossing the golden hills had been eventful. Four soldiers had been injured after a run-in with the poisonous lizard Euryleia had called a basilisk, and there had been skirmishes with a troop of violent baboons and a huge ground python.

John let his mind clear. Too much thinking led to a muddled mind, his father used to say, so he focused on the sounds around him. A distant voice could be heard: a Scottish warrior singing a lament, whose melody soothed John's thoughts, but the water was too cold to rest in, so he made his wash quick.

On the way back up, he passed Mata's empty pool and spotted two spiral impressions in the mud, which stayed in his mind as the conversation flowed around him in the main cave.

'...your song reminded me of home.'

'I swear I saw soldiers when you sang.'

'No,' the Scottish soldier replied, 'you're pulling my chain.'

'One was a big bloke with red hair and a squint like this.'

Mata was still complaining: 'The waterfall blocks out too much light.'

'Don't worry; we'll be heading out soon.' John calmed the big Maori and joined Crossley, who was with Randeep and Lavalle.

'Has anyone else had any… changes?' Randeep asked.

Lavalle was the first to reply, 'Apart from John's arm and Althorn's speed, no.'

'How is your arm now, John?' Randeep asked.

'Well, I guess I could say it's better, but it never actually hurt.' John held his arm up, which looked like a short-muzzled gun had been melted onto his elbow.

'Still, can't be much fun, hey buddy?' Crossley slapped him on the shoulder.

'What was your last battle like, John?' Randeep asked.

John swallowed. 'Well, my war was territorial, fought along lines.' He spoke with a slight stutter, not used to the attention. 'We dug trenches – been there for over a year, defending a command station.' John's courage grew as he spoke. 'I looked after the Lewis gun… it's not like the Vickers, which gets fixed in place – we had to carry it on raids to defend the flanks.'

'You had a crew though, right?' Crossley asked.

John nodded. 'But I could fire and load it myself,' John said and remembered the crater.

'So what does this gun do?' Randeep asked.

'It fires these,' Crossley unclipped a round from John's cache and threw it to the Sikh swordsman, '.303 calibre.'

'Arrowheads?' Randeep passed it on.

'Bullets,' John answered. 'It fires about five hundred a minute if you can change the magazines quick enough.'

Murmurs spread and a group built around John, eager to see his gun.

'And it fires how far?' Randeep asked.

'Seven hundred paces.'

Some of the soldiers gasped.

'But now all it does is hinder our friend.' Lavalle passed the bullet back to its owner.

'You never know,' Crossley smiled, 'it might end up firing fingers instead of bullets!'

John laughed but was horrified by the thought.

A commotion was building behind Crossley, where a whirlwind span through the cave, writing a grey trail of dust up to Lavalle, where the colours caught up and merged into the shape of a man.

'Althorn,' Lavalle said. 'What news?'

'There is much to tell.' Althorn leant on his knees and caught his breath. 'This rainforest ends after the next peak, followed by a pine forest.'

'And beyond that?' Lavalle asked.

'Did you see the silver gates?' a lancer called out.

'No gates. There's a cliff and a descent, then mist.'

'And beyond the mist?' Crossley asked.

Althorn sat down. 'A shore of one of the largest rivers I have ever seen.'

John dropped his head and wondered how much more walking he could take.

'You are sure this is the way we have to travel?' Mata asked.

'Yeah,' Crossley joined in. 'Who's to say we haven't already missed the silver gates?'

A low hum ran around the group.

'Althorn has been on many scouting missions,' Lavalle said. 'If the silver gates were near, he would have seen them.'

'But how do we know for sure?' Crossley asked.

'A sign is what we need – like the obelisk.'

'But we're running out of time!'

'Listen,' Althorn held out his palms. 'I'm sure we'll know when we're near the silver gates. As for the river – there is no sign of a ford.'

'So, we have to cross the damn thing?' said Crossley. 'Paddle the Mississippi without a boat?'

'It seems so,' Althorn said.

'Okay, so what do we know about the water?' Crossley asked.

'It's fed by the waterfall and other rivers,' Althorn replied.

'Currents? Depth? Salinity? We need to check all these things out.' Crossley stood, hands on hips.

'We can organise that when we get to the river.' Lavalle gave Crossley a look he saved for the American. 'We must pack and get moving.'

'This is pointless, goddamit!' Everyone looked at Crossley. 'We carry on like good little soldiers – obeying orders that were written on a block of stone, for Christ sake. Why?'

John sighed. 'Why us?'

The looks on the other soldiers' faces suggested they were thinking the same thing.

'*Those who stand against you fall in great numbers.*' Lavalle recalled the passage from the obelisk.

'It's true.' A Thracian held his javelin proudly. 'I am the greatest warrior of my tribe. We are prized by the Macedonians, who pay us well.'

'I'm the sharpest shot in my battalion,' a rifleman said.

'And I am considered one of the finest swordsmen in the Levant,' Lavalle boasted.

'Really?' Crossley asked with sarcasm.

'Yes.' He squinted at Crossley. 'And I'm sure your... skills were equally deadly during your war.'

Crossley nodded. 'I must have killed a few hundred troops.'

'I have killed many enemy soldiers.' Mata nodded.

'Too many to count.' Althorn's eyes hardened.

Images of enemy soldiers' bodies lining the crater came back to John. 'I couldn't say how many I killed. I just aimed and fired. I could have shot that many, I guess.'

'You are the youngest here,' Lavalle pointed out, 'and your weapon was incredibly proficient.'

'But you couldn't have killed hundreds of men with your sword,' John replied.

'Not just my sword: my lance, my horse, my mace and shield. Have you seen an armoured warhorse run full speed into seven rows of foot soldiers?'

John shook his head and turned to Euryleia. 'And you?'

She nodded her head solemnly.

These were proud warriors, John thought, but still felt the guilt of taking the lives of others.

An hour's march on, with the roar of the waterfall now behind them, Crossley and John compared their wars.

'Yes, well,' John said. 'I was pushed into the army, to be honest.'

'Really?'

'My grandfather was a decorated soldier – he believed in fighting for your country. He fought in the Crimea.' John didn't want to explain on which side his grandfather fought, so he asked, 'How about you? Why did you sign up?'

'I'd have been conscripted to fight sooner or later,' Crossley said. 'I thought I may as well have some choice in what I wanted to do. I always liked playing with explosives, so…'

'Did you meet any British troops?' John asked.

'Hell, yeah, all over the place! There was this one time your boys helped me out of a fix.' Crossley launched into a tale of being on Sicily, blowing up watchtowers around some bay, and various other exploits. As Crossley's tales melted into one another, the group filed out of the thick woodland, dripping with vegetation, and into a pine forest where the ground cover was thinner, giving them a better view around.

'We have a good chance of finding something to eat in here,' Lavalle said.

'A perfect hunting ground,' Euryleia agreed and stepped off the path, her silent feet leaving no trail.

'She'd make someone a good wife.' Crossley nudged John. 'Even goes hunting for you, eh?'

John smiled but stayed silent, not wanting to tempt the wrath of Lavalle.

A few minutes later, deep in the forest, Mata shouted from the back of the line. 'Somebody's running towards us!'

'Euryleia?' Lavalle stopped and called out. 'Euryleia!'

'Quick, group up!' Althorn shouted.

The Day Watch moved into a tight formation of blades, primed arrow tips and spears with John at the centre, cradling his gun.

With a yell, Euryleia appeared, bursting through a bush some fifty paces back.

'Run!' she shouted.

'What is it?' Althorn called out.

'Wolves!'

Half the group sprinted away immediately.

'Run, everyone!' Althorn ushered the remaining troops away.

'Come on, Mata!' John shouted to the Maori, who started to jog.

Euryleia overtook John as he heard thumping paws and howls. Althorn was already long gone and John had lost sight of the others as they ran down the bending track.

But the forest remained empty.

John stopped to look back.

'Come on, Mata. Keep–'

John froze when he saw movement in the ground behind Mata: patches of brown pine needles were rising and falling out of the dry soil and moving at him with speed. On one flank, John saw grey fur appear and sink back down.

'Keep running!' John shouted at Mata.

Mata shook his head, slowing down to turn and stand in a defensive pose. The sound of running paws grew louder as a pair of wolves rose up out of the earth as if emerging from a sea of soil. Mata slipped his club from his belt. John looked around, but everyone had gone. Two more wolves rose out of the dirt, their white eyes glaring and mouths foaming, and John stood frozen to the spot, watching helplessly as the wolves closed in on Mata.

Then something bizarre happened.

Mata grew in size. His fingers lengthened, winding around his club. And dark shapes tore through his arms and back.

'What happened?' Crossley asked between puffs of his cigarette when John and Mata had finally caught up with the group.

John looked at Mata for an explanation, but the large Maori was busy drinking water.

'Erm.' John felt his cheeks redden as the rest of the group turned to him. 'The wolves are dead,' he said.

John avoided Crossley's eyes and took a furtive glance at Mata. He swore he could see a new set of markings on his shoulder.

How could he describe what he'd seen? John thought as Lavalle ushered them on. In his mind's eye he could still see Mata exploding into a tangle of vines and deadly branches, throwing and tearing the wolves apart like rag dolls.

Chapter 5

Samas sat against the back of the cave with a clear view of the exit ahead of him. Despite the imminent danger it felt cosy, with the light from Li's visor giving the shelter a warm ambience. He watched the soldiers cleaning blades, repairing armour or repacking belongings, and wondered why Sakarbaal, the tattooed fighter with the trident, was rubbing his tattoos with the skin of a purple fruit.

'Where is he from?' Samas asked Li, who sat nearby projecting shapes onto a wall.

'He's a Canaanite or Phoenician, as you would know his people, possibly Carthaginian or Punic? A North African empire – before the Romans wiped them out, of course.'

'Romans?' Samas was confused by Li's endless list of people and places he had never heard of.

'It's a long story…'

'Another one I won't want to hear, no doubt.' Samas shook his head and watched the Assyrian archer Marodeen pluck a bird, selecting the best feathers to replace shabby flights on his arrows.

'Hey, nice work there.' The archer with the longbow joined Marodeen. 'It's good to meet an archer who can actually fletch.'

The Assyrian remained focused on his work. 'Professionals know their weapons.'

'I'm Mark Bowman.' The English archer held out his hand. 'But you can call me Bowman.'

'I'm Marodeen.'

Bowman hovered. 'Any chance I can have some feathers?'

Marodeen didn't look up. 'I need them all.'

'Right.' Bowman backed off. 'I'll just have to catch one myself then.'

Samas watched Bowman stalk off like a scolded child, sending a hurt glance over his shoulder at Marodeen. It wasn't good to let bad feelings stew like this, Samas thought. They were only beginning to understand the challenges this small army would face and they needed to be a solid fighting unit if they were to survive. He started thinking of ways he could improve the morale in the group… games maybe, or pairing the soldiers up? Competitions during training had always worked well but they didn't have time for drills here as they marched for the silver gates. The ideas slowed as he became drowsy, his eyelids closed and he fell asleep.

Samas sat up and stared at the cave mouth, just visible in the early-morning light. Something had woken him, but what? A deep rumble shook the ground, and he looked around: the other soldiers were stirring, weary eyes searching for answers; dust and small stones fell from the cave roof like snow. Samas had felt earthquakes before, knew they could flatten cities, so he jumped up and grabbed his weapons and shield.

'Get outside!' Samas shouted, as an almighty thunderclap shook the cave. 'Come on!' He shook the nearest warriors awake and pushed the soldiers in his way.

Blocks of rock were falling from the cave ceiling and cracks were running up the walls.

'Move!' Samas shouted in his battlefield voice and held his shield over his head as the stones rained down.

A large block slipped from the cave mouth wall and Samas leapt out of its way just in time. He pulled a swordsman out of the rubble, bruised and dusty, then caught his breath, brushed the dust off his armour and counted his men: three were missing as far as he could tell.

'Li!' he shouted and ran over to where the Chinese soldier surveyed the landscape. 'We're missing three men.'

'In the cave,' Li replied and put a hand on Samas' shoulder.

He shook it off and fought his urge to run in and save them. 'Then we have to–'

'We must wait for aftershocks,' Li said.

Samas cursed under his breath, knowing it was the right thing to do.

The oncoming dawn lit glades of cacti as the Night Watch neared the end of their night journey. Not one to hold grudges, Samas didn't blame Li for the loss of three men, but felt he could have saved one if he had been quick enough.

'We must be near the golden hills,' he said to Li.

'It would appear so.'

A shout from the left flank caught their attention. It was Olan, the Viking, and Samas was soon beside him.

'I'm fine – I tripped.' The Viking brushed himself down and picked up the offending item. 'Feels like metal.'

'It looks like a shield.' Li's visor cast a light on it. 'Possibly Roman.'

'One of the day travellers?' Samas asked.

Li nodded. 'It has to be.'

'Did you say it was Roman?' Sakarbaal interrupted.

'Yes.'

'Dido's pelt!' He laughed. 'I knew there'd be good news soon.'

Samas looked at him, unsure how to respond.

'Believe me,' Sakarbaal grinned his malicious smile, 'one less Roman in the world is a good thing. Is there blood? If only I could have been here to see the dirty bastard die!'

Samas took the crushed piece of metal from Olan, cursing the lack of moonlight. 'Are these toothmarks?' He fingered the holes, picked out a tooth and handed it to Li.

'Seems to be a shark tooth. But how did it get here, on the edge of this forest?' Li asked.

'We must be near a sea,' Samas said.

'No,' Li said.

'An animal with similar teeth?' Samas asked.

'What if it's still here?' Sakarbaal lifted his trident.

'No,' Mihran replied. 'If the shield belonged to the Day Watch, the attack happened hours ago.'

'Still, we should get out of the forest,' Li said, 'into the open.'

As they wound out of the forest, Samas came across a golden chest plate covered in eagle motifs.

'I'll swap!' Olan snatched the breastplate before Samas could protest and handed him a Roman sword. 'Looks like gold.' Olan tried it on, tightening the leather straps over each shoulder.

Samas shrugged, happy to keep the peace.

'Quiet!' Li hissed. 'Something's coming!'

Samas sprinted into the open with Olan at his side.

'Archers ready.' Samas spoke in a low voice, and his men responded with a series of squeaking strings and bows.

'What is it?' Mihran asked Li.

'A shark – *Carcharodon carcharias* – and it's swimming through the air,' Li replied matter of factly.

The unmistakeable silhouette of a shark slipped out of the trees and headed straight for them.

'Loose!' Samas yelled and a small cloud of arrows flew at the shark, most glancing off the tough skin. Marodeen's arrow missed by a distance and veered into the dark sky.

'Draw swords! Spearmen ready!' Samas shouted.

Samas eyed Marodeen then looked back to his wild arrow, which had flipped back on itself. Samas had never seen anything like it. Was it the wind? The arrow wavered then headed straight for the shark, speeding up before plunging into its eye.

'Good shot!' Samas shouted in surprise, leaving Marodeen rubbing his thick beard.

'Impressive,' Bowman nodded.

The shark's scream pierced the evening air as it thrashed about, snapping the arrow against a tree.

'Loose!' A second volley of arrows scratched and irritated the shark.

'Captain, I can see thermal residue in the ground.' Samas realised Li was talking to him. 'It looks like the Day Watch used explosives to scare off the shark.'

'Can you?' Samas gestured to the laser rifle.

'Sure.' Li unclipped the slender gun and fired a series of fireballs at the flying predator.

The first explosion left a burning blue light in Samas' vision. The rest he didn't see but heard clearly enough. When he regained his sight the shark had disappeared into the trees.

'Good work!' Samas said and rubbed his eyes.

'Uphill!' Mihran ordered.

'Archers to the rear,' Samas commanded. 'Signal if it returns.'

'Why didn't you attack with the first wave?' Mihran asked Li.

Samas heard Li sigh, but doubted Mihran had noticed. 'After killing the elephant I assumed I was to hold back.'

'No,' Mihran replied, 'no more holding back.'

Li nodded and they walked on.

Why couldn't he talk to Mihran like that? Samas thought. He had little time for Mihran, but if they were to lead together, they needed a better relationship. The trouble was, every time Mihran spoke, Samas pictured a general from his Persian army: haughty and ungracious. He had been high-born too, Samas thought. Power was the one thing Mihran took for granted. He would have been given the right to subjugate others from birth and would never give that up. Here, away from the safety of the structured world of his tribe and army, those rights were not certain any more, and Samas threatened his power.

With that thought, Samas walked a little lighter on his feet.

'This is far enough.' Lavalle spoke to the group with weary eyes. 'We should make camp.'

Althorn appeared by his side in a blur. 'I have found shelter,' he gestured and sped off again.

John tightened the strap holding his arm and longed for somewhere dry to lie down and sleep. Night had fallen hours ago and the winding forest path that ran up and downhill had made their journey hard going but Althorn insisted the river was just one day's walk away. No one mentioned Mata and the wolves, but it hadn't stopped John from thinking about it. Images of whipping green tendrils revisited him as he walked. John had tried to make eye contact with Mata, but he kept his distance.

'The land drops away from here.' Althorn appeared and pointed to a sandy cliff lined with rows of caves, which were clearly not natural. 'So it's a great view when light.'

'Looks like these were made for us!' Crossley shone his torch into the first few caves, which stood six feet tall and ten feet deep.

'Are these ruins?' Euryleia asked and touched a wall.

'They definitely look man-made.' John inspected a wall. 'But why six sides? Why not square or arched?'

'Who knows?' Lavalle pushed past and settled in the first cave. 'What I need is sleep.'

Euryleia followed the crusader, and the other soldiers leapt at the next few caves, pushing past one another like children trying to get to the best dormitory bed. Lavalle's glare told them his cave was full.

'We'll only get three in at the most,' someone grumbled.

'Don't worry – there's plenty more.' Crossley lit the long row up with his torch.

John watched Mata walk to one of the caves furthest from the group, so he joined Althorn and Randeep. He curled up with his bag for a pillow and was asleep in seconds.

'Who's there?' John's voice boomed in the small cave.

He sat up and rubbed his eyes. It was light outside and the cave was silent. What had woken him? Possibly Althorn when he left, seeing as his place was empty.

Beyond the hexagonal cave entrance, John saw a mist rising through the forest canopy, which lay below the cave's vantage point. The hazy sun's mellow heat warmed the shelters, and John felt a feeling of contentment wash over him. Despite the danger of this land, he preferred it to the destroyed towns and flooded trenches of Belgium and France. He glanced at his gun-arm, which lay bare since he'd ripped off the shirt sleeve. It had changed again: the corners of the muzzle looked softer, with organic curves, and his wrist was more metal than flesh now. He had tried fitting the discus-shaped magazine back in, in case it could still fire bullets, but the hole had distorted, making it useless. He could feel the gun though. Not the ghost presence of his fingers, as an amputee would, but he could sense the inner components of the gun instead, which felt comforting.

John crept out onto the earthen platform in front of the caves where the trees had been deliberately cut down. A distant bird sang a fluting tune and he instinctively searched for the creature: he'd learnt any sound could be a threat here.

'The caves are definitely man-made.' Crossley appeared from behind a tree, zipping his fly.

John felt his heart jump.

'You can see the marks where the builders used some kind of slicing tool to carve them out of the limestone,' the American continued.

John pointed at the stumps. 'They've cut these down too.'

'I'm telling you – there has to be someone else living here,' Crossley said.

'You think other soldiers were here before us?' John asked.

Crossley shook his head. 'Who knows? I would have said no, but this place is kinda strange.' He sat next to John and gazed out as the dawn light spread across the tree tops. 'Knowing this place, they were probably built by some kind of weird monkey or oversized crab!' He laughed.

'A bit like the Lost World, this place,' John said.

'You read the book?'

'No.' John wasn't a big reader. 'Some of my mates in the barracks talked about it – they'd read it. Dinosaurs and monkey men in South America.'

'Yeah, it's a good yarn. I guess you wouldn't have heard of Asimov or Heinlein, or read any of the sci-fi mags we've got in the US, but I reckon this place is more like something H.G. Wells would have dreamt up.'

'I've heard of him.' John smiled. 'The lads were talking about *The Time Machine* the other day.' His face lit up. 'Do you think that's how we got here?'

Crossley shrugged. 'Maybe.' He looked around. 'This could be Earth in the future. Maybe humans are extinct and we've been brought in to repopulate the planet, or protect it?'

'So, people in our future brought us here but didn't stay to talk to us?' John asked with a wry smile.

'No, it doesn't sound too convincing.' Crossley rubbed his temples and smiled. 'We could have been put in hibernation though – no time machine needed. Don't know by who, but that'd work.'

'Now you're just guessing.' John looked out across the woodland. 'Whoever brought us here must have had a bloody good reason to go to all this trouble.'

The sound of a snapped twig made them turn to see Lavalle exiting his cave.

'A nice little love nest over there, hey?' Crossley whispered to John.

'Good morning.' The muscular knight stretched as he greeted the men. 'Damn cramped in that cave – not good for my back.'

Crossley raised his eyebrows at John, who shook his head, imploring him not to tease Lavalle.

'Too cramped for you to get your sword out and try some lunges?' Crossley asked with a straight face.

'Yes, of course.' Lavalle gave the American his usual look. 'Why would I want to?'

John turned his laugh into a cough and stood up. 'Sorry, cold air on my chest.'

Crossley started to say something else but a shout caught their attention. It was coming from Mata's end of the caves.

'Help!' The cry was muffled.

The men ran towards the yell, past sleeping soldiers, to a blood-splattered cave. A decapitated body lay on the floor near a Chinese soldier, who struggled with two enormous blades swiping in and out of the back wall.

'God's mercy!' Lavalle leapt forward with his sword to fend off the sharp blades.

Crossley and John rushed in but could do little in the cramped space.

Two large compound eyes could be seen through the torn wall.

'It's a giant bug!' Crossley shouted and pulled an orange toadstool from his bag.

The huge insect snapped and tore at the Chinese soldier with its razor-sharp mandibles. With a lunge, it caught him around the waist and sliced him in two, spilling his intestines onto the ground.

Lavalle jabbed his broadsword into the insect's eye.

'Get back!' Crossley grabbed at Lavalle. 'Or you'll be next… stand clear!' Crossley shouted and lobbed a toadstool into the cave.

The explosion was magnified in the small chamber and sent a blast of debris over them, but John had turned in time to avoid a face full of stones.

'What did you do that for, you imbecile?' Lavalle roared, dusting himself off.

'We had to kill it,' Crossley replied.

'Well now you've woken up the whole damn nest.'

John looked up to see row after row of hexagonal caves lined on top of one another, leading up the entire cliff face. 'There must be hundreds of them.'

More screams could be heard and John rushed to Mata's cave in time to see a pair of glistening jaws piercing through the rear of the cave.

Lavalle bellowed, 'Everyone out of the caves and into the forest as fast as you can.'

A low humming sound was coming from the giant colony, so John grabbed his bag and ran, catching glimpses of jaws and clawed feet bursting through the walls of each cave he passed.

'Bloody giant wasps,' he heard Crossley muttering ahead. 'What's next? A troop of groundhogs with machetes?'

'Downhill!' Lavalle led them into the forest.

The humming noise was getting louder. With a glance back, John saw a line of wasps the size of fighter planes streaming out of the nest.

They were at the forest edge when the first insects attacked, grabbing the stragglers and stabbing with their stings.

'Don't stop!' John shouted to a medieval lancer who struck out at the flying beasts with his long spear.

'I'll hold them off!' The lancer jabbed one attacker in the abdomen, sending it falling to the ground in a wild panic of thrashing legs and pincers.

The buzzing grew louder in response.

'You're just making them worse!' John shouted, but it was too late.

Three wasps descended and pierced the lancer with their metre-long stings.

'John!' Crossley shouted from the forest edge. 'Hurry up!'

Once again, there was nothing John could do and he sprinted into the safety of the dark forest.

'We've gotta keep moving.' Crossley pointed into the forest.

'Aye, they're tenacious beasties,' said the Scottish warrior. 'They won't give up.'

'Right then,' said Lavalle, 'follow me!'

Althorn appeared between John and Mata. 'You'll need to be quick – they're crawling in.' He vanished and appeared next to Lavalle. 'Get deeper into the wood.'

What felt like an age later, the line of soldiers filed out of the forest and onto a long, sandy beach.

'Wow,' John said, squinting in the light.

Small waves folded softly into the sand and palms swayed in the breeze.

John dropped his bag and fell to his knees. 'This is beautiful.'

'Wait a minute.' Crossley's loud voice pierced the serene moment. 'That's no river – it's a sea!'

Althorn looked blank. 'What's a sea?'

'Are you serious?' Crossley growled.

Althorn shrugged.

'Great, so now we have to cross–'

'Quiet!' Lavalle shouted and pointed to the sky.

John looked up and shielded his eyes with his good hand to see a line of dark silhouettes descending from the clouds.

'I want to talk to you about the future,' Samas said to Li as they walked ahead of the main party.

'Go on,' Li replied with no emotion.

'What was war like in your time?' Samas asked.

'To be honest, we fight over the same thing – power. Power over trade, water or oil. But the fighting is very different from your time. We fight in cities, not on plains. Anyone in the open would be killed by tracker robots or vaporised by cosmo-tanks…'

Samas frowned as Li's words made no sense.

'Automated fighting machines,' Li explained.

Samas nodded, picturing wooden constructions firing exploding spears. 'And in the cities you fight with guns and explosions?'

'Yes.'

'Hand-to-hand combat? Face to face?'

'Yes.'

'And they let women fight?'

Li paused. 'Yes – in fact, where I come from, the best soldiers are women.'

Samas waited a few strides before asking, 'When are you going to tell the rest of the group you're a woman?'

'I'm not,' Li answered quickly. 'The last thing we need is more disruption.'

'But you will tell them eventually?'

Li didn't answer.

The path eventually stopped at a cliff edge.

'There's a rough track down there.' Bowman stood at the edge of the two-hundred-foot-high cliff in the hazy dusk light. 'It zigzags down. It'll be tight.'

Samas couldn't see any path.

'After you then, sure-foot!' Sakarbaal patted Bowman on the shoulder. 'Don't worry – we're right behind you.' He laughed.

Bowman made tentative steps down the narrow ledge, avoiding the piles of scree and loose stone.

'Careful there!' Samas shouted.

The rest of the Night Watch stared down, holding their collective breath as the Englishman picked out a safe route.

'It's fine!' he shouted back up from a ledge. 'Come on!' he beckoned.

'Why not?' Sakarbaal stepped down onto the precarious path, using his trident for balance, followed by the rest of the group.

Samas studied the cliff. Rocks jutted out, capturing soil for shrubs, whose roots secured the meandering path. Samas' turn came, and he cautiously positioned his sandalled feet on the dusty path which had been flattened by the first soldiers. He kept one eye on the path and another on the men up front.

'Woah!' Olan steadied himself after a slip that sent shards of rock into the forest below.

'This bit's a bit hairy,' Bowman shouted up.

'Dido's pelt!' Samas heard Sakarbaal join Bowman at a resting point. 'We're not even halfway down.'

The air cooled and an evening mist rose from the thick forest below.

'We should have made ropes,' Samas mumbled to himself. 'Don't rush – take your time!' He called down and took his eyes off the path. With a twist of the ankle, he slipped… the weight of his shield pulled him away from the cliff and he fell.

Down.

Through thin air.

It felt like time stood still as Samas saw shocked faces above him – Li; Mihran; Bowman; Sakarbaal – felt a wave of calm wash over him, found himself staring up the cliff face and into the dark clouds above. He stopped thrashing his arms and legs. What will be, will be, he thought. Then he slammed into a ledge with an explosion that shook his bones and darkness consumed him.

His next sensation was pain. It came in the form of light. He saw a low, grey light pulsing. Was that his heartbeat or his pounding head? Then a lightning strike ripped across his vision. What was that? Samas could feel something sticking into him. He tried to move and the lightning flashed again. Where was the pain? He moved his legs, then his arms. They were stuck but if he… there was the flash again.

This wasn't good.

He tried to open his eyes but they remained stubbornly closed. What was he afraid of seeing? He'd seen worse in battle. He heard voices and a spray of stones clattered near his feet.

'He's down here!'

Who was that? Sakarbaal?

'I can't get across to him.'

'I can make it from here,' another voice replied.

Samas forced his eyes open and craned his neck but couldn't see either of them. Was it Bowman? The pain in his arm throbbed, so he tried to shift his weight but was pinned down. Why couldn't he move?

'Samas!' Bowman came into view, sliding down to where he lay.

'I–' Samas tried to move, but the pain made him dizzy. He held his breath, trying not to vomit.

'Are you hurt?' Bowman asked.

'My arm…'

'If that's all, you got away lightly – it wasn't a race, you know. No prizes for getting down first.'

Samas started to laugh but a pain in his side stopped him. 'Maybe my ribs as well.'

Sakarbaal was beside Bowman now. 'We'll have to lift him out – sit him against the cliff.'

'Easier said than done. It's lucky these plants broke your fall,' Bowman said. 'And having your shield on your back.'

'My shield!' Samas would be lost without his weapons. 'Has it broken?'

'Don't worry, let's concentrate on you,' Bowman answered. 'Ready?'

Sakarbaal nodded. 'Ready. One arm and one leg each… easy… come on.'

The men carefully laid Samas on the dusty ledge.

'I could have predicted it would be you.' Mihran appeared, wearing a look of distaste.

Samas stared back and said nothing. If I can face an army, he thought, I can face you. And if I can face you, I can face this pain. As if in response, a shot of pain darted along his wrist, causing him to wince. I'll fight again, he thought.

'We'll see,' Mihran said, then turned to Sakarbaal. 'Make a stretcher.' He ushered the rest of the soldiers along. 'Keep moving.'

Samas looked at Mihran in confusion. Had he just replied to what Samas had been thinking? No, it must have been a trick of the mind, he thought, I must have said it out loud.

Sleep took Samas again.

When he woke, Li was scanning his body. 'You've got bruising on your lower back which will heal with heat-wave treatment.'

Samas' eyes widened as he envisioned red-hot coals.

'Your main issues are the broken ribs and arm.' She motioned towards Samas' left arm, which he cradled.

Samas looked at it, wondering how Li would fix it.

'Is it a clean break?' Mihran asked.

'Yes, both bones, no shards or fractures.'

'Then we must put a splint on it and let it heal naturally,' Mihran suggested, to Samas' relief.

'We can use clay to make a cast,' Li said. 'The clay in the cliff is high in gypsum and sand.'

Mihran nodded. 'Make it quick – we must keep moving.'

Li gave Samas a sedative before setting his arm, and the next time he woke he was lying in a bed of ferns by the shore of a lake. His arm felt tight and a tingling sensation ran down his side but he didn't move for fear of setting off more pain. He looked up: dusk was coming.

'Something's happening down the coast.' Bowman appeared and Mihran stood up with a flourish of red robes. 'I heard shouts and…'

'What is it?' Samas asked but Mihran held up his hand.

Li scanned the forest canopy. 'I see a swarm of large hornets in attack formation.'

'When you say large, how large?' someone out of Samas' view asked.

'Taller than a man,' Li replied.

'Target practice?' Bowman smiled at Marodeen, who didn't look impressed.

Li followed the line of flight. 'A group of soldiers are being attacked on the beach. What shall we do?'

All eyes turned to their injured battle leader, Samas.

'I think I'll sit this one out.' Samas smiled at Mihran. 'Commander, it's over to you.'

The giant wasps swarmed over the rocks where the Day Watch hid and fought sword to pincer. John was pinned down in a gap, his feet slipping in the sand as he struck out at a snapping insect. He gripped the metal body of the gun with his left hand and jabbed the muzzle at the wasp's eye.

'Get away!' he shouted and threw a handful of sand.

With a wild shriek, the wasp leapt back, revealing the hazy sky. Shaken but still fighting fit, John peeked over a rock to see the wasp writhing in the sand, clawing at a spear in its abdomen.

'Finish it off!' A cry came from behind John and Randeep leapt out to deftly decapitate the wasp with his curved sword.

John tapped his gun-arm and said to Crossley, 'If this bloody thing was working, I'd have killed twenty by now.'

Crossley shrugged. 'Twenty's nothing.'

'A brief respite and they'll be back,' Lavalle said, catching his breath.

John stared at the yellow gore dripping off the knight's broadsword.

'Where's Althorn?' John asked.

'Deploying ammo to the archers,' said Lavalle.

'Where from?' John asked.

Crossley pointed to a faint blur criss-crossing the battlefield. 'He's picking up missed arrows.'

The buzzing noise was getting louder again.

Lavalle rallied the unit. 'Same again – heads down, aim for the waist or eyes. Crossley, you and John finish off any brought to ground.'

The sky darkened as two lines of wasps descended.

'They're throwing everything they've got at us!' Crossley shouted.

John could make out a spray of arrows and quivering spears flying out of the palms where Euryleia's group lay hidden, but only a couple of wasps were hit. He tensed his hand and rubbed his gun, wishing he could use it again as the wasps arrived, diving in sting first.

'Gotcha!' The Scottish warrior cut a sting in half with a swipe of his blade.

The wasp shrieked and scrambled on the rocks in pain where, in a flash of blue, Randeep leapt up to slice the beast's head off and kick the flailing body onto the sand.

He was a true hero, John thought.

Another wasp attacked and John ducked down as its long sting darted past, scraping the rock by his head. For some reason, his grandfather's words came back to him from the day he'd practically frog-marched John to the army office: 'You defend your people, you defend your land. Every man able to walk should be fighting tooth and nail!'

John looked around. Everyone was swiping, jabbing or blocking with all their strength. What if someone died when there was something he could have done? He looked at Crossley, who was throwing stones at the nearest wasp. John's hand dropped to feel for stones on the ground but felt the satchel instead.

'Oi, Crossley!' he shouted and held up the bag.

Crossley grinned. 'I thought we'd run out!'

Leaning on a shoulder-high rock, John breathed in deeply, took out a toadstool and counted. 'One, two, three...' He lobbed the first one like a hand grenade and rolled over the rock onto his feet. 'Come on, you bastards!' he yelled as he ran, throwing explosive fungi with his good arm.

Crossley was soon beside him. 'Give 'em hell, Johnny!' he shouted as his pitching arm delivered a devastating throw: de-winging a wasp and sending it crashing into two others.

'Don't call me Johnny!' John shouted as he ran across the sand with no destination in mind.

One toadstool missed its target and blew a crater out of the beach, covering Crossley with sand.

'Hey, watch it!' he shouted.

Wasps detached themselves from the main fight and followed John, but were met with balls of fire. Wings, striped abdomens and heads lay scattered along the beach next to human limbs and corpses. After two minutes of running and dodging, John was disorientated. A few throws later, his gun felt twice as heavy and the wet sand pulled at his feet. He stumbled and panted hard as his lungs grew heavy.

'Come on!' Crossley beckoned towards the palms where the archers were hiding, but John's legs were slowing down.

His vision started to blur, so he stopped for a second. His head was thumping with all the noise: the buzzing; shouting; explosions. Visions of one of his old battles tried to invade the space behind his eyes, but he was too drained to concentrate on them. He strained and tensed his muscles, forcing his body to move, and felt a click in his gun-arm as though one of his lost tendons had pulled an internal mechanism.

With a solid thump, a wasp landed on the sand in front of him, followed by two more.

'Oh shit,' John mumbled and stepped backwards.

He thrust his hand into the satchel but only one toadstool remained. One throw might injure two wasps, but others would be on him in a second. He had to get to the palm trees, he thought, as a new wasp hovered menacingly overhead, swinging its sting at John's shoulder.

'Get back!' John shouted and swiped his gun-arm, but the weight of the gun pulled him over and the wasp's sting scratched his right shoulder, tearing at his shirt.

'Damn it!' He threw the last toadstool and watched it fall short, showering the advancing wasps with sand, infuriating them.

They charged at John with pincers gnashing... but a line of light, brighter than the sun, tore a smoking hole through one head, then the other. Both wasps collapsed in the sand. John stared in disbelief and turned to where the beam had come from. Scores of soldiers were advancing along the beach, surrounded by a wave of fire and green light.

Chapter 6

Following the group of night-travelling soldiers through the forest, Delta-Six had gathered data supporting his theory that they were trapped in a virtual prison. The soldiers were showing changes to their physical appearance picked up by his sensors. Growth spurts, increased bone density and bizarre mutations, which suggested a degradation of the virtual world. The night group discussed other events which suggested similar glitches: arrows acting like birds; flying sharks; extinct beasts.

Despite the evidence though, the world still felt real to Delta-Six.

'Maybe my emotions are warping my judgement?' he told his log as he kept out of earshot of the soldiers. 'I try to concentrate on the facts. But it doesn't tie up. I'm the most advanced soldier here, but is that because the virtual world doesn't have the capacity to create more advanced beings or, judging by how my war was advancing with avatars in the asteroid belt... am I the last soldier to fight on Earth?'

When Delta-Six found a safe place to rest, he thought about how he had changed since arriving in this land. His suit and body had started to merge, his thoughts felt less restricted and even his dreams were different here. Back home he would have the same dream every two or three nights: a dream of resting in the sunlight on a veranda overlooking the green fields of recolonised Europe with a gorgeous woman; children playing in the long garden with a retro-dog; a warm sun; a good life.

Delta-Six's logs didn't record the last time he'd had that dream.

Now he thought about it, the dream was clearly tied to the performance rewards that led to their retirement package. If Delta-Six completed his allocated tours with distinction he would have a pretty, fertile wife and a villa on the Elysium plains. Perform below par and he would end up in a regen-colony on the edge of the wasteland with a stick-thin, toothless wife, spending the rest of their lives drawing out toxins on a reed farm.

As Delta-Six drifted off to sleep in his night hammock, he wondered about the other Deltas and the original soldier all Deltas had been cloned from. What happened to him? Did he retire to Elysium? Did Elysium even exist?

Mihran was at point, leading the wedge of soldiers across the beach to attack the giant wasps. He would show Samas he could fight as well as command, he thought, as his feet pounded the sand. Ahead, the cloud of huge wasps harangued the humans stuck in their rock fort and light from explosions turned the wasps to silhouettes as two shapes ran from the rocks to the trees. Mihran recognised the short men from the obelisk hill and noted their bravery as they drew several wasps away from the swarm.

Mihran was ready to join in. He had left his long cloak with the ration bags and injured soldiers, and his shoulders felt loose, his arms strong.

'Release!' he shouted and the archers and riflemen he'd distributed on the flanks of the battalion fired their wild array of missiles.

Li's rifle was by far the most efficient, and wasp carcases were soon falling from the sky. As a result, the wasp swarm spilt and a section turned to focus on Mihran's army. He pulled his sword from its sheath and felt the strength in its weight. His energy was high as the thought of previous battles surged through him and he relished the feeling of being one with his weapon again.

The first few wasps flew straight over Mihran and his compatriots, homing in on the archers, who gravitated towards Li for cover.

'Left wing!' Mihran shouted as he ran, but nobody looked at him. 'Olan!' he shouted, and the big Viking caught his gaze. 'Defend the archers!'

Olan grimaced before breaking his run to head back, taking a couple of men with him.

Then the second wave of wasps came, diving in sting first at Mihran and those about him. Mihran kept running and only swung his sword at the last second. He missed, but so did the wasp, which hovered menacingly above, ready to attack again.

Mihran swung his sword, in defence as much as attack. He could see the wasps' weak point was their waist, but it was midway between their sting and jaws. A second wasp joined the attack as the sound of wild buzzing and people shouting grew around Mihran. He parried, ducked and jabbed until he saw his moment – a quick slice and he took off one wasp's wing, sending it spiralling away. He turned on the second and, with a quick feint and slice, cut its abdomen off. The scream was almost human, he thought, as the creature flew away to crash into the sea, leaving a trail of brown liquid in its wake.

Mihran caught his breath and scanned the battle around him. He watched his soldiers fight and observed how the warriors who fared the best were those who had naturally paired with another. Those on their own were easily picked off and those in larger groups got in each other's way. It was the fighting pairs who were turning the tide. More wasps had come, but they were too few now and were being chased by the humans who had escaped their fort.

The battle would be over soon.

As the last few wasps were being cleared up, Mihran cleaned his sword on a cloth, resheathed it and walked to meet the soldiers they had saved.

A tall man carrying a longsword was first to greet him – Sir William Lavalle, he recognised, the man who'd argued against travelling at night.

Lavalle gave a nod and said, 'I see you travel during the day now.'

'It's lucky for you we did,' Mihran replied and gave a wry smile, 'I doubt you would have lasted until nightfall.'

'So the bird's feathers give the arrows the power to think?'

John heard Lavalle's voice and kept his eyes closed. He wasn't in pain, but his head felt numb.

'Yes.' A voice John didn't recognise answered the knight. 'But only in flight.'

A new voice joined in. 'You should have seen the first arrow hit the shark!'

'You fought the shark too?' Althorn was with the group.

John opened his heavy eyes and saw dancing daggers. Steadily, his eyes focused on wafting palm fronds lit by a fire. It was night and they were still on the beach. Images of the wasps came to John and he closed his eyes.

'What did you say your name was?' the new voice asked.

'Sir William Lavalle, and you?'

'Mark Bowman, archer.'

'Yes, I can see that,' Lavalle replied.

'But did you see my arrows?' Bowman asked. 'After Marodeen's arrow hit the shark I re-fletched mine and, well… you saw the flames, didn't you?'

John remembered the orange trails across the sky and the soldiers advancing. He'd recognised some of them from the obelisk hill – the ones who'd wanted to travel by night.

'They were your arrows?' Lavalle sounded impressed. 'A useful weapon.'

John tried to move but his right arm was stuck to the ground. He licked his lips and pictured a glass of cold, fresh water.

'Hey, John's awake!' Crossley was soon by his side. 'Can you hear me, John?'

'Quick, get Euryleia,' Lavalle said.

'Hey, give him some air,' Crossley said.

John blinked a couple of times. 'Water…'

'Here you go buddy.' Crossley lifted John's head and brought a canteen to his lips.

The water gave John strength. He looked at the faces around him: Mata, Althorn, Lavalle, Crossley and some people he vaguely recognised. The weakness in his body pulsed up and down both arms.

'Thank God you're better,' Lavalle said.

'You've been talking in your sleep,' Crossley said. 'You kept saying "*Don't call me Johnny*". I didn't realise you found it so annoying.'

John managed a smile but the dizziness was returning.

'Euryleia's been looking after you,' Althorn said.

'Don't worry,' Mata said. 'She's not using the red root she used on me.'

John nodded but his eyes weighed heavy and darkness fell.

Mihran had been quiet since the battle with the wasps. His thoughts had taken him to the dunes of his youth and the cities of his war days. His memories were fresher now – more real. He had dwelled in them for days, but now he played mental games in his head: mathematical conundrums; memory tests; battle formations. He developed a game of duels between members of the expanded group, to see who would win. The more he practised, the more he became lost in his solitary world.

'So you've changed your mind?' Samas appeared next to Mihran.

He took a breath before answering, 'Yes.' What was it about Samas that riled him so? An image of a former – and totally incompetent – captain came to him. 'Our original logic was flawed – we have lost thirty soldiers, the Day Watch twenty. If we had travelled in daylight we would number more than our current 160.'

Mihran wondered what the Babylonian was thinking and felt a wave of light rush through his mind.

'So day travel had benefits?' Samas asked.

Mihran examined the light around Samas' head and picked out shapes, then replied, 'The uniform temperature makes day travel comfortable and the random threats here are difficult to defend against during the night.'

'You mean it's better when we can see our enemy?'

'Yes,' Mihran saw an image of the elephant they had fought in the light around Samas' head.

Samas moved to sit on a rock and Mihran fought to keep hold of the light link. He watched the image flicker from the elephant to a dusty battlefield and then to Li's face.

'Did you have any idea Li is a woman?' Samas asked.

Mihran broke the link with a shallow gasp. The images were his thoughts? 'No, I had no idea… but we are stronger with her.'

Samas frowned.

'And we're stronger with the day travellers in our ranks,' Mihran continued.

The overview of the group in the back of Mihran's mind had expanded to include the Day Watch, taking in skills, weapons and age, just as he had done with the Night Watch.

'So who will lead us now?' Samas asked.

'I will.' Mihran straightened his back.

'And what about Lavalle? He leads the Day Watch.'

'I will lead,' Mihran whispered. 'I am the Commander.'

Samas stood up, apparently ready for an argument. 'We are all fighting men. None of us are used to hiding in tents or lookout hills.'

Samas was right, and he'd commanded and fought well during the battle. If Mihran was to weigh up the true strength of this battalion, he would have to be honest, put personal feelings aside.

'And yet we are changing, aren't we?'

'Yes.' Samas' shoulders dropped.

'Our positive attributes are being enhanced and our weaknesses strengthened,' Mihran said.

Samas looked along the beach and Mihran followed suit. Scores of men and women. Ultimately, everyone was out for themselves, Mihran knew that, but by working together they increased their chance of survival.

Mihran opened his mind to Samas' thoughts. Images of ships and rough seas appeared. Obviously no sailor. New pictures emerged: children saluting him; an army bigger than any Mihran had seen before; metal clashing; arrows piercing; yells; blood; hooves thundering; spears thrusting… and a light Mihran remembered all too well. Samas was haunted by his last moments on the battlefield. How many others still dwelled in their past? Mihran sniffed. He had cut his last day off with ease – it was just another battle. These men had to do likewise if they were to fight effectively as a unit.

He turned to focus on another soldier: a Russian swordsman, whose head was mostly filled with images of naked women – real memories or daydreams, Mihran couldn't tell. How about someone else? John Greene was nearer now, so he focused on his thoughts: a young boy surrounded by fruit and vegetables, laughing; an old man in a chair, shouting; symbols on a medal; a body under a bloody sheet; a woman's scream; silhouettes crawling towards him.

Mihran pulled away and fought to catch his breath. He blinked, unaware how much energy it had taken out of him. He smiled: it was exhilarating. Like the first time he had ridden a horse.

'Is this God's will?' he asked the sky. 'Why have I been given this gift?'

A blur of movement caught his eye and Mihran instinctively

reached for the mind like casting out a fishing net. Pictures came: an obelisk hidden beneath rocks; water lapping around its sandy base; a dark room; a knife; a woman; blood and a flash.

Very interesting, Althorn, Mihran thought, and walked to where the blur was heading – to a group of Day Watch soldiers.

The swirl of sand slowed to form the shape of the Celt cut-throat. 'Lavalle, I have found something you need to see.'

Lavalle raised his head.

Mihran joined them. 'Is this something I need to know?'

'I'm sure I can handle it, thank you.' Lavalle turned away.

'No, I insist,' Mihran said. He had to know everything if he was going to be in charge – and in control. Information was a weapon and he needed to be well armed. 'We are one group now.'

'Right, yes.' Lavalle turned to Althorn. 'So, what have you found?'

Althorn spoke quietly and Mihran already knew what he was going to say.

'I have found another obelisk.'

Olan was sitting on a log with Bowman, watching the sea lap against the sandy shore, when he heard Li calling, 'Gather round!'

Small groups of warriors moved up the beach towards Li, who stood away from where Euryleia tended the injured soldiers. Olan studied the group and recognised more faces from the obelisk hill. Since the battle, they had foraged and eaten as one unit, but many kept to their original friendship groups.

'Listen up!' Li's voice was clear without shouting. 'We have decided to continue to travel by day.'

'But there's nowhere left to travel to!' a voice shouted out, sending laughter around the crowd.

'Which leads me to my second point,' Li replied. 'We have new information. Mihran…'

Mihran stepped forward, hands on hips, revealing his sword. Now Olan had seen him in action, his respect for the Arab had gone up several notches.

'Earlier today, while scouting this… endless coast, Althorn discovered a set of obelisks.'

A murmur rose from the soldiers and Olan stared down the coast but could see nothing.

'Subsequent surveys show these obelisks are scattered along the shoreline and the message is clear – if we are to reach the silver gates we must cross this sea.' Mihran gestured and Olan turned to stare at the placid waters.

'Where to?' someone asked.

Li replied, 'The obelisk says we must leave the safety of our homeland to venture to lands anew.'

'And what're we going to sail on?' asked another.

'We can build rafts,' Crossley's voice cut above the others, 'but is this what we want to do? Seriously?'

'What do you mean?' Lavalle asked. 'The obelisk says–'

'I get what the obelisk says,' Crossley replied, 'but I wanna know why we're being pushed around like toys? Why are we agreeing to that? I mean, who's really in charge here?'

A silence fell and Olan stared across the open water again. He had ventured out to sea a hundred times and the thought of taking a new voyage excited him. Maybe some of the men around him were scared of the ocean? Many of his crew had been on their first voyage, but had been taught to hide it.

'There's nothing to fear,' Olan said and stepped forward so everyone could see him. 'The sea looks calm and–'

'I'm not scared,' Crossley replied, 'I'm just asking why we should go in the first place? I mean, we read the first obelisk and trotted off the hill like good little Boy Scouts, following some–'

'And what happened next?' Mihran cut Crossley off. 'The hill was demolished. I think the message was clear. We move on or suffer the consequences.' He waited for a response but got none. 'I resent these orders we are forced to follow, as much as you,' Mihran said, 'but until we are in a position to negotiate our position, I suggest we obey.'

'I agree,' Samas said and was followed by several other soldiers.

'So I suggest we get to work on our craft,' Mihran said. 'Crossley, we could use your expertise, but if you would rather stay behind, that is your decision.'

Olan watched the short American, who said nothing and lit another of his cigarettes. He was right to argue, Olan thought. They could keep marching and fighting but, without any reward or purpose, even the most loyal soldier would soon start questioning their orders.

A crash of timber woke John.

'...coming along well. Li has been cutting palms with her rifle,' Crossley was saying. 'The density's as low as balsa, so we'll need less wood.'

'And the other soldiers?' Lavalle asked.

'All good workers – Olan's pretty handy with the axe,' Crossley replied.

An odd silence followed.

'Why are you looking at me like that?' Lavalle sounded angry.

John turned his head and managed to open his eyes to watch the men.

'Well, he's a Viking, isn't he?'

'Yes.'

'So he could be your ancestor – Li told me they settled Normandy and then conquered England, so...'

'Ah, yes,' Lavalle looked over at the large Norseman. 'I hadn't thought about it like that.'

'It's quite neat when you think about it,' Crossley continued. 'I mean, he could be your great, great, great whatever and any of you could be my ancestors, what with all the Europeans who–'

Lavalle shook his head. 'No. I don't think so,' he said vehemently and walked off.

John smiled. His head and body felt less heavy now and he wondered how long he had been asleep.

'We need to speed up!' a deep voice shouted.

John caught a glimpse of Mihran's maroon robes flowing in the sea breeze. Olan was nearby, binding palm trunks with green vines, while other soldiers were laying out poles and collecting purple bladders from the high-tide mark. Beyond them, a soldier with a clay cast on one arm was talking to the future soldier with the mask. John looked at his arm: it was almost all gun now. We're all changing, he thought, and remembered Mata and the wolves. But why?

'You're awake!' Mata's voice drew his attention.

John eased himself up onto his good elbow. 'Yes.'

'Take it easy.' Mata helped John to sit up against a palm. 'Drink?'

'Thanks.' John took a sip from Mata's canteen.

He could see more now. Three other soldiers lay wounded beside him with missing limbs or with Euryleia's poultices strapped to wounds.

'How many dead?' John asked.

'Seven,' Mata replied. 'Myrcin the lancer and Jarha the Egyptian.'

'How many of us will make it to the gates?' John asked.

Mata looked to the sea horizon and shrugged, then nodded at John's arm. 'Euryleia thinks the poison from the sting sped up your changes.'

'Changing into what though?' John raised both arms with a wince. 'This'll never fire again, that's for sure.' The gun-arm was only a few inches longer than his left arm now. 'It feels lighter.'

'He's awake then?' John recognised the voice of the archer who had been talking to Lavalle. 'Li tells me you're English like me. I'm Bowman.'

John dropped his arms and looked at Bowman. He could easily have been one of the lads back in his battalion. 'Yes, London born and bred. How about you?

'Wisbury, south of Lincoln. Not that I've spent much time there recently.'

John smiled. 'Tell me about it – I've been the wrong side of the Channel for years.'

Bowman smiled back. 'I would shake your hand but…'

John instinctively moved his coat to cover his arm.

'No it's alright, friend, I've seen stranger, believe me!' Bowman said.

Mata stood up.

'Have I been asleep long?' John asked.

'One night since the battle,' Mata replied.

'So we still have time to get to the silver gates?'

'Depends how big this sea is.' Mata stared out to sea again.

'And how far the gates are once we find land,' Bowman said.

'I'd like to see the rafts,' John said.

'Come on then,' Mata helped him to his feet.

They took it slow across the beach and John rested, leaning against Mata as they watched the hive of activity, the soldiers strapping leaf-wrapped packets of food, spare weapons and gourds of water to the rafts.

John felt his energy come back. 'Let's get closer.'

Mata helped him over to where Olan worked the last trunks into place. 'You must be John,' he said, with a glance at his arm. 'I'm Olan.'

'Hello,' John said.

Olan smiled, and looked at Mata. 'Have you got shorter?'

Mata's face was like carved stone. Then he burst out laughing: his tattoos wrinkling.

'What?' Olan looked at John. 'What did I say?'

John shrugged.

Mata's laugh slowed to a smile. 'Of all the changes, you ask if I'm shorter? Ha! No, my friend,' Mata patted the Viking on his shoulder. 'You have grown.'

'Really?'

John stared up at both tall warriors. They both looked huge to him.

Samas came over, having heard the conversation. 'We can't have grown – our clothes would be too small.'

'Well, we couldn't have shrunk or ours would be too big,' Mata replied.

'I know who can settle this.' Samas beckoned Li over. 'Li – you scanned us when you first arrived on the hill, correct?'

'Yes.' Li's visor stayed down.

'Well, how do we look now?' Olan asked, opening his arms.

Li's visor sent a blue, criss-cross pattern across Olan. 'Interesting…'

'Well?' Samas asked.

'Mata and John have the same dimensions as before,' Li replied. 'While you, Samas, are ten percent larger than when we arrived.'

'And me?' Olan asked.

'Even bigger – fourteen percent extra body mass.'

Lavalle was drawn over too. 'Excuse me, madam, but how do you know this?'

He drew strange looks.

'Madam?' John looked at Li.

'I can only suggest it was the…'

'Elephant steaks!' Olan shouted.

'Well, it could have been the food. Who's to know what's driving these changes?' Li said. 'When populations of a species diverge, environmental forces work differently on each group, causing them to change physiologically as they adapt to their new environment – but that's over several generations, not individual lifetimes.'

An array of blank faces stared at Li and a silence held until she turned to Olan. 'It could have been the elephant meat, yes.'

Mata turned to Lavalle. 'More importantly, why did you call Li a madam?'

Lavalle smiled. 'Well, my painted friend, where I come from, ladies are treated with respect and I merely…'

'Is it true?' John turned to Li. 'Are you…?'

'A woman?' Li said, with a glance at Samas, 'Yes.' And her visor slid back to reveal a truly beautiful, feminine face.

Chapter 7

Dakaniha had a dilemma. He was tracking a warrior he desperately wanted to learn from, but whose martial skills terrified him. Although he had yet to set eyes on him, Dakaniha could tell from the trail of destruction that teaming up with this man could mean the difference between life and death in this new, dangerous land he found himself in, so he had followed the track of footprints: a trail of broken twigs and broken bodies.

For days, Dakaniha had followed this trail, finding pieces of discarded clothing with loops of leather that suggested the owner was well armed. In a small clearing, he'd discovered the body of a large, striped beast that, judging by its wounds and the tracks in the dusty ground, had been slain by two warriors, a third individual joining them after the fight. None were the man he tracked. He found three sets of bloody clothes nearby. Their footwear matched the footprints near the beast, yet Dakaniha assumed all three deaths had been the work of the man he was tracking. If these men had killed the huge carnivore, and the man he pursued had killed them, he had to be an even greater warrior!

He'd had his own encounters with beasts. Dakaniha came across a lethargic stream where he took off his rawhide armour and poured the cool water over his shaved head. Thoughts of his wife, Adsila, and his young daughter, Ayasha, had come to him: they were waiting patiently for him, so he would have to be patient in order to return to them.

It was then that he'd seen the creature.

A galitsohidv? Dakaniha thought as he marvelled at the beast's lethal-looking horns.

It had noticed him. With a twitch of an ear and a trio of hoof stomps, it charged, full speed. Dakaniha had scared off lone wolves and hungry bears, but this animal was not going to be frightened by sticks of fire and its hide was too thick for his arrows. It bore down on him with a thundering gallop, leaving him two options – run or climb. So he did both. He scrambled up the low branches of the nearest tree as the heavyweight dashed beneath, ripping up clods of earth and snorting as it passed. Dakaniha was back on the ground in a second, running in the opposite direction and hoping the beast was not as good at tracking as he was.

Deeper into the forest he'd travelled until finally he'd come across another, intertwining path. So now, as the light faded and dusk closed in, he crouched to study the trail. The footprints weren't those of a British soldier, yet they weren't Aniyunwiya or those of the great warrior.

Will this land give me no clues? Dakaniha asked the canopy of leaves above.

As he lowered his head, he caught a glimpse of light in his peripheral vision. A campfire! Dakaniha closed in, with soft steps, avoiding dry leaves and twigs. He crouched nearby and saw a white man by the fire, which flickered and glinted off the bronze chest plate and helmet lying by the soldier's side. He had the wrong clothing to be British and had no rifle. Creeping closer, Dakaniha saw a long spear and a round shield and saw the man was wrapped in a red cape.

The stranger spoke, but used words Dakaniha didn't recognise, then tilted his head to one side and smiled.

Dakaniha stood to his full height and stepped into the light of the fire. 'I am Dakaniha of the Aniyunwiya people. Your people call us Cherokee.' He stood patiently, waiting for a reply.

The man spoke again and studied Dakaniha's bow and axe with obvious interest, but Dakaniha didn't recognise a single word.

'I am Dakaniha.' He stabbed his chest with a forefinger.

The man smiled then laughed a little, shaking his ponytail, then gestured to the fire.

Dakaniha frowned. Who was this man? A scout from another invading army? A new soldier fighting for the British?

The long-haired soldier gestured to the fire again and pointed to the ground. Then he tossed a cooked leg of bird to Dakaniha, who caught the charred meat and frowned. He weighed up the stranger's motives and, deciding he would be able to defend himself if attacked, sat down to tuck into the meat. It tasted good.

Chapter 7

'We should leave,' Dakaniha said the next morning as he shook the dust off his cloak and pulled it over his shoulders.

The long-haired soldier stretched, pointed at the hazy sky and made a comment Dakaniha couldn't understand.

He squinted at the foreigner, trying to make sense of his words. 'We go this way.' He led the man to the great warrior's trail, pointing out the shoe prints and pieces of broken twig. 'This belongs to a brave warrior who killed three dangerous men.'

The soldier casually swung his long spear over his shoulder, gave Dakaniha his broad smile and started jogging along the trail.

By dusk, there was still no sign of the warrior.

On the second morning, the pair entered a range of hills covered in orange and yellow cacti.

Dakaniha stood on the peak of the first hill and scanned the horizon but there was nothing he recognised. The twigs on the trail had been replaced by snapped cactus spines. They followed the trail, where the hills formed a rolling plateau, until Dakaniha found new tracks that merged with the path.

'They've walked over the footprints,' Dakaniha said, growing anxious, and his pounding heartbeat sounded loud in his ears, along with another sound carried by the wind.

'Somebody is in trouble,' Dakaniha said and looked to the stranger to see if he could hear it too.

He tapped his ear and pointed off the path.

They followed the calls to a shallow valley where the cacti grew thin. A red ground vine covered the dusty soil and, at the centre of the dell, sat a dark, ridged crater, staring at the sky like a pupil in a giant eye.

Dakaniha jogged behind his companion and eyed the enclosing hills warily. He rubbed his left temple. Something didn't feel right here. They jogged to the crater and Dakaniha stared into the abyss to see three pairs of eyes peering back up. The hole was twenty paces across with steep sides lined with shards of white glass, like the mouth of a giant subterranean beast. A voice shouted from the darkness but it was another garbled mess Dakaniha didn't understand.

The long-haired warrior had walked out of view but reappeared carrying an armful of red vines. Dakaniha took one and pulled on it to test its strength.

'This might work,' he said, tied two lengths together and lowered one end into the hole.

The trapped soldiers were still shouting as Dakaniha and the stranger took the strain and felt the weight on the other end of the vine. After a few yelps and growls from the pit, a black face appeared and clambered over the lip.

Dakaniha looked at the African with wide eyes and the man gave him a similar stare. Dakaniha saw glistening cuts on his forearms and shins but he seemed more concerned with getting everyone out of the hole.

The next soldier was another African, whose face carried a deep wound on his swollen eye.

Finally, a soldier with a round helmet pulled himself over the crater's ridge. He spoke with a rapid tongue and Dakaniha had no idea what he was saying. After several failed attempts and several cautious glances to the sky, the soldier pulled a mushroom from a bag and offered it to the long-haired soldier, who declined. Dakaniha refused as well and was ready to draw his dagger when the soldier blew a dust from the mushroom in his face.

Dakaniha stepped back, coughing and sneezing. A distant boom made him turn but he saw nothing in the sky. He scanned the landscape for cannon smoke but it was clear. By the time he had turned a full circle, the words of the saved soldiers had become clear.

'...two bodies down there, but we have to leave them.' The round-helmeted soldier spoke with authority.

'What happened to them?' the long-haired warrior asked.

'One was killed by the bird and the other died when she fell into the pit.'

Dakaniha scowled at each soldier, confused. 'What sorcery is this?' he asked.

'Ah, it worked!' The soldier who had blown the spores at Dakaniha gave him a nod. 'I am Tode of the Golden Horde, my thanks for rescuing us.'

'I am Dakaniha of the Aniyunwiya,' he replied, still confused.

'This fungus,' Tode held up a grey mushroom, 'gives us the power to communicate.'

Dakaniha looked to the long-haired soldier, who seemed to accept the idea.

'I'm Kastor of Sparta,' he said and gave his broad smile. 'Nice to understand you at last.'

'Yes,' Dakaniha replied.

'And I am Osayimwese of the Oyo Empire,' the first African said.

'You are injured,' Kastor looked from man to man as they side-stepped down the crater.

'We were cut by the eggshells when we climbed up,' said Osayimwese, and he pulled a sliver of white stone from his belt and his eyes lit up. 'But I managed to take a piece.'

Dakaniha turned to the soldier with the swollen eye, but he was running away from the crater. A flash of lightning lit up a dark shape in the clouds, followed by a distant crackle of thunder.

Tode looked up to the cloudy sky and said, 'We must leave this place.'

Dakaniha watched in horror as a huge eagle descended from the clouds, its enormous talons gripping two struggling bodies. He had his bow strung in an instant.

'We must find cover!' Tode cried.

'There is no cover!' Kastor shouted and stood beside Dakaniha, switching the grip on his spear.

Long lines of lightning spat at the giant bird's back as it raised its enormous wings to slow its descent and dropped its prey into the pit. With a thrust of its wings, it arched around and released a high-pitched scream.

'Hold your ground!' Kastor shouted as the bird swept in to attack.

With forty paces between the diving eagle and the men, Dakaniha released an arrow. The eagle dipped its head and the arrow grazed its white feathered tail. Then Kastor's long spear flew true but only clipped a talon. Another arrow left Dakaniha's bow, followed by another from behind. Both hit the bird in the chest, but its speed only increased as its talons came down to grab the warriors. A long spear struck the eagle's wing, sending it into a lopsided lunge.

'Get down!' Kastor shouted as the bird brought its immense talons down on them.

Dakaniha rolled away and saw Kastor swiping with his sword.

A shriek from behind caused them to turn and the bird took off.

'It's got Askum!' Osayimwese shouted.

Dakaniha and Tode fired arrows at the bird as it grabbed the half-blind African with one talon and powered its enormous wings to take off again.

'We must regroup!' Kastor shouted.

'Here,' Kastor threw Osayimwese his spear. 'We have to attack it when it reaches the pit.'

The group ran back to the crater, watching as the eagle swooped down to drop Askum into the hole. Dakaniha took the right flank and fired as soon as he came into range, while Osayimwese ran straight for the bird, under the cover of Tode's arrows.

'Keep it grounded!' Kastor yelled.

Kastor and Osayimwese released their spears, piercing the eagle's back and side. The bird flapped its wings wildly and dropped to the floor to rip out the offending lances.

Kastor held his sword and shield tight and leapt in.

Maddened with injury, the eagle snapped its hooked beak at Kastor while Dakaniha ran to attack from behind.

Tode fired arrow after arrow and Osayimwese jabbed at the huge bird of prey with his spear, but it only had eyes for the Spartan. With jarred movements, Kastor shuffled to either side, swinging his sword, then lunged at the breast of the eagle. In response, the bird snapped at the sword, catching it in its beak and tossing it to one side.

'Damn it!' Kastor shouted as he disappeared from view under the eagle.

With his arrows barely scratching the bird, Dakaniha ran and leapt on its back: his axe hooked into the flesh of a wing while he stabbed frantically with his knife. Wild with fury, the eagle shrieked and rolled to the ground, knocking Dakaniha off, who scrambled away. The bird turned on him, but its head suddenly snapped to one side. A loud crack echoed around the valley and the giant bird fell dead on its side.

Kastor was on it in a flash, plunging his retrieved sword deep into the eagle's chest.

Dakaniha stood panting, not sure if he could believe the fight was over. He walked over to see blood pouring from the bird's eye.

'Who killed the tlanuwa?' he asked.

Osayimwese looked blank and Tode was scanning the horizon. 'Over there,' he raised his head.

Dakaniha turned to see a silhouette with a long rifle but, before he could shout, the soldier had fled.

Gal-qadan sat patiently on the grass, cleaning and sharpening his knife, as he often did while he thought about what he would like to do next. The motion of sweeping the whetstone back and forth along the knife had an almost hypnotic quality. His mind drifted and images of the men he had killed came and went, followed by those of his horse and his men, and he wondered how he came to be in this place.

His last memory before his arrival had been his journey returning to Mongolia with his host of mounted soldiers, following a winter of plundering Rus towns. A band of rebels had attacked on horseback, streaming down the foothills of the Ural Mountains like an avalanche. With little time to prepare, his men had fought in their full winter gear.

Gal-qadan had charged through the snow, his bow singing in his ear as he took out two horsemen before the rebels released a single arrow. Pass after pass, he and his men rode hard, firing and dodging until his horse started to slow: their steeds had no energy for their lethal retreat and counter-attack tactic. Instead, Gal-qadan plunged straight into the melee, his lance in one hand and his sword in the other.

Two frantic minutes later, with his lance stuck in the chest of one horseman and his shining scimitar held high above his head, a brilliant-white flash had blinded Gal-qadan and he'd found himself here, on this grassy hillside.

Gal-qadan thought about all the ways he could have lost his memory – hallucinations brought on by frostbite, dehydration or an internal wound? Had the flash been one of the exploding missiles the Han used? He removed his fur hat and replaced his helmet. He took off two layers of woollen clothing, but kept his lacquered leather armour, which led down to a set of iron fish-scale plates connecting his belt to his leather boots. These boots had lasted well, he thought, through countless raids on the Rus, travels across Kyrgyz, all the way from the Eastern open plains: his homeland.

Born on the edge of the Gobi desert where his nomadic tribe bred goats and horses, Gal-qadan, or 'cliff of steel' in his native tongue, had been raised to be as tough as the desert. His father had cast him out the day the supreme Khan took control of all tribes and summoned men for his army, a month before Gal-qadan's thirteenth birthday. Bullied by the soldiers, Gal-qadan had become a servant boy to the cavalry archers who made up the Khan's mobile army. Knowing nothing better, he'd cleaned horses, cooked food and endured the backhand of any officer who didn't like the look of him.

Then something changed.

It was a week after a steed had caught him on the side of the head with a wild hoof and Gal-qadan's skull still ached.

'Clean my horse, pig-boy!' A Mongol officer whipped him while he worked, trying to get a response out of the stubborn desert boy. 'Make sure you do a good job or I'll be feeding you horse shit for breakfast,' the officer spat.

Gal-qadan kept his head down and cleaned, avoiding eye contact. The treatment was nothing new, but this time, as his head throbbed, he heard a voice and a whip-crack opened a line of blood on his neck. The voice spoke, pulsed with the pain in his head, and seemed to say the same word over and over… kill, kill, kill.

That night, under the cover of darkness, the officer became Gal-qadan's first kill: his throat slit while he slept. Just like slaughtering sheep, Gal-qadan had thought, and wondered why he didn't feel any emotion. When he was younger, he had felt sad for the death of an animal, but now he only felt calm.

With a clear mind, Gal-qadan had taken the officer's weapons, strapped on his armour and leather boots – then fled on a spare horse. Two days later, he was riding west with another unit. Despite the odd-fitting armour, nobody questioned him, and he soon found himself in battle. With speed, Gal-qadan learnt to master the sword and bow, on horseback and on foot. Cold and fast, Gal-qadan's fearless fighting style earned the respect of his unit and, within two years, he was promoted to lead his own troop of horsemen. Through his leadership and cold-minded ruthlessness, over the next thirty years they became one of the most formidable and trusted units in the Khan's cavalry.

Gal-qadan smiled at the thought of his first kill, but it faded when he lamented the loss of his horse, which carried his rations, battleaxe and land bow, leaving him with just his small bow, quiver and sword.

Free from his winter clothing, he strode downhill into the forest, stepping over the smouldering limbs of dead soldiers.

Gal-qadan was well travelled but he couldn't picture any forest similar to this. From the shores of the Black Sea to the coast of China, nothing here was recognisable. The trees looked deciduous but, without a mountain range or a recognisable mammal or bird, he was lost. One thing was for sure – he had never seen or heard of the golden hills he could see in the distance.

With an eye on the trees and an ear open for the sound of fresh water, Gal-qadan picked up twigs as he walked and snapped them every few steps. They felt like birds' necks, he thought, and smiled.

'Well, at least we'll be eating well tonight.' Kastor gave a broad smile and pointed his bloody sword at the fallen bird.

'You want to eat it after it feasted on human flesh?' Tode asked.

Kastor shrugged. 'I can't see much else to eat. What do you want? A bit of leg?' He patted a muscular leg and made a slicing motion.

The men ignored him as Dakaniha pulled his axe out of the bird's back.

'We don't have time,' Tode said. 'We must keep walking.'

'What do you mean *we don't have time*?' Kastor asked, looking serious now.

Dakaniha stood and watched, still unsure how he could understand these foreigners.

'The message on the obelisk said we have fourteen days to reach the silver gates.'

'What obelisk?' Kastor and Dakaniha asked in unison.

'On the hill,' Tode replied.

'I remember the hill, but no obelisk,' said Dakaniha.

'Are you not searching for the gates?' Osayimwese asked.

'No,' Dakaniha said, 'I am tracking a great warrior. He travels light and has killed many, including three swordsmen who killed a striped beast.'

'And he knows the location of the gates?' Osayimwese asked.

'I'm sure he will have the answers we seek.'

'Are you suggesting we don't set camp and eat?' Kastor asked.

'No,' Tode answered sharply and looked up. 'We will find this leader and make for the silver gates.'

'Who made you in charge?' Kastor asked, staring at Tode.

'In charge? I'm just stating the obvious course of action,' Tode held the Spartan's stare. 'Do you have other options?'

'No.' Kastor didn't look fazed, Dakaniha thought. 'But, what happens if we don't get to the gates in time?'

Tode shrugged. 'Of that, I have no idea.'

'Stop!' Dakaniha crouched and the other three followed suit.

They had been walking for half a day through the tall orange cacti and hadn't come across another soul, until now.

'What is it?' Tode whispered.

Dakaniha showed two fingers and pointed to the right.

Tode nodded and pointed at Kastor, then at the ground. 'Don't move,' he whispered.

Dakaniha started his advance. Keeping low, beneath the wild orange cacti, he slid forwards to the brow of the nearest incline. Through the vegetation he could see two people staring at the ground. Slowly and silently, Dakaniha crept forward until he was within earshot.

'...should just take his weapons and go.'

'All he has is this metal stick – what use is it?'

'Shh, I think I can–'

The sound of pounding feet made Dakaniha turn as a blur of movement flashed past. Violent shouts filled the air as someone attacked the men. Dakaniha jumped up and rushed in, axe in hand, and stopped with a glare.

'What are you doing?' he asked.

Kastor was kneeling on one of the warriors, holding his hands behind his back, while the other lay dribbling into the dust. 'You three were taking your time, so…'

Tode and Osayimwese walked through the cacti to join them.

'Kastor, do you understand what *don't move* means?' The Mongol fixed his eyes on the Spartan.

Kastor laughed and pulled his captive's arms tighter. 'You think I'm taking orders from you? Look,' he motioned at the third person on the floor, lying in a pool of blood. 'These two are dangerous – they killed him, so I knew it would take a real soldier to capture them.'

Osayimwese stepped forward. 'You are saying I'm not a real soldier?' He raised his spear.

'Listen, I'm a little busy right now,' Kastor replied. 'But sure, if you want a fight, we can settle this later.'

The three men stared at him in silence.

Dakaniha watched Kastor look from man to man. 'Listen, I didn't mean to insult you but…'

The soldier underneath the Spartan mumbled and Kastor pushed his face in the dirt.

Tode slipped his jacket off and stretched his neck.

'What? You really want to do this now?' Kastor said. 'I could have all three of you disarmed in a heartbeat.'

'Do you want to prove that?' Osayimwese pulled out a dagger and spun his spear.

'I was trained to kill from the age of–' Kastor said.

Dakaniha saw Tode's hand reach for the hilt of his sword.

'I'm being serious,' Kastor continued. 'What I learnt before the age of twelve is more than–'

Osayimwese spat on the ground and Dakaniha bent down to pick up the rifle by the dead man's side.

Kastor shrugged and smacked his captive on the back of the head with his sword hilt, knocking him out cold. 'I guess I'll have to teach you. Lesson number one.' Dakaniha was impressed by Kastor's speed as he rolled away and, in a swift move, slipped his arm into the straps of his shield and grabbed his spear.

'Don't threaten to fight…' Kastor said as, with a spin and a lunge, the blunt end of his spear came down hard on Tode's knuckles, shoving his sword back in its scabbard, '…unless you mean…' the Spartan spun again, ducking Osayimwese's spear jabs, '…to draw…' Kastor swiped at Osayimwese's knee with his spear shaft, then slammed his shield into his face, '…blood.'

Dakaniha fired the dead soldier's gun in the air, releasing a deafening bang, and the men froze. 'This is a pointless fight,' he said.

Kastor tilted his head to one side then looked at Osayimwese, who reached for his spear. 'Don't even think about it.'

'We *are* all soldiers,' Dakaniha said. 'And we rely on each other… we fight alongside, not against one another.' He waited a few seconds. 'If you disagree, you can leave.'

'No thanks,' Kastor grinned. 'You are far too entertaining – I would start missing you after a few days.'

'Then we leave this disagreement here, now,' Tode said.

Kastor nodded and lowered his spear. 'I was enjoying myself, but yes.'

Osayimwese wiped the blood from his nose. 'I *am* a real soldier.'

The Spartan sighed. 'Yes, you are a real soldier, but I… come on, let's sort these two out and get moving.' Kastor kicked the leg of the musketeer. 'Well, he's dead.'

The spearman on the floor moved and mumbled, 'We didn't kill him.'

'What?' Tode stood over him, eyeing up his golden armour.

'He was dead when we found him.'

Dakaniha said, 'Our leader must have killed him! I told you – even armed with this gun, this soldier was defeated.'

'Maybe,' Tode answered.

'What if he wants to kill us?' Osayimwese asked.

'Why?' Dakaniha shook his head. 'I say we give these two men the chance to join us.'

'Let these murderers join us?' Kastor said. 'No way.'

'There is more chance of survival in a larger group,' Osayimwese said.

'Then let's vote if they should join us.' Dakaniha raised his hand.

Tode looked to Osayimwese and, with a smile in Kastor's direction, they both nodded.

'It's getting dark,' Tode said. 'We should set up camp.'

'Just one more hill,' Dakaniha said, and picked up the pace at the front.

He looked over his shoulder to the dozen men behind him: the lone travellers who had joined his search for a leader. The Incan and Mayan kept their distance from Kastor, as did Osayimwese.

'There, on the next ridge!' Osayimwese pointed to a dot of yellow light.

Dakaniha couldn't hide his excitement. 'Our leader's camp!'

Leaving the group of soldiers behind, hoping to savour this moment, he jogged up the low hill and stopped to slow his breath, scratch his itchy temples and peer between the bulbous cactus leaves. A yellow glow reflected on the cap of the hill. Creeping forward, silently stepping around the protruding cacti, Dakaniha coughed politely before stepping into the firelight.

'Oh...'

The fireside was empty. He circled the fire, picked out the most recent footprints and followed the trail with his eyes. In the dusk light, Dakaniha could see the most likely path, downhill then up. He breathed in sharply and ran back down to the waiting group of soldiers.

'There's another fire, in the distance.' He spoke quickly. 'We must go to it.'

'As long as we get a meal after all this walking,' Osayimwese whispered.

But when they reached the next fire, again they found nothing.

'Is this a trap?' Osayimwese asked.

'There!' Kastor pointed. 'Another fire.' It would take them diagonally away from their path.

'Why is he doing this?' the Mayan asked.

'We must follow,' Dakaniha insisted. 'What else can we do?'

'Nice trick!' A voice called out as Gal-qadan sat at his original fire, which had burnt down to red coals – ideal for roasting. 'I recognised it.'

Gal-qadan had the arrow in his bow pointing at the stranger and both men stared at one another, unsure of what to say.

'This land has many surprises.' The stranger spoke in a reverent tone. 'But I didn't expect to meet an ancestor.' Slowly, he bent down to place his bow and quiver on the ground. 'Hail, Great Leader, I am Tode.'

Gal-qadan remained tense, assessing the stranger, reluctant to let him share his fire. I could just kill him, he thought. Take his weapons and food. Maybe his boots as well. But this man could have knowledge of the land, which would be an advantage. But what about the others in the group? Could he trust them? The rush of questions overwhelmed Gal-qadan. So far, he had been alone and managed to push away most thoughts but, in the presence of another human, the floodgates opened.

Gal-qadan lowered his bow. He was no fool. Knowledge of this foreign land was more useful than a meal. Plus this soldier was a worthy companion if he had figured out his game of fires.

'Come,' Gal-qadan beckoned.

'Thank you, Khan.' Tode sat down.

'Why "Khan"?'

Tode replied. 'My companions and I search for a leader to guide us through this strange country.'

Gal-qadan's stare intensified.

'We have seen what you have accomplished and require guidance,' Tode continued.

Gal-qadan grunted and turned to his food. What had he accomplished? He had simply walked from one place to the next, yet they expected answers from him!

Kill, kill. The familiar sound pounded through his head.

'Where are you from?' Gal-qadan asked to distract himself from the murderous voices.

'I am of the Golden Horde,' Tode said. 'Our empire is centred around our capital, Sarai Batu.'

'The western wing of the empire,' Gal-qadan whispered to the glowing fire, accepting this man was from an age after his. 'So the empire was divided after the Khan's death?'

'Yes, Batu and Orda were given…'

'Enough!' Gal-qadan held up a palm: he had never been interested in politics, only fighting. He sighed. He had planned to have eaten and been away from the fire within the hour, timing his departure to just after the motley crew had completed his ring of fires and found themselves back at the first fire.

'These soldiers who travel with you. Are they from your Golden Horde?'

'No.' Tode gave a sharp headshake. 'They come from distant lands… and ages, I suspect. They have good weapons and their skills are varied.'

'Do any possess gunpowder?' Gal-qadan asked between mouthfuls.

'Yes, Khan,' Tode replied.

Gal-qadan narrowed his eyes. So there is more here than just a group of lost men. He looked into the red coals of his fire and imagined what he could achieve with such an army.

Chapter 8

Delta-Six surveyed the beach and lake from his vantage point up a tall, evenly branched tree. What he had assumed were silver gates, during his flight from the obelisk hill, was an illusion created by whatever lay on the other side of the lake. Even from here, it was difficult to see what lay beyond.

'Start log,' he said. 'My sixth day here and still no sign of the silver gates.' He climbed down as he spoke, relaying his recent thoughts. 'I've been thinking about the mutations I witnessed in the soldiers: Althorn's speed, the Maori soaking water through his feet and John Greene's arm and machine gun. The changes echo how my suit has merged with my body. Is this a glitch in the virtual prison or are these changes actually taking place?'

Delta-Six took a last look at the soldiers building rafts further down the beach then jumped down from the lowest branch.

'Not all of the changes are physical,' he continued. 'Mihran, in the night troop, has developed an incredible ability to process data. After sampling his speech, my analysis suggests he is reciting and amending an algorithm of great complexity as he builds and rewrites a multi-layered equation. But what for? Why are any of these changes taking place? Are these others just creations for my sake or have they have been imprisoned by the Guevarians as well?'

During his training, Delta-Six had been told that a prisoner of a virtual prison would experience time at a slowed-down rate of two to one. Even with the body kept at an optimum rate, a VR system could only contain a mind for a maximum of three days.

'I've been here six days.' Delta-Six recorded his log a few hours later as he watched the combined Day and Night Watches build and supply their rafts. 'There are no signs of scenery degradation or data glitches, so one more day without anomalies and I will have to accept this land is real.'

Keeping out of sight of the other soldiers, Delta-Six crossed the beach and slipped into the water to test his mech-gills, which, with his jetpack, aligned with the thicker aquatic environment, allowing him to swim and, he hoped, hitch a ride under one of the rafts.

John lay on the gently bobbing raft, leaning against his ammunition bag and watching the distant mauve horizon merge with the green-tinged sky. It was good to be sailing away from a land full of danger, he thought. The trenches may have been horrific, but at least he'd been able to escape to relative safety every four days. In this land, John and his comrades had been surrounded by life-threatening events day and night.

'And you had no idea Li was a woman?' John heard Crossley tease Olan.

'No! She was… dominant. She was in charge.'

John turned to see the Viking blush.

'And what's wrong with that?' Crossley asked.

Olan shook his head and laughed. 'There's nothing wrong with a strong woman.'

John thought of Rosie and sighed. What sort of woman would she have become? She would have made a great mother, he thought, and one day they would have taken over running his parents' shop. He watched the hypnotic shapes of the sea and pictured Joe with his parents. What would they make of his adventures when he got home? Joe would believe every word, but his parents? No, he would have to hold back and just tell them the dull parts: the bits they expected to hear. He just had to get through these two weeks and he'd be back in England.

John took in a lungful of sea air to calm his speeding heart. The last time he'd been at sea was at the beginning of the war, when he'd crossed the Channel. He gripped a vine and turned to watch the other rafts. There were twenty bobbing across the sea, pulled by an unseen tide. Each raft carried ten or twelve soldiers – all eyeing the waters around them suspiciously. Samas and Mihran were in deep discussion on one raft, while Lavalle and Euryleia sat together on another. Randeep's raft was bobbing awkwardly, as though the weight was distributed unevenly.

'They'll drift away if they stay like that,' John said.

'Who?' Crossley asked.

John pointed. 'Look how it lists.'

Crossley squinted and shook his head. 'We balanced the weight. Something must have shifted.' He shrugged. 'They'll use the paddles if they have to.'

John cast a glance at Mata on the other side of their raft and swore he saw a finger stretch and twirl a loop before twisting back down again.

'Mata?' John asked. 'Are you alright?'

Mata looked up, like a child playing with a knife. 'Yes.' the word came too quickly and he shook his head. 'Well, I feel better, I just…'

Mata slid across the raft to sit next to John.

'Hey, watch it!' Crossley shouted. 'Move a box back if you're going to do that.'

Mata shoved a box so hard it nearly knocked Crossley off the raft then looked at John. 'Like you, it's hard to accept, this new… change.'

John rubbed his gun-arm and nodded.

'Only, I don't carry it on the outside like you… and I fear my emotions taking over again.'

John pictured the broken bodies of the wolves: the vines, the blood and the sound of snapping bones.

'So you try to control it?'

'I will train myself to use it.' Mata nodded as though he'd just made his mind up.

'Good idea. It's best to face these things,' John said and remembered the day he'd left for war, when he had kept a smile on his face, for Joe more than anyone.

'Face the enemy square on, John,' his father had said, showing some rare emotion. 'And come back in one piece, eh?'

Fear had been John's real enemy. His stomach tightened as memories from the crater came back. He'd been able to control his fear then, hadn't he? Alone in the mud. He knew he was going to die but he kept fighting: firing and reloading. He'd been strong fighting the wasps as well, hadn't he?

John looked back to Randeep's raft, which had caught up with the group.

'What in Odin's name is that?' Olan pointed.

John followed the Viking's finger to what he had assumed was an orange sunset.

'It must be land!' Mata stood up to get a better look.

'Don't rock the raft,' Crossley shouted. 'Come on!'

On a neighbouring raft, Bowman cupped his eyes and stared at the horizon.

'Bowman!' Olan called out. 'What do you see?'

'It's land,' the archer shouted back, 'but not a beach. A cliff maybe?'

John found himself holding his breath as the rafts drifted closer to one another, pulled together by a rip current at increasing speed. Then an immense set of red cliffs revealed themselves, towering from sea to cloud, with a shimmering light emanating from within.

'What's that?' John pointed to a dark line running down the wall.

'Is it a waterfall?' Mata asked.

'God knows.' Crossley sat down next to John. 'But we're heading straight for it, so we'd better get ready for a rough ride!'

John could see the other rafts had their oars ready.

'Everyone – hold fast!' Crossley shouted as the current pulled them in.

'It's a gap!' Bowman shouted. 'And we're going through!'

John wound his arm tight in the vines as they were pulled through the gap in the cliffs like bath toys drawn to a plughole. With a rush of hot air, the rafts flew in on a mass of roiling water. The open sound of the sea was cut off and the turbulence jostled the boats where currents fought with one another.

The water calmed and the long line of rafts cruised through a red ravine in silence. Some hundred paces wide, the current kept the rafts away from the walls and, looking deep into the clear water, John was sure he could see the red stone continue beneath for several leagues.

'Of all the things I've seen,' Crossley said with a shake of the head.

'It doesn't look natural, that's for sure.' Li could be heard three rafts behind. 'And it must have some purpose.'

They cruised on, their every sound echoing down the long gulley, until Mihran shouted from the front raft. 'It's opening up!'

John squinted to see a white line ahead.

'And it's speeding up.' Mata pointed to the widening gap between each raft.

The fleet rushed through the last stretch of the chasm on a bed of white water and, when they popped out the other side, John found himself staring at a huge, mist-shrouded lake.

'Look, another entrance over there.' Bowman pointed to a dark line in the cliffs.

'And another.' Althorn pointed to the other side.

The rafts rocked rhythmically as they traversed the vast lake, revealing their skirt of purple bladders with each bob. They spotted more potential entrances or exits along the way, each one disappearing behind a blanket of mist.

'They're identical,' Bowman shouted from his raft, 'and all flowing into the lake.'

'Where's the current taking us then?' Crossley asked, looking ahead into the mist.

'There must be a river leading from the lake,' Mata said. 'Look, there are no cliffs over there.'

'Hey, did you see–' John said, sure he'd seen a flash of light under the water.

The others turned to him.

'I saw lights,' John said, keeping his eyes on the water.

'There!' Mata pointed off to starboard. 'Two flashes.'

'Did you see that shadow?' John said. 'Deep down.'

Crossley was rapidly unstrapping the bamboo paddles and handing them out. 'Yeah, I saw it. We need to move!'

'I don't like ships without sides!' Olan started working his oar like a professional.

Unable to row, John stared into the waters, searching for shapes among the waves and ripples. 'Another flash!' he pointed. 'Whatever's down there must have weapons.'

As he spoke, a smooth, snake-like tail curled out of the water five metres away and splashed a nearby raft.

'Hold tight!' Bowman yelled and they gripped boxes as the wave rocked the raft.

John heard an explosion and spun around to see Li firing red-hot beams into the water, sending up plumes of steam where each pulse hit.

'Loose!' A call came from another raft, where archers were firing at the water.

Smoke from rifles was mixing with the haze of the lake, clouding everyone's view.

'Where is it?' Crossley asked.

'There's more than one.' Mata pointed to the raft where Mihran and other soldiers frantically rowed away from a bulge in the lake, which rose to reveal a scaly mass of flesh, covered in sharp barbs.

Crossley turned to paddle, missing the moment the creature fired a cloud of darts at the soldiers, but John saw a swordsman struck in the neck and topple off his raft.

'Shit!' John scrambled backwards, kicking his ammo bag off the side. 'No!' He lunged forward to grab the handle but it slipped under.

'Keep back!' Mata grabbed John and pulled him to the centre of the raft.

'But my–' John saw bubbles where his bag had been.

'It's not worth dying for,' Mata said and looked up in shock. 'Tane-Mahuta!'

John's stomach tightened as a thick, snake-like body rose from the water revealing a large, scaly head.

Clinging to the bottom of the raft, Delta-Six was busy taking notes on the bizarre geology of the narrow gorge and the lake floor, when the first shape appeared. It swam up from the darkness below, circled once then descended out of sight. A second, longer silhouette followed, then another from the opposite direction. Delta-Six's scans showed they were a diverse range of predators – fish, invertebrate, insectoid – none of which showed any physiological connection to any animals on his database.

Then one of the creatures attacked the lead raft. Delta-Six watched the bodies fall into the water, some pulled down by the weight of their armour, others dragged down and torn apart by smaller predators drawn in by the commotion.

Delta-Six fired his pulse weapon as one came close to him, burning off a fin, but the second creature – an eel-like beast – was tenacious and took three blasts to its stone head before retreating. He saw the long beam of another pulse rifle shearing through water and beast alike, but it was too little. The soldiers were defenceless in this environment, and the creatures kept coming. He had to draw the attackers away.

Delta-Six swam free of the raft and fired on two of the largest beasts as he powered past. The distraction worked and, after a couple more blasts, they were irritated enough to chase him. He set his sensors to maximum and dived deep, pulling the beasts with him. As the light faded, he only had his screen and the feel of his sensors to guide him. He hadn't noticed it before, but he could feel the readings from his suit's sensors. And something was getting close.

Yellow lights blinked on Delta-Six's screen, followed by a blow to his side and a flash of pain. New lights filled his screen, indicating various pain-reducing chemicals were being pumped into his body, and his legs fell limp. Fighting to stay conscious, he pushed all energy to his propulsion unit and activated his emergency evacuation procedure. A new red sign appeared, telling him what he already knew: Injured. Medical assistance required.

John looked out across the mist-layered lake. Broken trunks, vines and purple bladders bobbed in the shallow waves that tickled the stony beach. The seventeen rafts that had survived the journey had disappeared overnight. Crouched down to nurture his fire back to life, John surveyed the surviving soldiers. Scores sat in huddles around fires dug into the stones of the barren shore.

It had been dark when they had found land. Li's roll-call suggested they had lost nine men during the attack, which had stopped as quickly as it had started.

'How many days do we have left?' John asked Mihran.

The red-cloaked Commander stirred the embers with a stick, seemingly lost in his thoughts.

'Mihran?'

'Yes?' He looked at John and squinted. Then spoke as if woken from a dream. 'We have seven days to reach the silver gates and this feels like a centrepoint… the hub, the channels through the cliffs are like spokes leading from the north.' He turned and John followed his view to the featureless grassland that lined the southern shore of the lake.

'Halfway then,' Crossley said and kicked a stone.

'Do we have time to commemorate the dead?' John asked Crossley, who sat beside him.

Crossley shrugged, lost for words for once.

As with most battles, images came back to John as his brain tried to accept what had happened. Images blurred with the stories from the others: men dragged underwater by beasts with wild eyes and vicious teeth; bodies torn apart; blood and screams; the surviving rafts paddling out of the mist to safety.

'We should have distributed the soldiers more evenly,' Mihran said to Lavalle. 'One soldier with a firearm on each raft.'

'And at least one spearman,' Lavalle added.

The safety of hindsight was a strange thing, John thought. The next battle would be different and new lessons would be learnt.

'Nobody could have predicted the attack,' Li said.

Mihran shot a glance at Lavalle. 'Who have we lost?'

'Nine at the last count. Cruickshanks, Bazhenov, Ndleleni of the Masai, Marodeen…'

'Marodeen?' Mihran sighed.

'I found Marodeen's quiver, but no bow.' Bowman held a leather satchel.

Crossley folded his arms. 'What does it matter how many we lost? We have to get to the goddam gates in a few days or God knows what'll happen to us.' He looked around at the scattered soldiers. 'We're in this together and we must decide together.'

'Yeah!' a few warriors called out.

'Crossley's right.' Li stood up and held her hands out. 'We need to have an open discussion. Do we stay as one group? And who will lead us?'

Crossley crouched next to John and shook his head. 'We've been through all this before. Hey, where's your ammo bag?'

'Lost it,' John replied.

'What!' Crossley was up on his feet. 'That was my last stash of smokes. Seriously, can this day get any worse?'

'Enough!' Mihran's deep voice silenced Crossley. 'We have no time for a discussion. I will answer your questions.'

The crowd held their tongues and stared at the tall Arab.

'We will travel as one group – anyone wishing to travel alone should know they are fifteen times more likely to die. Secondly, we will travel day and night, as our terrain dictates.' Mihran turned slowly, taking the time to look at each soldier. 'I will be your leader,' and he stabbed a forefinger at his ornate chest plate.

'What? We don't even get a vote?' Crossley stood, arms outstretched.

Mihran focused on Crossley for a few silent seconds then said, 'David Michael Crossley.'

Crossley's eyes widened.

'A leader should know his team's weaknesses and strengths – how to bring out their full potential and when they are likely to fail.' Mihran swept his cloak back and rested a hand on the hilt of his sword. 'Your strengths have yet to be realised. We need explosives. As for Sicily…'

Crossley gasped.

'…we will talk about that when the time is right.' Mihran turned to Mata. 'Mata, your new skills need to be refined, but you are a formidable warrior.' He passed Randeep with a squint and looked to Olan. 'We must talk of your past also, my friend.'

Murmurs cascaded across the beach, where soldiers made wisecracks or smiled like children watching a magician.

'And what of food?' Li asked.

'We will glean what we can from the sea but must move quickly. Ah…' Mihran gestured to a whirlwind drifting towards them along the beach.

Althorn's shape appeared next to Mihran and he looked concerned. 'I have found something you need to see.'

'Let me guess,' Crossley had his hands on his hips. 'Another obelisk?'

Althorn raised an eyebrow. 'Well, yes.'

'I don't trust them,' Crossley said as he and John bagged up rations. 'I mean, Lavalle put Cruickshanks on the same raft with Bellvedere, for God's sake!' He made his usual fake laugh.

John pushed more dried seaweed into the bag hanging off his gun-arm. The shore of the lake was strewn with the black strips that Li had analysed for their nutritional value. Good stuff apparently.

'Who do you think gave Cruickshanks that black eye?' Crossley asked.

John guessed, 'Bellvedere?'

'Damn right it was! Then there was Foxhole and Rodriguez – they can't stand the sight of each other, but they put them on the same raft. Ha! I'm surprised Lavalle didn't put me on his raft!' Crossley dumped his bag on the pile of rations and picked up the last bag of red roots. 'Hey, Mata. You think this gave you your er… powers?'

'Yes.' The Maori spoke without looking up.

'Euryleia said it must have seeped into his blood from the poultice,' John added.

Crossley looked at John's gun-arm. 'And that wasp sting sped up whatever's going on with your arm?'

John nodded.

'So what's to stop me cutting open my arm and squeezing some root juice in?' Crossley asked.

'Nothing, go ahead.' Lavalle appeared on the bank with his arms crossed. 'In fact, let me help you.' He leapt forward with his hand on his broadsword.

'No!' Crossley stepped back. 'It was just hypothetical, you know.'

'Oh, I'm sure it would be fine.' Lavalle grabbed Crossley by the wrist.

'Get off!' Crossley shouted, wriggling like a bullied schoolboy.

Lavalle pulled Crossley forward then let go, sending him stumbling head first into the dusty bank.

Crossley coughed and rolled over, brushing the dust out of his hair. 'Bloody Limey.'

'Are you alright?' John asked with a smile.

'Yeah, sure, I just–' Crossley sneezed. 'Don't worry, I'll–' He sneezed again then stared at the ground. 'That's strange.'

'Well,' Lavalle said, wearing a smirk. 'Now you're sure I can't assist you with any bloody enhancements, your presence is required – all of you.' Lavalle looked at John and Mata. 'We will all see the obelisk Althorn has found.'

Althorn, Samas and Mihran were already at the black obelisk when John arrived.

The soldiers were silently reading the message, or having it read to them.

Warriors. You have faced enemies past and present. You are now entering a land of foreign enemies who must be defeated for safe passage through the silver gates. Many tests lie ahead and only the greatest will be victorious.

'Great!' Crossley turned to John. 'Basically, there's nothing but trouble from now on.'

'Well, the last obelisk did say we were leaving a safe area,' John said.

'Is there anything we have missed?' Mihran asked Li, whose mask flashed with green lights and red dots.

'One obvious difference here.' Li swept her visor back and pointed to the script. 'The first message called us humans but this one calls us "warriors". It's less personal – more generic.'

Althorn spoke from the back of the group, 'There are more stones.'

'Where?' Lavalle asked.

'Along the coast. They have the same message.'

Mihran's eyes narrowed. 'They are here to welcome whoever crosses the lake, so the entrances to the lake must come from other islands.'

'Which means?' Randeep asked.

'Which means, we aren't the first here and we won't be the last,' Mihran replied.

'So it's a race!' Crossley beamed. 'Well, come on then – let's keep moving! If we get there first we'll get through the silver gates and–'

Lavalle cut him off: 'The obelisk says we have to fight.'

John saw fear in the exhausted faces of the soldiers who, he knew, held back the questions he wanted to ask. Where next? How far? When do we fight? And the same question they'd been asking from the moment they arrived here – who brought them here?

'What about these changes to our bodies?' a voice shouted out.

Randeep looked to Mihran. 'We should create a list of everyone who has changed since arriving here.'

'I agree,' Mihran said. 'Li will do so, but we must focus on our journey. We have new challenges ahead and must adapt. We have all fought wars – a thousand wars in a thousand different ways, yet we need to find new ways of fighting. I believe this is why we have been given our powers.'

'And what about those who don't have powers?' a voice called out.

'Survival of the fittest,' Crossley whispered to John.

'Do we all have to change in order to survive?' Bowman added.

Mihran looked unsure.

'The truth is, we don't know.' Samas spoke, his broken arm hidden under his cloak. 'We can't tell what our strengths and weaknesses are until we know the enemy we are facing.'

'Whoever we fight will have powers too,' Sakarbaal said, leaning on his trident.

His comments sent a wave of murmurs through the crowd.

'Listen!' Lavalle held his hands high for silence. 'We cannot allow ourselves to be disheartened. We are soldiers marching a warpath! Battles lie ahead and we must unite as one force if we are going to survive!' He stared at the quiet mass.

'Whose orders do we follow?' someone shouted.

Samas looked at Lavalle and then Mihran. 'We need an organised command structure.' He looked around the group. 'We need to have a clear chain of command if we are going to form a solid fighting unit.'

A few friendly cheers backed Samas up.

'We need an archery captain!' Bowman called out. 'Samas commanded the infantry but we need someone to take control of the archers.'

'And the spearmen!'

'And slingers.'

John shook his head. With so many varied fighters, it was going to be impossible to rank soldiers side by side with anyone of similar fighting style or power.

'Enough!' Mihran held up a hand. 'Our armies have different ranks and reporting lines, so I have created my own. You will be grouped under your respective captains and they will report directly to me, as Commander. Seeing as we have no cavalry, Lavalle will be in charge of resources.'

'Quartermaster? Comfy job,' Crossley whispered to John.

'Samas will command the infantry,' said Mihran.

'I guess that's us.' Crossley looked at Mata.

'Li will command the archers and other projectile warriors. Riflemen, spearmen and so on.'

'And Althorn will be in charge of scouting parties,' Mihran finished.

'I thought you'd be in that group, Crossley.' John smiled. 'I mean, what exactly is it you do?'

'You know very well, my friend.' He looked at Mata, who really had no idea what a sapper was. 'Let's just say, those toadstools were fun but you guys are going to be in for a treat when I get my hands on some decent explosives!'

Mihran pointed to the vast hinterland ahead. 'Now we move.'

'Ah, good old Shanks' pony.' John grimaced, swinging his bag of rations and satchel over a shoulder. 'At least my blisters have hardened up.'

Crossley looked down at John's feet. 'It's a pity our boots haven't evolved too, eh? What are your feet like, Mata?'

The Maori turned a bare foot over to reveal a mat of wiry, twisted roots protruding from his sole.

'Jeez!' Crossley leant in for a better look. 'That's just plain weird.'

'But comfortable.' Mata gave a broad smile.

They set off in an arrowhead formation, with John and his pals at the front of Samas' group and behind Li's archers, who had Bowman on point.

'So, Crossley,' John said, 'why did Mihran mention Sicily?'

Crossley's jaw clenched. 'I don't want to talk about it.' He looked back through the crowd. 'Just something that happened a few months ago.'

'Right.' John didn't want to push it further. 'Well, what happened with Lavalle on the beach then? That was odd.'

'Nothing, no, it was nothing.' Crossley glanced at John and sighed.

'Okay… look, I don't want everyone knowing, but when I sneezed I… I could see underground.'

John studied Crossley's face, waiting for a smile.

Mata looked over with a scowl. 'Do not mock us, Crossley.'

'Look, this is why I didn't want to say anything. I mean, come on!' Crossley kept his voice low. 'There I was complaining about no adaptations and, wham, the next second I can see through rocks.'

John shook his head and looked away. Crossley was quite convincing this time.

'I'm not kidding.'

'So, what's it like then?' John decided to humour him.

'Well, I need to practise,' Crossley replied.

Mata raised an eyebrow.

'It happens when I sneeze, okay? And it works a bit when I cough and… well, it's like a three-dimensional image of what's beneath the ground, you know? Like when we were back at the wasp nest and we could see the forest below?'

'Yes.' John pictured it.

'Only there's no forest underground. Just different rocks and animal burrows.'

'How far can you see down?' John was beginning to take him seriously.

Crossley shrugged. 'I don't know. Three or four metres?'

'It might come in useful,' John said, struggling to think of examples.

'Yeah right.' Crossley shook his head. 'I finally get a skill and it's a dud!'

John cast a look over his shoulder, past the host of soldiers walking behind him. It hadn't taken long for the haze of the lake to merge with the ever-present shimmer of the sky. Off to the flank, the flat, featureless landscape spread out as far as the eye could see, and John couldn't truly say whether they'd been walking in a straight line or in a circle for the past few hours.

'It never ends,' he said.

'It has to.' Crossley spoke with a hoarse voice.

John heard him coughing every few minutes, testing out his new skill. Maybe he was telling the truth after all?

'Another crater!' a voice at the front called out and the group parted, walking around a black and perfectly symmetrical circle some fifteen paces wide.

John shivered, remembering his crater. 'Anything under there?' he asked Crossley to distract his thoughts.

Crossley cleared his throat. 'No, just compressed earth. If anything died in there it was burnt to a crisp. One hell of an incendiary.' Crossley shook his head and smiled. 'I wouldn't mind getting my hands on some of that!'

Twenty minutes later, a new call came from Bowman, 'Objects ahead!'

'Single file!' Mihran shouted from the rear.

Each soldier peered around the person ahead, trying to get a view.

'What on earth?' Crossley said when they passed the first, bleached carcase.

John swallowed. 'Like some kind of dinosaur.'

The twisted bones lay cracked in a pool of grey ash. The teeth, horns and eye sockets in a monstrous skull sent shivers down John's back. Then they passed a mass of intertwined bodies: a skeleton like the first, covered with four or five dog-like bodies.

'You can still see the fur,' Crossley said.

But no flesh remained on the corpses.

It reminded John of when his battalion had charged the German lines after a barrage of heavy artillery. In the mud and coarse grass of no-man's-land, bodies had lain untouched for weeks. The rain, wind and sun had weathered the clothes while the rats, beetles and flies had taken care of the flesh. Ghastly white skulls had grinned at John as he passed: their helmet straps holding their jaws tight.

'Why doesn't it smell?' John asked but no one answered.

The number of bodies along the path increased as the line of humans filed through the remnants of a battle. Shattered weapons lay next to splintered skeletons and torn, isolated limbs told of the violence that had taken place here.

Crossley darted out to pick up a shining object and slipped his find inside his coat.

'My readings show the battle took place two months ago.' John could hear Li ahead.

'Really?' Lavalle responded. 'It looks like an ancient conflict.'

'Diversion!' Bowman called out and the line veered off to the left to avoid a concentration of bodies.

John shook his head at the sight: scores of carcases – dog and dinosaur as he thought of them – lay crushed and broken in a mound of desiccated flesh.

'This was the centre,' Samas said some way behind John. 'I've seen it before: the crush of foot soldiers.'

'But no one took care of the bodies,' John said.

'The weapons have been taken,' Li said. 'The armour too, so someone must have been here.'

'It would be wise to take any weapons we see.' Mihran was scanning the ground. 'But take care if you leave the path.' Mihran sounded like a teacher on a field trip.

John was tempted but held back. Who knew what lay out there? Unexploded bombs, hidden creatures or objects full of the horrific trickery of this land. Crossley had no qualms and was darting in and out of the bodies every time he saw a glint of metal.

John raised his eyebrows. 'Maybe we shouldn't be playing around with this stuff, eh?'

Crossley shrugged and looked at John's arm. 'Who knows what to trust, eh?'

They passed a group of soldiers studying and pulling at a sleek metal object two men high.

'Some kind of missile launcher,' Crossley said, and ran to join the group.

John kept his hand in his pocket and walked on. The number of dead dwindled, replaced by craters and the smaller dog-like carcases with bolts sticking out of their chests.

'Water break!' Lavalle shouted as soon as they left the battle site and split into groups to share their discoveries and water.

'We must make efforts to maintain our direction,' John overheard

Mihran saying to Li. 'There are no stars to guide us and this empty landscape can fool us.'

'I have been leaving markers,' Li answered.

Mihran's left eyebrow raised a touch. 'Good.'

'And I'll scan ahead for any useful geographic markers.' She walked away to take readings.

John followed her, intrigued by Li's future technological apparatus, just as he'd been with Delta-Six. She was pressing buttons on a wrist strap and occasionally tapping her helmet.

John heard Li talk to herself. 'That's odd.'

John stepped forward. 'What is it?'

Li turned sharply. 'Oh, nothing... just a frequency I don't recognise.'

'A frequency?' John had no idea what she was talking about.

'A new setting. Number one is full power, two fires out pulses and three freezes objects... this new one allows me to manipulate particles.'

John saw a mote of sand dancing in the air a few inches from Li's visor. 'Amazing.'

'Li,' Mihran shouted and the fleck of sand dropped to the ground. 'Bowman has spotted a sandstorm on the right flank. What can you see?'

Li turned. 'It's a sandstorm alright. Heading this way. An hour away.'

Crossley walked over to John. 'I bet that's what cleaned those bones so fast.'

John swallowed and stared at the brown haze on the horizon.

'Where's Althorn?' Lavalle asked.

'The other flank,' Li replied. 'He'll be able to outrun it.'

Mihran pulled his cloak around him. 'Without shelter our only choice is to keep moving.' He shouted at the reclining soldiers, 'Double pace – Samas, you lead.'

John felt panic rising in his chest. How could he run with his arm in this state? He pulled the sling straps tighter, bringing his gun-arm tighter against his chest. The bags over his neck balanced the weight and he trotted forward, picking up pace until he found a steady rhythm.

John's throat was dry and his back ached from the bouncing weight of his gun.

'Here it comes!' Crossley had wrapped a shirt around his head as the wind swirled around them. 'Put your gas mask on.'

'Good idea.' John turned his back to the scraping winds, tugged the bag-like mask free and pulled it over his head.

'You look like a damn teddy bear,' Crossley laughed.

John hated the claustrophobic mask but at least his eyes had stopped stinging.

Mihran's face was barely visible beneath his tightly bound robes as he urged everyone on but Mata was the least affected by the vicious winds and rough sand, as his skin turned bark-brown across his legs and face.

'We can't outrun it!' Samas shouted from behind his round shield, lashed to his cast.

Silhouettes of soldiers, leaning on spears, came and went from view as John pushed through the thickening clouds. Some walked together, arm in arm, while others stumbled blindly. The sand stung John's good hand and the winds pulled at his bag and arm, draining his energy. He scanned from left to right and back, searching for some-one – anyone. His heart pounded and his breathing was heavy. Where were they?

Then he saw Bowman. He was pointing and his voice faltered with the wind, '...ahead!'

A blast of wind swept away the nearest cloud of sand like a huge curtain to reveal a dark shape in the distance, nothing more than a smudge. Was it a rock? Not wanting to be left behind, John found the energy to jog towards a cluster of soldiers as another blast of clear air revealed their intended destination.

John could hear Crossley. 'It's a goddam castle!'

Chapter 9

Panzicosta leapt off the behemoth Lutamek, ignoring the sparks and smoke emanating from the exposed access consoles. The robot strained against its braces as Panzicosta stretched his legs and appendages, with satisfying cracks.

'This place smells like a Skrift's intestines,' he said to Millok, who descended gracefully from the front of the enslaved vehicle.

'How long since you last saw the Doctor?' Panzicosta asked, noting the shudder as Millok stared at the tall, grey-washed buildings of Abzicrutia: Doctor Cynigar's experiments had been far from pain-free, but it was every Brakari soldier's duty to improve – or be improved.

'Long enough for me to heal, General,' Millok replied and stepped over a muddy puddle. 'The roads are no better.'

'Or the sanitation,' said Panzicosta. 'Still, it has its purpose.' Panzicosta looked at Millok and held back a wave of sexual need. 'The Lutamek performed as you promised. Good bracing.'

'Thank you, General.'

Between the mud-coloured towers sat squat domes for those Brakari who longed to sleep in a moist and warm environment. Panzicosta watched Millok steer clear of these, obviously wary of the male attention she attracted.

A guard from the nearest watchtower scuttled over. 'Doctor Cynigar will be here shortly, General.'

'Good,' Panzicosta snapped. 'And my intelligence report?'

'Yes, General. The Draytor has been in contact.' The turquoise soldier with unusually large eyes read from a sliver of plastic. 'The new biped army call themselves 'humans' and have crossed the great lake. The Draytor remains undetected and awaits further orders.'

'Good.' Panzicosta walked a circle. 'We have the name of our enemy at last.'

'And your orders, General?'

'Tell the Draytor–'

'Panzicosta!' A high-pitched squeal cut him off. 'I see you are still resisting your adaptation?'

Panzicosta turned to greet a small, black-shelled creature who swam through the air. Spikes and fins wafted over the body of a long sea slug with a monkey's face.

'Doctor Cynigar, I…' Panzicosta started.

'You need time, yes, but how much time, I wonder? Will you be ready for the next war?' The Doctor's voice was clipped like that of an officer Panzicosta had once served under.

General Panzicosta's scales raised a touch but paused before flexing fully and snapping shut.

'Don't start bristling at me, young Brakari!' A wave of green electricity washed over the Doctor. 'Belsang wants every Brakari at their full potential and that means having more than your new knife arms and engorged pincers!'

Panzicosta took in air and deflated slowly. He had to stay calm. Doctor Cynigar was one of only two Brakari he was truly wary of. Who knew which adaptations and violent skills he had endowed upon himself?

'But you will find out from Belsang yourself if you are here to wake him?' The Doctor floated up to Panzicosta's eye level and kept a claw's length back.

'Yes, I intend to wake Belsang shortly,' Panzicosta replied.

'Any more news of this new species?' Doctor Cynigar asked.

'*Humans*, they call themselves.' Panzicosta grumbled and turned to the guard. 'Lieutenant, has the Draytor any intelligence on these humans' adaptations?'

'Speed, invisibility, merging with weapons,' the turquoise soldier replied.

'Nothing aerial?' the Doctor asked.

Panzicosta stretched a mandible. 'Doctor, aerial warfare is inhibited by the laws of this land. We are bound to do battle on land only.'

The Doctor swung round with a flash of luminescence. 'I'm well aware of the imposed rules, General, which is why I push them to their limit! One successful aerial adaptation would be worth a dozen land traits.'

Panzicosta raised his head a notch and refused to respond.

'And you, Millok,' Doctor Cynigar floated over, 'your new visage suits you.'

'Thank you, Doctor.' She crouched slightly. 'Everything has been as you said.'

'And you have been practising?'

'Yes, Doctor.'

'This is acceptable. Come with me for further testing, I wish to see proof and talk about your donation.' Doctor Cynigar swayed through the air to return to his laboratory. 'It's good to know some of our soldiers are enhancing the Brakari cause.'

Panzicosta's scales wavered.

'Goodbye, General.' Millok bowed and followed the Doctor through a low doorway.

Panzicosta dismissed the guard and was left with his thoughts. He paced a circle in the mud. 'The dirty little Lutamek stain,' he mumbled. 'When the battle is won, I'll turn him inside out and drown him in a bowl of his own faeces.' His scales opened and snapped with a clack. A thought came to him and two of the antennae on his head flicked upright.

'Lieutenant!' he shouted and the turquoise officer scuttled back. 'New orders for the Draytor.'

'Yes, General.'

'I want it to kill three humans every day. The human army must be weakened by the time it reaches us.'

John sat up, gasping for air. The remnants of his dream hung close to him and he thought he could still hear Rosie on their bed, screaming and covered in blood.

In the dull light he could see men running out of the room, so he followed. They rushed through the rooms of the castle and joined the back of the crowd as Lavalle spoke to the group.

'...killed in the night. Three of them. All beheaded.' He stood in the early-dawn light at the tall entrance.

John looked at the calm desert morning, which contrasted with the pure hell of last night. In the thick of the sandstorm, the last hundred steps had been tortuous: clambering around walls, through ditches and over rough ground. Anything designed to inhibit an army willing to attack the castle had slowed them down as they searched for shelter. Now, with the clouds of skin-lashing sand gone, John could see the symmetry and beauty of the defensive system.

'How were they beheaded?' Mihran pushed through and stared at Lavalle. 'Was it a sword? An execution?'

Lavalle dropped his head. 'Look for yourself.'

'The bodies were dragged here.' Mihran's voice trailed away.

John couldn't see – and realised after some neck-craning he didn't want to see three decapitated soldiers anyway. But who were they? Who hadn't made it to safety last night? He looked around. Mata's large frame was easy to spot and Crossley was in the thick of the action.

John relaxed, knowing his friends were safe, and felt an urge to go back into the castle. Like a thief sneaking into an empty bank, he walked back into the darkness: back to the drawings.

He had a little more natural light now than when he and Crossley had explored last night. He climbed the stone steps leading to the first floor, past the room where he'd seen Mihran and Li discussing military tactics, using images she projected onto a wall. One more room and… the drawings: black smudges and lines covering the grey stone wall to form a vast, crude picture of war. With the morning light creeping in, John made sense of what appeared to be the castle's final battle, drawn by the defenders. But who were the soldiers fighting and where were they now?

The drawing had been split into a triptych of war. In the first picture, the safe haven was being built by a group of tall, metallic creatures. Some towers reached five storeys high and, at the perimeter, they were digging a shallow moat and filling it with white stones.

John looked at the second panel. A swarm of giant leeches surrounded the castle, held back by the moat. The leeches were firing barbed shells which, according to the picture, grew into stone-eating polyps when they hit the walls and burrowed through to attack the robotic army within.

'I thought you'd be in here again.' Crossley's voice made John jump. 'I still think this last one was drawn in the last few hours of the battle.' Crossley pointed at the third panel.

It showed the castle close to ruins. The flatworm army was inside and tearing the robots apart. It also showed a group of robots rushing out on a final defensive attack. Suicidal, but their final chance for escape.

'I wonder if it worked?' John asked. 'Did they survive?'

'I don't think I'd want to find out,' Crossley replied.

But it wasn't the story of the robots' last stand that had drawn John back to the pictures. It was the solitary man standing on a nearby hill while the battle played out. Watching. Was this the person responsible for bringing them here? John wondered. Were these battles his entertainment?

'Time to go,' Crossley said.

'Did they find out what happened to the three men?' John asked as they descended the stairs.

'Someone – or something – decapitated them, then dragged their bodies and heads to the entrance,' Crossley said as they wound down to where the main group were waiting. 'My guess is it was those freaky-looking worms from the picture, but who knows? Li says everyone's accounted for apart from Althorn.'

'Oh,' John replied.

Mihran nodded at them. 'Right, we're all here. The same as yesterday. Li on point, triangular formation.'

They filed through the entrance and snaked around the array of broken battlements where John saw three mounds of soil. Each had a block of stone from the castle as a gravestone with a black handprint embossed on the front.

'Who were they?' John asked Crossley.

'Li reckons it was an Ethiopian, an Indonesian and an Irishman.'

'No obvious connection there,' John said and looked back to the castle.

'No, it just sounds like the beginning of a bad joke.' Crossley nudged John.

John shook his head and tried not to smile.

Unseen by John the night before, large metal cubes lay scattered across the barren earth around the broken castle.

'These must have been the robot defenders,' Mihran said to Li, a few steps ahead of John.

'Odd how they haven't rusted,' John pointed to the shiny hulks.

'The metal is non-ferrous,' Li answered. 'Plus the humidity is low here.'

Mihran slowed down to walk with John. 'Li showed me the triptych. They fought well against such a formidable aggressor.'

'Even the moat didn't stop them,' John said.

'Yes.' Mihran looked ahead to the white line running around the battlefield. 'But it showed they knew their enemy.'

'A valiant defeat is one step from a glorious victory.' John quoted one of his grandfather's sayings.

Mihran stared at John and said, 'Which suggests a glorious victory is only one step away from defeat.'

The moat was ten paces wide. Mihran bent down to touch and taste the white substance that lay a finger deep.

'It's salt.'

'Where did they get it from?' John asked.

'The lake I guess.' Crossley looked back, past the castle to the shimmering horizon. 'One helluva feat, getting it out here.'

'They needed it.' Mihran pointed to a dark patch on the other edge of the moat.

John could tell by its kite-like shape it was the desiccated remains of one of the large flatworms.

'Over here!' Li called out.

She was standing by a large pile of broken robot bodies which lay in a semicircle.

'This is where they breached the moat.'

A thick dark line ran from across the moat.

'There must be seven or eight dead,' John said.

Mihran spoke slowly and nodded. 'They sacrificed themselves for the good of the species.'

'They died to form a bridge?' John shook his head.

'What I don't understand is if we've been getting these... adaptations,' Crossley said, 'how come the leeches didn't evolve a way to hop the moat?'

'Maybe one did,' Li answered. 'But that wouldn't mean the rest could follow.'

'Sure.' Crossley walked over the crunchy salt, coughing rhythmically as he stepped.

'Rekarius!' General Panzicosta cursed as he squeezed his large shelled body through a dark and dusty tunnel.

His temper was amplified by the knowledge that this was only the third of twenty-seven archways leading to the subterranean Temple of Bekkrypt, designed to ensure guests showed reverence to Belsang. The long passageway sloped downwards and became slippery the nearer visitors got to the humid circular body of the temple, where the Brakari leader resided. But, despite the humiliation, Panzicosta ran through the rites as he slipped through another set of arches, knowing the process of reviving Belsang had to be followed meticulously, and so he pushed on with his incisor arms stabbing the mudstone walls for support.

The faint light-blue glow emanating from the temple's centre illuminated the crude etchings on the tunnel walls: lines of Brakari warriors in formation; Brakari fighting various foes; a large Lutamek being restrained; the building of Abzucrutia; concentric rings of Brakari warriors in prayer around a floating figure.

'I can't see why…' Panzicosta grumbled as he pushed his way through the final, tightest, arch and into the dome of the temple.

The air lay thick with moisture, which dripped from clumps of moss and algae growing across the struts supporting an immense domed ceiling. Shafts of light pierced the heavy air through geometrically positioned air holes in the roof, illuminating the colourful images covering the walls of the temple. Panzicosta ignored them and stared at his slumbering leader.

'Belsang.' He lowered his large, blue head to the glowing powder-blue figure that hovered above a black stone plinth at the centre of the shrine.

Unlike other Brakari, Belsang's body showed no obvious sign of a protective shell. His body was a quarter the size of Panzicosta's but swollen with fatty flesh. Eight bulging appendages ran symmetrically down his body, each ending with three pudgy digits rather than the lethal blades and pincers Panzicosta possessed. Each pair of arms or legs was folded, giving Belsang a patient demeanour, but Panzicosta knew the ruthless power that resided beneath the banal facade.

Panzicosta recalled the moment Belsang had transformed from fellow warrior to Brakari leader. Mid-battle and covered in his enemy's blood, Belsang had bellowed in pain as he imploded with the sound of a mighty crashing wave. His weapons had fallen to the ground, his armour plating had disappeared and what remained was a small and bloated Brakari bursting with raw energy. Belsang's transformation had been too late for victory, but as the new Dominus he had shown the Brakari a new path.

'Belsang the Great.' Panzicosta lowered his body and stretched his pincers across the slimy floor of the temple. 'I humbly prostrate my body before you in servitude. The Brakari army faces threats anew.'

The light in the room increased a notch and a twitch shook Belsang's body.

'We need you, Dominus, to unite our forces and bring us the victory we desire,' Panzicosta continued.

The sound of a tiny bell echoed around the vast chamber and Panzicosta pulled his body back to a crouched position.

Two of Belsang's seven eyes opened, along with his tiny mouth. 'Name the enemy.' His deep voice filled the temple.

'Humans.'

'Detail.'

'Soft-bellied, internal-skeleton bipeds with an average level of adaptation.' Panzicosta knew to keep his answers brief.

'Can they create soldiers?' Belsang asked.

'No.'

'Have they any allies?'

'No.' Panzicosta hoped not.

Belsang vibrated and a third eye snapped open. 'You have sent a Draytor.'

'Yes, Dominus, it will kill three humans every day until battle.'

'Your orders must be reversed. I sense a weakness in this species.' Belsang's voice reverberated around the temple.

'Dominus, I–'

Worms of electricity writhed across Belsang's body. 'If the Draytor kills too many, the enemy will be debilitated beyond survival and may not arrive at battle in sufficient numbers. Do you understand?'

'Yes, Dominus.' Panzicosta remained motionless.

'Preparations for war are under way?'

'Yes, Dominus.'

'Then leave my temple immediately.' Belsang rose a foot higher and another eye opened. 'Bring me my Vaalori steed. We march!'

John watched the soldiers scour the remains of the robot army, which lay scattered around the ruined castle. They clambered over metal carcases and ripped open hatches to explore inside, searching for valuable gadgets, advanced weapons or, more often than not, something that looked good hanging on a cord around their neck.

From a rise in the land beyond the salt moat, John surveyed the land. He had to admit it was a good viewing point: far from where the flatworms had made their attack but near enough to see the action. This was where the watcher had been standing, but any footprints had been wiped clean by the sandstorm. John slipped his hand between the buttons on his shirt and clasped the toy soldier. Had the watcher taken him away from Joe? He pictured his son's smile and had to breathe in deeply to calm his anger.

A yell caught his attention. Olan was beckoning Li and Lavalle to a cluster of robot bodies where other soldiers were pushing the blocks apart. A deep boom echoed as a metal hulk fell to the ground. As the dust cleared, Olan's discovery was plain to see, and John scampered down the hillside.

'Step back!' Lavalle was shouting. 'Olan – you found it, read what you can see.'

John stood on tiptoes to see Olan standing on an overturned robot next to a tall, white obelisk stone. It had a simple message inscribed in black.

Olan spoke aloud: 'Here the Platae were victorious over the Lutamek.'

John looked around for a friendly face. 'So these robots are the Lutamek?' he asked.

Nobody answered him.

Mihran climbed up next to Olan and stroked his beard before speaking. 'When we reached these shores, an obelisk decreed we must defeat an enemy.' He scanned the faces around him. 'We thought, naively, we would fight an army similar to ourselves.' He pointed to the nearest Lutamek hulk, blasted and torn apart. 'Now we have seen the kind of enemy we will face. This is why we must embrace our changes and do everything in our powers to become greater fighters. Stronger, faster, more accurate... flexible, impenetrable and unpredictable.'

'But we only have a few days,' Crossley said. 'How can we fight an army who live here?'

Mihran gave a rare smile and shook his head. 'Who is saying we are not prepared?' He tapped his temple. 'We *will* be victorious. But enough of this distraction – we must find our enemy before they find us. Back in formation and keep walking.'

Samas, Li and Lavalle ushered their groups away.

'Check this out.' Crossley jogged up to John. 'I'm guessing it's some kind of communicator unit.' He held up a fist-sized box covered in blue dials. 'I just need a power source to fire it up.'

'Great,' John said and looked away.

'Hey, what's up?'

'I don't know.' John shook his head. 'Everything's getting to me – my arm, Joe, this place...'

'And you don't want to fight?' Crossley asked.

John gave the American a sharp look. 'I'm not afraid, if that's what you're thinking.'

'No, I...' Crossley lowered his voice. 'Look, *I'm* afraid, if I'm honest.' He looked around. 'And I reckon just about everyone else feels the same. This place is freaky enough but the idea of fighting a huge robot army or a swarm of gigantic ants is enough to make Lavalle soil his armour.'

John gave half a smile.

'Even Randeep over there with his invisible sword is probably worried, right?'

'It's totally invisible now, is it?' John asked.

'Apparently. He won't show anyone – something about having to draw blood every time it's unsheathed. Hey, I wonder what those two are chatting about.' Crossley nodded to where Bowman was in deep conversation with Li. 'Let's earwig!' He sped up and John trailed after him.

'...known as the Black Sword. He was known for his temper and he never took prisoners.' Bowman was talking. 'They say his sword was black from the blood of a thousand beheadings.'

'It doesn't mean he killed the men,' Li replied.

'But I'm sure it's him!'

'Did you ever meet him?' Li asked.

'No, he died long before I was born.'

'He died? How?'

Bowman shrugged. 'They said he burnt for his sins.'

'He was burnt at the stake?'

'No.' Bowman was visibly agitated, like a boy caught telling lies. 'They just said he burnt – in the Holy Land – something to do with God's wrath.'

Crossley was looking at John, trying to get his attention. 'Who?' he mouthed.

John shook his head. 'Don't know.'

'Okay, I'll look into it. Head back, we need your eyes up front.' Li stepped out of the line to survey the soldiers, ignoring John and Crossley.

'It has to be Lavalle,' Crossley whispered a dozen steps later. 'He's got a temper, that's for sure!'

'Bowman thinks he's this Black Sword?' John asked.

'Yeah, and if he's right, Lavalle must have killed those soldiers last night.'

John shook his head. 'No, not Lavalle, he's–'

'He's what?' Crossley asked. 'You saw how he was with me.'

'Yes, but–'

'No, the more I think about it, it has to be him.' Crossley turned, bumping into Randeep, who was just behind. 'There's only one way to find out.'

'What are you going to do?' John called out, but got no reply.

Five minutes later, Bowman shouted, 'Another obelisk!'

The soldiers rushed forward, carrying John forward in the tide.

'Just like the last one.' Bowman was touching the white stone and black script.

'But no bodies,' Randeep said.

'Nothing for miles.' Samas gestured out across the featureless landscape.

'On this spot, the Nama-Gametiads and their allies were victorious over the Ilanos,' Bowman read.

'Allies?' Olan asked.

'It would appear,' Mihran said as he joined them, 'that all participants of the victorious army in a pitched battle are equal.'

'We could use a few allies,' Olan said.

'But what happens to the defeated tribe?' Euryleia asked. 'The ones that survive...'

'I presume they are bound to this land.' Mihran turned, distracted by raised voices at the back of the crowd.

'...don't care what you say – I want to know the truth.' John heard Crossley. 'Are you the Black Sword or not?'

'What is he doing now?' John pushed through the crowd to see Crossley goading Lavalle.

'I'm going to string you up, you little–' the crowd parted and Lavalle froze. 'Ah, another obelisk,' Lavalle said, looking uncomfortable.

'Tell us the truth!' Crossley stood with his hands on his hips. 'Are you the Black Sword?'

Lavalle shook his head. 'I don't see how this is relevant.'

'We need to know if we have a murderer in our army,' Bowman said.

'Did you kill the three men at the castle?' Randeep stepped forward with one hand on the hilt of his sword.

'No, of course I didn't.' Lavalle stared at the faces around him, finally fixing on Mihran.

'It's time we cleared this up,' Mihran said. 'Let's make this easy. Describe your last kill.'

'My last kill was during my crusade when I was in Damascus and...' Lavalle paused.

'And?' Mihran asked.

Lavalle breathed in deeply.

'Come on!' Crossley shouted.

'Be quiet!' Lavalle yelled back, then took a deep breath. 'So be it. I will hide nothing.' The knight looked directly at Euryleia, whose eyes stayed on him throughout his confession. 'During my crusade I was captured at Hattin alongside King Guy. We were taken to Damascus, where a number of my compatriots were executed.'

The crowd stood silent. To John, the war sounded like his: an elite class leading the masses to their death, fighting for a noble cause they cared little about.

'Many waited for their ransom to be paid, but I escaped. I rejoined my army and the crusade continued. A few days ago our army engaged Saladin's at Arsur, where he was defeated.' Lavalle's eyes lit up. 'I killed many enemy soldiers from my horse, with my lance, a further score on foot, with my sword.'

'The *black* sword!' Bowman shouted out.

'Do you know the history of your crusades?' Mihran cut to the chase.

Lavalle's head dropped a notch. 'Yes, Li has told me all I need to know.'

'Your victory was short-lived.'

'Yes.' Lavalle raised his head. 'But I live to fight on.'

'Why are you not wearing your armour?' Mihran asked.

Lavalle sighed. 'I was not wearing my armour during my last kill because...' he looked to Euryleia, who held his gaze, '...I was executing the captured soldiers who could not be ransomed.'

'You could have let them live?' Euryleia spoke quietly.

'We had barely enough food to feed ourselves, let alone–'

Mihran stopped Lavalle with a raised hand. 'And what of the blond man?'

'What?' Lavalle glared at Mihran. 'I didn't mention the…'

'Why did you kill him? Was he your enemy as well?'

'He was a traitor.'

Lavalle seemed smaller to John now.

'And yet you took great relish in cleaving through his neck.'

Lavalle looked to the dusty earth. When he looked up, Euryleia was gone. 'I was serving my god… my duty as a knight. I executed many men but, as God is my witness,' he pressed a fist to his chest, 'I have not killed a single man in this land.'

John noticed Mihran squint and tilt his head, before saying, 'I believe you.'

'What?' Bowman stepped out of the crowd. 'But he's the Black Sword – it has to be him.'

'He may be the Black Sword,' Mihran said. 'But he did not kill the three men at the fort.'

General Panzicosta leant against the outside wall of the Temple of Bekkrypt, wheezing with exhaustion.

'Bring me a bucket of Sorean blood,' he ordered a shiny-blue Brakari, who crouched a salute before springing away with speed. He looks like he hatched yesterday, Panzicosta thought.

Fifty metres down the earthen road, the gigantic five-legged elephant-like Vaalori ambled through a crowd of bellowing Brakari soldiers. Belsang sat cross-legged on a wooden howdah on the behemoth's broad back, with one pair of arms unfolded, waving at the crowd.

The cries rang out: 'Dominus!', 'Belsang!' and 'Victorio Brakarius!'

Panzicosta kicked a piece of mudstone through the gaping hole he had knocked in the temple wall.

Belsang was testing me, he thought, forcing me to use my adaptation. No. Only I choose when.

The diminutive soldier returned with a leather bucket of dark red liquid and placed it at Panzicosta's feet. With a movement quicker than the soldier expected, Panzicosta lashed out at the small Brakari, slicing through a leg. A high-pitched squeal cut the air and the scorpion-like Brakari scuttled off, leaving its torn limb in the dirt.

'Next time you will be faster,' the General spat and dropped his head into the warm liquid.

'We will need every soldier fit, General.' A soft voice caused Panzicosta to pause and twitch his scales.

'It'll grow back, Millok,' Panzicosta said and finished off his victuals. He turned to the female. 'Ah, another present from Doctor Cynigar? But at what cost? More eggs for the army?'

'Yes, impressive, aren't they?' Millok swayed from side to side, showing off the electric-blue stripes that adorned her sides.

She stepped forward and stumbled.

'I meant your lame foreleg.' Panzicosta bristled. 'And remember I am your superior, Millok. You may be light-headed after your… enhancement programme, but only talk when requested or I'll injure more than one leg.'

'Yes, General.' Millok bowed and a wave of white light ran down each stripe.

Panzicosta let the silence hold and watched the young female with a mix of sexual desire and admiration. How had such a soldier been selected to fight for the Brakari? She was nothing like the rest of the army.

'We travel for battle soon, so you must be healed in two days,' he said.

'Yes, General.' Millok nodded and took a look through the hole in the temple wall.

Panzicosta wheezed: 'Belsang is serious this time. We go to war and, whatever the outcome, we won't be coming back to this shithole again.'

Millok replied, 'Good.'

'Yes.' Panzicosta looked away. Any power he had accumulated during Belsang's hibernation was slipping from his grasp and he needed to regain control. 'You, messenger!'

A Brakari officer armed with a huge fighting claw turned. 'Yes, General.'

'I need you to send an order for the Draytor with the enemy. Order it to cease killing.'

'Yes, General.'

Panzicosta walked in a circle and thought out loud. 'We need more information about the enemy. But with the little time we have left it won't be enough, I...'

Millok trembled as though she were holding back advice, Panzicosta noticed, or was it the Doctor's chemicals? He stared down the street at Belsang on his black Vaalori as it turned the corner and disappeared from view.

'And order the scouts to retreat,' Panzicosta said.

'General?' the clawed officer asked.

'Retreat from their posts and form groups no bigger than five. We go to war. Order them to attack at will.'

'Yes, General.'

'And one last order for the Draytor.' Panzicosta closed his scales silently.

Millok looked up.

'I want to see the enemy in the flesh. Order it to bring me a live human.'

John stared at the long, sinuous limbs which lay scattered across the ground like huge chicken bones. They walked past the occasional intact body but, due to the bizarre anatomy, it was hard to tell where the head had been and what weapons these creatures had fought with.

'Nothing to glean here,' Crossley said and shook his head.

It was the third battlefield they'd passed.

Nothing lived in this desolate, grey, flat land, John thought, and looked back at the skeletons.

'Why is there only one army?' he asked.

Crossley shrugged. 'Maybe the losers were really small?'

'Or they turned to dust when they died?' Olan added.

John gave the dirt a scuffled kick, sending a cloud up to his shins.

Up ahead, past the densest concentration of bodies, John could see symmetrical lines in the ground. 'Are they...?'

'Ah, yeah I get it.' Crossley nodded.

Olan looked confused until the lines became rows of mounds. 'They buried their dead?'

'Probably after their enemy headed to the silver gates,' Crossley said. 'The obelisk called them the Frarex. They lost.'

John shivered at the thought of coming up against some of the creatures they'd seen on the battlefields. 'But we'll have to meet one of these armies at some point, won't we?'

'Sure.' A grin spread across Crossley's face. 'Poor devils, ha!'

'That's if the losers stay here,' Olan said.

'What if they die when they are defeated?' Euryleia said.

'Maybe the defeated soldiers just go back home?' Crossley said.

'I doubt it,' Samas replied. 'This land has little love for the weak.'

'Most of these sites have been looted,' John said. 'Which means someone must still be here.'

'Unless new armies like ours are picking the bones?' Crossley said.

'Or victorious armies plundering before leaving?' Olan added.

'Anyone here would be battle-hardened.' Euryleia stared out to the horizon.

Samas said, 'Listen, we're getting stronger every day and with a little more training we'll fight as one unit.' He held up his clay cast. 'John and I are both healing well.'

John raised his gun-arm and smiled. 'I think mine might be more permanent.'

Samas shrugged. 'Who knows? If I ever get this thing off.' He wrapped his knuckles against the rock-hard cast.

'The rate everyone heals here, it should be fixed the day after tomorrow,' Euryleia said and turned to John. 'How is your arm?'

'Well, it doesn't weigh as much as it did,' John replied. 'But I can't get the magazine in so I won't be much use when it comes to fighting.'

'No excuses, John, we'll all have a use, believe me,' Samas said. 'My shield arm's out of action but I'll still fight. How about fixing a spear to your gun?'

'I don't know how to fight with a spear and…'

'It's fine,' Euryleia cut in. 'We'll know what we need to do when the enemy attacks.'

'Could be at any moment.' Crossley pointed at a new patch of bizarre, dead creatures.

'Okay, I'll think about it,' John said, reminding himself to stay strong. 'What are you going to do, Crossley?'

The American grinned. 'I'm still waiting to get my hands on some decent explosives.'

'What we really need is water,' Euryleia said.

'And some food before our rations run out,' Samas added.

'Good luck,' Crossley said in his usual manner.

John looked around at the burnt and desolate plain. 'Somewhere to sleep tonight would be good as well.'

Samas craned his neck to see the men at the front of the line, who had stopped.

Bowman was waving. 'Althorn's back!'

'In that direction,' Althorn pointed to the right of their path, 'near a tributary of the lake, I came across a camp of tents, big as a forest, all torn and full of corpses.'

Althorn was covered in dust and stretched his legs while the group rested around him.

'They were killed in their sleep.'

Crossley raised his eyebrows at John.

'Who were the dead?' Lavalle asked.

Althorn shrugged. 'Another tribe of alien soldiers. Who knows how long they lay there.'

John tried not to show his fear. A memory came back to him from a raid into enemy territory after his battalion had taken a German trench. He'd stepped into an officers' mess and, to his horror, found it fully manned. Full of gassed enemy troops. They looked like they were sleeping, John had thought. Some held gas masks in their laps and others were slumped in their chairs.

'So you suggest we head ten degrees left and aim for this forest?' Mihran asked.

'It's our best chance of finding water,' Althorn replied.

John looked at Crossley. 'This plain must be huge if Althorn didn't leave it.'

'Sure, but it can't all be like this though, hey?'

'Come on then.' Samas called the battalion to its feet. 'Let's move!'

'During our first day in the forest, we used a wide formation to find water.' Lavalle talked to Mihran and Li as they walked.

Mihran shook his head. 'Too dangerous – the arrowhead will suffice.'

John saw Lavalle grimace as he pulled back to walk with the infantry. The public humiliation he'd received hadn't only cost him Euryleia, but his standing in the battalion.

John heard low growling noises and looked at Crossley. 'You'll give yourself a nosebleed if you keep doing that.' He sounded more like his grandfather than he would have liked.

'How else are we going to find water?' Crossley whispered back.

John spotted Mata on the right flank. 'I might know a way.'

The battalion reached what looked like a tree sculpted from stone. John picked a tiny black feather from the twisted rock and guessed it was a leaf.

'Water.' Mata pointed at a dry crack opened by a broad granite root.

'Can you sense anything?' Mihran asked Li, who was busy scanning the tree and ground.

'Possibly… this tree is alive. Very slow-growing. No free water.'

Crossley stood next to Li and cleared his throat. 'How about here.' He pointed to a gap between the dirt and root.

'Yes, the tree must have penetrated the rock to access an aquifer. Quick, get–' Li started.

But Mata was there first: his left arm stretched into a twisted mass of brown vines, curled through the crack and into the earth to open up a depression two paces wide.

Li turned to Crossley. 'How did you know?'

'I…' he stuttered. 'I know my geology obviously and…'

Randeep rushed forward. 'Do you have an ability we don't know about?'

'What? No! What gave you that idea? Anyways, you can't talk with your apparently invisible sword.'

'I haven't hidden anything and my oath is sacred.' Randeep stared at Crossley. 'All abilities must be known.'

'Okay, but…'

'Look!' John said and they turned to Mata, who breathed hard as he coiled his arm back out of the crevice.

The small crater had filled with trickles of fresh water, which transformed into a small pond.

Althorn rushed forward. 'Let me test it.' He dipped an elbow and rubbed some on his wrist and lips. 'It's good. And cold!'

'Stand in line!' Mihran bellowed when the nearest soldiers moved in to drink. 'Slake your thirst, refill your canteens, then move on – we must find shelter before dark.'

John stood next to Crossley, who was nervously staring at patches of the ground. 'What is it?' he asked as the American coughed, turned and coughed again.

'I'm not sure, but I think I've found something, maybe a–'

Crossley's last word was cut off as explosions erupted around the soldiers, filling the air with dust.

John's first instinct had been to hit the ground, assuming it was mortar fire. 'Get down!' he shouted and pulled Crossley with him.

Through the stinging dust, John saw large shapes rise from the ground and attack the nearest soldiers. Through their legs he saw dark-blue shells and snapping pincers. He lay paralysed with fear as the huge creatures snapped at archers and spearmen, who fought valiantly to keep the enemy back. A disembowelled rifleman was writhing and screaming in his own blood and excrement, and a huge claw came crashing down, splitting him in two. John looked away. Lightning flashed, burning John's eyes, and a beast fell to the ground with steam pouring from a hole in its head. He saw Li, picking them off with accurate shots.

On the other flank, Samas was defending against another blue creature and Mihran was beside him, slashing with his formidable sword: removing limb after limb before finally taking the head of the attacker.

Two minutes after it had begun, it was all over. Five blue bodies lay next to seven dead men.

The war between humans and Brakari had begun.

Chapter 10

'Victorio Brakarius,' Millok replied to a guard.

She maintained her strong striding walk through the gates of the barracks.

Any sign of weakness and the soldiers would attack her in an instant, she knew. They despised female fighters. It had been the same back home, where the soldiers would show her up on exercises or intimidate her in the barracks. She had kept her carapace tight and head down but they still taunted her with threats of forced mating and torture.

Millok kept her antennae low as she passed a group of older Brakari sharing war stories and scars.

'...and the Skrifts just tore him apart. What was he thinking?'

'Must have had air in his shell.'

Is this how my life will always be? Millok thought. The threat of violence keeping me silent? The main reason she had agreed to Doctor Cynigar's experiments was for protection. Hosting a collection of unknown and lethal adaptations gave the aggressive soldiers second thoughts about trying to mate with her. It had been worse back home. After one of the largest soldiers tried to do his worst, Millok had reacted as any soldier would. When his decapitated body had been found in the mud saunas, the bullying stopped.

Millok climbed the steep wooden steps to the guard tower situated in the corner of the barracks. Her foreleg still ached but her other limbs were strong enough to pull her sleek body up to the platform, where two young soldiers kept watch.

The youngest soldier advanced. 'You are not permitted–' he started, but the other soldier leapt forward and nudged his shell.

Millok tensed and let two shocks of blue light up the new streaks that ran across her grey shell.

'Captain Millok.' The soldier bowed and turned back.

She was getting used to her new name. Bitet had been her name since hatching, but her adaptations had given her new powers, so why not a new name as well?

'Leave me be,' she ordered and the guards scuttled back to their posts.

Millok cleared her spiracles with a sharp exhalation and drew in fresh air as she walked around the tower, peering through various openings. The barracks had been built into the tall grey walls at a corner of the city by the river, which brought a cool breeze from the central lake.

'Abzicrutia stinks,' she muttered to herself, sure she could see a brown haze rising from the streets and mud domes.

How fast it had been built, and how quickly it had become a festering pit of filth. Streams of sewage ran down the main streets where packs of the black, wolf-like Skrifts were straining at their chains, feeding on the Brakari waste. The smell of other enslaved creatures wafted up on the air and Millok shut her spiracles. Lining the walls were the holding cells where General Panzicosta held captive soldiers for interrogation. The rumours of what he did to them made her shudder. Limp-limbed Ilanos, low slithering Gartoniads, even the few furred Sorean who had survived Panzicosta's torture would be forced to fight with the Brakari, along with the restrained Lutamek robots. Millok tensed and felt a wave of guilt wash through her for the bracing she had used to keep the electronic behemoths at bay.

A snippet of conversation wafted up from the barracks below: '–told me a few of the scout groups haven't checked in and Glexar thinks they were killed by the human army.'

So the enemy draw near, Millok thought, and they're proving to be more dangerous than Panzicosta's Draytor gave them credit for.

Turning to the city's solitary entrance, a stone's throw from her watchtower, Millok watched a stream of light-blue hatchling soldiers leaving the city. They were full of energy, bounding down the dirt streets and chattering away to each other with clicks and warbles. Her antennae twitched and her stomach acids swirled as she fought her emotions. She tried to detach herself from it, like a good soldier, but no matter how you looked at it, the truth always came back to her: these were her children.

Millok's trade with Doctor Cynigar had been simple. She'd given her eggs to replace the troops the Brakari had lost through their wars, and she would receive advanced adaptations as compensation. She'd had little choice – they would have strapped her down and cut her eggs out if she'd said no – but her instincts remained intact. She felt she should be protecting her brood, at least until their shells had hardened.

Outside the walls, the bulky armour-headed troops of the soil massed together, burrowing into the dusty soil, creating mounds to rest in. A host of Lutamek were being chained together to form a land train and, beyond them, the tip of a tall white tent could be seen next to the bulky black shape of Belsang's Vaalori. Inside, the Brakari leader was drawing up plans.

Sounds of commotion below attracted the guards next to Millok but she ignored them. Battle was not far away. She moved around the watchtower's edge and found herself staring at the distant mist. On a clear day, you could see the slum that had grown around the great gates, and Millok had lost count of the number of armies she had seen make the victorious march through to the other side. She no longer let herself daydream about what lay beyond. It didn't matter any more. What did she really have left to live for? She flexed her sore leg and felt the pain jolt through her nerves. Would she be fit enough to fight?

A sound made her turn – it was one of the guards.

'Captain Millok?' he repeated.

He was young too, she thought, but not one of hers.

'Yes,' she replied.

'It's General Panzicosta – he requests your presence.'

Gal-qadan smiled as he watched his soldiers file through the last clumps of orange cacti and into the dark pine forest. In close combat, his enemies would be powerless against this small but deadly force.

'We need more men,' he growled at Tode.

'I shall ask the scouts to look for lone warriors,' Tode replied.

'And horses. Can these men ride horses?' Gal-qadan asked.

'Yes, Khan. Dakaniha assures me he was one of his clan's greatest riders.'

'I would like to see if it's true.' Gal-qadan kept his face stone hard as he stared at Dakaniha and his compatriots, who talked out of earshot at the front of the line.

Gal-qadan had watched the men bicker and taken note. It wouldn't be good to let wounds fester. For now though, their objective was clear: find food and water and maintain the direction the Japanese swordsmen had been taking.

'Send the archers to hunt.' Gal-qadan ordered Tode away.

Gal-qadan felt content on his own, here at the back of the line, from where he could peer up through the dark forest canopy in private. He didn't want his men to know his secret: he had to keep up the pretence that he knew the way to the silver gates his men talked of.

'So is your great leader everything you thought he would be?' Kastor asked Dakaniha as they stood at a cliff top.

'His military prowess speaks for itself,' Dakaniha replied. 'And he led us out of the cactus lands.'

'True.' Kastor nodded. 'But is he really a leader? And what does he know about this land?'

'He survived on his own while others perished,' Dakaniha replied and pointed at the canopy of deciduous trees at the bottom of the cliff. 'This forest is different.'

'And it goes on forever!' said an Ottoman soldier, as the rest of the group arrived at the cliff top.

'How much further, Great Leader?' Dakaniha asked.

'Distance should not concern you, only how we get there,' Tode said.

'But we only have fourteen days,' the Mayan warrior said.

Gal-qadan glared at the man.

'We must find a way down the cliff. You three,' Gal-qadan pointed at Kastor, Dakaniha and Osayimwese, 'descend here.' He pointed to a goat path that zigzagged down the cliff face. 'Everyone else, this way.' He pointed to a landslip which had created a rocky slope down to the cliff base.

'Really?' Kastor stood with hands on hips. 'You go that way and we go–'

'Come on!' Dakaniha was already a few steps down the path.

Kastor shook his head and followed, using his long spear for balance.

Dakaniha didn't care if Kastor thought him too eager to impress Gal-qadan. The Mongol was a great soldier and any warrior wishing to improve their skills could learn from such a man.

His feet pattered rhythmically against the sandy soil of the cliff, but slid to a stop when he heard yelling from the forest below. Movement could be seen through the branches and leaves: somebody running.

'What's happening?' Kastor caught up.

'There.' Osayimwese pointed down to a dark figure speeding through the woodland.

'Is that the soldier who killed the Roc?' Kastor asked.

'Looks like it. He's being chased.'

Seven dark-grey shapes rose out of the soil of the woodland floor, closing in on the running man.

'Wolves,' Dakaniha said.

'We must save him!' Osayimwese raised his spear and looked at Kastor, as if to challenge him.

'You're on!' the Spartan grinned and scampered down the cliff path.

Dakaniha ignored the two spearmen and strung his bow. He stepped and slid down the steep hillside to a better vantage point. Below, the dark shadow of the rifleman burst out into the opening lining the cliff base. The man's clothes reminded Dakaniha of his enemy – the British – and his conscience told him he should not be saving this man.

No, he thought, I owe him a debt no matter who he is.

Ignoring his itching temples, Dakaniha slipped an arrow into his bow and aimed behind the running man. As soon as a fleck of grey fur rose from the ground, he fired four paces ahead, then at the next wolf when it revealed itself. Exhaling with each arrow, Dakaniha had little time to see if he had hit each target, and only stopped when Kastor and Osayimwese jumped in to attack, releasing their javelins in unison and unsheathing their swords to charge the wolves. Their yells echoed up the cliff as Kastor pummelled a wolf with his shield and jabbed with his short sword. Osayimwese tried a different tack when his wolf turned on him: with a deft feint, he dodged the flying claws and nicked the wolf's belly with his sword and eggshell dagger. Isolated, Osayimwese and the wolf repeated their fight to the death until, on his third attempt, Osayimwese stabbed the beast through the heart.

They had distracted some wolves but three remained focused on the rifleman, who scrambled up the cliff, trying to gain safety on a rocky ledge near the cliff's base.

Dakaniha looked over to Gal-qadan and the rest of the group. They were too far away to help and Dakaniha watched in horror as the rifleman stumbled on the loose rocks. The lead wolf pounced with teeth bared. Then a flash lit up the cliff, followed by an explosion that echoed like an avalanche.

When Dakaniha's eyes had recovered he saw that the wolf was dead by the rifleman's side and the surviving wolves were running back to the woods, slipping into the safety of the earth. He slowly slid down to where the rifleman rested, noticing odd shapes in the rock plateau around him.

'Are you hurt?' he asked the stranger.

The man squinted from beneath his peaked hat and said something in a language Dakaniha had heard before but couldn't understand. One word did stand out though: Cherokee.

Dakaniha bristled. 'Aniyunwiya,' he replied with a snap and pulled a mushroom from his satchel. Tode had given him it shortly after blowing the spores in his face and Dakaniha repeated the process now.

The man coughed and aimed his gun at Dakaniha, who held his hands up and waited for the dust to work its power.

'Take your time,' Dakaniha said as he put the mushroom away, 'and wait until you can understand me.'

The man's face calmed, he lowered his rifle and rubbed his nose. 'Say, what was that?' he asked.

Dakaniha gestured at the forest. 'Another gift from this strange land.'

'Like those wolves? Hell, it looks like the Unionists got men from every goddam creed searching this land, and now the wildlife don't want me here either.' The stranger looked at the rifle Dakaniha had taken from the dead soldier. 'Say, are you one of Stand Watie's men?'

'No, I...' Dakaniha started.

'Well, I'm Ethan Turner... a sharpshooter.' He patted his rifle. 'And I'd appreciate it if you could point me in the direction of the nearest Fed outpost.'

Dakaniha stared at the stranger's long, thin limbs and grey skin. He had seen the same colour on British soldiers who had been blown up by powder kegs.

'I'm not sure where we are,' Dakaniha replied. 'We're searching for the silver gates.'

'Silver gates?' Ethan looked up. 'What in hell's name are you talkin' about?'

'Our chief–'

Kastor hopped up to join them. 'They're all dead or gone!' he pointed at the scattering of dead wolves.

'You're wounded.' Dakaniha pointed to a cut on Kastor's knee that dripped blood onto the smooth rock.

'Oh, it's nothing – just a scratch,' Kastor said.

'Osayimwese?' Dakaniha asked.

'He's fine.' Kastor wrinkled his nose. 'He's not bad with a spear, you know.'

Gal-qadan and the rest of the group descended the scree fall to join them on the rocky platform.

'That was an impressive fight,' a bearded swordsman said, nodding and smiling. 'Good work!'

Kastor tilted his head. 'Next time we'll charge a fee.'

'This is Ethan Turner.' Dakaniha felt obliged to introduce the newcomer. 'He is the man who killed the eagle.'

Ethan pulled the cap on his hat down further and mumbled, 'Damned light burns my eyes.'

Gal-qadan mumbled, 'He can join us.'

'I prefer to work alone,' Ethan kept his head low, trying to avoid eye contact, 'but if you guys are heading to the nearest outpost I could tag along.'

'There are no outposts here,' Dakaniha said.

'Okay then.' Ethan sighed and stood to his full height. At nearly two metres tall, he towered over the men around him. 'I've never heard of no silver gates, but if you're heading my way I could use some company.'

Gal-qadan remained on the rock and took in the group that were now under his command. Ethan's rifle was a worthy addition, he thought, and he weighed up the men as they shared rations and stories. While he thought, Gal-qadan rubbed a spot of Kastor's blood into the rock with the tip of his bow. The curves and shapes in the rock seemed familiar and he bent down to take a closer look. A line of a leg here, a head there and an eye. Horses? he thought, and his gaze flicked to another drip of blood, which had been absorbed into the rock near what looked like a horse's fetlock.

It twitched.

Gal-qadan gasped and looked at his battalion. No one had noticed and they continued their buzz of chatter. He took a step back and scanned the fossils beneath his feet: horse-like creatures lay in various death poses within the dark stone, with hooves and long legs at odd angles.

If a drop of blood gave life to one muscle?

'Tode,' Gal-qadan snapped. 'Order the men to forage for food. Send some for fresh water.'

'Yes, Khan,' Tode replied and started ordering the men into groups.

Before they moved out of sight into the forest, Gal-qadan whittled down his options. He could provide more blood himself or… he weighed up his men's weapons and usefulness. One man stood aloof from the group. He could be sacrificed.

'I need that man for another job,' Gal-qadan said and Tode beckoned the soldier over.

The Mayan blinked and stayed silent beside Gal-qadan as he waited for Tode and the others to move further into the forest.

'We need soldiers,' Gal-qadan said, 'but we need horses more. Can you ride?'

The Mayan looked blank. 'I don't know what horses are, I…'

Gal-qadan held a hand up to silence him and unclipped his dagger, but the Mayan had noticed and drew his weapon in response.

'Look.' Gal-qadan pointed to the forest to distract him and swiped at the Mayan, but he was too fast and countered the attack.

Gal-qadan cursed himself for not attacking sooner and raised his arm to defend against the Mayan, who had swung his axe. Gal-qadan dodged and swiped with his knife, but the Mayan's handle was longer, giving him a greater reach. Incensed, Gal-qadan rushed and took the Mayan by surprise, tackling him to the ground, but Gal-qadan fell awkwardly and the Mayan had room to swing his weapon, which came crashing down. Gal-qadan held an arm up in defence and watched in disbelief as the razor-sharp stone axe bounced off his forearm with a shower of sparks.

The Mayan stumbled back in confusion and swung again. Gal-qadan defended and the sparks flew again. His skin was as tough as metal! A new energy surged through Gal-qadan. They grappled on the rock ledge, but Gal-qadan felt invincible now and the fight slowly turned in his favour. Blades clashed and sparks leapt around them until Gal-qadan saw an opening and took it. With a flash of steel, Gal-qadan painted a red line across the soldier's throat and blood cascaded down his chest, splashing maroon dots onto the rock. The Mayan gurgled and grabbed at his opened throat as Gal-qadan struck again, slicing at his arm and then his calf, sending the Mayan crashing to the ground.

The dying warrior eventually stopped convulsing, yet the blood poured from his opened veins, pooling in the crevasses and curves scattered across the rock. Gal-qadan gave a rare smile, and scanned the forest. Nobody was in sight, so he threw the Mayan's weapon into a pile of rocks and rolled the body over, spreading blood on more dry rock. Shapes jolted beneath his feet as Gal-qadan set to work, hacking away and distributing limbs to dry areas.

When he had covered most of the fossilised mass, Gal-qadan climbed up the cliff to watch the rock come to life. A curve of leg vibrated here and a circle blinked there, followed by spasms and mini-earthquakes which shook the dust and crumbled the stone. A sound could be heard, muffled at first but becoming clearer: tock, tock, tock-a-tock. Stones were shaking free from the rumbling mass and small boulders rolled onto the grassy floor. Then a leg broke free from its stone prison, clawing at thin air. Stones rolled, shaken by equine heads rising out of the dust and hindquarters struggling with wild kicks.

Gal-qadan listened to the animal's sound. Tocka, tocka, tock-tock. He pictured hooves clashing against the rocks but a head broke free and he saw a large set of sharpened incisors gnashing together: tocka, tocka.

'Steady!' Gal-qadan shouted as the beast flung its head about: its wild eyes staring about in fear.

The animal chomped in panic, shaking a foreleg free, then the other. It was clear by their teeth that these horses were not grass eaters. These will be better than any steppe horse, Gal-qadan thought, and found his cheeks aching from his wide grin. His breathing sped up with the excitement and turned into a deep laugh.

'Run free!' he shouted.

With a deep crack, the ledge gave way and crashed onto the grass below. Gal-qadan caught glimpses of heads and legs, wild eyes and teeth, but the dust billowed up, masking the host of freed beasts who screamed and chomped in exultation. When the cloud settled, the grass was covered with nothing more than grey stones and cracked boulders, covering what was left of the Mayan's body.

Gal-qadan scanned the forest but the only movement he saw were his men returning to the cliff, drawn back by the sound of the landslide.

'What happened?' Tode asked after sprinting back with Kastor and Dakaniha.

'The horses were in the rocks,' Gal-qadan replied. 'The man with me died in the rockslide when they broke free.'

He watched the men's face to see if they believed the lie, then clambered down the rocks to the grass floor and kept alert.

'There!' Gal-qadan pointed to their left flank, where sounds echoed through the forest: crashing branches and running hooves.

Time to break them in, Gal-qadan thought, and pulled a rope free from his belt.

'Tocka!' he shouted. 'To-cka, to-cka!' He tied a lasso and swung it through the air. Here they come; he could hear the hooves getting nearer. 'Tock-a, tock-a!'

Then the sound stopped.

Strange how the floor still rumbled, Gal-qadan thought. Then, with a flash of white, the herd rushed out of the forest with eyes of tigers and teeth of sharks. Gal-qadan stood his ground and released his lasso but it failed to snare a head. A bite caught him on the shoulder, slicing into his armour, but it slipped off his toughened skin.

As soon as they came, they disappeared.

'Amazing!' Gal-qadan staggered backwards.

The equine predators wheeled around and sped in for another attack. Gal-qadan braced himself, refusing to unsheathe a weapon. He heard yelling behind but focused on the wild animals rushing at him: jostling and barging one another to be in the lead.

Then something changed – he sensed it in the animals' eyes. Their expressions softened and the front runners braked hard, digging their strong hooves into the grassy earth. A tsunami of dirt billowed up as the herd came to a sliding stop.

'They obey me!' Gal-qadan said, his eyes wide with excitement.

'No.' Kastor was standing behind him. 'They obey me.'

'But, I must break them.' Gal-qadan felt anger rise and his right hand twitch for his sword.

'They won't be broken,' Kastor replied. 'They are equals and have the right to choose. These… tocka, will not be led.'

'Tocka?' Gal-qadan breathed deeply and weighed up his options. He could kill Kastor for insubordination. He wouldn't allow this kind of arrogant behaviour in his army.

One of the taller equines, some sixteen hands high, stepped forward and offered its muzzle to Kastor. Gal-qadan took a deep breath and controlled his ego. He still held power. If he ruled the Spartan, he ruled the beasts. Without the Spartan, he would have no horses.

'Will they carry men?' Gal-qadan asked.

'I'm not sure,' the Spartan said as he patted the soft muzzle and grinned, 'but we can ask them.'

Two hours later, Gal-qadan's troop rode through the last stretch of forest on their steeds and found themselves at the shore of an enormous waterway. Gal-qadan studied the detritus left along the sandy beach: vines, sea bladders and lumps of wood.

Tode joined Gal-qadan after scouting the beach. 'There was a battle here. Craters suggest gunpowder, and there are bodies of giant insects.'

Gal-qadan nodded and more men joined them.

'What will we do?' Dakaniha asked.

Gal-qadan glowered at him and clenched his fist. These men asked much of him and it made him feel... trapped. He paused to let his anger slide and noted how easier it had become in the past few days. It was true what Tode had said: Dakaniha was an accomplished rider. He could be useful.

Scanning down the beach, Gal-qadan saw a group of a dozen men in red coats dragging wood onto the beach. If they were heading across the water, and the mess on the beach suggested others had built rafts, it left him no option.

'Gather your belongings and make them waterproof,' Gal-qadan spoke slowly. 'Tie the bladders to your weapons. The tocka will take us.' He nodded to the water.

'What?' Kastor shouted. 'You don't even know if they can swim.'

Gal-qadan shrugged. 'Ask them.'

General Panzicosta watched Millok's sleek, grey body descend the watchtower ladder and felt stirrings beneath his carapace. They didn't have the domed halls of sex slaves here, so Panzicosta's sexual frustration had built up since settling in Abzicrutia. The only way he had found to reduce tension was to inflict pain on others. The power he had over his captives was addictive. With it he could incite fear – he chose when to cause pain and when a creature would die. If the torture helped the Brakari cause then it was a bonus.

'General Panzicosta.' Millok bowed and her new stripes flashed.

'Your leg is still weak.' Panzicosta had only seen the leg wobble once, but could tell by Millok's open spiracles that maintaining the illusion of fitness was tiring her.

'Yes, General, but growing stronger by the hour,' she replied.

An answer for everything, Panzicosta thought. 'Good, we need every soldier fighting fit for the forthcoming battle. Now,' he raised his body up and stalked over to the barrack gates, 'we have much to discuss. Good and bad.' He walked on, expecting Millok to follow him.

They left the barracks, past the makeshift huts leaning against the mud-brick walls of the city.

'If you haven't already heard,' Panzicosta kept his voice low, 'three of the seventeen scouting parties have not reported back.' He waited for a response, eager to know how fast the gossip was travelling through the army.

'I have heard rumours, General,' Millok replied, keeping her head low.

'Where?' Panzicosta stopped and loomed over the female.

'In the watchtower.'

With a snort, Panzicosta resumed his walk. 'Belsang put it down to communication issues. But three? We must be under attack.' The General stretched his long blue back to crack a shell in place. 'I say we weaken them, but Belsang wants them in large numbers for our great victory.'

'A risky strategy.' Millok spoke softly.

'Yes.' Panzicosta decided not to chastise her for speaking openly: she was here to help and provide a sounding board for his thoughts. 'Victory will be ours, but at what cost?'

Perimeter guards were approaching, so Panzicosta remained silent.

'General. Captain.' The pair of young Brakari crouched between huts to let them pass.

Panzicosta noticed Millok inhale as they passed.

'Of the remaining scouts,' Panzicosta continued, 'fifteen report nothing… but two have seen separate groups of humans making their way across the plains.'

Millok slowed her stride for a second. 'There are more of them?' She skipped to catch up.

'Not in great numbers, but I fear we may have underestimated their capacity to evolve and survive.' Panzicosta saw the mud-brick holding cells up ahead and felt a tingle run through his pincers. 'We should take the fight to them before they create alliances with any surviving species.'

Panzicosta felt distracted by the stench of unwashed vertebrates and their faeces. They passed the first cell, which had been built to form a box with no lid. Inside, three starved and beaten Sorean soldiers whimpered and slept, their fur and muzzles burnt and torn. In the next cell, whose windowless walls were high enough to trap their captives but low enough for Panzicosta to retrieve them, two red, twisted and tentacled creatures lay in their own mess. One wasn't moving, so Panzicosta halted and sniffed. 'Krotank!' he bellowed.

A bulky and scarred Brakari scurried out of a doorway down the path. 'Yes, General!'

'Why is this creature dead?' Panzicosta barked.

'It was alive this morning, General, I checked–'

Panzicosta thumped Krotank with a thick, spring-loaded pincer, flinging him back onto his shell. 'I decide when they die, do you understand?'

'Yes, General!' Krotank wriggled to right himself. 'It won't happen again.'

'You are right it won't happen again,' Panzicosta hissed, 'or you'll have a cell of your own.' Panzicosta snorted and retracted his thumping pincer. 'Go!' he shouted and turned to check Millok was still behind him. 'This will not be tolerated.'

He continued past the remaining cells to a building capped with a thick, wooden roof. 'The good news is I have heard from the Draytor.' He punched the door open and a thick waft of foul air drifted out. 'The Draytor is close to capturing a human soldier. So,' Panzicosta gestured for Millok to enter the dark and damp building, 'we must prepare for their visit.'

Inside, it took a second for Panzicosta's variety of eyes to adjust to the low light. The slicing blades, rusted manacles and holding tables came into view, alongside pails of blood, lumps of fur and long-lost limbs.

Chapter 11

'I can't see any bodies,' John said as a new battlefield appeared on the horizon.

'Plenty of graves though.' Crossley pointed to a series of mounds spread out in a random fashion, unlike the previous regimented graves.

'Some have a stick at one end.' Euryleia pointed.

'To mark the head?' Lavalle tried to catch her eye but she walked away.

'They were big.' Crossley coughed. 'Humanoid.'

'The others have a stone,' John said.

Mihran stared at the white obelisk, then spoke to Li: 'Scan this field as you have the others. I need more data and then–'

'Halt!' A deep voice boomed and a silhouette appeared of a tall biped.

'Friend or foe?' Bowman was nearest but received no reply.

John held his breath and took a step back. Even in the low light he recognised the figure.

'What is your name?' Mihran stepped forward, his scarlet robes flowing in the breeze.

'I am Peronicus-Rax,' the tall creature replied.

'The watcher,' John whispered and stared at the one large eye in his oval head, just like in the pictures.

Peronicus-Rax stood over eight feet tall, and his body was festooned with a variety of weapons and trinkets, dangling from belts and hooks. He didn't move, yet the thickness of his limbs suggested great strength.

'What happened here?' Mihran asked.

'Battle, war, death,' Peronicus-Rax replied.

'And then?'

'I buried them where they fell.' His voice was deep and full of sorrow.

Li stepped forward to get a better view. 'How long have you been here?'

'Long enough.' He winced and bent away in pain. 'Desist your scanning, female.'

'Sorry, I…' Li looked away.

'Your species is new to this land and you have questions.' He looked from soldier to soldier. 'I have answers but I doubt you want to hear them.'

'We would appreciate any information you have,' Mihran answered.

'Do you have shelter?' Lavalle asked.

'Yes, but be careful not to draw attention.'

Crossley looked at John and mouthed, 'What does he mean?'

'There must be other armies about,' John whispered back.

Peronicus-Rax strode off and John kept an eye on him, wondering what drew this creature to death.

'This place feels creepier than the other battlefields,' Crossley whispered. 'I mean… he buried *all* of these guys?'

John agreed. 'Maybe that's why he brings us here?' John replied.

'I don't know. It's more like he's here to clear up, like some kinda priest.'

'We can't trust him,' John said.

'Why?' Crossley asked.

'He's drawn to death.' John tried to find the words. 'He looks for death… he's dangerous.'

Crossley pointed ahead to the view unfolding in the low light. 'But we've got somewhere to sleep tonight.'

The ground dropped away to reveal what looked like an elephant graveyard. Huge, motionless creatures lay scattered across the dusty valley floor. At first, John thought they were sleeping, but their loose skins flapped in the wind.

They descended the shallow incline and John stared up at the huge creatures, wondering if they'd been warriors or beasts of burden. Each carcase bore no obvious face or limbs, just a bulk of desiccated flesh, and a spicy odour wafted from the bodies.

'Smells like cinnamon,' John overheard someone say, and he had to agree it wasn't a bad smell.

'Like a pod of beached whales.' Mata stared up as he walked

through the rows of bodies, each of which stood three times taller than him and fifty paces long.

'They're long dead by the look of it.' John pointed to one body where the skin hung in tatters to reveal a rigid, rib-like structure within.

Li was busy scanning a carcase. 'Their organs were scavenged or wasted away, and the dry air has turned their skins to leather. A perfect tent.'

'Whale tents in the desert.' Crossley laughed and shook his head.

'We just need an entrance,' Lavalle said, slipped his longsword from its scabbard and slit a diagonal cut between two ribs, 'and the tent is ours.'

The knight pulled back a flap and John half expected a cloud of bats to stream out. Instead, a gust of sweet odour greeted his nostrils.

'And maybe a second door for ventilation.' Lavalle disappeared into the dark cavity and shouted back, 'The floor is dry!'

'Right then,' Crossley stepped in. 'Time for some shut-eye.'

John followed into the dark cavernous belly. The exhausted soldiers who filed in behind him filled the leathery floor with their slumbering bodies. So, as he'd done for days now, John put his bag down for a pillow, unstrapped his gun-arm and lay on his back.

His mind wandered. He wanted to know more about the watcher – Peronicus-Rax. Was he one of a race of advanced aliens who had brought them here? More importantly, did he have the answer to how John could get back home to England and Joe?

Minutes passed as John's thoughts wandered and he stared at the ribs above. As his eyes adjusted to the darkness, the smallest sounds around him grew into larger sounds in his head – a creak here or a swish there. The breathing of the men slowed and they snuffled or snored as they drifted off. Then a rustle outside caught his attention, footsteps… followed by a pair of quiet voices.

John was up straight away and tiptoed over the prostrate soldiers to the tent's opening, where he hid in the shadows. From this distance he could just make out the deep voice of Peronicus-Rax, but who was he talking to?

'...fought in many wars, but these were our match,' Peronicus-Rax said.

'Why did you bury them?' It was Mihran.

Typical Mihran, John thought, always asking questions.

'I was the last survivor,' Peronicus-Rax replied.

'And yet, you buried your enemies as well,' Mihran said.

'Yes, they deserved that.'

Was Peronicus-Rax just another soldier? John wondered. Another pawn pushed around by whoever was playing this game?

'How did you survive?' Mihran asked.

'I was lucky and–' Peronicus-Rax shuddered like he had when Li had scanned him. 'Stop!'

Mihran stumbled backwards and clutched his head. 'I...'

'Do not enter a mind without permission!' Peronicus-Rax kept his voice quiet but sounded more threatening for it.

'I don't,' Mihran panted and John felt an urge to help his leader. It was the first time he'd seen him weakened like this. 'I'm still learning how to use this... gift.'

Without pity or anger, Peronicus-Rax spoke: 'Use it wisely. These gifts must be turned to your advantage in war. As leader, you must think of your battalion before yourself.'

Mihran was nodding, although breathing heavily still.

'You should refine your skills to keep in touch with your warriors. For example, did you know our conversation is being listened to?'

'No, I...' Mihran paused, then spun round to look in John's direction.

John pulled away from the tent flap, quickly tiptoed back and lay down. The sound of his pounding heart filled his ears as he waited for Peronicus-Rax or Mihran to burst in at any moment. John calmed his breathing and wiped his mind of all thoughts in case Mihran used his skills to find him, but all he could think about was Joe.

John woke with a gasp, unaware he'd fallen asleep. The tent was dark and full of the sounds of men breathing. He sat up and looked around, unable to shake the feeling that someone had been calling his name. A faint, high-pitched sound came from outside the tent, and John pictured a cat or puppy. He had to check it out, so crept out over the snoozing warriors, sure he heard a light pattering of feet running from the tent along with – was that a giggle? John stepped outside and, in the low light, caught a glimpse of a shadow disappearing behind the nearest tent. He coughed as a cloud of dust wafted over from the desert and then ran after the shadow.

'It can't be.' John caught sight of a leg and ran off in pursuit, holding his gun-arm against his chest.

He weaved around the tents and chased the little silhouette to where the tents opened up to reveal the open desert. John stopped to catch his breath and shook his head. Twenty paces away, standing on the rise of a hill with a cheeky smirk, stood a young boy no older than four years old.

'Joe?' John asked.

The boy's mouth broke into a full smile as he held John's gaze.

'My boy.' Tears filled John's eyes. 'You found me.'

He didn't question why or how. John just stared: drinking in the sight of his son. This was no picture or faint memory – it was Joe in the flesh! He wiped his eyes and, when he could see again, Joe had run up to the hill's brow.

'Wait!' John called out and started climbing.

Olan shook himself awake with a snort which, according to his wife, he always did when he slept on his back. It took a few seconds to recognise the lines of ribs above him; their bleached white lines glowing in the low dawn light. He licked his dry teeth and, with his trusty double-headed axe in one hand and his gleaming Incan chest plate in the other, stepped over the slumbering soldiers to the door flap. He noticed an empty space along the way but thought nothing of it.

The fresh air outside filled his lungs and cleared his mind. Thoughts of his wife, children and home village came to him just as they did every morning of this voyage. He had counted the days until he returned to his family, rich with plunder. But how long would it be now? Five more days, and then what? Just two more journeys, he had promised his wife, two raids would give him enough money to start trading furs and amber through the Eastern trade routes. Flashes of the butchery of war came to him: burning villages; earth pooled with blood; wailing children; frightened women; the dismembered bodies of fighting men.

He shook his head and made his way through the tents to where a winding line of small bushes scratched a living beside a clear, stone-bottomed brook. He dipped his elbow and splashed a little water onto his lips before drinking and refilling the goat's bladder – runes sewn into its handle gave him strength: his family name; his wife's name; and his children's.

For two generations, Olan's people had sent their warriors west to steal from the weak Britons and, being the tallest man in his village by the age of fifteen, Olan's parents had little choice in letting him go 'a viking'. Years later they said Olan was the strongest axe-man to set foot in a longboat, which was why so many men gambled and fought to be oarsmen in his ship.

His last raid, just a few days ago, had been like the rest: the fleet of twelve shallow-hulled ships had powered up the river with the tide when the clouds hid the moon. The scouts had told of decrepit guards defending a village nestling in the soft grassy hills of this timid and unthreatening country.

Not like this land, Olan thought, keeping one eye on the open desert. After a quick wash, he walked back to the tents to see Mihran and Samas stretching and talking.

'And you think they'll fight as one?' Samas said.

'We *will* fight in the next five days, so we need to be ready.' Mihran gave Olan a look. 'Our priority is to locate the gates, but we should think about training – manoeuvres and communication.'

Samas nodded and Olan wondered where the animosity between these two had gone.

'The water's clean.' Olan held up the bladder.

'Good. We breakfast then leave,' Mihran replied. 'Wake them.'

Olan smiled.

'Quietly.' The huge figure of Peronicus-Rax loomed up from behind.

'Yes, of course.' Olan felt like a child next to him and stepped away to the nearest tent.

'We haven't found out who decapitated the men at the castle,' Mihran said. 'And I'm not sure if it was one of our men.'

Olan felt Mihran staring at him as he walked away but, when he turned back, Mihran was looking elsewhere.

'There are many forces here who want your army reduced,' Peronicus-Rax said softly, 'and it seems your presence attracted unwanted attention – creatures were here in the night.'

'Who?' Mihran asked. 'Our enemy?'

'A potential enemy if you choose. They didn't stay for long,' Peronicus-Rax said.

Olan kept listening as he walked from tent to tent. 'Wake up, get up!'

'Which way to the silver gates?' Samas asked.

'In that direction,' Peronicus-Rax pointed.

Crossley was one of the first men Olan had woken. He joined the conversation. 'You've been to the silver gates?'

'I have seen them,' Peronicus-Rax replied.

Olan visited tents further away. 'Come on, time to get up,' he called and headed back to Mihran as Li gave her morning report.

'…supplies are low but we have a more pressing issue.'

'What is it?' Mihran asked.

'We have a soldier missing – John Greene.'

Olan looked at Li. Was she telling the truth or was she the killer? Olan had grown fond of the little Englishman.

'The short man with the arm-gun?' Mihran asked and Li nodded. 'Any sign of where he went?'

'I found two sets of footsteps leading out of the camp and over the dunes.'

'Listen.' Mihran raised his voice to get everyone's attention. 'We need to keep walking, but it appears John Greene left the camp last night.'

'What?' Crossley jumped up. 'He can't survive out there. Why the hell did he run off?'

Li shrugged. 'I don't know. He's taken his bags, so–'

'John needs to be with us.' Euryleia spoke out. 'He has no weapon and he's injured.'

'We've got to go get him.' Crossley was staring at Mihran. 'Come on!'

'No,' Mihran said firmly. 'We need you to find water in this desert – Mata too.'

'I will find him.' Lavalle stepped forward. 'Point me in his direction and I will track him down.'

Olan smiled. Did Lavalle really think finding John would restore Euryleia's faith in him?

'Yes.' Mihran stroked his beard. 'Anyone else?'

Randeep stepped forward. 'I will go.'

Olan shifted from foot to foot. It would be good to stretch his legs and get away from this monotonous march, but it could be dangerous and…

'Olan and Samas,' Mihran said, 'you will join Randeep and Lavalle.'

Olan caught a glimpse of Samas' face and recognised the old resentment rise in his eyes.

'Li will give you directions and instructions on how to locate us,' Mihran continued. 'Good luck.'

Olan grabbed his rations and strapped his chest plate to his back, with an extra leash for his axe. 'We'll be back in no time.' He patted Lavalle on the shoulder and tried to hide his smile.

As the four men jogged across the dry plain, Olan's first raid came back to him. He had been the youngest on his ship, wearing his father's armour and an iron amulet of Thor's hammer, which his mother had tied around his neck. When they hit land, Olan had held back while the other men charged the Saxon village and, by the time he walked through the broken wooden palisades and over the dead guards, the defeat was complete. But not the victory. Olan had watched in horror as his comrades hacked at defenceless people, burnt houses sheltering families and raped young women in the street. They tortured old men for their hidden silver and left the younger men writhing in agony, their wounds bleeding them dry.

His comrades had changed; Olan could see it in their eyes.

Shocked by the barbarity of his people and harassed by the sounds of torture and the stench of burning flesh, Olan had looked to the skies, asked Odin for answers. Was this how he was to act too? Attack the rich churches and monasteries, fight the men with swords? Olan had thought. Not this. Anything but this. He couldn't be like them… surely there was another way. But what could he do? He would never fight his own men and, looking at them, they enjoyed it too much to be talked out of it.

Solemn and confused, Olan had toured the village, wincing at the screams and moans. Out of desperation, and to shut him up, Olan lashed out at an elderly man who lay screaming in the mud. With an angry chop he beheaded the man. Shocked at his actions, but content he had ended the man's pain, Olan did the same with a young man dying from a stab wound. Then again and again. He couldn't understand their words but carried on, putting the people out of their misery. His countrymen looked on and laughed, soon naming him 'the beheader' but, with each hack, Olan felt another soul had been released. He couldn't protect them so he vowed next time he would kill the weak people before his comrades got to them. He would have to be fast and many would die but, standing in that burning village, he made his naive oath to the gods.

Over the years, Olan had kept his vow: cleanly killing as many villagers as possible before the rapists and sadists got to them. They had called him 'berserkir', but he wasn't. He felt every cut and bruise deeper than any man sharing his battlefield.

As Lavalle, Randeep and Samas paused for a water break, Olan's countless raids ran through his mind. Right up to his last battle. The flotilla had silently cruised up to the pontoons of the village and, as soon as his boat brushed the bank, Olan leapt onto land, his axe held high. Crashing through the barricade, Olan had been surprised to see soldiers drafted in by the villagers but he'd left them to his men. He scared the women and children out of the village with a yell and glare, and any men foolish enough to face him were hacked down. By the time the Viking vanguard had caught up, Olan had already saved a dozen lives.

Then the flash had taken him.

'We must keep moving,' Randeep said. The group of four stood now by a clump of shrubs a hundred paces from the forest Peronicus-Rax had warned them about.

'Don't worry,' said Samas. Always a calming influence, Olan thought. 'We'll find John soon enough and have him back with the others before night.' The Babylonian stared at the forest for a few long seconds. 'Plus if Peronicus is wary of this forest, we should be too.'

Randeep huffed and adjusted his blue turban. 'He's weak and these creatures will be nothing to worry about. Let's go – come on!' The swordsman was off.

Lavalle raised an eyebrow at Olan.

'Come on then.' Olan loosened the strap holding his axe.

They found Randeep crouched behind a tree. He beckoned them over and put a finger to his lips. Olan saw the issue.

'A village?' Lavalle whispered. 'How on earth is that here?'

Some fifty paces away through the open woodland, Olan could see several timber houses and a few upturned boats. 'It doesn't look defended.'

Samas was rubbing his chin. 'Do we just walk in and ask if anyone's seen John?'

Randeep looked tense. 'No, we must attack. They have him captive.'

'That would be unwise.' A voice made them turn and aim their weapons. Four shining blades pointed at a black and brown furred creature who stood no higher than Olan's elbow.

'Who are you?' Olan asked.

The cat-like humanoid wrinkled its muzzle and tilted its head inquisitively. 'I am Captain Jakan-tar of the Sorean and if you cross that fence you will be in great danger.'

John was still smiling. He couldn't believe that, after everything he'd been through – the trenches; the charges across no-man's-land; the crater; the bizarre events of the past ten days – Joe had found him. It didn't matter how. All John had wanted to do was hug his son and talk to him, but Joe kept running off.

When the morning light brought colour to the desert, Joe led him to a strip of green on the horizon. John had ignored his thirst and his stomach was too excited to be hungry. When they finally made it to the woodland, Joe pointed into the trees then disappeared into the darkness with a cheeky smile. John hadn't seen him since, although he'd called for him several times.

Not far from the wood's edge, John found a picket fence surrounding rows of wooden buildings, which looked oddly familiar.

Like a training camp, he thought, but spotted a flag. Was this a hospital?

He found the gate and was walking through the compound when a voice made him turn.

'What are you doing there, soldier?' As soon as he heard the clipped tones, John's back straightened and he turned on his heels.

'I, err… I'm looking for an officer, sir.' John could see by the crown on his shoulder he was being addressed by a major.

'Well you've found him.' The Major wore a thick, trim moustache and had piercing blue eyes which John couldn't hold for more than a second. 'Now, what are your orders and what in heaven's name have you done to your weapon?' The Major pointed a gloved hand at John's gun-arm.

'I lost my regiment, sir.'

A hundred thoughts whirled in John's head as he tried to make sense of what had had happened to him: the bizarre creatures; the wasps; the obelisks; the robot's castle. They had to be real, just like Crossley, Mata, Lavalle and the others, but how did that fit with… this place?

'And?' the Major barked.

John struggled to make sense of it. He saw a red cross on the nearest hut and it started to make sense. 'I was injured, sir.'

'Injured? Yes.' The Major sounded like Mihran, John thought. 'Rest and recuperation are the order of the day, what?' He nodded at the huts. 'It looks like you've bought your Blighty ticket, eh? Just head through and the nurses will help you out.'

John could hear laughter on the other side of the huts and caught a glimpse of someone wearing white.

'Yes, sir.' John started to walk off then remembered Joe. 'And my son, sir?'

The Major squinted and John avoided his stare. 'He'll be along shortly,' he replied and marched off.

John walked through the gap between the huts and saw nurses in their blue dresses and white pinafores attending to men in lounge chairs while, on the short grass beyond, men were running about and playing cricket. John had never really taken to the game but smiled all the same. He looked up at the hazy sky. Strange how it could be cloudy on such a sunny day, he thought.

A nurse raised a hand to shade her eyes and caught sight of him. 'Hello.' Her voice reminded John of Rosie's and his stomach fluttered. 'Have you just arrived?'

'Yes, I... the Major said to come through.'

'Right. Well, follow me and we'll have a look at you – it's your arm, isn't it?' The nurse's perfume wafted on the soft wind as she walked over and rested a hand on his shoulder.

'Yes.'

'We'll have you right as rain in no time.' The nurse led him into a whitewashed hut and picked up his bags. 'I'll take these. Have a seat.'

'Thanks.' John felt the urge to take off his shoes and thought of Joe. 'Will my son be here soon?'

'Oh, yes.' The nurse gave John a sweet smile. 'He's been telling us all about you. He's a lovely boy. A credit to you.'

'Well,' John felt himself blush as the nurse wrapped a bleached-white sling around his gun-arm, 'my parents have been raising him these past years, what with the war and all.'

'Yes, so sad about your wife. Here, please take this.' The nurse handed John a small pill and a glass of water.

'Rosie,' John said after swallowing.

'Yes, Rosie.' The nurse tied the sling tight. 'Ah, the doctor's here. I'll see you soon, John.'

'Oh, bye, and thanks.'

'John Greene?' A grey-haired man in a white coat was standing at his side, reading from a clipboard. The voice reminded him of Lavalle.

'Yes, sir.'

'No "sir" here, John, I'm just a doctor.' He ran a finger down the clipboard. 'Now, you were stationed at Ypres, is that right?'

'Yes, before…'

'Yes, yes, I don't need your whole war story, laddie, I just need to check you're our man. The boys can tell you where we are with the war, but I need you to rest. Get you on the mend.'

'Yes.' John turned back to the men outside, relaxing on loungers with a book or newspaper carelessly discarded on their chests.

'We're glad you're safe, John,' the doctor continued. 'We heard there was a spot of trouble last week with a breakout from the mental institution.'

John looked up. He felt woozy but something told him this was important, so he tried to focus.

'Many men escaped – shell-shocked, disillusioned, gassed, you name it – the word is they were terrorising the countryside dressed up as cowboys and Spartans, knights and Romans, if you could picture such a thing!'

'What?' John pictured Samas with his shield and Lavalle and his sword… but as each image came, it floated away in a mist.

'Yes, strange days, although I hear they are being rounded up as we speak.' He popped his pen back in his coat's top pocket and gave a reassuring smile. 'Don't worry, we'll look after you and I can guarantee you won't be going back to that God-awful war.'

'Great.' John blinked slowly and stared back out at the green grass and smiling faces. His eyelids were so heavy. 'But what about…' He saw the doctor leaving. 'What about Joe?'

Olan turned to Randeep, Lavalle and Samas, who looked as bemused as he felt.

'You are a captain?' Lavalle asked the short furred humanoid, whose arms looked too long for its short striped body.

'Yes.' Jakan-tar's muzzle twitched. 'Captain Jakan-tar of the Sorean, and my soldiers are trapped in that compound.' Jakan-tar pointed to where Olan saw wooden houses and upturned boats.

'Why don't you just break in and save them?' Randeep asked.

Jakan-tar sniffed before replying, 'I have no protection.'

'We believe one of our soldiers is also in the village,' Samas said.

'And we intend to save him,' Lavalle added.

'Then you will be captured.' Jakan-tar made a move to walk away. 'I have warned you.'

'But there must be a way.' Olan stepped forward. 'Please, can you help us?'

Jakan-tar's head dropped. 'I have been walking these woods for months. There is no way.'

'What happened?' Olan asked.

'We don't have time for this!' Randeep moved forward. 'Let's just get John out and be done with it.'

'We lost our battle.' Jakan-tar ignored Randeep. 'And wandered this dead land searching for somewhere to heal our wounded. The first soldier rushed in here and…'

'And?' Olan felt like crouching as though talking to a child, but held back.

'They are trapped. Healed, but trapped all the same,' Jakan-tar said.

'Have you been able to contact them?' Samas asked.

'I can see them but when I go near the village I feel the pull, my thoughts are changed and…'

'Can you show us?' Olan asked.

Jakan-tar led the group to the edge of the village, where they peeked through the vines and low branches. 'This is as near as I dare go,' the Captain whispered.

Olan felt his stomach tighten as he stared upon a perfect image of home. Nostalgia rose inside and he felt the urge to run out of the forest.

'My god.' Lavalle shook his head. 'The castle looks impenetrable… and the women and children in the meadow – it's a veritable Land of Cockayne!'

'What?' Olan looked at the knight and then back at the fjord-side village. 'I can see the women and children but no castle – is it on the shore?'

'What shore?' Lavalle frowned. 'It's on the hilltop surrounded by gorse and thick woodland.'

'All I see on the hill is the farmstead,' Samas said. 'With vineyards and olive groves lining the slopes, but no forest or shore.'

Olan looked at Randeep but he said nothing.

Jakan-tar had kept back. 'You all see something different to me. I see the burrow entrances and the smithies smelting in the open. I see my soldiers' abandoned weapons strung up on signposts and I see the younglings. What are these women you talk of?'

'The females.' Lavalle said. 'The childbearers. Our wives and loved ones…'

Olan suspected Lavalle was thinking about Euryleia.

'I don't understand,' Jakan-tar replied. 'We Sorean reproduce equally.'

Randeep sighed and whispered, 'As interesting as this is, we aren't saving John.' He made a move to go through the undergrowth.

'No, don't go nearer!' Olan whispered.

The Sikh swordsman gave him a sneer and held his position. 'Why?'

Jakan-tar's fur twitched and it pointed a clawed hand. 'Look!'

Olan saw a newcomer stroll down the shore to where a group of fishermen were hauling in a net, surrounded by women with salt and barrels. They were friendly with the man as he patted them on the back.

'It's one of them – one of the Frarex,' Jakan-tar said.

'The Frarex?' Samas asked. 'Why do I recognise that name?'

'It was on one of the obelisks,' Lavalle answered. 'They lost their battle.'

'Yes,' Jakan-tar said. 'And they renounced violence.'

'They what? How?' Olan asked.

'They destroyed their weapons and set this trap to entice other soldiers: a place where they would forget how to fight and settle down.'

'Sirens,' Olan heard Lavalle whisper.

'Still, there must be a way in,' Samas said.

'You will fall for their spell and become trapped, just like them.' It sounded like Jakan-tar was losing patience.

Olan's compatriots were fighting the urge to rush forward to free the captive soldiers. It was tempting but he also felt an affinity towards these Frarex, who had suppressed their bloodlust and saved countless lives through their peaceful ways. 'How would we know who was the enemy and who were innocent?' he asked.

'You wouldn't,' Jakan-tar replied. 'The Frarex weave their charm between them – kill one and the others take the strain.'

Olan grunted and shook his head.

Lavalle looked around. 'Where's Randeep?'

The others looked around, but the Sikh couldn't be seen.

'I'll get him.' Olan pushed through the undergrowth.

Back in the open ground of the forest, Olan unclipped his axe and took swings at the low branches. 'Randeep?' he called out. 'Where are you, Randeep?' He heard a snapping twig and saw a flash of blue turban. 'Don't go in!' Olan jogged and ducked into the thick undergrowth.

Through the twisted branches he saw they were nearer to where the men hauled in their nets. How peaceful it looked, Olan thought. They had a good haul of fish too: mackerel. The smoking coals were ready and the racks stood empty. They could do with an extra pair of hands to pull the catch in and the nets probably needed fixing. When he was a boy, Olan had enjoyed weaving the gaps, sitting by the fjord in the shadow of the mountains, and letting his thoughts float and swirl with the fjord tide.

'Stop following me!' Randeep appeared and shoved Olan in the chest.

Something about his eyes looked different, Olan thought.

'We can't go in there.'

'I can,' Randeep snapped.

'They'll trap you–'

'I've had enough of this.' Randeep reached into the folds of his cloak, pulled out a silver box and aimed it at Olan.

Olan dropped to the ground as a red flash lit the air. He screamed as burning heat pummelled and pushed him into the ground. With a surge of energy, he flipped over. Another red flash lit the forest but missed Olan, and smoke billowed around him where dry leaves had caught fire.

He scrambled away and, when he looked back, Randeep was gone.

Behind the trunk of a red-leaved oak, Olan said a quick prayer. 'Valhalla be praised.' He kissed the hammer on his necklace. 'Thank you for your protection.'

He tugged his chest-plate straps to help him breathe, but instead of leather he felt metal.

'Olan?' A voice called from through the trees and Lavalle appeared. 'What in God's name happened?'

Olan shook his head, still catching his breath. 'Randeep fired some… weapon at me. He's gone.'

'What happened to your armour?' Samas pointed at Olan's chest. 'Has it melted?'

'I have no idea.' Olan looked down to see gold dripping down the straps.

The drips had run across his chest, forming a mesh-like chainmail.

'The chest plate saved you, but,' Samas paused, 'now it writhes like a thing possessed.'

Olan couldn't hold back the panic. 'What? Help me get it off!' He clawed at the straps.

'Lavalle, help me,' Samas said.

Lavalle's hands worked fast but the chest plate was stuck tight. 'The metal has covered the buckles. It's stuck.'

'Cut it off!' Olan shouted.

Lavalle pulled out his razor-sharp sword and slipped it under a strap but, when it cut into the leather, metal ran down to protect it. 'It's no good.'

Samas had a look. 'The metal is still spreading. Is it hot?'

Olan touched the liquid metal, which had covered half his chest. 'No, it's cold.'

'A living shield?' Lavalle shook his head.

Olan wondered where it would stop.

Jakan-tar had been standing aloof from the group but watched the expanding chest plate with interest. 'My people, the Sorean, are renowned blacksmiths.' Jakan-tar looked in the direction of the village. 'Our armour was abandoned by my soldiers – a bewildering array of shielding and protection, I can assure you. But I have never seen anything like this.'

Lavalle agreed. 'It grows but is cold.' It looked as though a thought came to him. 'You call yourself an expert?' Lavalle squinted at Jakan-tar. 'Yet you wear no armour.'

'You think so?' Jakan-tar's mouth wrinkled to reveal pointed teeth. 'Then try to cut me.'

Lavalle shook his head. 'I cannot. It would be–'

'Go on.'

Lavalle cricked his neck, lifted his longsword and made a half-hearted swipe.

'Attack me, don't tickle me!' Jakan-tar shouted at the knight.

Lavalle huffed and swung again, aiming for the chest. This time a green light flashed across Jakan-tar's fur where the blade had neared it.

'And again,' Jakan-tar ordered.

Lavalle lunged and swiped, aiming for the Sorean's flank. But this time his sword was parried by a green barrier and Jakan-tar was instantly covered in a full body suit of armour.

Olan laughed as Lavalle struggled to keep his balance with the rebounding sword. 'Now that's impressive!'

'How is it done?' Samas asked.

'I wear it here.' Jakan-tar pointed to a red marble pinned to its chest.

'Just that?' Samas asked. 'Is it heavy?'

'No, we are masters of this construction. It's very light.'

'Enough of this. Impressive as it may be,' Lavalle's cheeks were flushed, 'we must find Randeep and save John Greene.'

'Right then.' Samas shook his head and smiled at Olan.

The group sauntered back to the undergrowth surrounding the village, past where Randeep's second shot had set the leaves aflame.

'I'm sure we can work together,' Olan said to Jakan-tar, 'to save John and your soldiers.'

'If we can get in, we will save all the trapped soldiers,' Samas added.

Jakan-tar replied. 'I only care for my soldiers.'

'Maybe a trade would be in order?' Olan looked ahead to Lavalle. 'I'm sure some armour would come in useful.'

Lavalle ignored the comment and crouched down by a bush at the town's perimeter.

After a wary glance at his golden chest plate, which had grown to cover his back and abdomen, Olan peered through. 'It's changed!' he whispered.

'No, the castle is still there,' Lavalle gestured.

Samas shrugged. 'I see more people in the fields.'

'The burrows look the same,' Jakan-tar added.

Olan swallowed and rubbed his forehead, 'But the fishing village has gone.'

Am I already trapped and fooled by this ruse? Olan asked himself. Is this Loki's work?

'What do you see?' Jakan-tar's eyes grew large.

'I see,' Olan looked around, finding the best way to explain it, 'nothing special.'

'Explain.'

'It's just a clearing in the forest. A few ramshackle huts over there.' He pointed. 'And a strip of grass where creatures of different shapes and sizes are miming out tasks… a hunchbacked ogre is casting a net, a large blue-shelled lobster is digging a hole next to a group of small black squirrels who are lying stretched out.'

'You must be seeing it in its true form,' Jakan-tar said.

'Can you see John?' Samas asked.

'No. There are so many people, I… there are the Sorean!'

'Where?' Jakan-tar was by Olan's side.

'A group are lying together behind that tall white creature.'

'All I see is the hill of the barrow.'

'They must think they are underground.' Olan watched as the thin white humanoid sprinkled dust over the sleeping Sorean with its elongated fingers. 'And I think I know which ones are the Frarex.'

'So we know who to attack?' said Lavalle.

'But we will still be trapped,' Samas replied.

'Over there.' Olan pointed. 'Randeep. He's walking to one of the huts. He's too quick.' As Olan stared, Randeep's clothes changed. 'Odin's eye! He just changed into Mihran… and now he's you, Lavalle.'

'What?' Lavalle squinted.

'I thought he smelt peculiar,' Jakan-tar said with a shrug. 'But you all do.'

'What do you mean?' Samas asked as Olan kept his eyes on Randeep as he finally fixed his shape and entered the hut.

'He is a shape-shifter,' Jakan-tar answered.

'And he's had us all fooled?' Lavalle whispered.

Olan felt his heart sink as he watched on, unable to do anything. 'Not just us.'

The shape of Crossley left the hut and with him, smiling and chatting, walked John Greene.

Olan edged forward tentatively.

'How do you feel now?' Jakan-tar whispered from ten strides behind, hidden in the undergrowth.

How do I feel? Olan asked himself. Scared would be one word. He kept his gaze fixed on the open grassland ahead, where a wide variety of alien soldiers slept or carried baskets of food. Interspersed among them, the tall ghostly shapes of the Frarex wove their enslaving magic.

'I'm fine,' Olan replied. 'It still looks the same.'

He had grown fond of the shore-side fishing village, and seeing the encampment in its true form made him feel sick. All these deluded creatures playing in mud.

'I'll take it five steps at a time.'

What he saw now had to be influenced by the chest plate, Olan thought, even though he couldn't see how such a thing was possible. More magic of the gods, he supposed. When Randeep – or the shapeshifter who had taken his place – shot that red flame at him, the energy must have been absorbed by the chest plate. Like the lightning in Thor's hammer.

Olan heard a soft padding sound and turned to see Jakan-tar running up to him with bounding strides.

'What are you doing?'

Jakan-tar swayed with a paw on its head as the effects of the charmed village grew strong. 'They left… cut Randeep off… had an idea.' The Sorean held out a short dagger and stumbled.

Olan leapt to catch the cat-like Captain and held it in his arms. Both its eyes were closed and its head rolled like one of his dogs back home.

'Wake up!' He shook Jakan-tar and the knife-bearing arm swung over, tapping against Olan's chest plate and sticking as though magnetised.

Jakan-tar woke instantly and looked at Olan, then at the village and gave a low sigh. 'My poor soldiers. This is the truth?' Olan watched Jakan-tar's large eyes quiver. 'This is how they have lived all these months.'

'Yes,' Olan whispered.

Jakan-tar looked up. 'Put me down – I want to walk... but I must be connected to you.'

'How does this work?' Olan asked.

'My theory is your armour has shielded your heart and, more importantly, your stomach from the Frarex weapon.'

'My stomach?' Olan asked.

'You remember the feeling you had when you first saw the village – the tightening... the nostalgia?'

'Yes.'

'It was their drug. Somehow your armour gives you immunity,' Jakan-tar said.

'And it shares it with you through the metal?' Olan asked, hoping he was understanding correctly.

'Most likely it's connected to my armour and... let's keep walking, I have another theory I want to test.'

Olan followed the small, furred Sorean, who walked, with its dagger, at Olan's side. If he wasn't carrying his war axe, anyone would think Jakan-tar held him captive.

'Where are we going?' Olan whispered.

'Silence,' Jakan-tar replied.

Olan grumbled and slung his axe over his shoulder. They walked past a group of green-skinned, dolphin-like aliens patting each other with their stumpy appendages. The creatures didn't react as they passed. Next came three long red worms playing a game with a cube of wood. Jakan-tar avoided the Sorean soldiers and headed straight for the centre of the settlement, where six white Frarex rested in a ramshackle wooden lodge.

'No!' Olan whispered, but Jakan-tar pushed on.

Only when they were a few strides from the Frarex did they stop. Olan waited and calmed his breathing. Were these aliens blind? Or asleep? He had to be cautious – one false move could mean spending the rest of his life writhing in the mud.

'Kar!' Jakan-tar coughed loudly.

The Frarex didn't move. Olan spun around to see if anyone else had heard, but the enslaved soldiers frolicked and rolled as before. The furred Sorean were still huddled in their make-believe burrow and the white Frarex scattered their dust as before, like tall wandering monks. In the distance, Olan caught a glimpse of a human in a grey suit he recognised from the obelisk hill.

'They can't hear us,' Jakan-tar said.

'Or see us,' Olan added.

Jakan-tar pulled out a new blade. 'And now we break their spell.'

Olan winced. Could he really do this? Could he kill these peaceful beasts while they slept? Their intentions had been good after all – they only wanted peace.

Jakan-tar looked up at him. 'Why do you wait? I can't attack if you don't move.'

'I...' Olan tried to find the words but failed.

'They are using these soldiers for their own needs.' The Sorean pointed at the nearest group of sleeping aliens and ghostly Frarex. 'They farm their energy in return for dreams.'

It was all about power. Images of the men Olan had fought with came back to him: violent men who raped, killed and tortured the weak and unarmed. It was always about power – the power they held over others. These Frarex were no different, Olan thought. An anger rose in his chest but he fought to control it. No, he thought, this is not my fight.

'My blade will not be bloodied today,' he said to Jakan-tar, who stared up but dared not break away from its magnetic link. 'But justice will be served.'

'We need more!' Jakan-tar hissed, urging Olan on.

'There's another group over here,' Olan replied and strode around a tiny pond to where a host of Sorean snuggled in a pile, while a ghostly Frarex stood nearby, farming their energy.

Following Olan's plan, the duo had woken individual Sorean from each group by joining them to their magnetic shield using whatever metal weapon or object they could find. The Frarex hadn't noticed individual soldiers waking from each spell but, as more soldiers disappeared from their grasp, they grew agitated, sensing the loss of energy. As the web of interconnected soldiers grew around Olan and Jakan-tar though, so did the anger of the freed slaves as they saw how they had been tricked and abused by the Frarex.

Now Olan could hold them no longer, the web broke and the Sorean unleashed their bloody revenge.

Olan watched in awe and fear as a bizarre mix of fighting species released their wrath on their enslavers. Caught by surprise, wallowing in their self-indulgence, the Frarex were cut down before they could weave new spells and, with each dead Frarex, a new group of enslaved soldiers rose from their slumber to join in. A small rebellion would have been quashed, Olan had no doubt, but the scores of freed soldiers were systematically isolating the Frarex. And annihilating them.

Olan kept his own axe sheathed. The Frarex might not be innocent, but Olan felt no need to fight them when he had other priorities. As the liberated soldiers swept through the Frarex camp, Olan rushed to the hut where he had seen the shape-shifter who, in Crossley's form, had led John Greene away into the forest. The crude wooden hut was empty and Olan couldn't see any sign that John had been there. He ran through the mud, searching for footprints, but was too late. His only hope was that Lavalle and Samas had cut them off on the other side of the forest.

Olan returned to the battle to see the last few Frarex fighting with clouds of invisibility and poisonous gases, but they were vastly outnumbered, and the Sorean fought with a manic intensity that would surely soon overwhelm them.

'Three Frarex escaped.' Jakan-tar was panting hard when Olan found it, flanked by two equally tired Sorean soldiers.

'It's not worth chasing them down,' Olan replied and sat on a fallen tree.

Jakan-tar's fur wrinkled in a way that Olan assumed to be a shrug. 'Perhaps we should save our energy.'

'The battle is won,' Olan answered.

Across the muddy glade, groups of other alien soldiers gravitated to their own and rested in groups. Freed slaves stared into the flames of the burning stack of Frarex bodies with a mix of anger and loss. From what Olan had been told by the survivors, they had been living a life of bliss. The shock of being torn back into the real, dirty world had been severe, and Olan wondered how many could deal with returning to their real lives.

Jakan-tar looked at Olan's clean blade. 'I would have enjoyed fighting alongside you, Olan Baardsson.'

'And I would have been honoured to fight alongside you, Captain Jakan-tar,' Olan replied.

'My soldiers wish to repay you for your help,' Jakan-tar said. 'Without you, I would still be wandering the perimeter and my army would be in the mud.' Jakan-tar gestured for the Sorean soldiers to leave them in peace.

'Thank you but–'

'All we can offer is armour, but seeing as you have armour enough,' Jakan-tar gestured at the enchanted chest plate, 'we offer our assistance in defeating your enemy.'

Olan looked into Jakan-tar's eyes. 'Really?' He had seen the Sorean in battle and knew Mihran would be impressed: they fought like tiny berserkers, with animal ferocity and unending stamina.

Jakan-tar looked out on the Sorean army, who Olan guessed numbered over eighty. 'We are a proud people and, like you, wish to leave this land. I believe we will make good allies.'

Olan took the offer in. Jakan-tar had respected him for his decision not to fight. But how would these creatures fit into the human army? Olan sighed. Sometimes you just know when it's the right thing to do.

'Your enemies are our enemies,' Olan replied. 'And we *will* make good allies.'

Chapter 12

Delta-Six twitched a finger, ready to press a button on his wrist, but remembered he could activate his systems through thought now. He selected his medical systems and gave himself a boost of painkiller for his leg. Within two seconds, he was walking normally again and sped up his journey across the great plain. As he walked, Delta-Six ran through any recordings he had made over the past few days as he struggled to make sense of what had happened to him. His memory records had been compromised, either by the poison from the creature in the lake or by the beings who had captured him.

'What if the hallucinations were a ruse to distract me while the VR prison was reset?' he asked, adding to his vocal notes. 'I still can't accept this place is real.'

Delta-Six was unsure how he had been tricked into believing he was in Elysium, with his future wife and... it was just like his dream. He wanted to go back but knew it had been an illusion. All video recordings from his time in the forest village proved that. Now he needed to focus and survive.

He had grown used to drinking his mineral supplements, which his suit was using as it morphed with his body. But he didn't understand why he was changing. And why were the other soldiers mutating? Was there a conscious mind behind it, making up for deficiencies or enhancing strong features? Or was it random?

He scanned the plain, where he had found scores of victory obelisks and battle debris. The sheer range of technologies and bodies at each site was overwhelming: so many forms of life and even more methods of destroying it.

'I don't know if it's the removal of my mental filters or the scale of war here, but I feel... insignificant,' Delta-Six said. 'My entire life has been a futile gesture which has done little but cause destruction. What have I achieved? Have I built anything or created anything new? After my death, how would anyone know I existed?'

Delta-Six focused on his body – he could feel a tingling sensation down his right side, which meant his sensors had picked up movement in that direction. He swung around but nothing could be seen. His senses tingled again: he was being surrounded. Various options ran through his mind as he switched to combat mode. A shot of adrenaline sped his heart up, followed by streams of lines on his screen, predicting escape routes. But before he could select one, clouds of soil exploded and five blue armoured beasts burst out of the ground, firing darts.

Delta-Six's defence system kicked in, creating a sub-sonic sound shield as he rapidly shot back with his wrist cannon, killing one attacker with a single shot that left a steaming hole through its carapace. Darts were deflected and bolts of energy absorbed by Delta-Six's shield as he rolled for cover, fired again and moved, repeating over and over until a gap appeared in the ring around him and he ran through it. His shield was losing energy and he felt barbs glance off his metallic skin. He turned and fired again, killing one more. Then, in a cloud of dust, the two remaining creatures disappeared down their tunnels.

Dakaniha woke from a fitful dream. He sat up, stared at the bodies scattered along the coast of the lake and rubbed the itchy scabs on his temples as visions haunted him: mouths; razor-sharp teeth; scaly bodies. He recalled the rough feel of the skin of a beast gliding beneath his legs and shivered.

The tocka had abandoned them in the water, leaving Gal-qadan's men gripping their floating purple bladders. Losing energy, Dakaniha had slipped underwater and seen the tocka swimming in formation to attack the submarine beasts. Black blood spread through the water before the tocka returned.

A noise made Dakaniha turn.

'I said, are you okay?' Kastor was standing over him.

'Yes,' Dakaniha replied and surveyed the beach.

Bodies of men lay scattered like stones. The tocka slept in a circle some fifty paces away with their heads towards the bodies of the two who hadn't survived.

What will this day bring? Dakaniha thought. He searched the

clouds for the sun and cursed the land. Why did it seem brighter today?

'Well, we're alive then.' Ethan sat up and rubbed his grey face.

Dakaniha felt a pang of pity for the man who, back home, would have been his enemy. He wondered if the American was suffering from the skin disease he had seen in the Southern tribes. From what he could remember it would be a painful death.

'We survived when many fell,' Dakaniha answered. 'We are lucky to see today's light.'

'Amen to that,' replied Ethan.

Tode joined the group. 'How many did we lose?'

'Four,' Kastor replied, 'and two tocka.'

Dakaniha sighed and spent a moment in silence for their lost comrades.

'This one remembers me,' Dakaniha heard Osayimwese say as the men rode the tocka up the beach ridge, with Kastor's steed taking the lead.

The ground flattened out at the top, presenting them with a long and featureless horizon.

'What's your plan, Great Leader?' Dakaniha asked Gal-qadan, whose face remained ever emotionless, like carved stone.

The Mongol surveyed the land ahead and pointed. 'We are cut off by this river.' Dakaniha could just make out a faint grey line to the right. 'And this river.' Another curved line snaked on the left flank. 'So we continue straight, through the mire.' Gal-qadan gave his tocka a sharp kick with his heels but it stayed still. Gal-qadan growled and reluctantly turned to Kastor.

'Right.' The Spartan held back a smile. He patted his tocka and the band of archers, riflemen and swordsmen let their carnivorous steeds pick out the driest path through the meandering streams and bogs that peppered the sodden lowland.

'Do we need to find grass for the tocka?' a rifleman to Dakaniha's right asked.

'No, they fed well last night,' Tode replied.

Dakaniha rubbed his hands on his trousers, convinced he could still feel the water-beast's blood on his skin. It was good to be on dry land, but something tickled the nape of his neck, like they were being watched. He looked around but his nervous glances caught nothing moving in the flat landscape. He scratched at his temples and peeled tiny scabs from under his headband. Was it lice? He pulled the headband off and saw Ethan had moved up to ride beside him. The journey was always quicker when you had someone to talk to, he thought, but his gut tightened: Ethan was his people's enemy. Then he pictured his mother's father. Maybe he could learn from his enemy as he had done? Guns and horses were the European's weapons, but Dakaniha's people had mastered them. Was there more to learn?

'Your rifle,' Dakaniha started a conversation, 'I haven't seen that type before.'

'Well, ha!' Ethan nodded at the musket strapped to Dakaniha's back. 'Compared to some guns this is pretty new.'

'This was not mine.' Dakaniha felt his cheeks flush. 'I… found it.'

'Okay, I get it,' Ethan nodded. 'Well, this is a Whitworth.' He patted his rifle. 'Only us who trade with the British got hold of 'em. The bullets whistle but I can take the tail off a chipmunk at a hundred paces.'

Dakaniha wanted to ask Ethan why he needed to shoot tails off rodents but held his tongue.

'It's saved my life a few times and taken more than its fair share of others'.' Ethan's face looked grim as though the weight of each life still pulled at him.

'And your war?'

Ethan laughed. 'Well, they call it civil but it's anything but civil, believe me!'

'It must be far from my land – I haven't heard of it,' Dakaniha replied.

That shocked Ethan, who peered at Dakaniha as though waiting for a joke.

'What is it?' Dakaniha asked after several side glances.

'The whole of the United States is at war – south versus north – and you ain't heard of it?'

Dakaniha squinted at Ethan. 'What country is this, United States?'

'Jeez.' Ethan shook his head. 'We're fighting from Richmond to Chattanooga – that's Cherokee country ain't it?'

Dakaniha shrugged. 'Sounds like a fishing village.'

'Chickamauga?' Ethan asked.

'No.' Dakaniha thought of the larger settlements that Ethan was bound to have heard of. 'Do you know Keowee?' he suggested.

'No… the British burnt it down a hundred years ago, why–' Ethan looked at the other warriors in the group, then back to Dakaniha. 'Say, you ain't from my time, are ya?'

'I don't understand,' Dakaniha replied.

'You're an ancestor.' Ethan looked to the grey sky, wide-eyed. 'Is that why I'm here?' He spoke to the clouds. 'To repent for my sins?' He looked back to Dakaniha. 'I had to make them pay. I know the good book says do not take revenge but leave room for God's wrath, but they had to pay. My family, my wife, my children… they deserved vengeance.'

As Ethan's voice trailed off, Dakaniha stared at his comrades. How could they be from different ages? Different nations travelling to one country maybe but not different generations.

Dakaniha saw the tocka ahead were slowing to form a fan shape around Kastor and Gal-qadan's steeds.

'–and then he just stopped,' Dakaniha caught the end of Kastor's sentence.

Gal-qadan pointed to a series of round mud mounds in the ground. 'We haven't seen these before – I don't trust them.'

Always so wary, Dakaniha thought.

Kastor shrugged and said, 'Well, the tocka won't go nearer so we'll have to go–'

An explosion erupted ahead of them, followed by more behind and on each flank. Lumps of mud rained down on them and Dakaniha gripped the thick mane of his tocka as it jostled and shimmied. The shocked herd were the closest he had ever seen to panic.

'There!'

Dakaniha saw a monstrous blue creature charging at them with a wild, snapping array of pincers and claws.

They were surrounded.

'Weapons!' Tode shouted.

Dakaniha set an arrow in his bow, controlled his breath and fired at the nearest creature. The bow sang its sweet note and the arrow flew true but glanced off the animal's armour. Dakaniha tried to calm his nerves but didn't know what to do against such an enemy. He looked for Gal-qadan but couldn't see him. Should he dismount and find space to attack with his knife? His head pounded and his temples itched. The tocka beneath him clawed at the ground... then a strange thing happened.

Light came pouring in.

It wasn't a new light, just more light. Then shapes and colour. Although he couldn't see it, Dakaniha felt two new eyes open on the side of his head. He could see all around now. Front and back. He couldn't say why, but it made him feel safe. Impenetrable. Stronger.

He gave his tocka a dig of his heels and it leapt forward, teeth bared: charging to attack.

John's head was pounding. He was tired, his mouth was dry and his stomach growled with hunger. Had he banged his head? It felt like he'd been asleep for a week and strange dreams were swimming before him: Joe; kind nurses; men playing cricket; Crossley's smile; Rosie's eyes; lights and... what was that smell? It was worse than Jess's stable.

Cautiously, John stretched his dry eyelids open and focused on a small square of light. A window? He was lying on his back and he could see shadows and silhouettes but nothing held any colour or shape. A closed door. Was he in an operating theatre? The doctor hadn't said they would operate, but Crossley had taken him to find Joe and... yes it was coming back now. They'd walked away from the field hospital, out of the woods. Why Joe had been at a field hospital, John had no idea – or why he and Crossley had travelled on a metal contraption like the tanks the army had started to use. Only this one was driven by what looked like a blue lobster... and there John's memory stopped.

He heard a sound from another room, so dropped his head and

closed his eyes. With no memory of how he got here, John knew he was in danger.

'…they have what?' A deep voice growled in anger.

'Steeds, General. Animals to carry them across the plain of battles,' a higher-pitched voice replied.

'Their main army will grow in number unless we…' the first voice trailed off.

John tried to move his legs but something was holding them at the knee. His left arm felt the same while his right arm… clicked when he tensed his fingers. His gun-arm. John visualised his fingers inside the gun, as he'd done before, and could feel shapes forming.

The door burst open to reveal a tall, navy-blue creature.

'It wakes.' A mouth of bizarre mandibles snapped in the centre of a face that reminded John of a fish he'd seen at Billingsgate market. The rest of its body was scorpion-like.

'Please join me.' The huge beast talked to a smaller, grey scorpion-like animal that scuttled into a dark corner, leaving a trail of electric-blue light in the air.

'Our first human.'

The blue animal's legs scraped and clicked against the floor as it walked over and leant over John.

Without warning, a claw punched the table and flipped John up to a standing position. His body tensed against the ties that held him. He was face to face with this thing, whose enormous creaking shell glistened and pulsated before him.

Stay strong, John told himself.

'And I sense I am your first Brakari?' the creature asked.

So this was the enemy they would face, John thought. He nodded, trying not to show his fear.

'What's this? He bares his teeth… anger? Defence?'

Stay calm, John told himself, no point in angering it.

'A smile perhaps?' The Brakari rocked back on its legs. 'I amuse you, do I?' It turned to the smaller creature. 'Do I look amusing to you, Captain Millok?'

'No, General.'

It snapped back to John. 'Then what is it that amuses you… what is your name?'

'John Greene.'

You must stay strong, he told himself. If you're the first human they've seen you must show these Brakari what great warriors we are. They must be scared of us.

'Well,' the inquisitor snorted. 'I am General Panzicosta of the Brakari army and I intend to find out every detail about your little army before we destroy it.'

'I can tell you what I know but it won't be of any use,' John replied. 'We're changing all the time.' He thought of Mihran and Lavalle and tried to emulate their arrogance and style. 'Many dangerous adaptations and defences – unbreakable by any army.'

Panzicosta's mouth-pieces stretched and his short pincer arm gestured at the table. 'Good, good.' He seemed unperturbed by John's boasts. 'I'm sure that will all be useful and help the Brakari cause. Look around you, John Greene.' He pointed at a long white arm hanging from the wall next to a dog-like head. 'And here.' Panzicosta pointed to the other side of the room.

John strained to turn his head to see wooden tables lining the walls covered in machinery and metallic objects that reminded him of the gear Crossley had taken from the dead robots near the castle. A metallic box that twinkled with tiny lights looked damaged where someone had broken into it and, next to it, a group of marbles reflected iridescent shades against the wall.

'Others have come before you and all have been broken.' Panzicosta stalked over to a table and grabbed the metal box in a claw. 'The technology held in this allowed us to enslave the Lutamek.' He cast the box back, scattering the coloured marbles. 'And these Sorean shields, ingenious in deflecting any attack, are virtually useless now we understand their workings.'

John fought to find a suitable reply. How could his friends fight against an army of monsters like this with the weapons it had at its disposal?

'You still won't defeat us,' John said and clenched his jaw.

'Yes, you have spirit, I like that. Now… as entertaining as I find this, it's time I learnt a little about human anatomy.' He raised a long, thin pincer with a cutting edge. 'I have always enjoyed dissecting animals with internal skeletons.'

The snaking line of soldiers had wound its way through the barren desert for three hours after leaving Peronicus-Rax's behemoth tents. Euryleia had walked in a comfortable silence alongside Mata, but had been sent ahead to divine for water.

'Althorn's scouting for shelter,' Euryleia heard Crossley tell Bowman.

She turned to where a hazy green line lay smudged against the horizon and felt her stomach tighten. Was Lavalle still alive? She controlled a pang of guilt. It was his decision to go after John; she hadn't forced him. Anyway, he wasn't the man he claimed to be – he was the Black Sword: the killer of unarmed men and innocents.

When had he ever claimed to be anything but a soldier? another voice in Euryleia's head asked. All soldiers kill.

No. She pushed the thought away. He let me down.

And yet you miss him.

'Euryleia,' Li called out and moved up through the line.

'Yes,' Euryleia snapped.

'I need to talk to you about adaptations.'

'Ah, yes. The amnesty.' Euryleia didn't like talking to Li when she had her visor down. Who knew what she was really thinking when all you could see was a warped reflection of your own face?

'It makes sense after Crossley hid his, and we need every advantage,' Li said.

Euryleia nodded but kept her eyes fixed ahead. How old was Li? She had to be ten years younger than her, yet she talked to her like she was her mother.

'So, have you had any changes? Any new skills or feelings?' Li asked.

Other than wanting to smash your visor with my fist? Euryleia thought, but stifled her anger, worried Mihran was listening to her mind. All these bizarre changes were hard to get used to.

'No, nothing new. I heal quickly, but everyone heals fast here.'

'Yes.' Li dragged the word out like she always did when she was concentrating on something else.

Euryleia bristled. 'And you? Have you got any new skills?'

'Nothing of any use,' Li answered in her monotone voice. 'The sensors in my visor have picked up new frequencies that allow me to manipulate micro-particles.'

Euryleia kept silent. She didn't want to sound ignorant, but hadn't understood a word.

'I can move pieces of dirt about,' Li explained. 'I'll keep experimenting with it.'

Euryleia tutted and pointed at the line ahead. 'Why are we stretched out like this? It's dangerous – anyone can pick us off or divide us.'

'Peronicus-Rax suggested it.'

'One night of shelter and we trust him?'

'Mihran does,' Li said, 'plus he gave us some valuable intelligence.'

'Such as?' Euryleia asked.

Li pressed a button on her helmet and her visor flipped open. 'He knows where the silver gates are.'

'And we're heading in the right direction?' Euryleia asked.

Li nodded and Euryleia saw a man stumble up ahead. There were more immediate things to worry about.

'The stony ground is taking a toll on our footwear and the injured are struggling,' she said.

'We're getting low on food as well,' Li said.

Euryleia glanced at Li, then back at the horizon. She looked genuinely concerned. 'And then we fight.' She was missing her horse almost as much as she missed having Lavalle to talk to and laugh with.

'An army marches on its stomach,' Li said.

'Who said that?' Euryleia asked.

'A French general many centuries before my time.'

'What is French?' Euryleia asked.

Their eyes met and Li gave a little smile, making Euryleia smile in return.

'What a ridiculous situation we're in,' Li said.

'Yes,' Euryleia sighed. 'Forced to fight under the leadership of men.' She shook her head.

'Well, Mihran has a remarkable military mind.'

'Really?'

Li nodded. 'It's part of his adaptation – he's memorised every piece of tactical military text in my memory banks and taken details from every battle we've passed.'

'To what benefit?' Euryleia asked.

'He'll use the models – or predictions – for whatever situation we find ourselves in.'

Euryleia raised her eyebrows. 'That's good in theory, but in the madness of battle how will each fighter know where to go and who to attack?'

Li shrugged. 'I asked the same thing and he said he's working on it.'

Euryleia shook her head. Back home, her people chose their war leaders on merit and fighting ability: man or woman. Experience was key but strength of mind, foresight and adaptability in the face of defeat were worth a dozen strong, armed men.

'I have analysed the battles too,' Li's voice was quieter now, 'and found interesting connections.'

Euryleia raised her head. 'Such as?'

'In our group, we are all land-based fighters. No navy or air, space or cyber. It's the same for every other species that has fought here. All land-based.'

'Does that mean there are other human soldiers out there?' Euryleia asked.

'Possibly. Or someone wants us to stay on the ground.' She flipped her visor back down. 'Listen, I need to ask the others about their adaptations. Mihran wants a report soon.'

Euryleia nodded and Li sped off. She had seen Delta-Six fly from the obelisk hill but she had never seen a battle on water or in the air and the thought bewildered her, just as the foreign weapons of her new comrades did. Lavalle was straightforward compared to the rest: a strong man with a deadly weapon. One extra pair of eyes in battle and a sword she could trust. It had all been said in their first look. But now the trust was gone, what was left?

What did she expect? the other voice asked. Did he have to tell her everything? Wasn't it better to leave some things unknown?

Euryleia looked ahead to where the vanguard had stopped. By the time she was within earshot, orders were being delivered.

'Althorn says an enemy is approaching,' Mihran said. 'We need natural protection. Li, I want two flanks of projectile launchers. I'll stay with the main army and command in the absence of Samas and Lavalle.'

Euryleia slipped her bow from her shoulder.

'The enemy number fifteen and are large and armoured with metal casing,' Althorn said. 'That's all I saw before–'

'Wait a minute,' Crossley cut in. 'Large and armoured with metal casing? Did they look like the bodies around the castle?'

Althorn shrugged. 'Possibly, I...'

Li tapped furiously on her wrist pad and projected an image of a large robot.

Althorn stared at the picture and rubbed his beard. 'Yes, they could be the same.'

'Seriously?' Crossley had his hands on his hips. 'We're going to fight fifteen gigantic robots?' He looked around the group. 'Shouldn't we try something else? Like running away?'

Althorn squinted at Crossley. 'I have followed them for some time and they have tracked us with ease – we won't be able to outrun them.'

Euryleia looked to the horizon, where a thin cloud of dust was building.

'Come on.' Crossley was red-faced. 'We must be able to do something. If we had explosives, I could knock up a few mines but... Li: surely your laser rifle will make easy work of them, right? Like with those blue lobster things?'

'I'll do my best but–'

'Where's Mata?' Crossley turned around.

'Enough!' Mihran turned to the horizon, where Euryleia could now see dark shapes. 'We must stand and fight. Without victory we will never leave this land.' He pointed to a series of red rocks that rose out of the yellow earth like tombstones. 'We take shelter here.'

'Yeah, how are they gonna help against robots?' Crossley's shoulders slumped. 'Shit. Okay, someone give me a weapon then or I'll have to rely on these trinkets.' He fingered the scavenged diodes hanging around his neck.

'Here,' Sakarbaal pointed to a pile of spare bows and spears, 'take your pick.'

Crossley shook his head and pulled a handgun from a shoulder holster, mumbling, 'Goddam ancient crap.'

Euryleia was in the thick of the group as they split into groups of archers and riflemen, with the bulk of the swordsmen between the two. She couldn't see anything on the horizon, yet felt vibrations through her feet.

'More on the left flank,' Mihran shouted, crouching behind one of the red stones. 'Now take shelter and – where have they gone?'

Euryleia had an arrow in her bow and half a dozen stabbed into the ground beside her.

'They're cloaked,' Li shouted.

'Where are they?' Crossley shouted.

'Hold!' Mihran shouted. 'Expect an attack any–'

In an instant, the desert, the red stones and the hazy green sky vanished in an orange flash so bright that Euryleia thought she could see the insides of her eyes. Time slowed as shapes and senses came to her in flashes: stone; silhouettes; the sky; the ground; burning.

Pain.

Nothing made sense.

Pain.

It all happened in a single breath.

Darkness descended.

When the light came back, the fighting was over. Euryleia rolled over and cradled her arm where a sharp pain burnt. She looked around for shelter but all she saw were bodies and smoke. The smell of burning flesh invaded her nostrils and she heaved.

Don't panic, she told herself. First thing: injuries.

Euryleia looked down at her wrist, where the pain was sharpest, and this time she couldn't hold back the vomit. Where her hand had been, she now saw a charred and bloody mess of flesh and bone.

They should have surrendered straight away, Mihran thought. Before the battle started, seventeen of his thirty-six scenarios had suggested surrender, but he had pushed them to the back of his mind, along with the eight that ended with the human army's complete destruction. He needed to find a smoother way to process his predictions and receive live information from his troops during battle, he thought.

When the lightning attack hit them, Mihran had struggled to keep up with the strategies and models. As one soldier died, his model shifted, but not fast enough for him to communicate any changes.

'Retreat and combine forces!' he had shouted, but nobody heard over the explosions and laser fire that ripped through the air like violent thunder.

Desperate for some coordination, Mihran had thrown his thoughts at an archer, trying to get him to focus his attack on the flank, but nothing changed. He tried another, but they ignored him. Determined to make it work, Mihran tried to project the image of an approaching robot to a group of swordsmen who were about to mount what would have been a suicidal attack. They paused and held back – it worked!

Just as Mihran was getting used to the method, the attack stopped as suddenly as it had started and the voice of the robot's leader drifted across the smoke-shrouded and cratered desert.

'Put your weapons down and you will not be harmed.'

'Cease!' Mihran shouted. 'Cease your firing! We surrender.' He walked out with his arms raised high.

An eager crossbowman released a metal-tipped bolt at the silhouette of one of the robots and was given an accurate laser burst to the ear in return.

'Put your weapons down!' Mihran ordered, shouting over the man's screams.

He took in the damage to his troops. Limbs and torsos told of the dead, while several were lying injured: Euryleia was on the ground, clutching the burnt stump of her left hand and, on the other flank, Li floated in a blue bubble.

He faced the aggressors, searching for something he could learn from their audacious attack. 'We submit,' he shouted. Smoke drifted on the lazy desert breeze as the dark silhouettes became fifteen robot warriors, each standing twice as tall as Mihran.

'Disarm,' the voice boomed again and a large red robot walked forward.

Mihran overheard Crossley, who was still hiding. 'Jeez, if these guys lost to the flatworms think how dangerous those little bastards must have been!'

Determined to show strength for the human army, Mihran spoke clearly. 'Why do you cease your attack?'

A rasping voice responded. 'You will not survive this fight and we are not interested in victory.'

'You are not interested in victory?' Mihran repeated.

'This skirmish will not count as a true battle.' A short orange robot spoke with a precise accent. 'We will not gain our freedom through your defeat.'

Mihran raised his eyebrows and looked to Li, as if to say 'Make a note of that,' but she was still trapped and unable to respond.

'Please release my soldier.' Mihran pointed to the blue bubble.

'When you return the belongings of our clan,' a yellow automaton said.

'What belongings?' Mihran asked.

'Those taken from the stronghold where our kin died. These parts belonged to our fallen comrades.'

'How do you know we have them?' Mihran asked to buy time.

'We tracked them to your position.'

'And your army's name?' Mihran asked.

'We are the Lutamek.'

'Ah.' Mihran turned to his troops. 'Bring forward anything taken from the castle.'

It was better not to argue with these metallic behemoths, plus a thought had come to him.

'Here.' An archer walked forward and threw a lump of metal at the nearest robot's feet.

The orange robot scanned the item with a blue pulse of light from its left eye. 'Seven-zero-eight's acronometric valve intensity monitor.' It picked the object up and deposited it in a hole in its arm.

More humans stepped forward and discarded treasured objects at the feet of the Lutamek.

The orange robot spoke once the items had been identified. 'You have five more items. Please return them.'

Nobody moved.

'If you wish, sir,' the red Lutamek addressed the orange robot, 'I can neutralise the offending alien.'

'No,' it replied. 'I need them intact, maybe maim the individual. One limb–'

'Okay, okay.' Crossley ran forward with his hands up, giving Mihran a sheepish look as he passed. 'Here you go.' The American threw down a copper-coloured box then opened his pockets, pulling out an assortment of metallic components. 'Couldn't get any of them to work anyway.'

'These are accepted,' said the Lutamek leader.

'Now release my soldier,' Mihran ordered.

A turquoise Lutamek twitched and the bubble disappeared, dropping Li to the ground.

'I couldn't hear a thing, what's going on?' she asked.

'Please see to the injured,' Mihran said and turned to the robot leader. 'My thanks. And now?'

'We are an honest race,' the leader spoke slowly, 'and believe in trade.'

'Yet you attacked us without asking for your belongings,' Mihran said.

'Yeah,' Crossley joined in, 'shoot first and ask questions later.'

Mihran held his hand up to silence him.

'We were witness to your defence against the Brakari scout patrol,' the robot replied, 'and are aware of your association with the one-eyed humanoid who did nothing to aid us during our battle.'

'Peronicus-Rax is a peaceful individual,' Mihran said.

'I will make a record of his name,' one of the Lutamek murmured.

'And I will remember the name of the Brakari,' Mihran replied, understanding how they had been outclassed so quickly by these fighting machines: they had seen the humans in action and had neutralised the most dangerous soldier first. 'These Brakari were just scouts?' he asked.

'Yes, their stronghold lies beyond the plain, near the silver gates,' the Lutamek leader replied.

And yet the Lutamek don't fight for their freedom, Mihran thought. He felt he had gleaned more information from the Lutamek than they had from him: tracing the parts of their fallen comrades, tracking a scouting party of another species and the intensity of their attack all suggested more was going on here.

'You are a new species,' the Lutamek leader said. 'Our trade is to answer any questions you have.'

'Well, if you could tell us who brought us here and why all these strange things are happening to us that'd be great,' Crossley said before Mihran could respond.

A high-pitched warble came from the orange robot and the yellow leader turned. 'Keep our transmission audible Nine-zero-five. No, I do not believe this information would threaten our mission.' The leader looked at Crossley, then Mihran. 'We do not know who brought us, or yourselves, here. Our location is also unknown to us. As for your changes,' the leader beckoned a lean white robot over, 'Ten-ten, scan and relay all adaptational sources.'

'Yes, Two-zero-three,' the robot replied and sprayed a fast pulsing light over Crossley, criss-crossing his body from head to boots. Then it switched to the soldier behind him, then Samas and so on. Mihran breathed out in relief when his scan finished with no sense that anything had touched him.

'Scan complete,' the white robot said a minute later.

'Results?'

'All individuals have ingested a fungal symbiont,' Ten-ten's rough voice held Mihran's attention, 'which has established a net of hyphae throughout their neural pathways, enhancing the language centres.'

Mihran's eyes widened. For the first time since arriving here, he was getting real answers. 'And each individual's unique adaptations?' he asked.

Ten-ten pointed a long metallic finger at Crossley. 'An increased sinus cavity combined with vocal cord extension has enabled you to create and read sonic waves.'

'Does that mean I can see in the dark as well?' Crossley asked, but Ten-ten had already moved on to Althorn.

'Your body has an enhanced metabolic rate, utilising eighty-nine percent of all energy consumed through enhanced glycolysis and partial carbon recovery from carbon dioxide.'

'So rather than being invisible,' Mihran said, 'you are simply moving at an incredible speed.'

'You,' the robot turned to an archer, 'have an enhanced visual cortex that allows you to see and predict atmospheric and enemy movements to a greater degree of accuracy, similar to our shard missile systems.'

'Ten-ten,' the Lutamek leader, Two-zero-three, said, 'please keep the information limited and relevant. Code Ecta.'

'Yes, sir.' Ten-ten turned back to the archer. 'Your enhanced eyes give you accurate aim.' Then to Mihran, 'A second symbiont has enhanced your mental capabilities.' Then Bowman, 'During the battle, your missiles showed signs of enhanced cognitive behaviour.'

When Ten-ten had finished, every member of the human battalion felt they had been told a little more than they would have liked.

'Just like getting bad news from the doctor.' Crossley sat on a rock and stared at the earth. 'My sinus cavity is bigger, so what's happened to my brain?'

Nobody answered.

Unlike the rest of the small army, Mihran pushed aside the reality of microscopic growths linking the subsections of his brain. He was more intrigued by the Lutamek army and their mission. 'Lutamek leader, Two-zero-three, your exchange of knowledge is gratefully received, and I apologise for any offence caused – we meant no disrespect to your lost comrades.'

'The trade is complete,' Two-zero-three replied. 'You have distracted us long enough.'

The robots holding the perimeter were already moving away.

'I understand.' Mihran nodded. 'You have more Brakari scouts to track, no doubt?'

Every Lutamek stopped instantly.

'You have information?' Two-zero-three asked.

Mihran stood silent as he calculated the odds of certainty. His question had revealed a clue. If only he could read their minds, he thought, but remembered the pain from trying to read Peronicus-Rax. He would have to take a gamble instead.

Two-zero-three appeared impatient and asked, 'You want more from us, human?'

'No.' Mihran stroked his beard. 'I was thinking about how we can help you on your mission... to free your comrades captured by the Brakari army.'

Chapter 13

Althorn sat by the coals of a dying fire, keeping watch and rubbing his engorged leg muscles, which ached from the previous day's running. Around him, soldiers slept within a perimeter circle of small fires, outside which the huge Lutamek rested and recharged. He'd been awake half the night, tending to the injured and dying who lay scattered across their desert camp. Now, a glow on the edge of the featureless plain signalled the start of his eleventh day in this land of war and death.

In the morning light it was like seeing his sleeping comrades for the first time: their faces, weapons and clothing were as bizarre to him as some of the aliens they had encountered, yet he wasn't fazed by the differences – they only increased his thirst to learn more. When he scouted ahead he discovered so many things of wonder: landscapes; bodies; forts; creatures; and plants. It made him feel alive. That was why he volunteered to scout. The years had been creeping up on him, pouring sorrow into his bones and sapping the strength from his muscles, but now he had the energy of a man half his age – no, he had more energy than ever before! He could run for hours on end, faster than an avalanche or so fast nothing could see him. The only problem was the amount of food and water he had to consume.

The thought made his belly rumble.

'Going for a break,' he whispered to an Assyrian soldier sharpening his spear blade.

The man gave a nod, and Althorn tiptoed through the wispy fires and past the large silhouettes of the Lutamek. He kept an eye on their lights, which flickered along their back ridges and legs. One of them was on watch, but he couldn't tell which. They could all be awake and have eyes all over their body for all he could tell.

He sped off, leaving a tiny whirlwind of dust in his wake.

The Lutamek were an odd fit in Althorn's mind. They weren't what he considered true allies – or true creatures for that matter. When they had attacked he had been fast enough to dodge the laser fire and divert some of their metallic missiles, but his attacks with his blade had barely dented their shells.

'I don't want them to touch me.' Euryleia had flatly refused when the Lutamek offered medical assistance.

'But you're seriously injured,' Althorn had argued.

'No help,' she snapped and coated her blackened stump with a green paste from her bag and tied a tight strip of cloth around her wrist.

Others took the aid: gels to heal burns, beams of red light to fix broken bones. Some even accepted metal limbs to replace those lost in the fight.

'They're turning us into them!' Althorn had protested to Mihran but he would have none of it.

'We are stronger when healed,' he had replied. 'And we are stronger together.'

Althorn travelled far in a few minutes and paused to light a fire in a protected hollow before speeding off again to a watering hole half a day's march back. As he neared he saw movement: dark shapes slipping around the edge of the depression Mata had created with his root-like arms. Without slowing, Althorn circled silently and watched the silhouettes in the dawn light. Were they dangerous? You could never be sure in this land. He closed in to see three deer sipping from the puddle. They looked harmless enough, so he circled once more before leaping in at a ferocious speed, grabbing the largest deer by its hind leg and whipping it away. He snapped the neck as he ran and held back his desire to bite into the fresh flesh.

A few minutes later he was back by his fire, gutting and roasting the dead animal.

'Typical.' Crossley shook his head as Althorn rejoined the group. 'You turn up just when we finish packing.'

'Sorry, I…' Althorn held back a burp, '…I needed to scout ahead and check the traps.' He held up the two small deer he had gone back for after his breakfast.

Crossley nodded with a smile. 'That'll do for lunch!'

'Gut, quarter and distribute them among the provisions,' Li said as she walked past.

Althorn handed the deer over and spotted Euryleia, who stared across the desert with her arm cradled against her chest. 'How is it?' he asked as he would a daughter.

Euryleia looked up with vacant eyes and Althorn could see her loss. She needed Lavalle.

She gave a smile. 'It tingles,' she said.

'Everyone heals fast here, Euryleia.'

'But I'll never fire my bow again.' Her brow was heavy. 'What use will I be in battle?' Tears were forming in her eyes.

'Let me take a look.' Althorn crouched next to her and held out his palm.

Euryleia looked away for a second then offered her wrist, keeping her head turned away. Resting her elbow on his leg, Althorn tenderly unwrapped the bandages, wary of what he would find beneath: redness or pus would indicate an infection and any protruding bone or weeping flesh would mean more pain in order to heal the wound.

'Has Li looked at it?' he asked as the layers peeled away.

Euryleia shook her head.

The last few layers were moist with a green liquid.

'And this is your paste?'

'Yes.'

Althorn took extra care not to tear any healing flesh but, as the last layer came free, he wasn't prepared for what he would see. 'Oh, I–'

'What?' Euryleia looked.

This land offered plenty to scare and frighten Althorn, but it never held back from amazing him. They stared at the blackened wrist in amazement and then at each other. Euryleia laughed.

'It's…'

'Growing back,' Althorn said in disbelief.

At the end of Euryleia's scorched wrist grew a tiny baby-like hand.

'Maybe you will fire your bow again.' Althorn smiled.

'Yes.' Tears ran from Euryleia's eyes and she wrapped the bandage back over then raised her head, distracted by something behind him. 'Look.'

'Althorn?' Mihran called out and Althorn turned to see the red silhouette of their commander beckoning him.

Althorn patted Euryleia on the shoulder. 'See you later.'

'Follow me.' Mihran walked Althorn away from the camp.

Away from human ears and Lutamek sensors, Althorn thought.

'The way forward,' Mihran stared into Althorn's eyes, 'how does it look?'

Althorn looked out at the horizon to avoid Mihran's gaze: there was something about his eyes he could never quite trust. 'Ahead is the same barren land, scattered with the dead. A few dips.' He pointed to the horizon. 'But mostly flat. We can reach the far hills by nightfall.'

'It might be best to take our time,' Mihran said.

'Why?' Althorn asked.

The Commander squinted. 'What if our location is known?'

'A trap?'

'Maybe.' Mihran turned away, as he always did when anyone asked him too many questions, and gestured to where Euryleia was sitting. 'You look after her well.'

Althorn nodded.

'As though she were a daughter to you… or sister.' He let the comment hang.

Althorn didn't know what to say. Did Mihran know? He kept his eyes fixed on Euryleia for fear of betraying his true emotions. The image of his sister, which had haunted him for days, came to him: her pained face; the recognition in her eyes; a slight smile on her lips; the line across her throat. It had been ten years since he had seen her taken by the men who had destroyed his clan.

'Yes,' Althorn replied, 'she needs to be looked after.'

Through the pain of grief and the acidic burn of shame that had eaten at him since his blade had taken her life, Althorn felt a new emotion rising like a sun in the winter months: he felt proud of his sister. She had done well for a slave with no family – she had married a king no less! And the crying child must have been his nephew or niece. A future king or queen.

'Good,' Mihran replied. 'Your skills are essential in our army, Althorn, not just your speed but in keeping us together.'

'Thank you, I–' Althorn started but the shaking ground silenced him.

The huge shape of Two-zero-three, the Lutamek leader, came close. 'Humans.'

'Yes,' Mihran replied.

'You offer us a distraction, yet you plan a delay – are you going back on your word?'

Had Two-zero-three been listening to their conversation? Althorn saw Mihran's nostrils flare.

'My men have been walking for ten days. We are preparing for battle, but your attack set us back.'

'Our scans show your soldiers are in good physical condition. Why do you delay?'

Mihran looked around to see who was listening, then replied in a hushed voice. 'It is psychological strength we are building not just the physical. What would you know of biological strength?'

'We have organic components,' Two-zero-three replied without apparent emotion. 'Our ancestors were organic, multilimbed bipeds similar to yourselves. They developed implants, metallic limbs and ionic neural pathways... until the mechanical replaced ninety-eight percent of the biological.'

Mihran nodded. 'Then you should appreciate our need for rest.'

The robot took a second before responding. 'We will proceed ahead of you to clear the path of Brakari scouts.'

'We appreciate the offer,' Mihran replied. 'It would be most helpful.' He turned. 'Althorn?'

'Yes.'

'A change to our plans – if our path is cleared we need every soldier back before tomorrow's dawn. I need you to find the rescue party and, if they have him, John Greene.'

The day after the battle with the blue creatures, Gal-qadan's band of warriors entered a forest of tall trees and thick undergrowth. Gal-qadan felt uneasy: this was easy ambush territory and the crunch of hooves on dry twigs broadcast their presence for miles.

When a clearing appeared, the leading soldiers rushed forward to catch a glimpse of the hazy sky and feel the wind on their faces.

'No!' Gal-qadan barked. 'We go around!' He had learnt that death lurked in every glade.

Some men ignored him, desperate for a release from the claustrophobic forest, but it was too late: they had already alerted a new enemy who closed in on them. Gal-qadan felt the muscles in his tocka's back tense. He looked to Kastor, whose tocka was making low noises to call the herd together, and out of the shadows a faint red glow appeared. The unearthly light neared and formed shapes, growing in definition as they drew closer.

'What are they?' Dakaniha whispered to Gal-qadan, who responded by slipping the bow off his shoulder.

Gal-qadan's eyes grew accustomed to the blood-red shade emanating from each creature to see long arms and thick legs. They were no bigger than an average man, carrying an array of unrecognisable weapons in their oversized hands. The sound of swords unsheathing and stretched bow strings filled the glade as the red enemy neared.

Gal-qadan gave sharp orders to his men. 'Archers.'

Around him, Dakaniha, Tode and other bowmen drew their taut bowstrings to their ears. He looked at Ethan, with his long rifle primed and aimed.

Gal-qadan loaded his own bow. 'Release!' he yelled.

A volley of arrows whipped through the air, following the whistling bullet from Ethan's gun, but Gal-qadan watched in confusion as the missiles passed through the red aliens and smashed into the trees beyond. Kastor and Osayimwese's spears met the same end.

'Release!' Gal-qadan shouted again, not believing his eyes. The second volley fared the same. How could he defeat an enemy he couldn't touch?

The red enemy broke into an attacking run. At fifty paces away each red beast threw, launched or spat some kind of missile. Explosions rocked the ground around Gal-qadan's men as the tocka were sent into disarray.

Gal-qadan turned to retreat and caught sight of a white mist curling through the trees, but ignored it. 'We're surrounded!' he shouted. 'Divide and retreat!'

Those who could command their tocka drove them left or right, with the remaining tocka obediently following. The sound of exploding trees rang in Gal-qadan's ears as the red army's missiles grew more destructive. He cast a look back and saw the mist again. It had drifted into the clearing, mingling with the smoke from the explosions. Something about the way it twisted and twirled kept Gal-qadan's attention, so he slowed his tocka and the others joined suit.

Three shapes formed from the mist: legs, arms and heads became clear. Layer upon layer of detail built until three robed samurai warriors could be seen, holding glinting swords above their heads. The red army was distracted and turned to fire but the swordsmen were already on them. High-pitched yells echoed through the air as the samurai leapt in at the enemy, slicing them to pieces with power and deft accuracy.

'Our allies,' Gal-qadan spoke to no one in particular.

'What shall we do, Khan?' Tode asked.

What could they do? Their weapons were useless and the samurai looked unharmed and full of energy as they fought. What Gal-qadan would give to have those men in his army! He had to give them a sign, he thought, to show they were on the same side.

'We must assist!' He kicked at his tocka and it leapt forward. 'Attack! Everyone attack!'

Gal-qadan wandered amongst the dismembered alien corpses, staring at the strange forms and marvelling at the ferocity and skill with which they had been despatched.

'No sign of the swordsmen,' Tode reported.

Gal-qadan nodded. 'Spirit warriors,' he whispered.

'Khan?'

Gal-qadan shook his head and mounted his tocka. 'We move on.'

His men looked tired and weren't talking as much as earlier, which was a relief. Dakaniha, with his ridiculous four eyes, looked pleased with himself, while Ethan, the rifleman, looked greyer than before, but only when fatigue set in would Gal-qadan be concerned.

'So why did our weapons pass through them if the swordsmen could kill them?' Dakaniha asked what Gal-qadan had been unable to answer. Only when the samurai had injured a red creature could Gal-qadan's troops physically attack them.

'My guess is shielding,' Tode answered.

'No,' Dakaniha replied. 'They had no shields.'

'None we could see,' Tode replied. 'But what if their shields did the opposite to ours – let the arrows through?'

'Weapons of the gods?' Kastor joined the conversation.

'Something like that,' Tode said.

And yet the samurai were able to bring down those shields, Gal-qadan thought. He *had* to have them in his army. A cold shiver ran across his shoulders and he looked back into the hazy forest. Never ignore a cold feeling, he thought, but only saw damp trees.

'So why didn't we take one of their shields?' Dakaniha asked.

'Did you see any?' Kastor responded. 'Because I didn't.'

'He's right, it was just flesh and armour,' Tode said.

As they left the forest, Gal-qadan saw grass hummocks, suggesting they were on the fringes of a great plain: his kind of territory. But when he reached the edge, his men had stopped in a huddle.

'What is it this time?' Gal-qadan asked.

Was this another argument? Gal-qadan half hoped so. He would be obliged to kill someone to restore his authority. But who would he kill? He needed control of the tocka but doubted they would let him ride if he killed Kastor. Dakaniha maybe? He had been of little practical use and, for some reason, his extra eyes offended him.

Dakaniha sat proud on his tocka. 'I have found a trail, Great Leader.'

'Made by whom?' Gal-qadan snapped back.

Dakaniha straightened his back. 'Made by another group of humans, Great Leader.'

John opened his eyes. His head was dizzy and his body ached but from what, he couldn't remember. Maybe he'd been drugged? His last memory was of the huge creature interrogating him… threatening him. John could picture his ugly, fish-like face covered in eyes and mouthparts, but couldn't remember anything else. John's body shuddered and his breathing sped up as panic seeped into his muscles. He pulled against his restraints and looked around. What if that thing came back?

He heard his father's voice. 'Take your time, son.'

He always said that when he learnt something new and John had used the same phrase when Joe took his first steps. The thought calmed him down, but tears filled his eyes: Rosie should have been with him to share those moments. Their son had needed his mother. Why did she have to die? The same question over and over. Anger rushed through John and he stretched, rattling the metal restraints.

'Damn it,' he gasped.

With a resigned sigh, he blinked away his tears. His bed was raised, giving him a good view of the room, and he could see a few trophy-like body parts nailed to the wall near a set of lethal-looking metal implements. John shivered and felt his left leg twitch. He had to get out of here.

A noise made him turn. They were back. He could hear the telltale scraping sound and pictured them: the large angry one; the tiny one with flashing sides who hid in the corner; the thickset one with the scarred face. Panic was rising again and John pulled on his chains.

He could hear a voice, '...still alive?'

'–gave him some Penchack to take the memories away.'

'Good.'

John relaxed a little. Maybe he could reason with these two and ask them to let him out? All he wanted to do was get back to his army so he could get to the silver gates and back to Joe. He strained his neck, looking for anything he could reach to prise the metal clasps off his wrists. There was nothing within reach on the tables and all he saw on the walls were more body parts... John stopped and stared. His throat dried, his eyes widened and, without meaning to, he made a whimpering sound.

Nailed to the mud-brick wall hung the bottom half of his left leg.

John's eyesight blurred.

He didn't feel pain, but instinctively looked to his feet and shook his legs. He didn't care who heard him. One leg rattled its fixings while the other felt stuck. Stretching and peering down, he could just make out the tip of his right boot. Not his left.

John stared back at the leg on the wall.

First his arm got swallowed by his machine gun and now he'd lost a leg? How could he go home like this? What would his parents say? His grandfather would just have more reasons to put him down. More importantly, what would Joe think of him? Would he be scared? How could he hug his son like this, or run with him?

John's left hand formed a fist as he strained against his bonds again. The mechanisms in his gun-arm clicked and he felt warmth grow inside the gun. Light flooded the room and John closed his eyes. He heard claws scraping across the ground and wheezing sounds.

'It's awake.'

'Yes.'

'How long until Panzicosta returns?'

'Hours. Probably after sundown,' replied the distorted voice of the scarred beast. 'He likes to leave them to regain energy. It delays their death.'

'And you're sure you'll be fine, Krotank?'

Krotank coughed. 'My fighting days are numbered and I grow tired of this world. As soon as you are free of the walls I'll head into the plains.'

'Are you certain?'

Krotank replied, 'There's much to explore here. That's all I ever wanted, you know? To explore. Then I was called up in the army and, well, we ended up here.'

'Your time was one of our bloodiest.'

'The expansionists and the eradication of the Crarl, yes, but when was our history ever peaceful?' Krotank replied.

As John listened, he realised these Brakari weren't natives of this land – they were fighting for their survival too! Which meant they must have lost their battle or they wouldn't still be here. The thought gave him strength. The Brakari had lost, which meant his people could beat them.

John opened his eyes. 'Excuse me?'

'Yes?' A sleek grey head appeared by his side. It wasn't as hideous as the large creature who had tortured him, but its numerous eyes and mouth pincers weren't pretty either.

'What have you done to me? To my leg?'

'General Panzicosta…'

'I don't care about the bloody General,' John bellowed, feeling his anger grow. Once again, he acted as he thought Mihran or Lavalle would. 'I demand my freedom.'

'Well that's interesting because…'

'Release me now!'

The small Brakari tilted its head to one side. 'Are you fit enough to travel?'

'I–' John cast a look at the wall where his amputated leg hung. 'I don't know. No.' John tried to control his panic. 'What do you want with me?'

'You misunderstand me, John Greene.' The creature moved and the metal clasps snapped open. 'I have come to free you.'

John took his time to slide off the bed and stared at the creatures. Then he stretched to retrieve his amputated leg, leaning over a table with the stump of his right leg sticking out impotently.

'You won't be able to use it,' Krotank said. 'It's been embalmed.'

John stopped and rested on a table.

'Drained of all liquids, then pumped full of–'

'Yes, I get the picture.' John had never felt like this before. It was beyond anger. He felt infiltrated and abused… dirty and less than an animal. 'What else did you bastards do to me?'

'It wasn't us,' the feminine creature replied.

'But you let that thing cut my leg off and God knows what else…' John slipped his good hand down his trousers to check everything was in place. 'Oh, thank God.' His shoulders relaxed.

'General Panzicosta is very…' The female paused. 'It would be best to start from the beginning.'

John turned to look at her. Although smaller than his torturer, at four foot tall and six foot long, she still intimidated John in the small room.

'I am Millok and we,' she turned to Krotank, 'have given you drugs to remove all pain and memories of your time with the General.'

John was ready for an argument but the words sunk in and his head dropped a notch. 'Thank you.'

'We are…' Millok started.

'Rebelling against our leader's cause,' Krotank finished the sentence.

'Rebels?' John whispered. Could he trust them? What if it was another trap, like when he followed Joe to the hospital and then Crossley? This time he would be prepared, he told himself. Or ready to escape at the first chance.

'We can take you back to your army,' Millok said.

'Why can't you just let me go.' John looked at the doorway that stood ajar. 'I can make it on my own, thanks.'

With a hop, John moved towards the exit, but the weight of his gun-arm pulled him into a table, knocking off the marbles he'd seen earlier. Weren't these some kind of shield? John thought and grabbed a few. If he could get back to his army, maybe Mihran or Li would find a way to use them.

'Where are my bags?' he asked and shoved the marbles in his pocket.

'Here.' Krotank swung the satchels onto the table.

'I've got everything I need.' John scooped up more marbles.

'You cannot travel alone. Do you even know where you are?' Millok asked.

John peered through the tiny window, where a slither of the hazy sky could be seen. All he needed was a crutch and he could make a good go of it, he was sure.

'You are in a city, John Greene,' Millok said.

'A city?' John stared at the Brakari soldier.

How could he escape from a city full of creatures like the one who had tortured him? He pictured his father but couldn't remember any advice that would be useful now… his mother? Nothing. An image of the armchair by the fire came to John, and one of his grandfather. 'You're a useless boy, John,' he grumbled. 'You never take your time and you never ask for help – you just blunder on through without a care…'

He was right. Maybe now was the time to accept some help?

'Your name is Millok?' he asked.

'Yes,' she replied.

'You can call me John… I would appreciate your help.'

'Good,' Millok replied. 'We must make the most of the time before the general returns.'

John leant in the shadow of the uneven mud-brick wall that surrounded the city of Abzicrutia. He'd never seen such a place. Beside him, her eyes constantly scanning, Millok explained how the Brakari army had marched out to confront the humans, leaving behind only the slave soldiers too weak to fight.

'Can't we free them too?' John asked.

'Just keep moving,' she snapped.

Keeping close to the wall, they kept out of sight of the watchtowers where the last few Brakari soldiers stood guard.

'Stand back.'

John hopped away as Millok pulled up a section of ground, spilling debris, and rested a metal grate against the wall. 'Climb down,' she ordered.

John paused for a second.

Stay strong, he told himself, and descended foot first into the hole. A muddy and dark hole. Probably the sewers, going by the smell. It was preferable to the torture rack, he reminded himself, and, with his gun-arm strapped tight, he slipped along the tube.

'Back in the trenches again,' he muttered but Millok ignored him as she pulled back the grate.

'Out that way.' She gestured towards a dim grey light.

It took John a while to get a good rhythm going, crouching with one good hand and one foot. He slipped a few times, covering himself in whatever it was the Brakari defecated, but after ten minutes they reached the clean air and John could see leaves fluttering.

'Don't worry,' Millok said, urging John on, 'we can't be spotted from here.'

Tentatively, John stepped out and hopped to the nearest tree.

'Never again,' he grunted and sat on the ground to stretch his leg. Although the outlet was in the centre of a small copse of trees, the walls of the city were just a stone's throw away. 'And now what do we do?' he asked.

'There's a blind spot all the way to the trees.' Millok pointed towards the fringes of a forest some fifty paces away.

'After you then.' John pulled his straps tighter.

'We go together,' Millok said, looking around.

John noticed two new protrusions on her head, wafting.

'We must be quick.' She turned to John. 'Let me help you up.'

'No!' John cringed from the Brakari's touch. 'I'm fine,' he lied.

He reached for a low branch to get up. His left arm was getting stronger but the weight of his gun and bags and the lack of a left leg made it impossible to get up. 'Just do it, John!' he growled and pictured his grandfather. With a surge of anger, he pulled himself upright.

'You can lean on me.' Millok had been watching him. 'It would be quicker.'

It would, John thought, but that would be a sign of weakness. He spotted a forked branch and reached for it. 'No thanks, I'll use this.'

The branch snapped off.

'Quiet!' Millok hissed.

John tore off the loose twigs and wedged a stick under his armpit. 'Come on then!'

Millok scuttled ahead and John swung into action behind her, determined not to fall over. He took it easy to start with: footstep, crutch step. It would be easier if he had two, he thought, but how would he grip it with his gun-arm? His steps picked up as the ground sloped away from the city, faster and faster until the trees were around him.

'What's that thing?' John asked when he caught up with Millok and stared at the long metal vehicle she stood beside. A hum could be heard coming from an open panel where Millok tinkered.

'It's a machine,' Millok replied. 'It will take us to your army.'

The smell was familiar to John. Of course! Crossley had taken him on one of these when he left the hospital. 'I've seen it before,' John almost whispered.

Millok turned to him. 'Yes. The Draytor brought you here.'

'The what?' John asked.

'The shape-shifter. It brought you to General Panzicosta.'

A shape-shifter? That made sense. He knew it couldn't have been Crossley, but had never worked out *how* he had been tricked. His memory may have been wiped since the field hospital but, deep down, he knew it had all been make-believe and trickery. Anger stirred deep in John's chest again, but he had to control it – he needed to get clear from Abzicrutia and then worry about getting away from Millok.

'Right then,' John rested a hand on the metal behemoth and felt its warmth, 'where shall I–'

'Shh!' Millok hissed and crouched. Her feelers waved through the air with a noise that sounded like sniffing.

John stared into the forest, blood pounding through his ears, as he listened to every branch creak and leaf brush. Then he saw the unmistakable shape of General Panzicosta.

Chapter 14

'And they won?' Mihran asked Li, marvelling at the details of yet another battle she held in her database.

'Against all the odds,' Li replied, walking beside him. 'One in three killed, yet the English only lost five percent.'

Mihran remained silent. He felt comfortable being quiet with Li. She didn't expect him to reply to every question like the others. But still, he had questions. 'And it was down to one weapon: this longbow?'

'The range and sheer number of archers overwhelmed the French,' Li replied.

'But the hill was a factor too,' Mihran was speaking to himself now, 'and the arrogance of the leaders.'

Li knew when to stay silent too.

They had been walking for two hours, by Mihran's reckoning. The Lutamek robots had skilfully disappeared from sight and were scouring the land for potential enemies. The army was safer than it had ever been in this land, yet Mihran couldn't relax. Each step drew them closer to battle. He glanced at the ragtag group of soldiers. Heads were down and the injured were limping or being carried by their comrades. They needed to be stronger. They needed more firepower. They needed… an idea came to him.

'When we first arrived here, did you take notes on every soldier you saw?' Mihran asked.

'Yes,' Li replied, as ever without emotion.

'And you have logged every adaptation – every death?'

'Yes.'

While the group took a water break in the lee of a low hill, Mihran obtained all the information he needed and, in return, allowed Li to bounce her theories off him.

'So although the mutations appear random in nature, there is always a root cause or trigger and, as Ten-ten pointed out, these changes can be traced to biological enhancements.'

'Yes.' Mihran tried not to think about the fungal growth in his brain. Unlike the rest of the group, for whom only the language and aural areas were affected, his brain was riddled with mycelium, providing direct connections to distant cerebral regions. All the fungus wanted in return was a small amount of energy.

'I suggest we try an experiment to kick-start…' Li was still talking, he noticed, '…and measure the effects.'

Mihran took a moment to recall what she had been saying. Purposefully injure some of the troops to see if it triggers an adaptation? Mihran couldn't allow anything to weaken his army. He saw them as a frail web of connected parts: some weak, some strong, but all intertwined. Take some out and the balance would be warped.

'Not this close to battle – we can't risk any more injuries.'

'But the potential adaptations would outweigh the losses,' Li argued.

'*If* your theory is correct,' Mihran said.

'Yes, but–'

'We have been weakened.' Mihran stood, ready to resume their walk. 'But I have a plan. We're not desperate enough for your experiments yet, Li.'

It was another hour before they found anything of interest, after skirting more battle sites and obelisks that grew thin this side of the plain.

'I found another battlefield – looks a bit different to the others,' Bowman reported to Mihran. 'Only one set of bodies. No graves either.'

Mihran was intrigued. 'Let's detour to visit it.'

Bowman wasn't wrong. The obligatory white obelisk with its sharp, black script stood proud, with a ring of burnt bodies splayed out around it like a giant, dark flower.

'I suggest we walk around the bodies,' Li said.

'Can you read the obelisk from here?' Mihran asked.

Li tapped some buttons on her sleeve and started reading. 'Here the Stobardorian army was erased. They dishonoured the true warrior and refused to fight within the chosen time period.'

Mihran sighed. It was as he had predicted. He needed to turn this into an advantage.

'We knew we had to fight and now we know the consequences of not going to war,' he said to the whole group. 'We are fighters.' He let the words sink in. 'Now we know we must fight for our honour.'

Mumbles could be heard around the group. What did they fear? Mihran had resisted using his mind skills since his run-in with Peronicus-Rax, which had left him bruised, but Mihran had to try something. Gently, he pushed his mind out to feel his way around the group.

'Don't worry.' Mihran kept his eyes open as he talked and tentatively touched the minds of the men and women. He imagined a wide net reaching out, which was blue for some reason. He could sense emotions through it. They were scared: not of death, but of losing. 'Any army we meet has already lost a battle.' His mind net was spread thin but he could feel the emotions quicker than by delving into each person's mind. 'Our enemy will be weakened after losing. They will be demoralised,' he could feel the mood lighten, 'and they will lose again!' He saw heads rising and pulled back his mind. 'War is near. Victory is near!'

'Yeah!' Crossley was nodding with other soldiers who grunted in agreement.

Some didn't look convinced and Mihran had to work on them. 'But rather than wait for them to attack us,' Mihran pointed to the burnt remains, 'this reminds us we need to take the battle to them.'

He smiled as he walked away. The mind net, as he pictured it, felt easy to control and would give him new insight into the army as a whole. These people were parts in a bigger machine: a machine that he controlled.

'Wait!' Someone shouted and Mihran froze. 'Don't move a muscle.' It was Crossley, who was coughing now.

What was he doing? Was he challenging his authority? Mihran stayed still and pushed his mind out behind him to where he felt the American stood. He was excited and a touch scared.

'What is it?' Mihran asked.

'One step ahead of you, a finger's length under the ground,' Crossley coughed again, 'is a mine – an explosive.'

Mihran's breathing grew heavy. He was no longer in control.

Worse, he was relying on one of his men to help him. Mihran spoke quietly so few people could hear him. 'What shall I do?'

'Step backwards, but very carefully,' Crossley was almost whispering, 'softly.'

Mihran waited a second to show he was in control of his own actions, then slowly lifted his right foot and stepped half a pace back. It was the slightest of movements, yet the shift in weight triggered something in the ground ahead of him: he was sure he had seen movement.

Crossley coughed. 'Wait!' He coughed again. 'One of the sensor arms moved... slower this time.'

Mihran clenched his fists. With controlled effort, he lifted his left foot with such a slow movement he was unsure how high he had lifted it before he swept it back half a step.

'And again,' Crossley said before coughing. 'But watch your robes!'

Mihran raised his long coat then stepped back with his right foot and again with his left until he saw Crossley in his peripheral vision.

'You did it – thank God for that!' Crossley was laughing.

Mihran gave a little smile of thanks. It was good to know his men cared about his safety.

'I thought you were going to blow up all the explosives!' Crossley was on his knees now. 'Just give me some room and I'll dig it up.'

Mihran's eyes narrowed.

'Actually,' Crossley stared up at Mihran, 'can I use your sword?'

Mihran's teeth hurt as his jaws clamped together.

Crossley got the message. 'No? Okay. I'll use this stick but–'

'I can help you.' Li tapped buttons on her wrist. 'I can remove the sand, one layer at a time, and then...'

Mihran exhaled and unclenched his teeth. What if the rest of the land was littered with these devices? And why hadn't the Lutamek or Althorn set them off when they passed? He watched as Li used an unseen force to lift thin discs of sand from the ground. This would take some time.

Dusk was upon them by the time Bowman spotted the Lutamek

fighters, huddled on an incline. They had reached the gentle hills as Althorn had predicted.

'Are they walking?' Crossley asked. Mihran noticed the American had become more vocal since he and Li had managed to safely remove the explosives from the swathe of mines he had discovered.

'No,' Mihran answered, remembering the books he had studied with Li: dust low and spreading was the sign of infantry approaching.

'Right, so what are they doing?' Crossley asked.

'Resting by the look of it,' Li replied.

To Mihran they looked like nothing more than a series of low-lying buildings.

As they neared, a burning aroma came to them in wafts on the slow wind.

'Smells bad,' Crossley winced.

Mihran opened his mind net and pushed it forwards to feel for any conscious thoughts from the Lutamek. He had been developing the skill as the group walked, spreading it thinly across the land around the army in an attempt to pick up living creatures other than his troops.

Nothing. Not even a creature scuttling about – wait, he could feel something. It was different to his men. There were shapes pulsing… yellow. Peronicus-Rax had been orange and then blinding white when he attacked him. He would tread carefully and feel around each shape. Yes, it was them! He could see the waves of communication between them and feel the warmth of their organic parts. He could feel emotion too: they were tired and lonely. They pined for their lost comrades.

Mihran reeled in his mental net and whispered to the wind. 'I know what I have to do.'

Isao stood still and breathed in deeply. He didn't need to breathe but he missed the simple act, just like he missed eating and drinking. He soaked up the view: the light; the colours; the sounds; the smells. These were the few glorious minutes he and his comrades fought for: the space between the end of the battle and the inevitable return of the muffled veil that cursed them.

Around them lay the bodies of their red foes, shattered and broken. As ever, Isao and his companions were unscathed. They stood in a triangle with their weapons pointing to the earth. Hori was smiling but Masaharu's face wore a shadow of a frown.

The mist was returning.

Isao could feel it, like hearing the footsteps of the jailer returning with his key.

'Time to go,' Isao whispered to the other two, who nodded.

Their bushido code of honour had decreed they commit seppuku. If not, they could have fallen into enemy hands and been tortured for information. But had they known the true cost of their sacrifice, would they have carried it through? Isao shook his head to remove the thought. They were samurai: this was their burden.

As they slipped back into the shadow world, Isao took one last breath, savouring the pine forest. Then the colours of the real world disappeared.

'Did you see them?' Hori asked as they floated together through the clouded landscape, peppered with shadows of the real world.

'Yes,' Isao replied.

'They tried to help us,' Masaharu said, 'at the end.'

'They did help,' Hori said. 'They killed the injured.'

'But finished the battle too soon.' Isao already missed the colours: the scarlet of the enemy; the ochre of the earth; the jade of the leaves. This world lacked definition. Even Hori and Masaharu were poorly formed smudges of their true selves.

'We were given longer this time.' Hori sounded cheerful.

It was true. This had been their third battle and they had enjoyed more time in the real world.

'But only a few minutes,' Isao said.

'We are being rewarded,' Hori stated.

'And if we win more, will we be able to return?' Masaharu asked.

'You want to return?' Isao snapped at the wispy image, whose body flowed about him like robes in a storm.

'Yes.' Masaharu's eyes were sharp. 'If returning means I have regained my honour.'

Isao looked towards the shadows of Gal-qadan's troops riding their tocka. Was it possible to wash away one's wrongs with blood? It seemed wrong. And would they be able to return to their homeland after regaining corporeal form? Isao didn't know if he wanted to, not after the things he had seen. He had attained everything his family had wished for: a high position in the army; land; a beautiful wife. His status was envied by many yet, if he was honest, he wanted more. He had to be honest with himself. Life was short. His old life had ended and if he had a chance to live it again he would do things differently. He couldn't say how, but it would be different.

'Their steeds didn't fight.' Hori was talking to Masaharu and Isao focused on them to make sure they didn't get separated.

The tide that had pulled the three samurai since their deaths still tugged at them and could easily pull them in different directions.

'They are more intelligent than horses,' Masaharu replied.

'You think they knew not to attack?' Isao asked.

'Maybe,' Masaharu answered. 'But they didn't attack the injured either.'

'They have honour too,' Hori said.

Isao focused on the tocka at the rear of the line carrying the Mongol leader. He didn't trust the man: he had killed two soldiers in cold blood: one to raise the tocka and another during the battle who could have been saved.

'Will we fight again?' Hori asked.

'Of course!' Masaharu answered quickly.

'The tide grows strong,' Isao noted. 'And our enemies grow thick.'

'So we will be tested.'

'Yes,' Isao said.

'And we will have longer in the real world,' Masaharu said.

'Wait.' Isao could hear a voice.

'Up ahead,' Hori said, 'a beacon.'

An orange light pulsed in the sky.

Gal-qadan and his men had stopped and wore strained expressions. Some held their hands over their ears.

'Hold on to something. We need to focus,' Isao told his comrades. 'Focus and listen.'

Isao anchored his body to the shadow of a hazy tree. Then he heard the words: the call to arms.

John's good hand slipped under his shirt for Joe's tin soldier as he kept his eyes on the Brakari monster. Although he had no memory of the torture or pain, John's anger was still raw. A simple blast from his gun would give him some retribution, he thought, as the creature sniffed and loped through the long undergrowth to where Millok had tied down the large robot transporter. John's gun clicked and he imagined bullet shapes as Millok held up a foreleg, with a gesture that he assumed meant either 'stay silent' or 'don't move'. John decided to do both and groped for the cord around his neck. Where was it? He unbuttoned his shirt and found nothing. Had he lost it? And what were those marks on his stomach? Lines and circles around his belly button. He rubbed them but didn't feel any pain.

That bastard must have taken Joe's soldier!

'I know you are here,' Panzicosta's voice boomed, sending a shiver through John. 'You have braced the Lutamek well. Give me the human and you will be released, Millok.'

John looked at Millok. Surely she wouldn't give him up after everything she'd risked? Watching her gently vibrating carapace and shiny sets of eyes, there was no way to tell. She was waving her mouthparts, sniffing the air, and now her head shell was swelling. What was that sound? Like a distant rumble of artillery fire.

John swivelled to look at Panzicosta, who was holding his head low. Then the large shelled beast raised his head and roared. 'Bring him to me!'

Millok whispered, 'Trust me.'

'No,' John whispered back. 'What are you doing?'

She couldn't fight him, he was far too big. Was she going to give John up in exchange for her freedom?

Panzicosta's eyes fixed on her as she crawled out of the undergrowth, keeping the robot between them.

Maybe he should run while Panzicosta was distracted? John thought. But how far could he get on one leg? No, he had to stay here. Maybe his gun would fire? He tried to wriggle and flex what felt like his fingers deep inside the shortened Lewis gun. He felt for a trigger or firing mechanism, visualising the schematics and stripped-down pieces, but the gun had warped too much. All he could feel was a metal tube where he formed the shapes.

John looked up as Millok spoke.

'I will give you the human,' she was leaning up against the vibrating robot with her forelegs gripping a metal ridge, 'but you must give me complete freedom from the army. No more fighting.' She paused as though thinking. 'And give me access through the silver gates when you defeat the humans.'

Panzicosta huffed with derision. 'I will guarantee your safety and you can flee, but you will never have access through the silver gates unless you fight alongside the victorious.'

'Belsang would know a way,' Millok replied.

Panzicosta huffed again. 'Maybe, but…'

John fought every urge to crawl away. Why was he listening to these creatures discuss him like an unwanted pet? Why didn't he escape while he had the chance? He looked at Millok and knew the answer: he trusted her. She'd helped him escape when she could have fled on her own. True, she may have done it to annoy Panzicosta, but she'd also wiped John's memory of pain. She'd shown compassion.

'The human must come with me to finish the interrogation. Where is he?' Panzicosta growled.

John moved to one side, careful not to give away his position. Millok was balanced gracefully on two of her rear appendages while, unseen by Panzicosta, the other two poked at a section of the robot.

'He's over there.' Millok nodded in John's direction. 'John, it's safe to come out!'

Panzicosta made a step forward towards John.

'John!' Millok called again. 'Stand up.'

'I'm not bloody standing up!' John shouted and Panzicosta took a step towards Millok and the Lutamek.

'Come to me, human!' Panzicosta shouted.

Without warning, a blue flash leapt out of the robot and struck Panzicosta in the head, sending him flying backwards. John was up on his good knee, watching him writhe on the ground. Another blue shock ripped into him and his shape changed from a large blue scorpion to a wolf-like creature, and then to human form. Was that Crossley? Then Randeep. How could it be? Another bolt struck it and the creature changed three more times, finally finishing in what John assumed was its true form.

'It's the Draytor?' John hobbled forward on his stump and knee and stared at the multilimbed, wet-skinned animal that lay pulsing in a pool of slime.

'This is the creature that fooled you and brought you here,' Millok said.

John could feel his cheeks warm as his anger grew. His gun-arm clicked and warmed as he pictured twisting torpedoes of fire, ready to burn the quivering mess.

'I will kill it.' John focused on the jellied mass.

This creature was to blame for everything: Joe's tin soldier; his leg; the war; Rosie dying. He raised his arm, aimed the muzzle and fired, but a sound similar to a horse's fart erupted, followed by a weak puff of smoke.

'Damn it!' John fumed.

'Your weapon is faulty?' Millok asked.

'No, I…' John had no answer and felt his anger twist inside him. Did a soldier always have to kill? he wondered and took a deep breath.

'I will let it live,' he said, feeling a weight lift off him.

'Are you sure?' Millok asked.

'Yes.' John raised his eyebrows. 'Just give him another zap from that thing and we can go.'

Millok had fine-tuned the sound of the thundering Lutamek robot to a low rumble, allowing her and John to talk as they fled across the grassland plain. Although the bolted-on wheels were rudimentary, this was the fastest John had travelled since the train to Dover.

'How did you know it was the Draytor?' he asked Millok.

'I didn't.' She sat in front of John, claws gripping metal ridges while her pincers controlled the robot through exposed panels. 'I tested it with a sound weapon – any Brakari would have exhaled water, even Panzicosta.'

John stayed silent as hazy memories of riding the Lutamek with Crossley came back to him. He'd been drugged and fooled by that creature, yet he'd let it live.

'I had to attack it to know if it was a Draytor or Panzicosta,' Millok continued, 'so I overloaded the Lutamek systems, knowing it would release energy and...'

John couldn't hear any more. The vibrations beneath his leg and buttocks increased as the Lutamek jolted. Millok poked and twisted metal components inside the panels and the rumbling died down again.

John's head hurt. He was clinging on with his left arm and had his gun-arm wedged under a strap like on the raft. He was grateful to Millok for taking him away from the stinking city and for being alive, so why did he feel down?

He looked at the metal beneath him.

'Did it feel pain?' John asked.

'What? Yes – you saw it squirming on the ground.' Millok raised her voice.

'No. Did the Lutamek feel pain?' John asked. 'When you overloaded it?'

Millok turned her head to one side and three of her eyes focused on John's face. 'I don't know.'

'But it reacts,' John said and pictured Panzicosta leaning over him with his spikes. Strapped to the table, John had been vulnerable, just like the robot they were riding on.

'Millok, stop!' he shouted. 'This machine feels pain. You have to stop!'

He saw lines of small holes across her blue-shelled body open and close, then Millok brought the machine to a standstill.

'Yes, it feels pain. They have biological components connected to every major component and wired up to their power system. Every Lutamek I have ever braced has felt pain. I try to reduce it as much as I can but–'

'Why do it at all?' John asked, still gripping the handrail. 'Why torture and maim? Why fight?'

'For information and for victory. That's what we do.' Millok answered slowly and John sensed she didn't believe a word of it.

'And what happens afterwards?' John asked the question that had haunted him ever since he had first set eyes on the poisoned farmland and wrecked towns of Belgium. A lifetime to build. A day to destroy.

'That's for leaders to discuss, not the soldiers,' Millok replied.

John looked at markings on the huge robot and ran his fingers over a series of bumps: two, then eight, then four. Black pockmarks ran along one side of the shiny surface, like miniature craters, and the open panels looked like raw wounds with wires and dials hanging out.

'We're free now.' John looked up at Millok. 'Why can't this robot be free as well?'

Millok looked around before answering. 'Are you sure we're near your army? I promised to get you to safety, not abandon you.'

John shook his head. 'We'll walk.' He looked at his stump. 'I'll build a crutch. But this... soldier needs to be free.'

Millok's head dropped a notch. 'I'll use a time-delay brace so we're clear when it breaks free.'

'Good idea.' John guessed the first thing the Lutamek would do would be to try to find its kin, but who knew what its priorities would be: revenge was probably a close second. 'I'll just–' a wave of dizziness washed over him and his vision blurred, then an image came to him: a blue sphere, tinged white, green and brown. Was it a map?

'Are you okay?' Millok asked.

'Yes, I...' John focused on the image pushed into his mind and the word 'home' came to him. It wasn't spoken or seen but came with a warm comforting feeling.

He didn't expect the words that came next but instantly recognised the voice. He turned in the direction they came from and listened.

Since the day he'd taken his first life and become a man, Gal-qadan had only been surprised once. A man he had taken for dead had sprung up from a pile of bodies and stabbed him in the forearm. Gal-qadan had sliced the man's throat in a flash, but the rush of heartbeats that followed had made him feel truly alive.

The voice speaking in Gal-qadan's head now surprised him.

Mihran's words boomed, and Gal-qadan felt the same rush of euphoria: his body jolted, then filled with a delayed pulse of energy. He closed his eyes and, when the rush faded, listened to the words.

'...all soldiers of Earth to join forces. We will be victorious together.' There was a pause before the words started again. 'Listen. Listen carefully. This is a call to arms. All human soldiers must travel towards the beacon and...'

Gal-qadan opened his eyes. His men had stopped and the tocka stood patiently in a line. 'What's going on?' he shouted.

Tode turned. 'Do you not hear it, Khan?'

'Yes, of course I hear it.' He dug his heels in to spur his tocka on. 'But why have we stopped? We must keep moving.'

'Towards the beacon?' Tode asked.

Gal-qadan breathed sharply. Why was he constantly tested like this? Didn't any of his men realise how difficult it was for him to control his anger? If he was a weaker man he would have killed half of them by now.

'No. Not to the beacon.' He chose a new direction. 'That way.'

Kastor turned to face him. 'The trail we're following leads to the beacon. Why change direction now?'

The other soldiers turned too, bringing their tocka round to form a semicircle around Gal-qadan. All eyes were on him and his tocka nervously shifted its weight from hoof to hoof.

He was in charge, not them, Gal-qadan told himself. He needed to show leadership and strength. But what could he do faced with this?

'Why change our course?' Kastor asked again.

Gal-qadan fought the urge to draw his bow and shoot the Spartan. He pictured the long-haired swordsman falling off his tocka, and finishing him off with his short sword. He blinked to remove the thought. He had to maintain power. If the war the voice talked of was inevitable and they joined a larger army, what would he have control of? He had allies in his group, but Gal-qadan knew the majority of his men would not stay loyal. He needed something else.

'Khan?' Tode asked.

'Yes, I am Khan,' Gal-qadan spoke slowly as he worked out what he had to do, 'yet you question me.'

'We do because–' Kastor started but Gal-qadan cut him off.

'I haven't finished.' He counted to five before starting again. 'I have led you towards the silver gates. This is our mission.' He calmly looked from man to man, holding each gaze. 'Yet we are being distracted. How do we know this call to arms isn't a trap?'

'Why would they do that?' Kastor asked.

'Because they want the gates for themselves,' Gal-qadan replied quickly. 'You run towards the water like a young deer. Where are the wolves?'

Gal-qadan had their attention but had to make more ground. He slid off his tocka, giving it a friendly pat as he dismounted. 'We shall head to the beacon, but not this way.' He walked towards Kastor and stroked his tocka's muzzle as he had done a thousand times with his horses. He had seen what these beasts' teeth could do, but felt no fear. 'We head this way.' He nodded to the right again. 'So we can see for ourselves who calls us.'

'That sounds wise,' Dakaniha said.

Gal-qadan felt the momentum swinging back his way. 'But I ask one thing.'

'What?' Kastor's hand had moved to his sword handle.

Gal-qadan stared Kastor in the eye. 'That I ride your tocka and you ride mine.'

'What? No, I…'

'As the leader, I should ride the lead horse.' Gal-qadan kept stroking the tocka's muzzle.

'No, we've–'

'He is the Khan, Kastor,' Tode said, 'and he will lead us into battle.'

'Yes, but–' Kastor protested.

'He released the tocka,' Dakaniha added.

'Yes,' Gal-qadan looked in the lead tocka's eyes, 'it was I who freed you.'

'And you wouldn't be here if you hadn't followed me.' Dakaniha faced Kastor.

Osayimwese moved forward. 'Do you not have commanders in your army, Kastor? I thought you were a real soldier.'

Kastor raised a finger. 'Don't goad me, you know who the real soldier is here. And, yes, we have commanders, but they lead after earning the soldiers' respect.' He looked Gal-qadan in the eye.

Gal-qadan pictured his sword slipping through Kastor's wide mouth and out the back of his head.

Ethan leant over to Kastor and whispered something but Gal-qadan only caught the end, '...because they are your blood.'

Kastor nodded but remained seated. Gal-qadan knew the Spartan was a proud man. He had to give him a way to accept his order but save face. He smiled as he remembered an old trick.

'You have grown attached to your steed,' Gal-qadan said. 'But if I lead on mine, will the tocka follow? No. So I suggest we leave it to fate.' He picked a thumbnail-sized silver coin from a concealed pocket.

Kastor huffed but studied the coin all the same. 'You will pay me for my tocka?'

'No.' He turned the coin to show Arabic writing on one side and a symmetrical shape on the other. 'Choose a face.'

'Ah.' Kastor's grin returned. 'A bet!'

Gal-qadan rode the lead tocka at the head of his posse and Kastor took the rear. They had crossed a tract of open grassland and ventured into what looked like the remnants of a forest fire. A war had been fought here. Craters and bodies littered the ground and they passed a white obelisk surrounded by concentric circles of dark corpses, whose shining bones mimicked the obelisk.

Gal-qadan had allowed himself a smile for tricking Kastor, but now he had to focus on any present danger. 'Split into two units,' he ordered. 'I will take east; Tode, you take west.'

He gave his steed a subtle nudge with his heels, playing it safe with the tocka leader: one false move and the whole troop could abandon him. Gal-qadan had played his hand well but he needed something else to maintain his leadership. As the tocka walked sure-footedly through the metal and organic debris, Gal-qadan's eyes wandered. He caught glimpses of foreign weapons. That was what he needed – something so destructive that just having it in his possession ensured loyalty. He scoured the mess and stroked his tocka's mane to slow him down. He could see how the charred soldiers had met their deaths: the agony and the humiliation. But there were no weapons he could use here. Gal-qadan ushered his battalion on. Back to the flat grasslands: along their roundabout route to the beacon. The arrogant man would pay for assuming Gal-qadan could be summoned like this. This weapon he dreamt of would be the answer – something which, with the tocka, would give him negotiating power.

An hour later, another battlefield appeared on the horizon.

'Just like the last one, Khan,' Tode reported after scouting ahead. 'Shall we go around it?'

'No,' Gal-qadan snapped.

He *needed* a weapon.

'But the fields beyond lie thick with battle debris. Surely it will become impassable?' Tode said.

Gal-qadan felt his shoulders relax. There was so much possibility here. He looked ahead and saw the size of the next debris plain – he would need help.

'We go through, but everyone must look for anything of use.' He paused, wondering how much detail to give. 'We need supplies.'

'Food and water?' Tode asked.

Gal-qadan nodded. 'And arrows… missiles for each soldier.'

The pattern was repeated over and over: a new battlefield raised the chance of finding the weapon of Gal-qadan's desires. He had no time to stare at the bizarre alien physiologies of the dead: he only had eyes for their weapons. He picked up the odd blade or gun but in his mind he pictured a hand-held gun, like the rifles Dakaniha and Ethan carried but deadlier. His frustrations grew with each empty battlefield, while his battalion grew rich in trinkets and shields.

Gal-qadan reluctantly joined Tode after another fruitless search.

'Two more changes to report, Khan.'

Gal-qadan sighed, growing tired of his men's successes.

'Three tocka wandered off path and–'

Gal-qadan cut Tode off. 'Was that the explosion I heard?'

'Yes, Khan.'

'Are they dead?'

'No, Khan.' Tode's eyes lit up. 'They survived and now wear a coat of metal. Most fortunate.'

'Fortunate?' Gal-qadan looked away. It would make the tocka more of a threat. Useful when negotiating with the army leader.

He turned away. Maybe the next field would have what he was looking for? He had struggled enough, leading this band of complaining men through war, hunger and thirst. He deserved something in return.

Five battlefields later, when the green clouds above had turned a shade of peach, signalling the start of another long dusk, Gal-qadan found scores of squat bodies lying in a semicircle. Their feet pointed in the same direction, which told Gal-qadan they had been killed by the same weapon, belonging to their metallic, ball-shaped enemy. This was what he had been looking for! Gal-qadan's pulse raced and he turned his tocka to follow an invisible line from the set of dead feet to a patch of bare earth. He leapt down and kicked one of the spherical bodies, which rolled away with a tinny echo.

'There is nothing here,' he growled and looked across the field of debris.

Dakaniha and Tode were silently riding their tocka through a patch of bones, while Ethan rode atop a shallow ridge. Beyond him, Kastor was inspecting something of interest.

Anger built and Gal-qadan kicked another dead spheroid, wincing as his toe hit a hard object beneath. His tocka stepped away. Gal-qadan looked around but nobody had been watching. Still, he felt a tingle in his neck. He rolled the offending corpse away and spotted a dark line in the ground. He brushed away soil to reveal a ridge of metal and followed it, pushing more spheres out of the way. Had they died protecting this? Something nobody else had found? Breathing heavily, Gal-qadan cleared three corners and stepped back to stare at the triangle of metal embedded in the ground. He pounded it with his fists and forced his short sword under a corner, desperate to prise it free. He jabbed and poked at the corner – then stopped. A shape had appeared by his side. He turned to see his tocka, who gently tapped a hoof on the edge of the triangle and, with a hiss, a door hinged up, revealing a dark recess where two spherical creatures, as dead as those above ground, sat either side of a metal tube the length of his arm.

'At last.' Gal-qadan reached in to pick up the weapon.

He froze again. He could hear footsteps. He spun round with his sword aimed at the newcomer.

'That is not yours to take, human,' the deep voice spoke slowly.

Gal-qadan stared at the tall, thickset humanoid. The wind jingled trinkets hanging across its body and its one large eye stared down darkly.

Gal-qadan's head throbbed as he fought to control his anger. He may have been called rash or quick-tempered in the past, but he knew when he was outmuscled.

'I forbid you to take that weapon,' the tall warrior's voice boomed again.

Gal-qadan heard no malice in the voice but it implied great strength, so he placed the tubular weapon back beside its dead owners and faced the newcomer. He was too far away for a sword lunge and too near to string and fire an arrow.

'What authority do you have, stranger?' he asked.

'I protect the belongings of the dead,' it replied.

Gal-qadan glanced at the array of objects hooked on its armour: sharp implements hung alongside metal trinkets with winking lights, which jostled with colourful discs and tubes.

'Yet you take them yourself.' He gestured at a sphere dangling on a chain. 'What do you do with them?'

'I protect them.'

'From what?' Gal-qadan asked.

'Not what, whom,' the deep voice boomed. 'Anyone wishing to destroy them.'

Gal-qadan refrained from asking why.

'You have no authority in this land or any other. I, Gal-qadan, lead my army to war and we require provision and armaments.' Gal-qadan paused to stare into the large, unblinking eye, searching for a sign of anger or understanding. He pointed to a longsword hanging on its side. 'You have taken weapons from my people, yet you demand I leave this weapon here?'

'Yes.' It remained motionless.

Gal-qadan thought about his armoured skin and was weighing up how he would fare in a fight with the giant, when an idea came to him.

'If you wish to collect… protect this weapon,' Gal-qadan pointed to the tube in the vault by his feet, 'you may accompany us to our battle.'

The eye darkened.

'On victory, or death, I will bequeath it to you,' Gal-qadan said.

The eye lightened again.

'If not,' Gal-qadan said, 'my men will destroy you and the weapons you carry.' He swung his arm out to gesture at the soldiers on their tocka. 'No matter how powerful your weapons may be, we outnumber you.'

The tall soldier remained silent but took half a step back.

'My offer remains. I bequeath you the weapon on one condition.'

'Name it,' the tall being replied.

'Show me how to use it.'

Silence.

The dangling trinkets tinkled in the soft breeze and Gal-qadan stood tense, waiting for a physical attack.

The humanoid seemed to shrug. 'I will show you, human.'

'Good,' Gal-qadan replied.

The tall soldier shifted its footing to walk away. 'I wish to observe humans in battle. Who do you fight?'

Gal-qadan kept his stony face rigid. It was a good question. Who would they fight? Giants like him? Or bizarre enemies like the red aliens that could only be defeated by the samurai ghosts?

'They are unknown but will be defeated.'

'The unknown enemy is never defeated.'

'They will be with this weapon.' Gal-qadan pointed down into the pit. 'And then it will be yours.'

'It shall.'

Even though he had the weapon, Gal-qadan couldn't shake the feeling he had lost out.

Chapter 15

'So you could tell it wasn't human?' Althorn asked Jakan-tar as he led the company of Sorean, human and other freed soldiers across the open grassy plain to meet Mihran and the rest of the army.

'Yes.' The cat-like captain blinked, which Olan translated as a shrug. 'You humans have a... distinctive aroma.'

'Oh, thanks!' Olan laughed.

Olan had told Althorn about the events of the Frarex village in the woods and he needed to know more about the shape-shifter that had masqueraded as Randeep. 'You will tell us if we have more in our ranks?' he asked.

'Yes.' The Sorean's large eyes stared up at Althorn, unnerving him a little. 'We are allies.'

'Thank you.' Althorn faked a smile. He was unsure of these creatures. The army needed help but how deadly were these short fighters compared with the might of the Lutamek robots? And who was to say they would stay loyal?

Althorn stared back down the line of soldiers following him: Samas was discussing tactics with one of Jakan-tar's fighters, while Lavalle was way back, wearing his new, black armour. The Sorean had offered Lavalle one of their hidden shields, but the knight would only accept a true metal suit of armour. Olan said the Sorean were natural blacksmiths and had built a bespoke suit in half a day using a strange metal held in each Sorean shield. If Lavalle was to be believed, the resulting armour was lighter than his undergarments.

A pang of guilt tightened Althorn's stomach as he remembered he hadn't told Lavalle about Euryleia's injury.

When he had first seen the group, traipsing out of the forest and onto the plain, Althorn had circled, unsure whether Olan and the others had been taken hostage by the Sorean, who outnumbered them. He had sped in, triggering a dozen of the Sorean shields as he passed, which had impressed him, then lobbed explosives at the fringes and watched as Samas, Lavalle and Olan each drew their weapons alongside the strange cats.

This was war, he told them, so he had to be sure.

Jakan-tar spoke, pulling Althorn out of his thoughts. 'You understand it's likely the shape-shifter killed your comrade to get his sword?'

'Yes.' Althorn wondered if it had been the real Randeep who had killed the lion, then imagined Randeep's broken body in a distant forest. 'He was also Crossley, yet I know he lives.'

Jakan-tar tilted its head. 'They can replicate bodies, faces and voices but nothing that can be separated from their body.'

'How much further?' Olan changed the subject. He had admitted regretting not chasing after John when he had had the chance and was clearly disturbed by the conversation.

'Two ridges,' Althorn said. He waited a moment before saying, 'We all failed them, you know, John and Randeep.'

'And you will be more vigilant in future,' Jakan-tar said.

'Yes and I hope–' Althorn felt an odd sensation brush his mind. It felt like his head was underwater. He held a hand up and slowed his pace. 'One moment.' He knew what came next.

Althorn, can you hear me? It was Mihran's voice. Unlike his call-to-arms broadcast, this one-to-one communication made Althorn feel dizzy. He closed his eyes to concentrate.

I hear you. Althorn spoke in his head and pushed the words out as Mihran had explained.

What is your position? Mihran asked.

We will be with you before midday. Althorn kept his sentences short to save the emotional energy it took to form and project the words.

And the new soldiers?

Althorn fixed an image of Jakan-tar in his mind and pushed it towards Mihran with the words: *Small, but good weapons.*

Good, Mihran replied and Althorn's wave of nausea melted away.

He opened his eyes and saw Olan watching him with a look of concern. 'Are you sick? Do you need water?'

'Sorry. Water, yes.' Althorn stretched his neck. 'Mihran was talking to me and I find it difficult to talk back.'

'How is that possible?' Olan asked.

'He uses his call-to-arms voice,' Althorn explained.

'And he can talk to us one at a time?' Olan asked.

Althorn nodded and drank from a canteen. 'Maybe he'll speak to you next.' He smiled, hoping the big Viking would feel as sick as he did.

'Hey!' Crossley was the first to greet them when they wound their way into the shallow valley where the human army hid. Li and Mihran were some steps behind. 'Good to see you. Where's John?'

'We didn't find him,' Althorn said quietly.

Crossley peered at the Sorean warriors who waited patiently. 'But you found some pets, I see.'

Jakan-tar's eyes widened. 'Pets?' It walked up to Crossley and looked him up and down. 'No weapon I see. Shall we duel?'

Crossley ignored him and looked at Olan. 'They talk too? That's cute.'

Althorn shook his head.

Samas and Lavalle arrived from the back of the line, catching Crossley's attention. 'Hey, Euryleia!' he called out. 'Your knight in shining armour's back.'

Lavalle cricked his neck, avoiding Crossley's taunt, and walked straight to Mihran. 'Commander.'

'Lavalle.'

The broad knight stared across the encampment. 'There are fewer here than I expected.'

Mihran shrugged. 'This land is wide. Are you expecting anyone in particular?'

'Prester John.' Lavalle cut to the chase, as was his way, Althorn thought. 'We heard rumours of his army in the Levant but it never came. I assumed it had been brought here, with us.'

Li overheard. 'I don't think we can expect this army any time soon, Lavalle. I'm sorry.' She turned to Mihran. 'According to my records, Prester John and his army were mythical – probably created by a tenth-century European monarch frustrated by the power of the Pope.'

Mihran nodded and held Lavalle's stare for a moment. 'I think you should visit Euryleia.' He gestured to where the Amazon slept.

Althorn stepped away to keep his distance, as was his way, and watched Samas update Li on their mission's successes and failures. Then Olan introduced the Sorean.

'May I introduce Captain Jakan-tar of the Sorean.' Olan looked proud in his gleaming armour.

Jakan-tar stepped forward, staring Mihran in the eyes. 'Commander, I am grateful to your men for the release of my soldiers. The Sorean offer our weapons in alliance to secure victory and exit from this land.'

Althorn noticed Mihran held back a smile as he was being addressed: if ever there was a man who enjoyed the power of a ritual, it was him.

'Your offer humbles me and is welcome. Do you have any intelligence on our enemy, the Brakari?' Mihran asked.

Jakan-tar blinked. 'We had an encounter with the scouts of a shelled species…'

Althorn left the conversation to wander around the camp. The army had grown – maybe fifty more soldiers swelled their numbers. Some stayed in groups: a red-coated troop kept to themselves, as did ten or eleven Asian soldiers, whom he assumed from what he had learnt these past days were Chinese. Near a fire, Lavalle crouched with his arm around Euryleia and, near the centre, Li was showing Samas a silver box that had all the hallmarks of Lutamek design. A spout of dust shot out of the centre, rising to three times their height, and paused for a second before dropping with an audible patter.

'Damn it!' she cursed before trying again.

'Maybe start with a smaller amount,' Samas suggested as Althorn walked away.

Althorn had found it difficult to walk at his slow pace today and his stomach reminded him how long it had been since he last ate. Maybe he could dash away for a short spell and find another deer to roast?

Raised voices made him turn and Althorn saw Sakarbaal turning visible beside Mihran, leaving a line of irate warriors behind him. He had heard rumours the gladiator's tattoos were merging to form patterns but had no idea of their camouflage abilities.

Althorn sped over to listen.

'One Brakari coming this way – probably a scout,' Sakarbaal said, out of breath. 'What shall we do?'

Mihran replied with an open face, 'Why, capture it of course.'

The anticipation of finishing his work with the human soldier made General Panzicosta's shell vibrate. The soft-bellied vertebrate had squealed under his every slice and had even experienced pain through his metallic arm. Panzicosta pictured ripping the metal out of the human's body and felt another tremble. Such nervous creatures, these humans, he thought.

If he had any sense of remorse, he would have felt sorry for the species who would be the Brakari's final enemy, but he didn't feel pity – he relished the power he would have over them.

'Victorio Brakarius, General.' A freshly hatched guard bowed low as Panzicosta left through the gatehouse's inner gates.

Panzicosta resisted the urge to ram his bludgeoning claw through the youngling's head carapace for slowing him down.

'Victorio Brakarius,' he growled back.

The holding cells were just a few minutes' walk away and Panzicosta pictured his victim, chained up and bleeding. The vision cheered him up. The information John had given him had been useless as far as he could tell, but he had passed it on all the same. The last Brakari had left the city and would carry word of the humans' weaknesses to Belsang, but Panzicosta decided he would wait until morning to leave.

If these humans were as weak as their bodies and adaptations suggested, Panzicosta wouldn't have to use his adaptation after all. Simple physical violence would suffice. His mouth-pieces gnashed against each other. They would be victorious and Belsang would have no further use for Doctor Cynigar, who could be disposed of, or Millok, who would be forced to submit to him.

The holes across his dark shell exhaled at the sight of the holding cells. As he breathed in he sensed blood. Sorean blood, he was sure. He sped up and spotted a ragged body on the path ahead.

'How did you get here?' Panzicosta loomed over the half-burnt cat-like creature pulling itself along the dirt floor with its remaining arm.

It didn't have the strength to look up, let alone fight back, as Panzicosta scooped up the broken body with a wide claw and pressed its belly into his mouthparts. As he fed, small red spikes struck out of the dying body, but the enhancement was too weak to even scratch Panzicosta's shell.

'Better than Skrift meat,' he mumbled, sucked up the last of the intestines and tossed the drained carcase to one side.

Drunk on the impending torture and the taste of Sorean flesh, Panzicosta caught a glimpse of another injured warrior cowering in a waste pile and looked up to see the broken shell of a mollusc soldier making its way up the city wall.

'What is happening here?' he yelled, seeing the first cell's door hanging open. 'Krotank?'

Pincers scratched at the doors as he stalked from cell to cell, finding only dead and paralysed soldiers. Had the injured soldiers overpowered Krotank and escaped? An unseen adaptation perhaps? Panzicosta puffed out moist air as his anger grew. He reached the main building and rushed into the darkness: all eyes and claws open.

'Krotank?' he hissed, as he pushed through to the back room where John Greene had been held captive. 'Where is the human?' He punched a hole through the door with his claw.

He scanned the room: the leg was on the wall but the human's bags had gone. Anything else missing? The Lutamek box remained on the table, but the Sorean shields were missing. Panzicosta almost laughed: the shields were useless. Doctor Cynigar had isolated their weakness days ago and his blocking technology had been taken to the battlefield when Belsang left.

'So now,' General Panzicosta weighed up the likely scenarios of what had happened in his building: no signs of a struggle and no blood trail, 'I will find who betrayed me.'

'I can help you with that.'

Panzicosta swung round to see Krotank in the doorway, wearing his spiked battle armour. Panzicosta closed down his eyes pair by pair until only his fighting eyes remained open. This was the traitor? The throwback with his extra claw and scarred shell? The urge to inflict pain rose and shook the General's body with hormones.

'There's a lot you could learn from your ancestors, Panzicosta.' Krotank backed out of the doorway to the mud path outside. 'Humility, patience… selflessness.'

'Don't give me that crap.' Panzicosta sped forward to get his large body clear of the building. 'Our species left that behind with you half-breeds centuries ago.' He lunged forward to jab five of his sharpest pincers at Krotank, but each point was deflected. 'You will die for betraying me.'

'Perhaps,' Krotank replied as they circled. 'But in death there is life.'

'I didn't realise how much shit you talk.' Panzicosta feigned an attack to the left then jumped in with a hammering smash to Krotank's carapace. The spikes on the black armour bent but Krotank simply groaned and stabbed back with a razor claw, cutting a thin line down Panzicosta's shoulder shell.

Panzicosta leapt back. 'What happened to Millok?' he asked, assuming Krotank had killed her.

'You can find out for yourself.' Krotank circled, unwilling to be drawn in to an attack.

'Cryptic as well? Another thing I could learn from my ancestors?'

'No, but you could learn to do things for yourself rather than relying on others,' Krotank replied.

Panzicosta snorted. 'I'll take care of this problem myself, don't you worry.'

He struck out with every appendage: hammering, slicing and spearing at the tenacious fighter. A warm feeling spread through his claws as a yellow light spread across Krotank, who seemed uninjured by the blows and cuts. 'What is this?' Panzicosta tried to pull back but was stuck.

'Another lesson.' Krotank sounded out of breath. 'This time in concealment.'

The yellow light turned orange. Had Krotank hidden an adaptation? Panzicosta felt a pang of admiration for the old soldier as he was thrown back in a ball of flame and pain.

General Panzicosta opened an extra pair of eyes to make sense of the shapes in the poor light of the medical dome. His shell creaked as he walked and, as he passed an overturned metal table, he caught a glimpse of the brilliant yellow scars running across his carapace, glowing like a cracked egg containing fire. With slow precision, the large Brakari limped past empty mud craters and sulphur baths to a low table and picked through an array of open bottles. Each contained different quantities of liquid which varied in colour and viscosity. None were labelled but Panzicosta knew what he was looking for. He selected a jar of electric-blue water and threw the contents over his damaged shell, flinching as a hissing sound echoed around the low dome. The yellow fractures sealed, leaving the dark natural armour unblemished.

A noise from one of the shadowed alcoves made him turn. 'Who's there?' Panzicosta expected Doctor Cynigar to float out of the darkness and deliver some poisonous remark.

'General,' a weak voice replied, 'it is I...'

Panzicosta recognised the tones of the Draytor in its natural form. 'You are injured?' It was an odd prospect for a shape-shifter.

'Yes.' It was fighting for breath. 'Millok and the human, they–'

'I know they escaped.' Panzicosta opened a set of his most sensitive eyes and focused on a quivering silhouette slumped in a hollow set in the dome's thick walls. He sighed at the sight. He could have fun tearing this creature apart... so many unknown qualities and challenges.

'I had them fooled,' the Draytor continued, 'but they had a Lutamek and–'

Panzicosta edged forward, looming over the injured creature, wondering how he could shackle such a gelatinous beast. 'You know, there is nothing here that can heal you,' he lied, sowing the seeds of torture.

'I will heal in time,' the Draytor responded with defiance. Panzicosta liked that. The stronger they were, the longer it took to break them, which prolonged the ecstasy. 'What are your orders, General?'

'My orders?' It still believed it would live. 'My orders are–' a sharp jab spiked Panzicosta's mind.

Panzicosta. The word echoed around his head.

The General closed all but one set of eyes and concentrated to reply. *Yes, Dominus.*

War is upon us. Why are you still in Abzicrutia?

Panzicosta fought to control his thoughts and reactions. Despite the distance, there was a chance Belsang could read every nuance of his psyche. *I have been dealing with traitors, Dominus,* he replied.

Who?

Krotank and Millok.

Millok? After all we have done for her? A pause. *It's no loss. The plan moves forward – the humans* will *meet us at the predestined destination.*

General Panzicosta waited. What was it Belsang wanted? The usual, he suspected: a good soldier who followed orders and never questioned his authority.

He needed to reply. *I will leave within the hour, Dominus.*

Good. Have you seen Doctor Cynigar?

No, Panzicosta replied.

The Draytor? I cannot commune with it directly.

Panzicosta stared at the vulnerable creature before him. He couldn't lie to his leader. This had to be another sacrifice for the Brakari cause.

It is here with me. Injured by the traitors. His shell slumped: he would have enjoyed a little pre-battle warm-up with the changeling.

Order it to round up the remaining Brakari. It can use whatever shape necessary. I need an attack group to enter the battle at my signal.

I can lead the group, Dominus, Panzicosta replied, fighting to control his annoyance.

No. I need you here. Now.

Yes, Dominus, Panzicosta replied and waited. Was the conversation over? Belsang's messages always began with a stabbing pain but didn't end with any obvious sensation. Worried his thoughts were being read, he thought about war and about dusting off his spiked, thermantium armour, which had saved his shell countless times.

'General?' the squirming Draytor asked, 'are you injured?'

Panzicosta realised how long he had been standing over the creature and intimidating it without muttering a word. 'It's time to move.'

'Where?' the Draytor asked.

Panzicosta ignored it and scuttled back to the table of bottles. He found a tall vial of green liquid, returned to the Draytor and threw it over its gelatinous body. The creature hissed and fizzed as the liquid took effect, causing convulsions and growth spurts. It visibly grew before Panzicosta, who stepped back with a sneer.

'Heal,' Panzicosta growled. 'Then you will fight to your death.'

'Wait!'

Millok froze as John's whisper cut through the crisp night air.

What had he seen that she couldn't? His two eyes were limited to a tiny range of visual frequencies compared to her own numerous eyes, and when she scanned the land she saw no movement or body heat. Her antennae didn't sense any telltale humidity changes either. Maybe it was a noise? His species' evolutionary path had led to developing a high level of aural sensitivity. Prey tended to have sharper hearing.

John was huddled on the tree-bark sled behind her and caught her glance. 'Go,' he whispered, and Millok scuttled onwards through the tall grass, keeping her body low. The swish of the sled hid other sounds as she ran. The sound and the wide trail they left in their wake were two giveaways she needed to avoid. This was Brakari war territory and she was a traitor. Her shell pieces creaked as she remembered what had happened to the last suspected traitor.

'We will find your army once we pass the crater lands,' she'd told John before they set off. 'But there is one battlefield you must see first.'

'Why?' John had asked.

'You will understand when you see it.'

'But Mihran's message was clear.' John's voice had risen. 'We have to meet my army at the location before sundown tomorrow or we will lose them.'

'Don't worry. It's on the way there. It will be worth it.' Even if it is a risk, Millok had thought.

Now they covered ground quickly despite the sled, which bumped and jolted across the long grass, and Millok recognised landmarks from the maps she had seen in Abzicrutia. Any intelligence she picked up before joining the human army would be crucial for the humans to accept her.

'How much further?' John asked.

'Not far. We can rest soon.'

The ground levelled off and the valley beyond came into view.

'What are they?' John shouted and pointed to an irregular series of hummocks which filled one end of the shallow valley, near woodland.

'Graves,' Millok replied, and images of violence, fire and death flickered through her mind.

A serpentine river marked the other end of the valley but disappeared from view as Millok ran downhill to the white obelisk, where John rolled off the sled and propped himself up with his crutch to read the script.

'Here the allied forces of the Ladrof and Scarpinelloss defeated the Brakari.'

Millok watched the young human and tried to read his emotions through his body language. He straightened a little then turned. 'Who were the Ladrof and Scarpinelloss?'

'It doesn't matter who they were.' Millok sensed a metallic tang in her mouth. She needed water. 'They were victorious and left through the gates. It's the land that is important.'

John hobbled in a small circle to take in the surroundings. 'Why?'

'Because this is where Belsang will lead your army, John. This is where he intends to destroy your species.'

'How do you know?' he asked.

'I've seen the plans.' Millok had never been part of the discussions but had heard Panzicosta's grumbles and found discarded maps in his torture rooms.

'But,' John's knee wobbled and he sat down, 'how can your commander be sure we will come here?'

'He has his methods,' Millok replied and felt sorry for the poor tortured creature. 'We have to go,' she said, 'I can't tell if the Lutamek followed us, but we have left a clear trail.'

The Brakari army had war rituals and wouldn't taint the battlefield until the day of war, but what if Belsang's scouts were watching? Millok thought. John stared at her and she wondered if it was a look of tiredness or revulsion on his face as he dragged his body back onto the makeshift sled.

Off they went again, uphill and across the flat grassy plains, keeping to the low ridges. A thought came to Millok as she ran: what if the other humans were weak like John? He had spirit, but physically he was vulnerable. His vital organs were open to attack and severing his brain from his body would be easy. If all the human soldiers had the same weaknesses they were sure to lose to the Brakari army. Even the enslaved troops were tougher than these soft bipeds.

'We need to head in that direction,' John shouted, pointing to the left.

Millok adjusted her course accordingly. Apparently, John had been able to sense a beacon since hearing his commander's message. It was a good sign the humans had a communications system but it was nothing compared with what Belsang was capable of. The humans had only been in this world for a number of days after all, so why should she expect more?

'We should see them soon.' John was sitting upright, eagerly scanning the horizon.

Millok slowed as they passed over a ridge and the land beyond opened up before them: a vast skyline and everything in between tinged brown. No landmarks. No signs of life or an army.

'Are you sure this–' Millok skidded to a halt and raised her fighting claws. Something had been close: she had felt the swish of grass. She raised her antennae and tasted moisture.

John rolled off his sled and pulled himself up with his crutch.

'I heard him.' John laughed.

'Him?' Millok scanned the nearest clumps of dry grass for signs of movement. 'Can you see your army?'

'No, but they're here.' John was still smiling.

A new scent came to Millok: a forest odour of leaves and earth.

John was next to her now. 'It's alright. Just stay still and don't fight. I'll vouch for you.'

What could he see that she couldn't? Her spiracles gasped for air as she fought her instinct to run. What was that creaking sound? And why was the grass turning dark? Stay calm and trust him – you saved his life, Millok told herself, he will save yours.

Moving quicker than she could react, scores of green plant shoots leapt out from the swaying grass. Tendrils gripped her limbs and claws, rendering her immobile in a flash.

'John?' She had to control the urge to fight back.

'It's okay,' he replied as a mass of bark and green leaves rolled up the hill, tearing strips out of the ground with spiked roots.

'Hello, Mata, how are you?' John said.

A rush of wind tore a line through the grass. 'Althorn? Where are you?'

Millok watched a blur appear beside John and turn into a hooded human. 'John! We thought we'd lost you. Did you receive Mihran's message?'

'Yes. I managed to escape and followed the beacon.'

'What have they done to you?' Althorn pointed at his knotted trouser leg and turned to Millok. 'Is this creature responsible?'

'No,' John said. 'There's a lot to explain, but you can trust her.' He turned to the huge ball of tree and grass. 'Mata, please let her go – she is an ally.'

Althorn stared at Millok, who decided staying silent was her best option. 'Are you sure? She's one of them, isn't she? A Brakari.'

'Yes, but she helped me escape.' John looked at her. 'In fact, without her I doubt I'd still be alive.'

Althorn rubbed his bearded face. 'I believe you, John, but we have to be safe.' He turned. 'Mata, hold her but don't harm her. Let's get back to Mihran.'

The vines gripping Millok lifted her into the air and carried her downhill. The grassland ahead was a continuous band of dry prairie. Had they built tunnels? Millok wondered. But as they descended further, a distorted region became apparent. Maybe the humans didn't see it, but one pair of Millok's eyes saw a dome-like structure. They walked through a brown mist and the human army was revealed. Millok prepared herself for a hostile welcome. Scores of soldiers, who had been eating or cleaning weapons, turned to stare at her. The army wasn't large and the humans weren't well equipped or individually much bigger than John.

'...and it's a female, you say?' A tall human in red clothing was talking to John.

'Yes. Talk to her, but treat her well.'

The Commander walked to Millok and she remained calm. A pressure built in her head shell. Was he probing her neural pathways? It was a crude method but she opened up her recent memories to him.

'How is it you could see our protective dome?' he asked.

A crowd was growing around them. Millok knew she had to put on a show if she was to survive. 'No introductions, Commander?' she asked.

'What need is there? You are Millok. And I am known as Mihran. You are an enemy soldier. Our captive. Answer my question.'

Millok tensed but felt the tendrils tighten: this plant was stronger than it looked. 'I am a Brakari rebel. I have saved John Greene from certain death and I wish to join your army.'

'How do we know you are not a spy?' a short human in a brown uniform shouted.

'He has read my memories. What did you see, Commander?' Millok asked.

Mihran raised his chin. 'Answer my question and I shall tell you.'

Millok had to give him something. Not everything at once or she would no longer be useful. 'Your camouflage – the dome of dust surrounding your camp – uses a modulating frequency. Each time it shifts, the particles lose momentum for a split second. Brakari eyes spot this easily.'

Mihran whispered to a soldier, whose face was obscured by a reflective plate, and then returned his gaze. 'And this battlefield you showed John, you fought there?'

'Yes, I was present and I–'

Mihran turned and Millok focused on a blurred shape advancing on them. A human appeared next to him and she stayed silent.

'What is it, Sakarbaal?' Mihran asked. 'What news?'

'The Lutamek,' – he flicked his head – 'they've returned.'

'It's good to be back.' John bit another strip of venison from the chunk Euryleia had handed him.

'Well, it's good to have you back.' Crossley looked genuinely happy. 'Although you'll probably want to join the redcoats now they're here, right?' He gestured to where a dozen British soldiers camped round a fire using their maroon coats as blankets and tending their wounds with what John recognised as sphagnum moss.

'I doubt they'd have me.' John lifted his gun-arm. Why would they? he thought.

'That's their loss, my friend,' Crossley replied.

John felt a pang of guilt in his stomach. How could he have believed the Draytor who had taken him from the Frarex village was Crossley?

'What is it, John?' Euryleia asked when he found himself staring into the flames.

'I…' John didn't know where to begin. He hadn't told anyone his story yet.

Lavalle laid a hand on Euryleia's shoulder. 'He'll tell us in his own time.' The knight glanced at the knot in John's trouser leg.

'Sure.' Crossley sat with the fire between him and Lavalle. 'But there's no point bottling it all up, hey?' He looked at John. 'You're with friends now, so you can say what you want.'

John wrinkled his nose as he felt his eyes water. Crossley was right – these were his friends. He felt like he'd been through more with these men and women these past two weeks than during any battle in Belgium.

'I…' John's voice broke, so he coughed and started again. 'I thought I saw my son, Joe and–' A thought came to him. 'You know, when I first arrived here I thought my wife would be here – I thought we were all dead.' He paused and breathed in deeply. 'But it's just a trick. One big trick. I mean, what are we here for?'

'To fight,' Lavalle said.

Crossley shrugged. 'Probably.'

John took a sip of water. 'I thought I saw Joe, then I thought I saw you.' He looked at Crossley. 'Then the bastards who tricked me tied me up, stuck pins in me and cut off my leg.'

Silence. The faces said it all. John saw the trail of a tear run down Euryleia's cheek.

'It's not the pain,' John said. 'It's the loss. The emptiness.'

Lavalle stared into the fire and said, 'But there are always moments of hope.'

'True.' John nodded and looked to where Millok was guarded by Li, Samas and Sakarbaal. She looked uncomfortable as she floated in a prison of light: a gift from the Lutamek.

Behind them, Mihran and Althorn walked with the Lutamek robots. He tried to remember the names Crossley had told him. The leader was Two-zero-three and their doctor was Ten-ten and… was that Millok's robot?

'Give me a minute.' John pushed himself up. 'No, I'm fine.' He waved away helping hands, leant on his crutch and hopped towards the commanders, trying to cut them off before they reached Millok.

'…torturing my soldiers in the Brakari city,' Two-zero-three was talking, 'and we demand retribution.'

'And you shall have it,' Mihran replied. 'Just not today. Ah, John.'

'Commander.' John nodded and glanced at the Lutamek leader then back to Mihran. 'Millok saved me. You can't kill her.'

'John.' Mihran held a palm up. 'Nobody is talking about killing prisoners.'

'But we demand retribution,' Two-zero-three repeated. 'Your commander tells me the Brakari crippled you, and Two-eight-four tells me you do not desire revenge.'

'Two-eight-four?' John pictured the markings on the Lutamek they had freed.

'It was present when you chose not to kill the Draytor – is this a human weakness?'

'No, I…' John stuttered.

'Then you released Two-eight-four from imprisonment. Is this another weakness?' The Lutamek turned to Mihran. 'Is your army weak, Commander? Should we break our pact and search for other allies to help free our kin?'

Mihran clenched his teeth before replying, 'Do not test me. Our alliance will hold because you need us. The Brakari can overpower your systems. You offer us scouts and information. We offer you diversion and victory. We have one day left and *will* fight tomorrow.' He pointed at John. 'One of my men has already freed one of your soldiers. Proof of our intent. Instead of insulting us, please show gratitude.'

John stood dumbstruck. Had they really been here only thirteen days? It felt longer.

'Your information is correct,' Two-zero-three replied. 'The Brakari have the ability to control our components, which is why, despite our martial prowess, we cannot meet them in battle.'

Mihran's eyes narrowed. 'What we need is information.' He looked at Two-zero-three. 'And gratitude.'

Ten-ten gestured at John. 'I can construct him a leg.'

John felt his cheeks warm. Could they really give him his leg back? 'Yes, a leg would be good, but what about this?' He raised his gun-arm in its sling.

A blue light on Ten-ten's shoulder pulsed and a criss-cross pattern ran over his body. 'Interesting,' the robot said. 'But this change is irreversible.'

'Will the gun fire again?' Mihran asked.

'Perhaps,' Ten-ten replied. 'But not with the original ammunition.'

John sighed. 'Just the leg then, thank you.'

'Come. We can fix it now.'

Ten-ten walked away and John limped after him.

'Sit.' Ten-ten pointed to a rock. 'I have the measurements.'

John looked back at Mihran and Two-zero-three as they discussed the new tactics. A new Lutamek joined them and projected a map onto a scrap of bare earth. John recognised the Brakari battlefield Millok had shown him. The Sorean joined the discussions, along with some human soldiers.

A shape loomed over John and he looked up. 'Here.' It was Two-eight-four, the robot he had freed. It offered a piece of metal to John. 'For your leg.'

John shook his head. 'No, you need this more than me, after what they did to you.'

'To us both.' The metal didn't move. 'Take it.'

Reluctantly, John raised his good hand and took the warm tube of shiny metal. 'Thank you.' He looked in what he assumed were the robot's eyes.

'Thank you,' Two-eight-four replied and walked away.

'I'll see to him next.' Ten-ten took the metal rod with his mammoth hands.

John watched open-mouthed as the Lutamek's eight fingers twisted, screwed and welded pieces of dark-grey and black metal together and around each other. It was like watching an origami master. Out of the shapes a leg and foot were forming, with rotating ankles and flexible toes.

'Here.' Ten-ten held out its creation with a hint of pride in its voice. 'Please try it.'

John untied his trouser knot and pressed his stump into the warm cup at the top of the false leg. A tingle ran across his skin where it touched, making him shiver.

'The material is sensitive to organic components,' Ten-ten explained. 'It's how our inert body parts interact with our biological material.'

John nodded, not sure he completely understood. If he closed his eyes he could pretend he had his old leg back. He wiggled the metal toes and flexed the ankle. John lifted his leg and was surprised how light it was. He stepped forward and smiled.

'Good?' Ten-ten asked.

Better than good, John thought. 'Yes, thank you.'

John took a step, then another. He felt a smile creeping across his face. 'Yes!' He whispered and walked a circle, then walked to where the soldiers were watching shapes moving on the floor. 'What is it?' John asked Crossley and tried to get a better view.

'Movies of old battles apparently. The Brakari... evil-looking bastards.'

'Yes, I know.' John caught a glimpse of three blue-shelled Brakari circling a Lutamek and felt a shiver in his belly.

His hand slipped under his shirt and he remembered he'd lost Joe's tin soldier back in Panzicosta's torture hut. He looked at Millok, trussed up like an animal ready for slaughter, and an idea came to him.

He picked out Mihran and walked over to him. 'Commander, I...'

'Ah, your leg.' Mihran gave him the once-over. 'Good.'

'No, I wanted to say, I mean... What the Lutamek said about the Brakari controlling them, I think I know how to stop it... I saw a

Lutamek box.' John unhooked his bag and pulled out one of the marbles, which attracted a look from a Sorean. 'And I found these. The Brakari who tortured me said they are shields.'

Mihran stared at him.

'Millok can help me get back in and get it,' John said.

'No,' Mihran replied and nodded at the hooded figure at the edge of the group. 'Althorn will go.'

Chapter 16

Althorn watched the Lutamek's projection of miniature battles play out on the dusty floor. The squat Brakari soldiers had more weaponry and shielding than the scouts they had fought, which the Lutamek suggested had been clones and not the adapted, hardened warriors they were likely to fight on the battlefield tomorrow.

Tomorrow they would fight, Althorn thought. Would tomorrow be their last day in this land or would it be his last day alive?

Before becoming a paid killer, Althorn had fought many battles but, unlike other soldiers, the thrill of war had never gripped him. Every clash and scrap had been a terrifying fight for survival, not the artful display of sword dancing and heroism the song weavers sang about. He'd feared for his life more times than he could remember and, each time, had taken another's life in order to survive. That weighed heavy on him… he pictured his sister's dying eyes and shook his head.

'Althorn.' Mihran's voice made him turn quickly, sending his body into a blur.

'Commander.'

'Another mission.' Mihran flicked his head and Althorn walked with him. 'As you heard, the Lutamek cannot fight unless we find their shield generator. I want you to go to Abzicrutia and retrieve it.'

'Yes, Commander.' Althorn felt his stomach tense: being away meant he would have to communicate through Mihran's mental net.

'John can give you the details – question Millok as well. Then go. It's highly likely you'll intercept the Brakari army. I need to know everything about them.' Mihran wore a look that suggested he was expecting questions.

'Yes, Commander,' Althorn replied. 'If the city is abandoned and I know what I'm looking for, it will be fine.'

'Good.' Mihran nodded. 'And if you see anything else of interest…'

'Such as?' Althorn asked.

'The silver gates. Also, I have a theory there are more human soldiers out there. Other fighting species too – losers who are too few to fight a battle. If you find any…'

'Yes.' Althorn wasn't sure how he would be able to convince anyone to join their fight, but Olan had managed it with the Sorean. 'I'll try.'

Althorn was soon speeding across the grassy plain, following a memorised map. To his left he saw the deep greys and shadows of a tall ruined fortress. Beyond was the valley where the Brakari wanted to fight, according to John.

Althorn found himself drifting again, as he did when he felt tense, and ran at high speed. He had to loosen his shoulders and work the stress out. There was a lot riding on him. He had to report back on the Brakari army, locate the Lutamek shield and find new allies. All in half a day.

He tried to clear his mind and enjoy the moment: let the rushing wind wash away the weight of expectation. He thrived on the freedom and speed. Here he was. Anonymous. Invisible. Untouchable. He gave a wild howl as he sped through a long valley.

Then he saw a Brakari scout.

It was perched between two rocks at the head of the valley, its blue shell standing out against a world of dull browns. The Lutamek had told him to expect five scouts in each party, so Althorn skirted in a wide arc around the scout and sped to a nook hidden in a scattering of rocks. Here he could see in all directions and keep his back against solid rock. Everything was quiet. Althorn scanned the immense plain below and caught his first sight of the Brakari army. It was the largest army – the largest group of beings – he had ever seen. Hundreds of shadows moved in an arrow-shaped pattern. He squinted but, other than the odd shade of blue, he could only make out some large beasts among the throng. His eyes followed the trail back to where the ground met the hazy horizon and saw the silhouette of a city.

Althorn took a gulp of water and chewed on a lump of dried meat from his satchel. He needed to replenish his energy: it was time to contact Mihran. He sat still, closed his eyes and pictured the map the Lutamek had shown him. He imagined a red dot where he sat and marked a blue dot at the head of the valley where he had seen the scout. On the plain, he marked where Abzicrutia appeared and painted the shape of the Brakari army. He pushed the image back to where the human army waited and followed it up with the words: *Enemy moving into position.*

Althorn rested his head as the pressure headache came, followed by Mihran's voice. *More detail. Troop numbers. Allies. Weaponry.*

The pressure disappeared and Althorn opened his eyes, breathing deeply. Mihran was to the point as ever.

The Brakari army moved slowly across the plain, leaving a low cloud of dust in its wake. Ahead of the main group, isolated pockets of dust belonged to scouting parties, which was odd, because if they were that far ahead surely they would also be… He heard a noise, leapt up and ran away as fast as he could; painting an erratic path down the hill, then back up behind the rocks. He caught a glimpse of blue – that was all he needed – and sped off.

Continuing his unpredictable, snaking path, Althorn sped downhill to where the great Brakari army had trampled the grassland flat. There was less chance of running into scouts here, he thought. Plus he had to get a close look at the army before the scouts raised the alarm.

He closed in. The sheer number of creatures of varying sizes overwhelmed Althorn. He could estimate the numbers: a hundred light-blue scorpion Brakari; two packs of large, humpbacked wolves; scores of sparking Lutamek; a group of furred soldiers; at least fifty dark-blue Brakari and, in the centre, a lumbering mammoth, similar to the corpses they had camped inside with Peronicus-Rax. On its back a small creature gave off a phosphorescent blue light, which pulsed and pulled at Althorn as he sped past. It was a strange colour. Piercing, yet soft.

'No!' Althorn veered away, realising he was being drawn like a moth to a flame.

Had he strayed too near? His head started to ache like when Mihran talked to him, but he pushed the feeling away. He had to get to safety. He needed food and water, but had to keep running. If he slowed they would see him. His thoughts came and went as his energy waned. Shelter. He needed shelter. A small grove of trees was nearby, so he pulled in. His head was spinning as he slowed down to a run then a jog and stopped to take a sip from his canteen.

Must contact Mihran, he thought, but his head was so heavy. He just needed to stop and build the energy to talk to Mihran. Just a quick rest, he thought, and stumbled behind a tree where he rested his head on a root and closed his eyes.

Althorn didn't know how long he had been asleep. He hadn't dreamt but he felt a presence and looked up to see several pairs of eyes staring at him. He felt groggy and blinked as a wave of nausea ran through his belly.

He forced himself to focus.

'Escape,' a voice said.

But the eyes… he could see they were set in an odd-looking face whose features seemed to be in the wrong position. No teeth, but plenty of sharp, moving objects making sounds, surrounded by a glimmering, dark-blue shell.

Slowly, Althorn realised the creature was talking to him.

'…another human.' The large Brakari's mouthparts twisted and snapped. 'Just what I need after the last one was so rudely taken from me.'

'Can you see it?' Dakaniha asked Kastor, who crouched beside him as they peered over a mound of charred metal and bone.

'No, you say it's white?' Kastor asked.

Dakaniha nodded.

'Hard to see in the morning light.'

Dakaniha didn't need to turn to see the Spartan squinting. He had all four eyes open, giving him an almost full view of his surroundings. 'It's moving again. Long, thin arms and legs.'

'Ah, yes, I see it.' Kastor was smiling.

Dakaniha kept his front eyes fixed on the sinuous, bleached creature as a gangly comrade joined it. The creatures were skirting around the battle debris and closing in on where Gal-qadan's army slept. He had never seen one before but Dakaniha's people knew of such creatures.

'Come on.' Kastor beckoned him over.

They had been on sentry duty but Kastor wanted to search for the ghostly samurai who trailed Gal-qadan's men. They had seen no sign of the three hazy trails and there hadn't been a wisp of moist air to be seen when this threat had arrived, skulking and loping across the ground.

Kastor stopped and pointed. 'They're throwing something,' he whispered.

Dakaniha saw clouds of powder drifting on the morning breeze in the direction of the sleeping soldiers.

'They're too far away. They'll move closer,' Dakaniha whispered.

'Let's get in their way then!' Kastor beamed and unclipped his sword.

The two men kept low and tiptoed across to intercept the white creatures – but Dakaniha had second thoughts. What if these creatures really were the Yunwi-Tsunsdi his tribe knew of? Attacking them would be disastrous! Their army would be hounded every step of the way, through forest, prairie and mire.

They came to a gap and he caught a closer glimpse of them. No, these creatures were too big to be Yunwi-Tsunsdi. And ugly, with their long faces and hollow eyes.

Kastor made a series of quick hand signals and crawled off without looking back, leaving Dakaniha with no way to tell him it was a stupid plan. They needed more men. He threw a glance at the sleeping soldiers, less than twenty paces away. Should he wake them and scare off the white creatures? No, he and Kastor could take care of these two. Keeping his front eyes fixed on the white beings, Dakaniha slipped his bow free. A tickling sensation crept up his neck and he froze – something had moved behind him. Something in his peripheral vision. In one fluid movement, he pulled an arrow from his quiver, rolled onto his right shoulder and, as his back hit the floor, fired an arrow.

Everything slowed down.

He saw a white silhouette and an outstretched hand. His arrow disappeared through a thin cloud of dust and, when he opened his eyes, the arrow had hit home.

His wife's body lay, twitching, with his arrow in her chest. 'No!' Dakaniha shouted and the world sped up again. He scrambled over and pulled her limp body to his. Her eyes were empty, staring up to the clouds. Her head rolled back into the long grass, where flowers tangled with her long hair.

'Adsila,' he whispered, 'what have I done?'

He stroked her hair and stared at her face, absorbing every detail: her forehead; long eyelashes; straight nose; the curve of her lips; the arrow embedded in her chest. It was clear she would die.

He had killed her.

'What are you doing, you crazy fool?'

Dakaniha looked up and scowled at Kastor, who stood over him. 'This is my wife!' he shouted.

Even in his pain, Dakaniha could tell something was different about Kastor. His voice was the same but he wasn't European any more – he was Aniyunwiya. Even his clothes and weapons were Aniyunwiya.

'The other one is dead. What *are* you doing with this one?' Kastor said.

Dakaniha could feel his wife's breathing slow and turned to her. She looked so peaceful. Then a spasm took her and she coughed, bringing scarlet bubbles to her lips. 'No,' Dakaniha whimpered. So beautiful. How did she get here? He stared at the face he had longed to see for so long, absorbing each tiny detail.

Details that were changing.

Her nose was shrinking. Her hair was falling away.

'What's happening?' Dakaniha gripped her tight. He turned to Kastor, who was frowning, and said nothing. 'What can I do?' Dakaniha mumbled and stared at Adsila as her face lengthened and her eyes sunk to become two deep holes. He dropped her on the dusty ground and scrambled back as a white glow emanated through her skin.

'It's dead.' Kastor patted Dakaniha on the shoulder. 'Come on.'

'It?' Dakaniha pushed away Kastor's hand. 'That was my wife!' Even as he said the words, he knew it was wrong. How could it be his wife? He breathed heavily and rubbed his eyes, kneeling in the dust.

Behind them the rest of their army, woken by the shouting, was walking over. Among them, Gal-qadan stared with his harsh, unforgiving eyes. 'Are they dead?' he asked.

'Yes,' Kastor replied, cleaning his sword.

'Yes, Khan,' Dakaniha replied. He glanced back at his dead wife, but saw only the bleached body of a long-limbed creature with his arrow in its chest.

'And the samurai?' Gal-qadan asked.

'No sign of them,' Kastor replied.

'Then we proceed.' He pointed to the sky. 'Dawn is upon us.'

After a day spent in silence, this land's poor excuse for a sun was low behind its hazy blanket, and another night was approaching. New colours merged with the green of the sky and painted the rolling hills with pleasing shades, yet Dakaniha only thought of his wife. Even if it had been a trick, some hallucination, it had still felt like her. It had been her warmth and her scent. Now, Dakaniha just wanted to go home to the real Adsila. But what would he become if he rode off now and found his way back to his tribe? He would be a failed warrior. Someone who ran from war. A coward.

'We're nearly there.' Kastor looked back from his tocka and flashed his customary grin. 'I can feel it.'

The Spartan had been like that all day, throwing comments over his shoulder or slowing down to make conversation, but Dakaniha had remained silent. Still, he had learnt a thing or two from the information Kastor had gleaned from Gal-qadan and the huge alien who had joined their army for half a day before stomping off on his long, tree-trunk legs.

'I will watch you and will return for the weapon.' Those had been the giant's last words according to Kastor.

Dakaniha had seen the weapon in action. White light shot from the metal tube as though it harnessed the power of lightning.

But it didn't interest Dakaniha.

'We can't get anyone to ride the metal tocka,' Kastor said in another attempt to get him talking. 'And I can't blame them – too sore on your arse, surely?' He was grinning again. 'Oh well, if you won't talk, I'll do the talking for you…'

Dakaniha wished he could go back to before he could understand the chatty Spartan.

'...but nobody could work out why the holes would be like that – spaced out neatly. Probably made by water...'

Rather than tell Kastor to be quiet, Dakaniha played with his new eyes, opening their lids a fraction at a time or squinting and blinking. He could see a range of colours. Deep purples through to blue and, when fully open, he could detect a light that gave the tocka and humans warm colours: red in their core and green at their extremities. It was like he could see their souls.

Now, as the day ended, the colours were less vivid. Dakaniha's eyes were tired and they settled on Gal-qadan, who led the army. Every now and then the leader rubbed his forehead which, through Dakaniha's new eyes, pulsated red and pink.

They were climbing a long, steady hill with a set of rocks standing proud at its peak.

'...apparently Peronicus-Rax says our enemy will be an army of creatures with shells. Like the ones we fought in the marsh.' Kastor was still talking.

Dakaniha ignored him. He wasn't sure if it was the light, but something about the rocks ahead looked strange to him. He opened all four eyes and tilted his head. He was sure he saw patches of red on the rocks.

'So I said–'

'Stop!' Dakaniha silenced Kastor with an outstretched hand.

Their tocka kept walking but Dakaniha felt his steed's muscles tense: they sensed it too.

'We have to stop.' Dakaniha's neck tingled.

'But we're nearly there,' Kastor replied, 'I can feel the–' His words were cut off and his spear was in his hand.

The rocks on the hilltop had split into three separate shapes. Dakaniha could see legs, arms and heads, but they weren't human. They weren't even animal.

'Halt!' A voice boomed out from the silhouettes, followed by a blue light that held Dakaniha and his tocka still. He tried to turn his head but he was stuck. Even his tocka stopped mid-stride, as did the tocka ahead of them. The three shapes moved closer and Dakaniha saw movement behind them. Had these creatures been hiding in the ground? Why hadn't the tocka sensed them?

'Do not struggle,' the deep voice continued, 'you are not in danger.'

'*You* will be when you release me,' Kastor hissed.

Dakaniha focused on the nearest giant and fully opened all four eyes. Nothing. No, maybe a hint of orange, but nothing compared to the colour of humans and tocka. Were these giants made of metal?

'You will be scanned before entry.'

If these were the guards, Dakaniha thought, this new army was going to be impressive.

One of the metal men swept a blue light over each soldier and tocka and, one by one, they were allowed to pass, over the hilltop and into the valley beyond. Despite a few shouts and protests, the men rode on.

Dakaniha followed the trail and rode open-mouthed into the valley beyond and under a dust dome, which shaded a world teeming with human soldiers, cat-like creatures and metal giants. When every man had passed the metal guards, Gal-qadan led the diamond-shaped formation of tocka downhill to a man who stood proudly with hands on hips. Even in this light, Dakaniha could see the rich colour of the scarlet cloak that flowed about him in the evening breeze. Oddly, his head flashed a purple colour compared with the scores of soldiers who stood behind him, who were red, just like Gal-qadan's men.

'Welcome!' The red-robed man held his arms out.

Dakaniha recognised the voice from the call to arms. He turned to see Gal-qadan, who remained stony faced.

'Welcome to our army.' The man even had a red beard, Dakaniha noticed. 'And,' the man turned to face the soldiers who had congregated behind him, 'may I introduce Gal-qadan and his battalion of horsemen.'

Dakaniha gasped. How did he know his name? He turned to Gal-qadan who, for the first time, looked shocked.

'Gal-qadan,' the red man continued, 'is our new cavalry captain.'

John heard Joe's laughter and his shoes, which tapped an erratic rhythm on the bare floorboards. He pictured the scuffed sky-blue leather and the shiny buckles.

'Wake up, Daddy!'

John could tell Joe was smiling by the sound of his voice.

'I'm asleep,' John said with a smile and kept his eyes closed.

Something told him if he opened them Joe would disappear.

'But it's time to get up, Daddy.' He sounded serious now. 'It's time.'

'Time for what?' John asked, still smiling. 'Is it time for breakfast?'

'No, silly Daddy.' Joe giggled and swung his legs, knocking the bed. 'It's not breakfast time.' He giggled. 'It's time to fight.'

'What?' John sat up and opened his eyes. It was dark and he could feel bare earth beneath him.

Crossley was standing over him. 'Sorry buddy, I know you need your sleep, but we're outta here.'

'What? I…'

'Mihran says we need to leave. Battle day and all that jazz.' Crossley faked a smile and picked up a box. 'He wants us on the battle site with food in our bellies before it starts.' He shifted the box in his arms. 'Anyway, Samas needs this so…'

John muttered something unintelligible and Crossley walked off. The American's nervousness made John feel edgy and yet, for the first time in this land, he knew there would be no surprise attack or wild animals leaping out today. Today was their last day and they would fight. They had to fight! Crossley had told him about the burnt bodies: cowards were killed.

Joe was right, John thought, and looked around.

The whole camp was alive with soldiers packing bags, moving boxes and putting out fires. John could see the army had grown while he slept. More humans were dotted around the place, and were those horses? The silhouettes were unmistakable, but he couldn't hear them neighing.

'How are you?' Li walked over, her visor reflecting the light of the nearest fires. 'Are you good to travel?'

'Yes.' John tapped his leg. 'Good as new.'

'The injured soldiers are travelling with the Lutamek if you would prefer that?'

'No, I can walk. It's not that far anyway.' John wasn't in any pain and he didn't want to be lumped in with the injured men.

'If you're sure,' Li said.

'You can help me up though.' John offered his hand and Li pulled him up. 'One more metal limb and I'll turn into a Lutamek.' John lifted his gun-arm and gave a timid smile.

'What doesn't kill you…' Li started.

'You know that phrase?' John asked.

'Sure. My database is filled with historic information.'

'Right.' John pulled his strap tight, bringing his gun-arm against his chest, and a thought came to him. 'Do you think after all this – after we get through the silver gates – do you think we'll go home and I'll have my normal arm and leg back?'

'I…' Li hesitated.

'Honestly?' John looked at her.

Li flipped her visor up. She was more attractive than he'd remembered. 'Honestly? No. You have been physically injured. It's permanent.'

'What about Euryleia's hand?' John asked.

'A one-off.'

John glanced down at his metallic arm and leg. 'I don't want Joe to be scared of me.' He pictured Joe's frightened face.

'He won't be,' Li answered.

'How do you know? I mean, he's just a young boy and you don't know him. He's smart and brave but…'

'No.' Li's stare was hard. 'He won't see you like this because he won't ever see you, John.'

'What?' John's good knee felt weak. 'No, I have to get back to Joe. You don't understand – his mother died and he needs me.' His head felt light and, as he took a step forward, his leg wobbled.

Li grabbed him by the shoulders. 'Come on, take a seat.' She led him to a box and crouched beside him. 'Look. I'm not sure how to say this, John.'

The sounds around them disappeared and John looked into Li's eyes. She didn't want to hurt him, he could see that.

'This world is real. Your injuries are permanent.' She spoke slowly, as though talking to a child.

John nodded.

'You won't see your son again because he died a long, long time ago.'

John shook his head and blinked, pushing tears down his cheeks. 'No,' he mouthed.

Li continued, 'The Lutamek and I theorise we were taken from our planet and transported many light years away. That means a lot of time has passed. Do you understand, John?'

John sighed. He looked away, then back at Li and nodded. Of course time had passed. How else could he explain Crossley or Delta-Six being here? Or Li? Time passes and we all die, he knew that. He took a lungful of air. If he was honest, deep down John had already known he would never see Joe again but, as with Rosie, he'd allowed himself the tiniest hope he would. One day, he'd hoped, they would all be reunited as the family they should have been.

'You understand that decades passed between when you were taken from your war and when I was on Earth?' Li asked.

'Yes.'

'John, in my records I have details of a British soldier. Can I read them to you?'

John frowned. What was she talking about? He nodded.

'Lieutenant Joseph Viktor Greene.'

John's eyes widened. 'But that's Joe!'

'Born on the Fifteenth of April, 1912.'

'The day Rosie died…' John looked down as Li carried on.

'Enrolled in the British army 1939 at the outbreak of World War Two.'

Crossley's war. John looked over to where the American lifted boxes onto a makeshift trailer. Did he know Joe? Had they fought together during one of his battle tales?

'…Overlord, decorated for Operation…' Li listed a run of battles and medals John had never heard of.

Was she really talking about little Joe? John's stomach tingled with pride at what his son had achieved. Then his stomach tensed: his boy had been through what John had seen. He had seen death. Close personal death. He had killed men. Why? John's war had been the war to end all wars, yet the next generation had been dragged into the same carnage and destruction. His stomach was a tight ball, just like his good hand, which clenched a fist, and his gun-fingers clicked and twisted inside their metal prison.

'...married and had three children...'

They were the grandchildren John never met. He would have been a good grandfather; not like his own, John thought. Even giving Joe his grandfather's name as a middle name hadn't pleased the old whinger.

'...attended every memorial service at the Cenotaph until his death on the Tenth of October, 1996.'

He'd died.

His little Joe was dead.

Silent tears ran down John's cheeks.

Everything was empty and void of meaning. He stared at the ground: the colourless, featureless soil. This was how he'd felt when Rosie had died. Empty. Useless.

John had one purpose: Joe.

After Rosie died, everything John had endured had been for Joe: the trenches; the fighting; the killing. He'd stayed strong for Joe.

And now?

Everyone John ever knew or loved was dead and, when they were alive, they'd believed John had died in the war. They'd mourned him and Joe had gone on to live a full life without him. Without him or Rosie.

John had nothing to fight for now.

Li was still speaking. 'He probably visited the Cenotaph in your memory as much as his comrades'.'

John looked up and stared into Li's dark eyes. 'Cenotaph?'

'A monument for the missing. For those whose bodies were never found.'

John pictured Johnson. His serene face as he climbed out of the trench, never to be seen again. 'And he went there for me?' John asked.

Li held his gaze. 'You were reported as missing in action, John. They never found your body.'

'Well of course not.' John looked away and breathed in hard

through his nose. He could hear his gun clicking. 'Of course they didn't find my…' He stopped before he swore. '…I'm here,' he whispered.

'Everyone here has been taken from their loved ones, just like you, John.' Li looked up at the dark sky and said, 'And I can barely imagine the effort and technology involved in bringing us all here.'

John couldn't think of anything capable of transporting them here. He pictured the trains and ships, but anything bigger was too much to think about. His chest felt hot, as though his anger was being held captive behind his ribs. If he wanted to release it, he knew he could. He sensed what he had to do to channel that power, but he pictured Joe and his mind calmed.

'Do you know anything else about Joe?' he asked.

'No, that's everything I have,' Li said.

John stood up, feeling the strength return to his legs. 'Thank you, Li. I appreciate your honesty.' His arms felt stronger too. The toes on his false leg gripped the soil.

'Are you okay?' Li asked.

'Yes, I…' John looked around. 'I'm okay.' He spoke without thinking. He didn't know why but he felt like running. Jumping. He saw a box and felt the urge to smash it into pieces. He knew he could.

Li was still looking at John. 'It's just… without a purpose, I was worried you would…'

'No purpose?' John blinked. He tensed his shoulders and felt the strength of his gun-arm. 'Oh, I have a purpose.'

Li tilted her head.

'I will kill whoever brought me here.' He looked up into the dark clouds and clenched his jaw. 'They have nothing else they can take from me… and I will make them pay for taking me away from my son.'

John walked with his eyes fixed on his feet. A brown boot, a silver foot, a brown boot, a silver foot. His feet swung through the dry grass with different sounds: the boot swished through, while the metal of his Lutamek foot tinkled against the grass stems.

John looked up and saw Mata's large frame bobbing with each step.

His back was covered in thick grass blades that nodded with brown seed cases. The Maori had gone missing yesterday morning and had been found curled up in a hollow, covered in bees. Nobody had seen the flowers but, like John, Mata didn't want to talk about it.

Ahead of Mata, the Sorean skipped and loped through the grass with Olan and Jakan-tar in the lead, while, out of sight in the vanguard, the huge Lutamek robots scouted for trouble.

To John's left, the group of soldiers that had arrived in the night trotted on their steeds. Crossley had been talking to a Spartan who said the horses were called 'tocka', but John thought they looked like starved racehorses. The group's leader, a sour-faced Mongolian, had given five tocka to Mihran as a tribute. Some wore a metal coat, or was it their skin? Lavalle rode one of them, looking splendid in his pitch-black armour.

To John's right, Mihran rode his tocka at the head of a group of soldiers, with Millok floating above Li in her energy-field prison. John had tried to talk to the Brakari, but she'd only twitched in response, and John felt a twinge of regret when he saw her trapped body.

John recognised the shape of the hills ahead. 'Not much further,' he said to no one.

'What's that?' Crossley was behind him.

'Not much further to the battlefield,' John said.

'Right.' The American's face turned dark. 'Just when I was getting used to all this walking.' Crossley's face lightened. 'Hey, did I tell you about the robot I spoke to yesterday? Five-seven?'

John shook his head.

'So, I was walking the perimeter when I found him, I guess it's a him? Anyway… I found him drawing.' He paused for effect. 'He was the one who drew the pictures in the ruined castle.'

John glanced at Crossley.

'He was drawing Brakari soldiers and humans, just scratches in the soil, but they looked good. So, I asked him about the castle and, eventually, he got to telling me how the Platae beat them. You know? Those flatworms?'

John nodded.

'There were too many of them. They bred right in front of them and, if you shot one, you got two! They kept coming and when they landed on a Lutamek, they got *in* them.' Crossley's eyes were wide. 'They wriggled inside and ate their organs... the organic parts. Without those, the Lutamek were just machines. Nothing controlling the mechanical parts and nothing making decisions.'

John winced. That was how he felt right now. He was becoming more machine by the day. He glanced at Millok, trapped in her floating prison. She'd been good to him: saved him from a painful death. He should save her. He owed her that.

'I need to speak to Mihran,' John said and sped off across the grass.

'Wait!' Crossley shouted but didn't follow.

John focused on Mihran, riding his steed, as he quickstepped through the grass with alternating swishes and tinkles. He would change Mihran's mind. They *needed* Millok to fight on their side. They needed all the help they could get!

'Mihran!' John shouted. 'Commander!'

Scores of eyes turned to John and Mihran brought his tocka to a standstill. John blocked out the staring faces. He would never have done this during his war but a fire in his chest powered him now. 'Mihran, I need to speak to you.'

Mihran waved a finger and the line carried on past them. 'Yes?'

'It's about Millok.' They both watched her grey body float past. 'Something she told me... I think it's a trap.'

'A trap?' Mihran scowled at John for a moment then said, 'Walk with me.' He patted his tocka and it moved on.

'Millok told me about what the Brakari leader can do. Belsang,' John said. 'He'll push us where he wants us to go.'

Mihran replied, 'Belsang, yes, the Lutamek told me about him. I will not underestimate him. You have nothing to worry about. I have received word from Althorn.' Mihran tapped his temple. 'He has shown me the Brakari army and they are weaker than the Lutamek said. Fewer troops, less well armed. They are slower too, so,' Mihran pointed beyond the grey smudge on the horizon, 'we will be beyond your valley and onto the plain before they reach us.'

'Althorn told you that?'

'Yes, he thought-cast the images to me.'

Maybe it was true? They would make it past the valley and fight the Brakari on their own terms. But why did John's stomach still feel tight?

Ahead, a set of grey shapes loomed up.

'The Lutamek say it's an abandoned fort,' Mihran said. 'Stone pillars mostly.'

That's where we should fight them, John thought. Somewhere with shelter. Not out in the open.

'What about Millok?' John asked. 'We need every soldier we can get.'

'No.' Mihran looked away. 'I have plans for your Brakari friend.'

Chapter 17

'I'm glad you brought it to me before your interrogations were complete.'

Althorn listened to the words with his eyes closed and instinctively pictured a tall man with a wide mouth and thick neck speaking.

'Yes, Dominus.' A new voice spoke, not as deep, but something in the way he pronounced every syllable made Althorn shiver.

'I see you have tested its armour,' the leader said.

'These humans have no natural armour as such.'

Who was speaking? And where was he? Althorn tried to recall his recent memories.

'Any information?'

'Yes. It told me of its adaptation and of those within the human army.'

Memories were coming back to Althorn: sharp blades; fire; pain; a large blue creature looming over him. He tried to move but he lost consciousness again.

When he came to, he felt an odd sensation.

'You're sure this will wake it?'

'It worked last time, Dominus.'

'Don't waste water on it. Turn it.'

Althorn felt the world spin. He clenched his teeth as what felt like a thousand cuts screamed across his body. He breathed heavily but refused to yell out.

'It's awake, Dominus.'

From what he could feel with his hands, Althorn was tied to something hard and coarse.

'I sense it. Very easy to manipulate despite the cranial barrier,' the deep voice spoke. 'One simple tweak and I drained its energy.'

Althorn had to open his eyes, but feared what he would see. He stretched his legs and forced his eyelids open. Something was wrong. The colours looked fine but how near were the shapes? He focused on two creatures: a dark-blue scorpion-like beast and a powder-blue caterpillar of a creature. Althorn looked from side to side. Brakari soldiers were everywhere, resting, eating and wrestling.

'These simple neural patterns are easy to copy. I was able to send a message to the human commander,' the larva said, in deep tones, and Althorn realised this was the Brakari leader, Belsang.

'And your message?' The well-enunciated tones belonged to the huge shelled creature that had tortured him. Was this the same Brakari who had cut off John's leg?

Belsang gave a low chuckle. 'I sent simple lies. Soldier numbers, position, strength. Whatever they wanted to hear.'

'So they will be unprepared.'

'And will meet us on a field of our choosing.'

Althorn struggled against his ropes. He had to send a message to Mihran to warn him. A sharp sensation stabbed at his head and a voice spoke. *Your attempts would be futile.*

Althorn looked at Belsang, who turned to meet his gaze and flicked a white ball from claw to claw.

You can still see me?

Of course I can see you... Althorn stopped his thoughts. Antagonising the enemy would not benefit him.

'It appears,' Belsang spoke aloud, 'that both human eyes serve the same purpose. Imagine that!' Belsang's body rippled as he chuckled. 'One pair of eyes – *both* absorbing the same frequencies.'

Althorn blinked and fought to control his thoughts. Surely he could think inside his head without projecting the words? Or was Belsang constantly in his mind, reading every thought?

'What a limited life these creatures have,' Panzicosta replied. 'In many ways we will be doing them a favour when we destroy their species.'

Belsang stopped laughing and asked. 'Any regrowth?'

The huge Brakari stepped forward, clamped Althorn's head in one of his claws and stared into his face. 'None I can detect, Dominus. But if John Greene were recaptured we could see if he has the ability.'

'Yes,' Belsang snorted and pulsed a darker blue, 'Millok will pay for her insurrection. After all we did for her.'

The torturer moved away, leaving Althorn's nostrils stinging from his foetid breath. He felt energy coming back as his anger rose and he pulled against the restraints.

You haven't worked it out yet, have you?

Althorn watched Belsang casually flick the ball from claw to claw. As it spun in the air, Althorn caught a glimpse of blue. Was it? No, it couldn't be, surely he would feel pain if…

You humans really are quite slow. Yes, it is your eye.

'No!' Althorn shouted.

The Brakari soldiers either side of Belsang lunged at Althorn with their bladed claws and he jolted in shock. He had to calm down. He couldn't risk losing his other eye.

Belsang giggled, sending ripples of colour across his tiny, bloated body. 'General.'

The large Brakari stepped forward. 'Yes, Dominus.'

'The human has served its use for now – put it with the injured slaves, I may have a use for them during the battle.'

'Yes, Dominus. Victorio Brakarius!'

Althorn didn't fight back when the guards carried him away, and they didn't cut him from the plank when they threw him into a festering pit of dying creatures. Seconds later, he passed out.

When he came to, Althorn felt a rocking motion. In any other circumstance it would have sent him to sleep, but this movement disturbed him – a bumpy, side-to-side motion that reminded him of the rafts. Was he at sea? No, he could hear axles grinding and… was that a Lutamek sparking?

The smell of rotten flesh and bloodied fur lay thick about him, but he could deal with it. He opened his eyelids and raised his head. Here were the countless species of doomed soldiers captured by the Brakari. They were weak and broken, not yet finished but saved for some awful purpose. He remembered seeing these carts in the Brakari throng when he had been scouting and had assumed they were carrying food and tents, not bodies.

The thought of food made his stomach rumble.

He turned his head to get a better view and saw he was resting on the corpse of a Sorean soldier. Its vacant eyes were still open, staring up at the ever-clouded sky. Althorn pulled his arms in frustration, testing his restraints, but he was stuck tight to the plank. If he managed to free himself he could run clear of the Brakari army, but would he be quick enough to get out of Belsang's reach? He would have to wait, regain his energy and then – what was that sound? He could hear a rhythmic, knocking noise, but it wasn't coming from the cart or its wheels. He tilted his head and scanned the bodies. Past the white limbs of a groaning Frarex, two yellow, animal eyes stared out of the shadows.

Althorn met the gaze and the knocking stopped.

The eyes blinked and another pair appeared above the first. A four-eyed creature wasn't a surprise, but the sight gave Althorn an odd feeling.

One pair of eyes closed, followed by the other.

Althorn twisted his head, looking for movement, but only saw broken bodies. Then something vibrated beneath him, sending ripples up his arms. Without a sound, the pressure on his arms released.

'Don't move, One-eye,' a crackly voice whispered somewhere near Althorn's right ear. '*They* watch us, and *he* listens with his mind.'

Althorn held his tongue. The last thing he wanted was to attract Belsang's attention.

'You are free, One-eye, but stay still a while longer.'

Althorn felt movement beneath him and scanned the bodies for a sign of who had untied him. Five arm-lengths away a set of brown scales slipped between two bodies, like a snake in the undergrowth. Althorn looked around and noticed a new head. Small, with a pointed muzzle and, Althorn admitted, quite cute. Towards the nape of its neck he saw a set of soft scales.

'Thank you,' Althorn whispered and the creature's nose wrinkled in response.

A new voice spoke in Althorn's ear, making him jump. 'We accept your thanks.'

Althorn turned to see that the dead Sorean had been replaced by a brown, scaled creature identical to the one he had thanked. No four-eyed animal, but two, two-eyed captives.

'What do they want with us?' Althorn asked.

The brown animal lay still, but its mouth moved. 'Who knows? It doesn't concern my brother and I.'

'Why?' Althorn whispered.

'We won't let it get that far… not for those who can still fight.'

Althorn felt an energy rise in his chest. He was not alone. 'Are there more of you? Of us?'

'Some.'

'And me? What can I do?' Althorn asked.

'My brother and I will help you.'

'Help me?' Althorn asked. 'Escape?'

'No.' An eyelid opened a notch and a yellow eye stared into Althorn's remaining eye. 'We will help you kill the Brakari leader.'

John's mood switched between anger and despair. He wanted to free Millok from her prison so she could convince Mihran the army was walking into a trap but, when the heat of frustration subsided, John felt the immensity of what he had to do afterwards: how could he fight whoever had brought him here? He thought of Joe and his good hand slipped inside his shirt for the tin soldier. Finding nothing, his stomach tightened, his gun-arm clicked and his anger rose again.

The cycle continued as they passed the tall, grey remains of what Li said was an abandoned fortress. The place looked like a hundred smokestacks to John: all chimneys and no factory. Grubby and dark, but a good place to hide.

Soon it was behind them and, in his insular state, John would have forgotten about Crossley if he hadn't seen him hanging back by the grey columns with a couple of soldiers and a stack of boxes. John didn't wonder why because they were nearly at the valley. One slow climb and they would be there.

He had to do something fast.

John scanned the rows of soldiers, hoping someone would be able to help. Mata would listen and John could talk to Lavalle and Euryleia, but what good would it do? Nothing would change Mihran's mind.

As they closed in on the ridge of the hill, John saw a flash of metal where a Lutamek scout patrolled at point. The Lutamek! Didn't Mihran say they had to stay out of range of the Brakari? Without the shield generator Althorn had gone to retrieve, the robots would be enslaved and turned against them.

John spun around to where three Lutamek pulled carts loaded with limp humans and Sorean. He recognised one and ran downhill.

'Two-eight-four!' John called out and the large metal head flipped in his direction.

The Lutamek remained silent, its huge shape dwarfing John as he walked beside its elephantine legs.

'Two-eight-four, I need to talk to you, I…' John found himself lost for words. What was he going to ask? 'Listen, I need to ask a favour and–'

'I owe you nothing.' Two-eight-four cut him off.

'But this is about you and your… people. It's important.'

Two-eight-four looked at John.

'I think we're being led into a trap and the Lutamek need to be out of range or…'

'We will be enslaved? Yes, we are aware of the risks, but the Brakari army has not been sensed on any frequencies. We are safe.'

'No – it's not true.' John felt his anger rise again. Why would nobody listen to him? 'Millok told me the Brakari want to drive us into their first battle site and that's where we're going. It's just over this hill.' John pointed. 'We have to stop!'

'You want me to trust the Brakari who maimed my comrades and I?'

John wanted to say 'yes' but held his tongue.

'Would you trust General Panzicosta – the Brakari who tortured you?' Two-eight-four asked.

John raised his eyebrows. 'No, I wouldn't.'

'So.'

John wasn't going to give up. 'But that doesn't mean we're not in danger, I…'

An explosion on the ridge made them look up. Lights flashed where huge silhouettes sped along the horizon like immense puppets being dragged by impatient handlers.

'Lutamek against Lutamek?' Two-eight-four spoke quietly. 'It's not possible.'

But that was what they could see. Rockets, lasers and a host of weaponry John had never seen before were being unleashed by the Lutamek on each other. The tocka stopped and the human soldiers looked to Mihran for answers.

'What's happening?' John asked Two-eight-four, whose head flashed with lights. But John knew the answer. Millok had warned him. 'It's the Brakari, isn't it? They're here. I knew it!'

John charged off towards Li and heard Two-eight-four behind him. 'We must retreat. Retreat.'

Up ahead, Mihran was holding his head, while the battle on the ridge raged with incandescent showers. John cast a look back to see Two-eight-four bounding away, abandoning its trailer of injured soldiers. Elsewhere, other Lutamek did the same.

'I warned you!' John shouted at Mihran. 'But you didn't listen. They're here!' He pointed at the hilltop. 'The bloody enemy are here!'

Mihran held his eyes shut and massaged his temples. 'False messages?' His eyes snapped open. 'It has to be.'

'What are we going to do?' John asked.

Mihran looked down from his tocka at John. 'My orders? Why, we'll fight of course. No choice.'

'What?' John was panting. He stared at the army surrounding him: they were out of formation and waiting nervously. The captains galloped over on their tocka: Lavalle, Samas, Li and the Mongol cavalry captain, Gal-qadan.

'Commander.' Li was first to address Mihran.

'We must prepare for battle,' Mihran replied.

'But what about the Lutamek?' John pointed at the few surviving robot warriors fighting on the ridge.

'Nothing we can do. I await information and…' Mihran stared at an empty space in the grass where a blur of grass morphed into the shape of Sakarbaal. 'Report.'

'Their entire army stands on the other side of the valley,' Sakarbaal spoke between breaths.

'Let me see.' Mihran closed his eyes.

Sakarbaal closed his eyes and John watched the Carthaginian's face writhe.

'Yes.' Mihran looked stony faced.

'More than we thought?' Samas asked.

Mihran nodded.

Lavalle asked, 'Your orders?'

Mihran held up a palm. 'I must recalculate... some Lutamek survived and if Althorn returns soon, I...' Mihran suddenly looked up. 'Captains, return to your troops – prepare your units.'

'But...' John was too late: Mihran and the captains had ridden away.

A few minutes later, John stood among the foot soldiers, behind Samas on the right flank. Around him he heard murmurs of prayer and other pre-battle rituals. John heard vomiting and sighed. What could he do? He couldn't fight. They didn't have time to strap a spear to his gun and all the alien weapons they had picked up had been handed out.

'March!' Samas shouted and the grass was trampled in an orderly style as they climbed the hill.

Behind John and his comrades, Li led her clan of myriad archers and riflemen while, to his right, the mass of tocka, led by Gal-qadan and Lavalle, paced uphill. On the left, Olan stood tall among the Sorean. Ahead of them, the lonely figure of Mihran rode his tocka.

John was not used to seeing his enemy. The start of a battle to him was waiting: staring at the mud of the trench wall; eyeing up the sodden rungs of the wooden ladders. Here they marched to war in plain view. What about Millok? John thought and scanned the troops. Over his shoulder he saw the abandoned carts and cumbersome belongings, with Millok floating above them in her invisible prison. He wanted to free her, to return the favour, but it was too late. He couldn't run back. He had to fight, or he would be killed.

They all had to fight.

John knew he would do his duty as he'd done before. Face the enemy and lay his life down for the good of... who? The human race?

There was no chance of getting home and Joe was dead.

John's mood snapped back to anger. He had to fight today, but that didn't mean he had to fight now when he was of no use. He was more than just cannon fodder. If he was to get vengeance on whoever brought him here, they had to defeat the Brakari, so he had to do everything in his power to make sure his army won.

They reached the top of the hill and the view across the valley slowly revealed itself. More grass. Empty grass. The valley was bigger than John had remembered. Then the enemy. On the other side of the valley, squares of enemy soldiers stood in silence. When he focused on one square, John saw the blue Brakari and a variety of alien soldiers, including Lutamek, which sparked and twisted against their slave collars.

'That's a big army.'

John turned to see Mata, who had a broad smile lighting up his face. John tried not to stare at the black seed pods that hung over his body and asked, 'You're happy about facing such an army?'

'Of course.' Mata's eyes grew wide. 'More enemy to kill!'

John didn't understand.

'Forward!' A call came from the centre and the foot soldiers moved off the hilltop. There was a plateau halfway down the valley where, John guessed, they would pause.

As they drew closer, John saw the Brakari army in more detail. At the centre stood a huge elephant-like beast and, on its back sat a tiny, bright-blue creature who had to be the Brakari leader, Belsang. Around the beast sat an array of boxes and constructions.

'Formation!' Samas shouted and the men around John stepped into rows and columns. 'Halt!'

John was at the front. He took a peek down the line and felt tiny next to the scores of warriors, tall and brave. His heart was racing. He remembered a trick his mother had taught him: breathe in for a count of four and out for eight. In for four. Out for eight. John closed his eyes. His body was tricked and his heart slowed. He opened his eyes. The seething mass of alien fighters five hundred paces away hadn't disappeared.

'Why are they so quiet?' someone at the back asked.

'They're shittin' themselves of course!' someone replied and laughter ran through the ranks.

John allowed himself a little smile and relaxed.

Then he spotted someone tied to a post near the Brakari leader.

'Althorn?'

The colour of the hood was unmistakeable, but wasn't he in Abzicrutia? John squinted. It had to be him.

Without thinking, John left the ranks and ran in Mihran's direction.

Li ran over to intercept him. 'John, what are you doing?'

'Althorn – I saw Althorn.' He pointed.

Beeping sounds came from her visor.

'It's him,' Li said. 'I'll inform Mihran – get back in line.'

'But.' John didn't know which way to turn. He looked to Mihran, sitting proud on his tocka, and to Li, who was thought-casting Mihran.

This was his only chance. He ran straight towards Mihran and heard Li's footsteps behind him. John was close to Mihran when he heard the commander whisper, 'It's worse than I thought.'

'Commander?' Li had heard too.

Mihran spoke slowly. 'Li, release the Brakari prisoner. My plans for it were in vain.' His harsh eyes fixed on John. 'You are of no use here, John Greene, you must get the shield generator from the Brakari city.' His eyes grew distant. 'Because without the Lutamek, we *will* lose this battle.'

Mihran surveyed the virgin battlefield and felt his heart race. He fought to quash the panic in his chest that pulled his emotions and influenced his thoughts.

Calm.

He pictured endless sand dunes blanketed by the myriad stars of a desert night sky. Warm breezes and a citrus scent.

Why had he disregarded the possibility of being intercepted by the Brakari like this? Never underestimate the enemy. Or, remembering what he had learnt from Li, Sun Tzu had said: 'He who exercises no forethought but makes light of his opponents is sure to be captured by them.'

Mihran took a deep breath and looked for positives. The Brakari hadn't attacked yet. There was still time to prepare.

He scanned the enemy, knowing they were doing the same with his army. He took in the number and variety of enemy troops and combined it with the information relayed to him from his captains and scouts. Could he trust the scouts' information? Now he knew Althorn's message was false, Mihran set up a coded-word system for each of his captains when communicating with him via his thought-cast system.

He disregarded the scouts' information. Better to trust his eyes.

Mihran reduced his predictions to a few models of how the war would play out. When the battle started he would alter his primary model and, if necessary, replace it with a more suitable plan. Deaths, troop movements, successes and surprise attacks – they all fed into the model.

At the moment he saw only one thing: defeat.

Something was missing though. The valley had no abnormal features – the river to the right was a good barrier and the left was flanked by uneven ground and forest. Nothing out of the ordinary. Still, an instinct told him the left flank was weak. On the army's edge, the great swarm of cat-like Sorean stood with their swords glinting. Among them, Olan stood tall, having been taken into the Sorean army as one of their own.

Jakan-tar needs to strengthen the left side, Mihran thought-cast Olan.

Olan didn't respond but, after a few moments, the Sorean troops reshaped their rectangular formation to a wide triangle.

Perfect.

Mihran adjusted his primary model and scanned the bulk of his army: the infantry stood at the centre, fighting under Samas, behind them stood the projectile units under the command of Li, while Gal-qadan and Lavalle sat on their patient tocka steeds on the right. Although stationed together, Mihran had given Lavalle a quarter of the cavalry and specific instructions on how to act during the battle.

In contrast to the Sorean–human alliance, Belsang had his soldiers form compact shapes with spaces of bare earth between them. They had twelve units, which now changed formation in response to Mihran's changes. It was a good plan, Mihran thought. It made it hard to tell which troops were stationed where and made the army look smaller.

Deceptive.

On the far side of the valley, his counterpart, Belsang, floated above the back of a giant creature that Mihran had been told was a Vaalori. As dumb as it was huge, according to the Lutamek. But Belsang was not dumb. Mihran focused on the powder-blue alien: all limbs crossed and no sign of movement. Belsang had tricked Mihran with Althorn's message and he couldn't afford to be tricked again. He had to accept the powers he'd acquired since arriving in this land were nothing compared to Belsang's.

Do not be intimidated by the enemy. They have lost before and can lose again.

Mihran's army had secret strengths too. The Brakari had no idea of the violent nature hidden beneath the docile facade of the tocka. Or the humans for that matter. And Sakarbaal, who stood on the right flank, waited with an array of Crossley's incendiaries and mines. The Sorean would be fearless and their shield technology would even the odds, with the bag of shields John had found in Abzicrutia giving the human soldiers a better chance of surviving.

It was like a life-sized game of chess. Mihran had to think several moves ahead, knowing that one bad decision would mean defeat and death. A pang of nerves tightened his stomach, echoing the emotions of his first battle.

We've got movement in the centre, Samas thought-cast.

Mihran stared at the enemy. This was his last chance to look for detail – anything that gave a weakness away.

Watch them carefully. Learn your enemy. Look for surprises. Mihran cast the thought to his captains.

The Brakari soldiers were forming four diamond shapes with three triangular groups in between, with their points facing towards the rear. The quick reshuffle was a show of control and obedience, Mihran thought, as much as tactics. Belsang wanted to intimidate the humans, much like the Roman army machine had bullied their barbarian enemies.

It wasn't going to plan though.

Some of their dogs have escaped, Samas thought-cast.

Mihran saw three wolf-like creatures race down the enemy hill and splash through the stream, aiming for Samas' men. This was a chance to send a message back to Belsang, Mihran thought.

Send in Kastor and Osayimwese.

Mihran had paired the two warriors as fighting partners after sensing their conflict, which Gal-qadan should have dealt with days ago. Mihran wasn't surprised some of Gal-qadan's men had deserted their steeds for the infantry – he had seen the Mongol's thoughts and was fully aware of his capabilities.

The two armies watched in silence as the long-haired Spartan and the tall Oyo strolled out of the mass of soldiers. Kastor twirled his spear nonchalantly while Osayimwese stretched his neck and threw furtive glances at his partner. The three canines – which the Lutamek had told him were called Skrift – were far bigger than any dog Mihran had seen and beelined for the two humans as though sensing prey.

Forty seconds later, two bloodied bodies lay on the ground and the fight was over.

They fought well, bring them back in, Mihran thought-cast Samas.

It had been a good choice to pair them, Mihran thought, as he watched Kastor and Osayimwese with a smile. They stood, strong and proud, with their two long spears holding the third dead Skrift aloft while the other two beasts lay in pools of their own blood. The men had treated it as a competition and drawn. That was good – they would fight to outdo each other when the real battle began.

Now Mihran could concentrate on the enemy.

The mass of blue scorpion and lobster-like creatures brandished horrific weapons – slicing blades, maces and hammers – along with equally deadly spiked armour. Each misshapen claw or enhanced mandible represented an adaptation enhanced, according to the Lutamek, by a Brakari doctor who had developed cloning and evolution-advancement technologies.

They were desperate, Mihran thought. And clever.

He saw a number of freaks in the Brakari ranks, with disfigured heads and deformed arms. Some mimicked the more powerful, original soldiers. Could he write these soldiers off? Or did their wild nature pose more of a threat than the originals?

Mihran adapted his models accordingly.

I've analysed the troops in the triangle formations, Li thought-cast.

Report, Mihran replied.

Many equipped with shovel-like appendages. Flat-headed. Flippered feet. Suggest they are the moles.

Mihran had heard about these so-called moles from the Lutamek, who had built up some reliable knowledge whilst fighting Brakari scouting parties.

A glint of light beyond the river caught Mihran's eye from the direction of Abzicrutia. What if the Brakari had backup? Looking at the enslaved aliens amongst the army, the Brakari didn't seem likely to form an alliance with another species, but who knew how many estranged alien warrior clans roamed this land? Mihran adjusted his primary model to hold back Gal-qadan's cavalry. Then he studied the slave soldiers. He saw Lutamek and Sorean, neither of which looked in any fit state to fight, while every other species – low-lying creatures, bulky beasts and curious pyramid-shaped objects – were positioned in the centre of each diamond, which meant Belsang didn't trust them.

We've got movement, Samas thought-cast.

Mihran saw Brakari troops making space in the two centre diamonds.

Are they archers? Mihran asked Li and Samas.

Affirmative, Li replied.

Mihran focused on Belsang. What was he doing? He was swaying like a thing possessed.

Mihran tensed.

Prepare.

The shuffling on the opposite side of the valley stopped. Mihran heard a low humming sound as both armies hushed. He searched the enemy army as the sound rose in volume. Belsang was shaking violently: his arms and legs flailing about him. It had to be him. Mihran watched as, with one almighty fit, Belsang spat out a long tubular object that rose into the sky, leaving a trail of red behind it.

Mihran had no idea what it was but one thing was clear: the battle had started.

John stumbled as the cart ran away from him.

'Shit!' He ran to catch up, grabbed the trailing rope with his good hand and, with a sharp tug, had it under control again.

It was a simple cart of planks and metal wheels put together by the Lutamek to transport weapons and now Millok lay on it, groaning and twitching.

The battle valley was almost out of view when a screaming sound erupted and John pulled the cart to a stop. He turned in time to see a small black dot rise into the air above the human army. Mihran had ordered everyone to hold fire until absolutely necessary, so he wasn't surprised to see the missile fly without opposition, but did a double take when it paused mid-air and was joined by four streams of what looked like orange liquid shooting up from the Brakari army. He winced, remembering the gassed soldiers he'd seen. Was this chemical warfare?

He turned to Millok, sensing her stir and, despite himself, felt a glow of happiness. He was glad he'd repaid his debt and saved her but, more importantly, he was happy not to be on the battlefield. He sped the cart up again, casting a look back every dozen steps. The lava-like liquid had shot high in the air while, above it, the missile opened, releasing a cloud of shimmering white specks, which floated down with careless grace.

I must hurry, John told himself, as he pushed the cart over a rise and down the long hill which led to the wide plain beyond. He could follow the river to Abzicrutia, then he would need Millok.

An almighty flash lit the sky, followed by a deep explosion that he felt through the ground.

Millok's long, grey head rose and fell.

'The battle's started.' John tried to speak softly. 'You're safe now. We're heading to Abzicrutia.'

Millok's body tensed and, with a clash of shelled legs, she scrambled to her feet. 'No,' she whimpered, 'not back there.'

'It's fine,' John used the calming voice he used when Joe was upset, 'nobody's there. They're all fighting.'

Several sets of Millok's eyes focused on John. 'Are you sure?'

John shrugged. 'As sure as I can be. Why would anyone be left behind? They want to win, don't they?' John sped up as they hit the level ground, using the last bit of momentum from the hill. 'Surely Belsang would throw everything at us?'

'No.' Millok rested her head on the planks. 'Nothing is obvious with him. He deceives and punishes. I should be back there, fighting.'

'Mihran said he didn't need your knowledge.' John shook his head. 'I tried, honest.'

'Then what hope is there?' Millok asked.

John remained silent as the cart cruised across the flat plain. The wheels were good and had suspension, but he couldn't keep pushing this hard for long.

'You'll have to fight too,' Millok said.

'We'll get back in time to fight,' he spoke to himself as much as Millok, 'and if my gun's still not working, I'll find something else to–'

'Stop!' Millok hissed.

John let go of the cart and pulled the rope. 'What is it?'

'Movement. Up ahead.'

John squinted but could see only open grassland, the snaking line of the river to his left and a hazy smudge in the distance, which he assumed was Abzicrutia.

'We need to hide. Quick!' Millok said.

'Alright, give me a chance!' John pushed hard, stepping into each push, until he built up momentum to start jogging again.

'Over there.' Millok pointed at a set of low, purple rocks.

'Ready?' John flipped Millok off the cart behind the hip-high rocks and turned the cart on its back. 'Were we spotted?' he asked.

'They didn't change direction,' Millok replied, lying where she'd landed.

John was still catching his breath. 'Is it safe to look?'

'Allow me.' Millok extended one of her smaller eyes on a stalk and John waited, praying for them to pass.

'I recognise them... all original Brakari. Tower guards. Must have been held back for a surprise attack.'

'What? I have to tell Mihran.' John remembered Mihran's implicit ban on thought-casting. 'But–'

'There's nothing you can do now.' Millok's eye was turning, following the enemy party. 'Wait… one is different. The Draytor!'

John's gun-arm clicked. 'I should have killed it while I had the chance.'

Millok's eye curled back down and she faced him. 'Maybe.' She flexed her neck and put some weight on one of her forelegs.

'Can you walk?' John asked.

'Not yet. The force field froze my shell casings tight – it'll take some time for the muscles to be strong enough again to snap them open. But I have an idea.'

Minutes later, Millok and John sped through a shallow ford and were closing in on Abzicrutia. They took turns to power the cart: John would push and run from behind for a spell, then he would rest on the back step while Millok used her powerful arms to spin the wheels.

'If Abzicrutia's this close, why did your army take so long to get to the battlefield?' John asked.

'Deception,' Millok replied. 'Always deception.'

The towers and domes of Abzicrutia loomed ahead and John's stomach tightened. This was the last place he wanted to be but he knew the army was relying on him.

'We're going the wrong way,' John said, not recognising this side of the city.

'No,' Millok replied. 'We'll have to use the main entrance – there's no time for the tunnel.'

She was right. Who knew what was happening back at the battle? It could all be over by the time they made it back.

'Leave this here.' Millok steered the cart up to the side of a tower gate and straightened her legs with a series of cracks.

'Right then,' John strapped his webbing tight, 'after you.'

Millok stalked away with more clicks and groans and, by the time they'd made it into the city, she was walking normally again.

'There's no one here,' she whispered.

'Told you,' John replied.

Keeping the wall on their left, they crept past the domed sauna houses and towers he remembered from his escape. The smell hadn't changed and he considered putting his gas mask on.

'Oh no!' Millok rushed forward to a shape on the floor. Another Brakari by the look of the blue shell, but the limbs looked wrong. 'Krotank.' Millok stroked the Brakari's head. It was obvious she would get no reply. Half of his limbs had been severed or were hanging off the broken shell of his torso.

'Who did this?' John asked.

Millok didn't need to answer. 'Let's get what we need and get out of here.'

John saw a flash of orange pulse down Millok's side as he followed her inside the hut where he'd been tortured. His eyes adjusted and he realised he'd been holding his breath. Calm down, he told himself. The place was a mess compared with how he'd last seen it, with weapons, body parts and blades scattered across the floor.

'Where did you see the box?' Millok asked.

'Over there.' John pointed to the table where he'd found the marble-like Sorean shields. He paused and stared. Hanging on the wall in all its preserved horror was his petrified leg. He'd hoped Joe's tin soldier would be with it but the leg hung alone.

'Is this it?' Millok was holding a metallic box. Tiny lights twinkled across its chrome surface.

'Yes.'

'Let's go then.'

'Sure, just one second, I…' John scanned the tables and floor. 'It has to be here.'

'I'll be outside,' Millok said, leaving John alone.

He turned over boxes and nudged limbs with his metal foot, but he couldn't see the tin soldier. It was too dark. He heard a noise outside and drifted into the first room, still searching. Scraps of paper littered the floor and shelves. Nothing useful, like tactical plans or weapons lists, just sketches of broken bodies and numbers. Out of frustration he kicked a table leg and the whole thing collapsed.

'Shit!' He jumped back, surprised at the strength of his new metal leg.

Then he smiled. Joe's tin soldier lay on the floor, still on its leather thread. John grabbed it, hung it round his neck and ran out of the building. He was still smiling when his eyes adjusted to the outdoor light to see Millok crouched and poised to run. A few steps away, a small black-shelled creature covered in spikes floated menacingly. Green energy writhed over its skin as it spoke.

'And you must be the human, John Greene.'

Chapter 18

'Shields up!' Li shouted.

The tang in the air from the orange liquid above them was indescribable, but Li's warning systems had flashed the second they sensed the chemicals in the air.

It's explosive, she thought-cast to Mihran and the other captains.

Mihran replied, *Prepare for the worst.*

Li peered over Samas' infantrymen, who stood between her archers and the Brakari. The four, bloated beasts who had vomited the liquid into the sky were nowhere to be seen. Incapacitated or dead, she presumed. She peered up at the frozen amber dome, above which floated a cloud of white petals from Belsang's missile. The effect was menacing and implied total control.

Then the first petal hit the layer of amber explosive.

A spot of yellow appeared and Li's telescopic sight zoomed in to see a chemical reaction taking place. The orange liquid was rapidly absorbing energy from the white fragment and expanding its molecular structure, from solid to liquid.

Here it comes, she thought-cast. *Above the Sorean. Olan, watch out!*

Sections fell out of the orange sky, sending liquid flames on to the soldiers below. The Sorean dodged the falling drips, losing their formation as the first explosive hit the ground, showering them with flaming soil and triggering green and red shields into action.

With the allies distracted, the Brakari army opened fire. Rockets, arrows and incendiaries arched into the air.

They're attacking, Samas thought-cast.

Do we return fire? Li asked Mihran.

No, Mihran replied. *Hold position. They want to disrupt us, but we will learn from their attack. All captains – hold and defend.*

Then the rain came: barbed arrows of medieval quality slammed into the earth metres from where heat-seeking missiles spun into the human army, sending bodies flying.

We must do something! Samas was striding from side to side. *Or they'll pick us off one by one!*

Shall we intercept the missiles? Li asked.

Basic weapons only, Mihran replied. *Not your rifle, Li – give nothing away.*

Li ordered her archers to fire and Bowman's eagle-eyed arrows were soon snaking through the air, picking off missiles. New sections of the amber dome melted as more petals set off chain reactions, dripping explosives onto the troops below. If they could be shielded from the aerial onslaught they could concentrate on the Brakari, she thought. They needed a shield dome like the Lutamek had created on the grassland, but the equipment was back up the hill. An idea came to her, and Li flicked through her visor's frequencies to the new manipulative bandwidth. A series of drips were falling above her right flank, so she focused on one and tried to slow its fall. The archers beneath looked up in time and jumped for cover as the drip hit the ground. She had bought them a second or two but there was no way she could hold off every drip like that.

'Damn it!' Her frustration burst through.

And then something strange happened.

The debris from the explosion paused mid-air. Li daren't look away – it felt like she was holding the pieces. She raised her head and the fragments lifted up. 'Yes!' Her anger must have added energy to her commands. All she had to do was keep the fragments in mid-air then… she had an idea. She changed the frequency and held her breath before turning away. When she looked back, the soil and shrapnel were still in place, floating in mid-air.

We need dust, she thought-cast.

Questions came back from all quarters until Mihran replied, *Explain.*

Throw up dust, soil – anything – and I'll create a barrier, Li said.

We can't expose your skill, Mihran responded.

We need protection and we need it now! Samas joined in.

Mihran thought-cast the entire army at once. *All troops. Kick the ground – throw soil into the air.*

After a few bemused looks, the riflemen and spearmen around Li were scuffing the ground with their sandalled and booted feet, or throwing fistfuls of dirt into the air. The soldiers in Samas' group downhill were doing the same. Li had to be quick. She ran back a few paces to get a better view over the army and fixed her gaze on a portion of air above their heads. She trapped the debris and moved it high, close to the orange dome, then changed her frequency to fix it in place. Then again, leaving the next layer a fraction lower, and so on. Each layer was thin but she was steadily building a protective net of dust and soil.

The next orange drip hit her highest layer of dust and exploded, sending smaller drips onto the levels below, which exploded in turn. The cascade continued downwards until a fine spray of hot sparks showered the soldiers beneath, leaving no one injured.

We need more, Mihran thought-cast.

Li felt the rumble of trampling feet and worked quicker to send more layers of dust up to join the ever-thickening cover. In her peripheral vision she saw the missiles from the Brakari hit the outer edges of her dirt shield. It was working! She focused on the missiles too, absorbing them into the protective layer, then cleared the smoke from the battlefield and twisted it into a thin layer over the entire army.

Let's make it hard for them to see us, she thought-cast to the captains and Mihran.

Good work, Li, Mihran replied.

Li felt the army sigh with her. The battle had barely started and they had been given a shock, but now they could catch their breath, move the injured and prepare for what came next.

The Brakari were reshaping in response: the small triangular divisions were breaking up and forming one long, zigzag line. Li's visor zoomed to focus on the front line, which was made up of the Brakari with their shovel-like arms.

Moles, she thought-cast. *Big ones.*

Your orders, Commander? Gal-qadan asked.

Hold, Mihran replied. *It's time for Sakarbaal.*

Li looked to the right flank and imagined Sakarbaal nonchalantly leaning on his trident. She had seen the inventions Crossley had come up with: club-headed stakes; lances; discus-shaped devices.

Time to play, Sakarbaal thought-cast back, but he couldn't be seen. Li noticed movement in Samas' ranks: a slow wave of soldiers retreating back a few steps as stakes of varying heights appeared, sunk in the ground at random intervals across no-man's-land.

The zigzag line of large Brakari advanced using the downward slope to speed to a gallop. The ground trembled beneath their weight and then, after they splashed through the stream at the valley floor, the entire line dived into the ground with an explosion of soil and debris. When the dust settled, all Li saw was a line of holes.

What now? Samas thought-cast.

Hold, Mihran replied.

I estimate two minutes until the moles reach the line, Li added.

More missiles! Olan's voice entered her head.

Li scanned the Brakari army and picked out groups of red, bat-like creatures loading and firing cannons. Overhead, one of the missiles exploded, sending a green light across Li's dust shield. Had they developed a chemical to destroy her shield that quickly?

The dust shield is deteriorating, she thought-cast.

We must attack soon! Samas shouted.

Patience, Mihran responded. *More dust.*

The soldiers stamped and Li worked quickly to add new layers to the shield. She ran ideas through her mind as she worked. Mihran's strategy so far was to absorb every attack the enemy could throw at them, but what next? Wait or attack? 'Lure with bait: strike with chaos,' seemed most apt but, despite their discussions, she had no idea what Mihran's next move would be.

That'll hold it for a little longer, Li thought-cast.

In no-man's-land, snaking cracks and mounds were leading uphill towards the humans, which meant the Brakari-moles were close to breaking out to attack. Li held her breath as the cracks ran up to Sakarbaal's line of mines, which should be triggered by their movement... but the cracks continued, straight on towards Samas and his men.

'Weapons ready!' Samas shouted and took stock of his front line. His men were paired up, as Mihran had ordered. Some stood back, nervously, while others, like Kastor and Osayimwese, were on the front foot with their spears aimed at the mounds of earth that zigzagged towards them.

Why didn't the explosions work? Samas thought-cast.

Must be the trigger, Li replied.

Mihran said nothing, but Samas could see Li frantically tapping buttons on her wrist controls.

Too late to worry, he thought. It was time to fight and his men needed him.

'Strong arms, strong legs – get in line! Anwar, keep tight with your partner.' Samas berated a swordsman for drifting. 'Focus! Whatever comes out of the ground – kill it!'

The men roared or clashed steel against armour.

I think I can see the issue, Li thought-cast but nobody responded.

Samas cast a look at Dakaniha. Why had Mihran paired them? Dakaniha had given him some excuse about not wanting to fight on horseback, but their fighting styles were completely different: Dakaniha had a knife, an axe and wooden armour. It wasn't enough.

'Ready?' Samas asked, stern-faced, and pushed his helmet down tight.

Dakaniha nodded and opened all four eyes.

Then all hell broke loose. A slow god-drum made a steady beat from right to left as clouds of soil erupted every few metres, moving along the line Sakarbaal had planted.

There we go, Li thought-cast.

The explosions ripped along the valley, past the tocka and along Samas' front line, showering them with soil, all the way along to the Sorean on the left flank. When the dust settled, Samas stared at an immense trench, twice a man's height deep. Here and there, the blue shells of the Brakari-moles could be seen: the dead and the dying. But the explosion had been too late and half of the attack had made it through. Blue claws punched free and smashed into the grassy valley side, grasping for leverage to pull their armoured bodies out of the ground. These were big Brakari: taller than Samas and twice as long. It would be like fighting the metal tanks Crossley had talked about.

'Choose one and attack!' Samas shouted.

He saw pairs of soldiers rushing in to meet their opponents and held out a hand to stop Dakaniha. He pointed to a crack in the soil winding towards them like a slow-moving wave.

Li, Samas thought-cast. *Any help would be great.*

Sure, she replied. *Just trying to stop the sky from falling in…*

Samas looked up. The dust shield was spotted with green patches.

'Here it comes,' Dakaniha said and took a step forward.

Samas flexed his shoulders. The shield felt strong strapped to the rock-cast on his arm, while his right arm felt loose and free. He watched the soil rise ten strides away and, with an eruption of earth, blue claws punched out of the ground and dragged out their shelled body. All Samas could see were eyes, the points where the limbs met the body and the joins between the armoured plates: all the weak spots.

A claw smashed into the ground by Samas' feet and he leapt forward, lunging with his spear: the shaft slipped through his palm with practised grace and pierced one of the larger eyes, which popped with an explosion of black liquid.

'Rekarius!' the creature yelled.

Instinctively, Samas pulled the spear back, before the large hammer pincers could snap it. He ducked beneath another attacking claw and looked for Dakaniha, who stood on the other side of the massive creature.

'Attack its legs!' Samas shouted and rolled to avoid the digger's huge claw, which would have cut him in half.

Through the scuttling legs and thumping pincers, Samas saw Dakaniha skip and jump. There was no way he could get close enough to use his tiny weapons. With the mole's attention turned to Dakaniha, Samas ran to its rear end and stabbed at its hind legs. The shell was thicker than his shield and the gap between its leg plates and the carapace on its back was too tight to stab. Samas paused a second too long and was caught off guard as a leg swung out and clattered into his shield, sending him flying back into the dust. He grunted and picked himself up. The creature was getting tired and confused but hadn't become less dangerous.

Shall I use my rifle? Li thought-cast.

No, Mihran replied. *Incendiaries only.*

Samas leant on his spear to stand up. He saw patches of crimson blood across the battlefield. One digger was running rampant, but his men had it circled. A lone figure caught his attention: Mata. The broad Maori walked unscathed and unchallenged through the battlefield with a bemused look on his face, and his bizarre black seed pods shook on his body, like a heavy coat.

Heads up, here comes the fire, Olan messaged.

Before Samas could look up, the blue beast was facing him.

'Extinction time,' it growled and slashed at Samas.

Behind, Dakaniha lay dazed on the ground. Down came a shovel claw, then another, crashing into the dirt inches from Samas' sandalled feet. Quickly, he lunged for the eye as before, but with his shield held high, and rolled out of the move as a pincer caught him, slicing a red line across his shoulder.

'Too close.' Samas got back on his feet and saw Dakaniha do the same. 'Come on!' he shouted and threw his spear to him.

Without checking if he had caught it, Samas drew his sword and ran in for another attack. Down came the shovel blades, harder this time, and Samas turned and sliced between them, parrying the mouth pincers that jabbed at him from above. Samas was freer now and quicker. He was sure something was wrong with the beast – it wasn't moving like before. Samas ran out of its reach and stared back. One of its claws was wedged in the ground. Dakaniha had noticed too and was busy stabbing at its hind legs. Out of the corner of his eye, Samas saw movement and ducked away as an explosion tore into the shell of the Brakari-mole, which screamed as it fought wildly to release its embedded claw.

Nice shot, Samas thought-cast Li.

It wasn't us, she replied.

Samas looked up and saw an orange ball of flames dripping from the lava dome.

'Let's finish this!' Samas ran back in to stab at the beast's face.

He ducked one sweeping pincer, then another, but was too slow for the third, which punched into his shield arm, sending him crashing to the ground.

Dakaniha was by his side. 'Captain?'

'I'm fine,' Samas lied, feeling shooting pains down his side. He'd felt worse before, so knew the pain would go away.

'Your shield.' Dakaniha pointed.

Samas' rock-cast arm sported two leather straps and a spray of loose splinters.

'It doesn't matter.' He grimaced as Dakaniha pulled him up. His anger was rising and an energy with it. It washed away his pain. Even when the Brakari pulled its trapped claw free, Samas felt no fear. His battle calm was back.

'Attack!' he shouted and ran at the Brakari as they turned to face him.

A claw came swinging at his head and Samas fell and slid on the dusty ground, through the creature's legs and under its belly. He caught a view of Dakaniha pole-vaulting onto the creature's back. This was the moment! Samas stabbed at the beast's underbelly with his short sword, dodging the pincers slashing at him, but his blade bounced off the shell. A long, whip-like arm thrashed at Samas, knocking the sword out of his hand, so he did what was natural: he punched. His good hand bruised against the hard shell, but his plastered fist crunched into the underbelly with a satisfying hollow thump. He punched again. And again. Cracks were appearing. The whip-claw flicked at his face, so Samas grabbed it with his good hand and punched with his rock-fist, each blow sending shivers through the mighty beast.

With a shriek, the Brakari-mole scampered away, leaving Samas lying in the violet blood-splattered dust. He sat up and saw Dakaniha standing on its back as it ran off, reminding him of the elephant drivers of the Persian army. Dakaniha lifted both arms high, his axe and knife blades shining and, with one almighty strike, plunged them into the Brakari's neck, sending it crashing to the ground.

'Rekarius!' General Panzicosta swore as he watched the battle unfold.

His mouth-pieces twisted with contempt as he watched waves of aerial and ground attacks fail to break the human–Sorean army.

Both he and Belsang had assumed these soft-bellied warriors would be easily swept aside – not only were they physically weak but they had fallen into the trap with ease. So why did Belsang ignore his advice to launch a three-pronged attack? Aerial cover, slaves in the centre to absorb the bulk of the human army and Brakari soldiers on the flanks, free to use their abilities. But no, Belsang maintained his slow and steady range of attacks, reforming the troops and poking at the enemy like a scared hatchling eating its first live meal.

This was war, not a game!

Panzicosta had given up. He wouldn't admit it but he was sulking. The battle was not being fought the way he would have commanded it and he didn't want to be part of another defeat. Still, he waited, ready to kill when the need arose.

A Sorean messenger limped past and Panzicosta stretched out a rear leg to trip it up. He found himself hesitating for a second before leaning in to slice its tail off. The Sorean squirmed and looked up at Panzicosta with its large eyes. Was that hope he saw? Was this creature resigned to death and actually hoping for it?

'Go.' Panzicosta flicked the broken cat-like beast back onto its feet and pushed it away. 'Weak creatures.' He released a snort through his spiracles. The black armour fitted well but the lack of air holes made it hard to breathe. He looked at the hazy sky and found the dull sun beyond. At this rate, the battle would last all day. They needed a decisive victory or they would never leave this land.

Naturally, he thought of his last battle.

After half a day of failed attacks, defeat had become inevitable for the Brakari. Their leader, Kantoff, was desperately throwing every last troop at the Ladrof and Scarpinelloss alliance. Even when the white obelisk rose from the battlefield, surrounded by the dead and dying, Kantoff would have battled on: wasting more soldiers by attacking the victorious army on their journey to the silver gates. So Belsang had killed him before he had the chance.

After the battle, a legend had built up around Belsang. They said he'd killed five Ladrof warriors and bathed in their fluorescent blood.

But Panzicosta was there and knew the truth. Belsang had been larger back then, although not as broad as Panzicosta, and had cut his way through dozens of Scarpinelloss as the Brakari foot soldiers rushed the enemy position. The part about the blood was true, but it was Panzicosta who had sliced the Ladrof's belly open. The blood had a light of its own as it sprayed over Belsang, who had screamed in pain as his shell shrank and crushed his body within. Panzicosta was about to put him out of his misery when the shrieking stopped and Belsang imploded with the sound of a thunder clap. The white obelisk rose and Belsang had transformed into a tiny, glowing ball of raw energy. Belsang floated to Kantoff, decapitated him with a shock of white light and turned to pronounce, 'I am Dominus.'

Panzicosta had wondered what would have happened if he had been in the path of the Ladrof's blood. Would he have survived and evolved? Or would Belsang have struck him down as he writhed in pain? Either way, he couldn't help dreaming about becoming Dominus.

General. Belsang's words stabbed into Panzicosta's head.

Yes, Dominus.

Prepare to release the Skrift.

Yes, Dominus.

Panzicosta waited for the sensation of the icicle in his brain to retreat before allowing himself to think openly. What good would the Skrift do now? Look what had happened to the first three who had escaped and charged the humans – their bodies were the first to wet the ground.

'You,' Panzicosta shouted at the nearest Brakari in his battalion, 'tell Forshaq to whip the Skrift, I need them ready.'

'Yes, General.' The Brakari lowered his head and scampered across to the makeshift pens.

Starved and half mad, the Skrift would kill a handful of humans but it wouldn't be enough. This would be just another half-hearted skirmish. Panzicosta scanned his army and saw other captains on the move, ordering their troops in various directions. Weapons were being primed and, behind the rear lines, the red chemists were busy preparing more of Doctor Cynigar's potions.

Belsang hadn't moved and neither had his Vaalori. Beside it, Panzicosta could see the half-blind human, tied to a stake in the ground. A shiver ran through his shell. Maybe he could come back for him after the battle? His death could be part of the celebration party, along with John Greene's. Now that would be a treat.

The icicle drilled into his head again.

General.

Panzicosta's attention flicked to Belsang. Yes, *Dominus.*

Alpha formation. Belsang's voice came and went.

Alpha formation? Panzicosta was taken aback. Really?

Yes, Dominus, Panzicosta replied.

Finally, something big was going to happen.

Mihran sat on his tocka while his army battled the Brakari-moles and defended against the falling, flaming sky and incoming missiles. His head robotically scanned the battlefield: left to right, then back again. Everything he saw – every death, injury, new weapon or enemy movement – fed into his primary model. Each human or Sorean death was a push towards defeat or a new choice, while every Brakari loss added weight in their favour. The balance of the battle was calculated automatically as Mihran filtered the thought-cast messages coming to him. Some had code words but many didn't, which meant Belsang was trying to distract him so, in his head, Mihran was fighting a battle of his own.

Mihran had pushed each message away to start with and even replied with false messages of his own but the effort was draining. He needed a mental wall like Li's dust dome so, using some far corner of his well-connected brain, Mihran constructed a cloud of messages designed to interact with one another: false conversations between fake personalities. He created voices: some from his past, some new personas. As his skills improved and the voices interacted fluidly, the pace quickened until he had a bee swarm of voices shouting, answering and questioning one another. He released it into the ether of thought-cast frequencies where no human would hear, just anyone trying to listen in to his mind. And only one individual was doing that.

Mihran's shoulders relaxed. Freed from the intense filtering and counter-messaging, he was able to focus on individual soldiers. He watched Kastor and Osayimwese. They fought well, competing with each other to be the first to kill their Brakari-mole. Rather than dodging the pincer jabs and hammer blows, as Samas and Dakaniha had done, these two athletic warriors had systematically sliced off the enemy's limbs one by one. Even under enemy fire and with the sky falling in about them, they had been fearless: swapping positions and attacking with lightning speed every chance they could. Mihran recalled how Samas had wanted to split the pair up, but Mihran's instincts had been correct: competition drove them to new heights. While Samas and Dakaniha still fought to overpower their opponent, Kastor and Osayimwese's mole was dead and the two men were exchanging laughs and taunts.

Mihran let his eyes wander. The new trench cut by the explosives was good defensively, but the Brakari army beyond had plenty of warriors left, most of whom were the adapted soldiers he feared the most. Belsang was holding back his favourites. Mihran saw energy pulses running down their shells, much like they did along Millok's shell. Maybe, like John suggested, he should have asked her for information? But how would he have known what was true?

He turned to the right flank of the army, where Sakarbaal's mines had killed three out of every four Brakari-moles in front of Galqadan's cavalry, who had casually finished off the survivors without revealing the tocka's true carnivorous nature. Lavalle had held his horsemen back, defending the river, as ordered, although Mihran knew the knight was eager to charge into the melee and test his metal horse and obsidian armour.

On the left flank, where the Sorean fought, the delay in explosions had allowed more moles to break through. The cat-like soldiers had proven as vicious as Olan had told him: spinning and leaping over the cumbersome enemy, whose every other thump and slice bounced off the Sorean's invisible armour. But the Sorean were losing numbers.

Li, Mihran thought-cast. *The Sorean need support.*

Yes, Commander. A new cloud of dancing arrows, loaded spears and flaming incendiaries flew at the Brakari-moles.

Above them, the green disease had eaten through Li's dust shield, opening the skies, but it was too late. The last of Belsang's white petals had lit what remained of the frozen lava and the view to the clouds was clear again.

Then everything changed.

Commanded by an unheard order, the surviving Brakari-moles broke off in unison and scampered back downhill, diving into their underground tunnels.

They're regrouping, Samas thought-cast.

On the other side of the valley, Belsang's troops were reshaping again.

Samas' men caught their breath and the Sorean took the opportunity to rest, while Li's troops picked off the injured Brakari diggers who had strayed into the open.

Prepare for the next attack, Mihran ordered.

He re-evaluated the battle. So far, the human–Sorean alliance had seen off two attacks with varying success – the Sorean had lost ten percent of their number and the humans had lost less. Everyone's strength had been sapped by the encounter. The Brakari had lost a large number of diggers but the main Brakari army remained intact.

Mihran sighed. He knew the subterranean attack, just like the aerial attack before it, had been a test. They were being prodded like some vulnerable prey, softened up and made ready for an easy kill. Well, think again, Belsang, Mihran thought. I still have plenty more surprises to come! He looked to where Lavalle and his mounted soldiers waited patiently – yet to draw their swords. Confidence rose in the Arab's chest as he pictured each of the hidden secrets in his army: the tocka; Li's rifle; Gal-qadan's devastating weapon; Crossley's mission; and the Lutamek, if John could retrieve the box in time.

The Brakari army finished manoeuvring into a long rectangular block, less than a hundred paces from the trench, leaving a thin line of archers to their rear. It looked like Belsang was desperate enough to launch an all-out assault.

The floating blue Brakari leader opened his mouth, raised his arms and spoke with a voice that seemed to resonate through the very ground itself.

'I invoke the rite of the dead!' the words echoed around the valley, turning the heads of every soldier, 'which allows the formerly defeated party to bring back those lost in battle!'

Mihran's throat dried. Had Belsang acquired some greater knowledge of this strange land? Was he using a hidden rule to win this game of war?

Belsang swung his arms down and a deep vibration rang out across the battlefield.

Olan, ready the troops! Mihran watched with dread as the patch of lumpy ground off the left flank – the area he had been wary of – started to shake. Tussocks of grass rose and cracks crept across the ground's surface. The intensity of the earthquake grew, enlarging the cracks and shaking clumps of grass and soil, as though the ground was boiling.

Mihran gasped as the undulating surface spawned the broken bodies of dead Brakari soldiers.

John stared at the floating Brakari, who shivered as pulses of green energy ran over its black shell.

'Yes, I'm John Greene,' John spoke clearly. 'Who are you?' Despite his bravado, John was nervously making shapes inside his gun: spikes, corkscrews and cubes.

'Why don't you tell him, Millok?' The dark Brakari's voice jumped mid-sentence as a green shiver ran up his body. 'These are the animals you have sworn allegiance to? These soft-bellied cowards?'

'This–' Millok tried to speak but was cut off.

'I am Doctor Cynigar,' the creature bobbed a little higher, 'master of the biological and keyholder to the genetic lock. Am I not, Millok?'

'Yes.' Millok was crouched but not cowering, John noticed, and her spiracles were open. Was that a defensive or aggressive pose?

'I am responsible for the might of the Brakari army, am I not? And responsible for your excellent adaptations, which you intend to turn on your own kind.' One of Cynigar's back plates slid back and two sets of black, skeletal wings folded out. 'I know all your secrets, Millok, you have nothing to hide from me.' He floated forward a pace, keeping one pair of eyes on John. 'I know your weaknesses and your strengths.' He darted forward and back again, teasing Millok. 'If you do not return to the army I will have to kill you, do you understand?'

'You are mistaken, Cynigar.' Millok didn't sound nervous, which calmed John's nerves. 'What you know about me is limited… my skills have multiplied.'

'Impossible!' Cynigar shrieked and a ball of green energy erupted from his mouth, smashing a hole in the side of the nearest dome, sending dry mud over Millok. 'I have read your genetic map. Added to it, preened it and taken from it.'

'Like you took my eggs.' One of Millok's legs twitched, betraying her emotions.

'It was a trade.'

'A one-sided trade, Doctor, just like the society Belsang and Panzicosta have fostered here. It's nothing like the home world, where we were progressing… developing towards equality and–'

'In your time maybe,' Cynigar snarled. 'It was different in my time…'

John took a step back, unsure whether to stay and help or run away while the two Brakari fought it out. He would be of no use if he had to help Millok, and he needed to get the Lutamek box back to Mihran.

'Inequality is always going backwards,' Millok said.

'Nobody is equal!' Cynigar shrieked. 'Even hatchlings. I see it in the design. The patterns. The origin. It's all there if you take the time to look.'

'You're crazy, Cynigar.' Millok was sidestepping now, keeping her eyes on the doctor, who turned to face her. 'You were a soldier like us but you've been corrupted by this power.' She stretched to make herself taller. 'You are not a god, Cynigar.'

Another section of shell slipped back on Doctor Cynigar's body and a long, spiked tail unravelled from within. 'Not a god, no, but when you have seen what I have seen – the majesty of it all – then you would feel the power… the power over life and death.'

Millok was circling away from John. 'You have no right to that power, Cynigar. No right to choose who lives and who dies.'

'Or who is healthy? And who lives a full life?' Cynigar replied. 'A doctor has that right.' He shivered once more as a line of green energy writhed across his shell. 'What I have attained has been in the name of science and for the Brakari cause. Victorio Brakarius!' He darted forward and whipped his tail at Millok, who batted it away with ease.

'You've spent too long in the laboratory, Cynigar.'

'Not at all.' Cynigar was flitting around now, darting back and forth with random movements. He dipped at Millok again, scratching her carapace with one of his bladed wings.

John watched nervously, clicking his gun as Millok refused to retaliate. She crouched a little lower, John noticed, and the flaming stripes down her shell had returned.

'What's it going to be, Millok?' Cynigar taunted. 'Will you stab me with your enhanced chela? Spit the poison from your veins?' He leapt forward, jabbing with his tail, and missed. 'Will you use the sonic erupter I built in your empty egg chamber? Or use your speed to run away, leaving this defenceless creature to me?' Cynigar leapt at Millok and stabbed with his tail, catching her between the plates on a hind leg. She leapt back with a whistle from her spiracles.

John felt useless, watching from the doorway with his gun-arm making strange noises and his good hand gripping the tin soldier under his shirt. He had to be strong. Strong? he thought. No. I have nothing to be strong for. What I need is revenge – someone must pay for taking me from Joe… for leaving him alone. John felt heat building in his gun-arm and pictured the shapes he was nervously creating. If his gun worked like it had during his war he could give Cynigar a quick burst of fire, but when he'd fired it at the Draytor, the gun had gone off like a trumpet.

Cynigar attacked again and Millok fought back, scratching the doctor's black shell.

'I have other weapons.' Cynigar bobbed back and forth. 'But these will suffice.' A green wave ran up his body and he vomited a ball of electricity at Millok. For the first time, John saw a hint of Millok's powers as she leapt away with a flash of orange. She was quick, but not fast enough to avoid the shower of soil that rained down on her shell. 'You will tire soon,' Cynigar continued. 'And I will kill the human. I'm sure, by the rules of this land, that by killing you both –

as enemies of my army – I will be granted safe passage through the silver gates without risking myself on the battlefield.'

'Are you sure?' Millok replied. 'The battle's already started – it could be over now, for all you know.'

'No,' the Doctor replied. 'Belsang is in constant communication. He expects me shortly.'

John stepped nervously from foot to foot and wanted to distract Cynigar, but was scared he would turn on him. He concentrated on his gun-arm and pictured a smooth, long bullet spinning in the chamber. Could he fire it? He aimed the muzzle at Cynigar's back and waited.

Millok scuttled and dodged as she sparred with Cynigar, who leapt in again and again with a tail sting or a slash from a wing. If Millok was injured, John would have to push her on the cart back to the battle. They would never get back in time and… he fired. Everything slowed down. The recoil surprised John, but his back absorbed the blow and he kept his footing. He felt the bullet burn its way up the barrel and fly out with a blast of hot air. Time sped up again and the bullet smashed into Cynigar's left shoulder, cracking his shell and sending him flying towards the nearest building.

'Shit!' John shouted and shook his gun-arm. 'It's burning!'

'Fire again!' Millok shouted.

Cynigar spun around and bore down on him. His shoulder glowed pink. 'Self-healing shell,' he said. 'One of the adaptations I refused to give to you, Millok.'

John pictured another bullet rotating in the chamber. He gave it a three-pointed tip and fired it at Cynigar. With a jet of steam, it hissed out and hit Cynigar with a sharp crack, clipping his abdomen, spinning him through the air again.

'Keep firing,' Millok said, before slipping out of Cynigar's peripheral vision.

John built a new bullet and an odd thought came to him – where did the bullet's metal come from? Was it using metal from the gun itself? He fired again: a musket ball this time, which glanced off Cynigar's right wing, snapping a blade.

'Damn it,' John cursed as a hot burn ran up his arm.

He couldn't keep this up and it looked like Cynigar was barely affected by the shots. John needed something more powerful. He focused on Cynigar's belly plates and imagined drilling into them with a twisting motion.

Cynigar rushed at John with wing blades and whip flailing. John blasted out a corkscrew blade with a rush of hot smoke – but Cynigar was dead before it reached him.

Millok had leapt up and deftly sliced the doctor's head from his body with her razor-sharp forearm. John's corkscrew bullet hit a second later, tearing through the doctor's shell and into the soft tissue within.

'Teach you to threaten me, you freak!' Millok panted, as Cynigar's body hit the ground.

John didn't have time to congratulate her: his gun-arm felt like it was on fire. 'Water. Water!'

Millok pointed to a pail of liquid by the holding pens and John ran over and plunged his arm in with a hiss and a cloud of pink steam.

'What's this?' He looked down.

'Sorean blood,' Millok replied.

John shook his head, lost for words.

Chapter 19

'I made it... but it's not what I expected.' Delta-Six recorded his log while he hid in the shadow of a pile of bodies. 'I have more questions now.'

He could see the silver gates, some ten metres tall and thirty wide, surrounded by camps made by hundreds of alien soldiers who, like Delta-Six, had drifted here. Were these defeated soldiers?

He detoured, avoiding the sprawling huts and tents, and walked to the immense gates, which reached high into the low clouds. He scanned and studied the metal with little outcome. There was no obvious opening mechanism and, judging by the piles of ash at its feet, it was protected by a sophisticated security system.

Wary of receiving attention from the myriad and deadly looking soldiers gathered in the camp, Delta-Six retreated to a safe place, from where he watched the comings and goings.

As the hours, and days, passed, the gates remained closed. New soldiers joined the camp, mostly in small groups, but Delta-Six noted one group of red worm-like fighters leaving on a herd of huge beasts, laden with rocks and primitive catapults. Off to war, he guessed.

The white obelisk, which commemorated the Brakari's defeat, stood on an island of calm as the soil rose and fell around it like an undulating sea. Olan caught his breath and stared at the deformed and half-rotten Brakari soldiers rising from their war graves.

'Can you see those?' Olan pointed to the strings of vapour wisping from each warrior and into the sky.

'No,' the nearest Sorean replied.

Olan patted his gold chest plate and his eyes remained fixed on the rising creatures, which seemed to be pulled out of the ground by the white wisps. The Brakari walked with erratic movements as they came to attack, swinging their rusted blades and cracked claws with unpredictable speed.

'Formation!' Jakan-tar called its troops away from the dead Brakari-moles who woke from their short death.

What rite is this? Lavalle's voice echoed around Olan's head and he closed his eyes to focus.

Is there anything like this we can use? Samas asked.

Olan joined in. *I see strings. They are being worked like puppets.*

Belsang must be controlling them, Mihran said. *It's trickery.*

So kill him and they all fall? Samas replied. *We should send the cavalry wide to distract them, then my men will attack.*

The river's too close. Not enough room, Gal-qadan thought-cast for the first time.

I agree, Lavalle said.

Why can't Li shoot Belsang? Olan said.

Belsang has an energy shield, Li replied. *Even on full power, I won't penetrate it at this range.*

We must strengthen the left flank, Samas said.

Lavalle started. *Why can't we–*

SILENCE, Mihran thought-cast louder than before. *Prepare to defend and I will issue my orders.*

The voices faded and Olan opened his eyes. It always took him a second to deal with thought-casting. None of the other captains seemed to have that problem. Was it the chest plate filtering the messages, he wondered? His eyes refocused on the advancing enemy and he felt a presence by his side.

Jakan-tar looked up at him. 'We have an issue.' The green aura of the Sorean's shield was flashing. 'Our shields.'

Olan stepped back. 'What's happened to them?'

'Interference.' Jakan-tar nodded to where a gang of slave species clustered around the feet of Belsang's Vaalori, moving boxes with lights. 'They must have hacked into the shields they took from my captured soldiers.'

'The shields John brought back with him?' Olan asked.

'Your troops will be affected too,' Jakan-tar replied and walked away to join the front line. 'You must inform your commander.' His eyes lit up. 'Now we fight without shields, we fight with pure energy!'

Olan nodded and closed his eyes to thought-cast. *Mihran, the Sorean shields are failing.*

Samas, did you hear that? Mihran replied. *Do* not *trust the Sorean shields.*

Hearing you loud and clear, Samas responded.

Your orders, Commander? Lavalle asked.

Defend and hold, came Mihran's terse reply.

Olan's eyes flicked open. Defend and hold? How do you defend against an army of the dead?

The Sorean moved back from the uneven ground and created what Olan assumed was the defensive line Jakan-tar had told him about. It was an ancient method, he'd said, used by the first Sorean when their planet had been invaded by a self-replicating mechanoid species intent on consuming the Sorean planet's metallic resources for procreation. Like now, they'd been outnumbered and outgunned, but had defeated their enemy on the battlefield. Jakan-tar had gone on to explain how most of the Sorean's technology was derived from the remnants of the defeated mechanoid army, including their shields.

Now, with no trust in their technology, the front line of Sorean bore a sword in each arm while those behind, armed with long spears and curved halberds, held back, ready to thrust at a moment's notice. A wall of blades. Olan noticed the front warriors wore shield brooches donated by those behind in case they still worked.

Olan searched the battlefield and caught sight of Mata strolling casually through the melee. His tattooed body writhed as he ducked the blades of a Brakari-mole and swung his patu club in response. Only, he didn't use his arm: a long, thick tendril flicked out and smashed the club down on the mole's armoured head, cracking it with two vicious swipes. Mata paused mid-stride but didn't look back.

Back at the Sorean front line, the first Brakari smashed into the swinging blades, which held for a second before the weight of the attack was too much and the Sorean stumbled back. Flashes of colourful shields were lighting up the front line where Brakari claws and tails smashed into the Sorean soldiers, but Olan could see by the number of dead trampled and scattered across the grass that many shields were useless now. The picture repeated along the line and Olan felt a pain in his belly: the Sorean had put everything into fighting the diggers and for what? A realisation came to him: he had never defended a position before. All of his battles had been attacks. Destruction. He had killed the weak to save them from the evils of his brethren, but now what could he do to save the weak?

Fight. That was all he could do.

'Don't worry,' he shouted as he unclipped his battleaxe and ran to help the Sorean, 'we've killed them once before and we can kill them again!'

He focused on a rejuvenated Brakari-mole with a brave Sorean on its shoulders, who stabbed at its neck with a long blade. Even the Brakari's severed claws were attacking: flipping across the ground like beached sharks, snapping at ankles and feet. Olan rushed in with his axe high, shimmied to one side, then swung down, slicing between the neck and head plates. With one blow, the dead head was severed and fell on the floor with a hollow thud.

But the body fought on.

Olan parried a slicing arm and dug his axe into its remaining digging claw. The axe bit into the thick chitin and Olan fought to keep his feet as the arm pulled back. Dakaniha was beside him with all four eyes open, slashing at the shoulder joint with his knife, stabbing until the arm broke free.

'Thanks.' Olan stepped on the arm to wrench his axe free.

The body jumped and shook as it tried to dislodge the stubborn Sorean still on its back.

'We must stop the dead creatures before the rest of their army arrive.' Dakaniha pointed across the valley, where lines of live Brakari marched to the bottom. Only the trench stood in their way. Behind them, a pack of dark wolves rushed down the valley towards the centre of the human army.

'We'll have no energy left by the time they get here.' Olan took a step back and looked up at the white lines flowing from each dead Brakari through the air to Belsang. If he could cut the links the undead would have no power. But how? Olan felt for Thor's hammer hanging around his neck but his hand tapped his chest plate instead. His eyes widened. 'I've got an idea.' Olan pointed to where a Brakari-mole spun around, defending against a host of Sorean troops. 'I need to get on its back.'

Dakaniha blinked and opened his mouth to protest but was cut off.

'Just distract it and I'll do the rest.' Olan ran towards the large Brakari-mole with his axe high.

The Sorean who saw him coming stepped back and the Brakari spun to face him with blades slashing and its digging claw snapping wildly. Olan threw a glance to his left, where Dakaniha was fitting a long arrow to his bow. Olan dodged right, saw a flash of white and the enemy dipped as the arrow stabbed a foreleg. The angle was perfect: Olan ran up the leg with strong strides as another arrow made the Brakari-mole turn again. With a scramble, Olan was up on the shell and, with a burst of energy, leapt high and slashed the air with his axe. Two lines of diamond dust sparked and Olan felt a surge of energy rush through his chest plate.

When he landed, he stood on a motionless corpse.

'You did it!' Dakaniha leapt up beside him with a smile that turned into a frown. 'What did you do?'

Olan thumped a fist against his chest plate and looked up into the sky, where the detached wisp coiled back to Belsang. 'I'm not sure, but I think I'm going to have to do it again.' Olan jumped down and away from the nearest fighting. 'Give me a second.' He closed his eyes and thought-cast to Mihran and the captains. *Li, can you see the connections between the undead and Belsang?*

What connections? Mihran asked.

They're like fishing lines, Olan replied. *Cut them and they drop.*

You'd better cut them quick, Samas replied. *We've got wolves coming over the ridge and the rest of the army isn't far behind.*

Li?

Okay, I've found the frequency. I'm surprised anyone can see at that level.

Can you cut them? Samas asked.

Sure, Li replied. *Mihran, I think it's time to use my rifle.*

Agreed. Fire at will. And if you get close enough, take out Belsang.

Olan opened his eyes to see Dakaniha staring into the clouds, blinking his new eyes. 'I think I see them,' he muttered. 'Another has been cut.' He pointed.

Olan stared up and saw the second strand flailing back to where the powder-blue Brakari sat on his behemoth steed. Then another and another. He turned to Li's section of archers and could make out Li, crouched behind a rock, aiming her rifle and steadily picking off the connections.

'Great.' Olan turned to Dakaniha. 'Now we can fight the real soldiers!'

Mihran closed his eyes and checked the voices he had sent to counter Belsang's disruption. They were still talking and arguing. He removed the few rambling voices that had gone mad and started new voices in their place.

With no time to lose, his eyes snapped open and scanned the battlefield and he readjusted his models. The undead Brakari soldiers were crashing to the floor as Li severed the connections between the puppets and their master. She managed to get two or three shots away before someone in the Brakari army located her and sent rapid missiles her way. Soon she would be running out of hiding places.

Find a good spot and stay there, Mihran thought-cast to Li.

On the left flank, Olan was leaping from enemy to enemy, slicing the ghostly fibres and reducing the pressure on the Sorean. Jakan-tar's warriors had taken the brunt of the new attack and needed time to regroup before the wave of fresh, enhanced Brakari warriors entered the battle. The thick line of dark Brakari was already at the trench.

Mihran scanned Li's troops. One man stood out from the rest as he took potshots at the newcomers: Ethan Turner. Gal-qadan had said he was accurate, but Mihran had taken it as bluster. Whether it was the man's gun or his skill, Ethan was clearly hitting his mark with every shot. The bullets rarely killed but they were injuring and slowing down the oncoming Brakari. Mihran needed more soldiers like him: reliable and accurate.

Ethan, Mihran thought-cast, *get close and aim for Belsang.*

The American glanced back at Mihran, gave him a nod and ran downhill to find a clear shot.

Mihran let his main set of models run forward: five minutes; ten; thirty. None of them looked good. Forgetting the Lutamek, and as long as they had no more surprises from Belsang, the human–Sorean alliance would have to absorb every attack with minimum losses if they were to swing the battle in their favour.

Divide, demoralise, defeat.

Mihran caught a glimpse of movement beyond the river off the right flank. Brakari reinforcements?

Li, Mihran thought-cast. *I need you or Bowman to look beyond the right flank. Who is coming?*

He watched Li roll behind a mound as an incendiary hit where she had been standing, spraying her troops with lumps of metal and earth.

Sure, she replied. *I need a break.* She ran uphill and ducked behind some rocks, from where Mihran saw her peering out. *Okay, we've got twenty-three Brakari arriving. Dark-shelled.*

Mihran felt his heart speed up. More of the enhanced soldiers they had yet to face. How could he judge their impact on the battle? He looked to Lavalle and his small troop of mounted knights. They were tasked with defending the ford but would their numbers be enough?

He had no choice.

Lavalle, Mihran thought-cast. *Incoming enemy. Defend the–*

A violent explosion sent Mihran's tocka stumbling to one side and Mihran gripped its thick mane to avoid sliding off its muscular back. He turned to see a mass of thick smoke and rock debris where Li had been stationed.

Li? Mihran thought-cast and wheeled his tocka round. Instinctively it cantered towards the crater. *Li, can you hear me?*

Her archers were already at the rocks, wafting the smoke away and stepping in. After a few anxious seconds, Bowman strode out with a cloth at his face and Li's rifle in his hand. He shook his head.

Li was dead.

Mihran sat motionless for what felt like minutes. He looked out to the battle and saw a flash of light from Ethan's rifle, followed by a white bubble around Belsang. Eventually, Mihran blinked and looked at Bowman. 'Give the rifle to Ethan.' He pulled the tocka round and shouted over his shoulder, 'You're my captain now, Bowman.'

'Centenaur? Me?' the English archer asked and, when Mihran

didn't respond, puffed up his chest and rejoined what were now his troops.

Mihran headed back uphill. *Lavalle, defend the ford. You have twenty-three incoming enemy soldiers.* He couldn't afford to be emotional. He had to stick to the primary model and mould and tweak until victory was theirs. He resumed his original position and watched Lavalle detach his group from Gal-qadan's cavalry and move through the shallow ford.

Commander, you have to see this, Samas thought-cast and Mihran turned to focus on the centre of the battle.

A pack of dark wolf-like creatures scrambling over no-man's-land was being attacked by its own army. Catapults fired huge incendiaries that painted electric-blue arches across the sky before smashing into the wolves. Have they escaped? Mihran wondered. One of the creatures writhed on the ground after being hit. The blue energy rippled across its body, changing its shape and size: its rear legs straightened and bulked out, the head distorted and teeth lengthened. The deformed but re-energised beast rose to its feet with a snarl and leapt in to attack. They weren't being attacked: they were being forced to mutate.

Mihran ordered, *Attack before they are enhanced.*

Easy for you to say, Samas replied and ran to join his men in attacking the nearest freakish wolf.

Gal-qadan's voice came next. *The enemy have breached the pit.*

Here too, Olan replied from within the Sorean ranks that had reformed twenty paces uphill from their original position.

Defend and hold, Mihran ordered all his captains.

He studied his model and waited before releasing Gal-qadan's cavalry – they needed space, which they had now Lavalle and his knights had crossed the ford.

Gal-qadan, Mihran thought-cast. *You have room for a Cantabrian circle.* He sent an image of a moving circle of archer horsemen attacking the Brakari, hoping the Mongol knew the tactic. Gal-qadan didn't respond, but the tocka were soon moving. Within a minute, a line was looping back round and opened fire as the first Brakari clambered out of the trench. One Brakari emitted its own energy shield and the arrows bounced away harmlessly, while another lost its footing after an arrow exploded in its face, sending it back into the trench.

Different models fought for Mihran's attention now, including one he hadn't seen for some time and had ignored. Some suggested releasing the tocka to ride wide and hit the Brakari from behind, while other models suggested a full-blown attack. Most suggested dividing the attackers.

Bowman, Mihran thought-cast. *Direct all fire at the centre.*

Yes, Commander.

Arrows and spears leapt into the air, followed by smoke from various guns. The British contingent of redcoats was holding its own with a rally of rolling fire and Mihran was pleased to see that, even though he couldn't take out Belsang, Ethan Turner was making good use of Li's rifle. As Mihran watched, he blasted an enemy soldier: splitting its carapace with a violent crack.

Every minute they survived was a minute closer to victory.

On the Brakari side, a group of pyramid-shaped creatures were rolling into Sakarbaal's trench, locking together to form a bridge over which a dozen prime Brakari fighters now scuttled.

Samas, Olan, Mihran thought-cast. *Enemy coming thick where your troops meet. Bowman, send a squad to help.*

Yes, Commander, the archer replied.

Mihran sighed. They were being stretched on all sides. He watched Bowman's division unleash a second attack, which ripped into the Brakari as they made landfall off the living bridge. The archers fought on. Some, like Euryleia, had no powerful weapon, but their metal-tipped arrows injured and slowed down the Brakari assault, giving Samas and his men time to concentrate on one enemy at a time. But it wasn't enough. Mihran didn't need his models and predictions to see that. They were losing ground and losing numbers.

One of the redcoats had been hit by the Brakari's blue-electric arrows meant for the wolves and exploded into a mass of moss, which now rolled around the battlefield aimlessly. On the right wing, flashes and deep booms sounded as Lavalle and his knights engaged the new Brakari. Two of Gal-qadan's horsemen were down, although their tocka still ran with the moving circle. Mihran recognised Tode as one of the fallen, but not the other. The Cantabrian circle had served its purpose but the Brakari had breached the trench and were running amok now.

Gal-qadan, Mihran thought-cast. *Attack at will.*

Time to show them what the tocka could really do, he thought.

Commander. Olan's voice came through. *Something's happening in the forest.*

Mihran turned to see ghostly white shapes creeping out of the trees. Some had made it onto the battlefield itself, where they threw handfuls of dust to the wind.

Frarex? Mihran asked.

Not them, Olan replied. In *the forest.*

The canopies of trees within the dark forest were shaking and a low rumbling could be heard. Was it the Lutamek or more Brakari reinforcements? Whatever it was, Belsang seemed as unsure as Mihran. His giant steed turned in the direction of the newcomers and the Brakari on their right flank disengaged from the Sorean, ready for what was about to appear.

Then the new force revealed itself: a line of five-metre-tall, steel-armoured and tri-tusked rhino-like behemoths. They crashed through the last line of trees and into the open meadowland, shaking the ground and snorting like beasts possessed.

There must be thirty of them! Olan's voice echoed round Mihran's head.

Even Mihran's tocka took a step back when the huge animals burst onto the battlefield. From what Mihran could see, they carried red worms on their broad backs and came out of the forest in pairs: one carrying enormous baskets of large boulders and the other saddled with stout catapults.

Mihran threw a glance at Belsang, who was manoeuvring his steed back to face the fight, having evidently ordered his troops to re-engage with the humans. The newcomers were Brakari allies now.

For the first time in decades, Mihran swore.

All hell was breaking loose around Althorn as he fought to understand what his overloaded senses were telling him. The stench of burnt flesh and chemicals filled the air, sending his stomach into alternating bouts of hunger and sickness. He was sitting beside a cluster of trees near to where a pack of Brakari fired blazing weapons into the sky. Sorean and other smaller slaves ran across the grassy hillside with ammunition and messages. Monkey-like creatures were working a giant catapult nearby and lumbering Lutameks dragged nets of glass balls of blue liquid.

The battle had started.

Althorn stared out between the tree trunks across a valley. On the opposite side, a defensive line of broken earth ran across a scorched hillside. Behind it, various groups of humans fought through smoke and fire. Althorn saw lines of Brakari soldiers scrambling across the trench towards the bulk of the human army using bridges made by a horde of pyramid-shaped creatures.

Belsang had managed to trap them after all, Althorn thought, and by the look of Mihran's fragmented army, the Brakari were winning.

The drifting wind carried a tang of putrid decay and Althorn retched but brought nothing up. Whatever he had been drugged with was wearing off. His shoulders ached where he had been tied to a stake in the ground.

Without warning, the trunks in front of Althorn moved. He blinked and looked up – the five broad, grey pillars were supporting a huge beast far bigger than the elephants Samas had described to him. It was four men high and had long drapes of metal-tipped armour hanging down its sides. On its back sat a wooden platform, where Althorn could make out an unmistakable powder-blue glow.

'Belsang,' he murmured.

Why was the Brakari leader keeping him by his side? Was he being saved to trade if they lost the war? Surely not. This was a battle to the death and only the victorious gained freedom through the silver gates. Belsang would have another use for him and, knowing the Brakari, it wouldn't be pleasant. Althorn had to escape and… he remembered the two brown creatures from the cart. They'd said they would help him kill Belsang, but there was no sign of them.

Althorn twisted his neck to see what Belsang was looking at. Past where the Sorean were fighting, scores of large shapes emerged from a forest. Althorn felt his stomach tense at the sight and flinched as a Brakari soldier scuttled past.

'Your orders, Dominus?' it asked Belsang.

Belsang waited a moment before answering. 'I have spoken with their leader. They are allied to our cause.'

'But Brakari don't make alliances,' the Brakari responded.

'You question my authority?' One of Belsang's tiny arms pointed to the front line. 'Join the battle immediately or I will make you prise off your shell and feed yourself to my Vaalori, limb by limb.'

Belsang's huge steed sidestepped back into its original position and the officer cowered before it.

'Yes, Dominus. Victorio Brakarius!' It raised a claw and disappeared down the hill.

Althorn watched the horned beasts from the forest pair up on the open ground of the battlefield. Myriad worms scampered over their backs, lifting rocks into wooden catapults, and each giant beast let out a wild trumpet-like call. A cacophony of deep, whip-crack sounds followed and dozens of catapults fired in unison. A moment of silence held as huge shadows raced across the battlefield before the immense lumps of rock smashed into the human–Sorean army, sending up clouds of dust and body parts.

Althorn swallowed hard. Boulders crushed the Sorean soldiers, obliterating three or four men in Samas' section at a time. One boulder crashed into a huge mossy shape, sending a shower of water over the red-coated riflemen nearby. Was that Mata? No, Althorn searched and found Mata strolling across the other side of the battlefield.

The Maori looked oblivious to anything around him as he nonchalantly strode into the Brakari front line. Althorn watched in awe as Mata homed in on a large, long-legged Brakari equipped with two flaming claws. Roots spurted out of Mata's feet, raising him up. The Brakari flinched and Althorn heard two pops. Mata's seed pods, he presumed. Then Mata raised an arm and dark-green vines sprang from his hand. Flames leapt from the Brakari but the vines wrapped around its limbs. Mata raised the other arm and more vines shot out. The Brakari flashed electric pulses, fired white-hot flames and slashed with all manner of blades and claws, but Mata had him in a deadly embrace. Seconds later, the Brakari lay in pieces and Mata resumed his casual stroll along the trench.

Althorn sighed. Mata was deadly but there was only one of him. Pummelled by the catapulted rocks, the rest of the army was only just holding the line – and more Brakari were coming. Althorn's comrades needed him, yet here he was, shackled and half blinded. He pulled on his restraints and grunted as the ropes bit into his wrists.

His eye travelled up to Belsang and he remembered the way he had casually flicked his eyeball from claw to claw. The arrogance and contempt riled Althorn, and an urge for vengeance surged through his veins. He had to do something! His belly tightened and he felt a strength building. He felt the ball of anger and defiance that had been there since the day his people had been massacred and taken into slavery. Nothing would take that feeling of loss away from him. Althorn had learnt from his first kill that he could feel temporary relief. Each assassination and every murder: the slave owners; pillagers; tyrants; and rapists. Each of their deaths had only given him a moment of peace, but killing Belsang would right many wrongs. Would it set Althorn free of his pain?

It didn't matter. He had no choice. He had to escape and kill Belsang, or die trying.

With a quick look for nearby guards, Althorn pushed against the pole – and it moved. He shoved it again, looked down to see a gap appearing where the stake drove into the earth. He pushed again and wiggled, then grabbed the pole and lifted it. Crouching down, he raised the pole clear of its hole, but the weight pulled him over, into the mud. With a grunt, he shimmied down and slipped his tied hands off and under his feet. The knot was easy for his teeth and, before he knew it, Althorn was free and climbing up the armour of the giant Vaalori.

The battle raged on with explosions and screams echoing along the valley and Althorn had to stop to catch his breath and make sure he hadn't been spotted. There were slave species nearby, working with boxes covered in lights, but they seemed too drained to look up, so Althorn twisted a spike out of the armour and gripped it between his teeth.

A few more rungs and Althorn was on the platform, behind Belsang. He calmed his breathing and clenched the spike in his hand before moving in to kill, as he had done scores of times before. He would aim for the throat area beneath what, from behind, looked like Belsang's head.

He took two steps forward.

'It's a good view from up here, isn't it Althorn?'

A blue hand leapt out of Belsang's back and snatched the spike before Althorn had a chance to respond. He stepped back and lost his balance, slipping on the metal armour, but another blue hand appeared and grabbed him.

Belsang continued, 'Although, not good from your point of view, I imagine.'

Althorn looked at the hand gripping his wrist: a gnarled, alien hand.

It felt like an out-of-body experience: here he was next to the enemy leader but unable to kill him.

'No,' he replied, 'not a good view.'

'Stay a while and watch with me.'

'I...' Althorn looked down to see several Brakari officers pacing around the Vaalori's feet.

'Or not,' Belsang said, 'it's your choice. Staying would lengthen your pitiful life by a few moments.'

Althorn was lost for words.

'So be it.' Belsang raised his voice so the troops below could hear. 'Now is the time for a sacrifice. Victorio Brakarius!'

'Victorio Brakarius!' the voices called back.

'Take him.' Belsang let go of Althorn and he fell off the Vaalori.

A long second later, he hit the ground with a thud and everything went black.

'According to the message on the obelisk at the start of my journey, something must happen today.' Delta-Six started his log on what he calculated was his fourteenth day in what he now accepted was not a virtual prison.

'On another note, my mini-sat, Copan-One, has been in communication with me. I've managed to access its archived images and I believe it has information it wants to share. Here comes a live camera feed… it's hovering over a broad valley where two armies are locked in battle and… I can zoom in. I recognise the blue arachnids I fought in the desert. The sat's swinging round to face the other army and… I must help them.'

'What's wrong?' John asked Millok when they stopped for a water break behind a stand of rocks protruding from the grassy plain like worn teeth. 'Something on your mind?'

Millok's spiracles opened and closed before she replied, which John had learnt was a sign she was thinking.

'Two things,' she started. 'Doctor Cynigar. I know we saw his body but–'

'He's dead,' John cut in. 'You took off his head remember? Then my bullet ripped a hole through his body.'

Millok made an undecipherable head wobble.

'He's dead,' John repeated. 'What's the other thing?'

Millok looked up to the distant horizon. 'This battle… sometimes I forget what I'm fighting for.'

There was more, John could tell, but he didn't know how to get her to talk. All he could do was empathise. 'Well, I'm fighting to get to the gates so I can make whoever brought me here pay for taking me from my son.'

Millok turned to him. 'I will be fighting *against* my children.'

John held her alien gaze and tried to understand how she felt. 'There must be a way to…'

'I have to fight to get through the silver gates,' she replied. 'If I don't, I'll be stuck here with the Brakari survivors and they'll want revenge.'

'But you've already killed an enemy – you killed Doctor Cynigar,' John said.

Millok stood up. 'Maybe.'

'So, you want to kill more to make sure?' John asked.

'Let's go,' Millok replied, which John took as a 'yes' and climbed onto the cart.

John double-checked the Lutamek box and gripped the cart with his good hand. Now she was back to full fitness, Millok could cover the ground four times faster than John could run.

'John,' Millok turned to him before pulling away, 'you should never fight for vengeance.'

'You think fighting for a righteous cause is better?' John shook his head. 'I've done that and look where that got us. One bleeding war after the next.'

'No, you should fight for something you believe in,' Millok said. 'You should fight for your comrades – for your friends.' She turned and, after a tug, they were speeding across the plain again.

Millok had something there, John thought. Back in France, after the shine had gone and reality kicked in, the only thing John and his mates had fought for was each other: looking out for snipers; telling stories; keeping spirits up when they got tired.

John thought about Crossley, Mata and Althorn. His head dropped as a wave of shame washed over him. He was right to volunteer to retrieve the Lutamek box but had been selfish seeking safety and abandoning his comrades. What would his grandfather have said about that? He pictured the old man's red-cheeked face and brilliant-white hair as he spouted whatever had him fired up. 'There are no second places in war, John!'

Maybe his grandfather had been right. He'd been to war and seen death, just like John had. Maybe the old man had been tough on John because, however hard he was, the reality of war would be much harder. Life had proven to be just as hard, John realised, and his thoughts turned to Rosie… and Joe.

The wooden cart bumped and jolted across the prairie as John's feelings consolidated. He had something to fight for: justice. And he had something to die for: his friends.

They climbed the long hill to the war valley and a light wind carried odours of battle that John recognised as explosives, turned earth and burnt flesh.

'We stop here.' Millok pulled up and lay down.

'Are you sure?' John climbed off, ready to fight, but could hear the tinkle of the Brakari's holes gasping for oxygen. Millok needed rest. 'I'll get some practice in,' John said and walked away.

Like in the trenches, he picked a target fifty paces away, a rock, and prepared his weapon. There was no bipod, no circular ammunition case to clip on, nothing to oil and no water cooler to top up. 'Water!' He wished he'd kept the bucket from Abzicrutia to cool his gun-arm down. He scanned the gun for an air vent or some remnant of the cooling system but nothing could be found. If this weapon had evolved, like Li said they all had, why didn't it have a way to remove the heat?

He told himself to forget it and stood in a stable firing position.

Using what felt like his fingers, John pictured a pointed bullet of compressed air and felt the shape take form inside the gun body. The sensation of heat was rising too.

Concentrate, John told himself, and fired.

The gun didn't make a sound and neither did the rock. A line of bent grass to one side showed where his shot had disappeared. Just like when he had shot Doctor Cynigar, there were no bullet casings flying from his gun, so he wasn't sure if he was firing slivers of metal or compressed air. He tried again, forming the shape, spinning then shooting. And missed. He tried again, with shorter and longer bullets, spinning one way, then the other, until a shard of stone finally splintered off the rock target with a satisfying crack.

The sound startled Millok, who stood up.

'I'm rested,' she said. 'Let's go.'

Her voice sounded loud to John. 'Wait.' He held up his good hand. 'It's too quiet. Something's wrong.'

Millok followed John's eyes up the hill towards the battle valley beyond.

John's face dropped. 'We need to go. Now.' He clambered onto the cart as quickly as he could. 'Quick!'

Millok pulled the cart up the rest of the hill and, as they reached the apex, the valley came into view. A dark line of torn earth curved an arc around where John's army had been stationed and bodies of all sizes lay scattered across the valley, some ringed by scarlet, others in burnt craters, mostly on the human side of the battle.

Nothing moved.

John climbed off the cart. His good leg wobbled and he fell to the ground.

'We're too late.'

Chapter 20

He had no choice. That's what Mihran reminded himself as he spurred his tocka back across the grassland towards the vast silhouette of the ruined fortress where they had left Crossley. His primary model switched the moment the new species arrived from the forest. Even if he ignored that, the next three suggested retreat as well.

We will fight again, Mihran had thought-cast after ordering the retreat.

They had to. Lose now and they would be stuck in this land with an even smaller army and there was no way Mihran wanted to be trapped here and risk becoming what the Brakari had turned into.

It was the silver gates or death.

He looked up at the green sky. They had enough light to keep fighting: no sign of dusk yet.

Commander. Gal-qadan's harsh tones entered his head. *When do we turn to fight?*

Mihran had asked Gal-qadan to form the army's rearguard, alongside the mounted knights who had survived Lavalle's defence of the ford. The Mongol knew many tactics but was refusing to accept this was a true retreat.

Defend the rear then seek safety in the fort, Mihran thought-cast. *New orders will follow.* He turned to catch a glimpse of Gal-qadan's sneer.

In between Mihran and Gal-qadan, the mass of humans and Sorean ran, limped and scampered across the plain. It was a sorry sight. Many were falling behind and being picked off by the fastest Brakari. Mihran began thought-casting Li to ask her advice but stopped as memories of the explosion came back. There was no one else he trusted.

The dark shape of the ruined fort loomed ahead like an enormous temple. It reminded Mihran of the huge ruins his army had camped in during their campaigns across Mesopotamia and Syria, only this fort had been scarred by flame rather than sand and time. For a moment, Mihran allowed himself to picture what this grand ruin had once been, just as he had done on those desert nights under the stars. He imagined an impenetrable gleaming fortress upon which armies had thrown their might: tall buttresses where skeletal metal now stood and imposing towers where stone now tottered as though leaning against the sky.

Everything returns to dust.

Ahead, Crossley and a number of soldiers stood by a fire with the giant pillars looming behind like a leafless forest. Mihran knew he had to take care and led his tocka on a winding path marked with yellow dots around what looked like deep trenches criss-crossing the ground in front of the ruin.

'I hope it slows them down,' he said as he pulled the tocka to a halt. 'Have you searched the fort?'

'Sure,' Crossley replied. 'We've got deep foundations – deeper than I can see anyway – and there are over five hundred pillars.'

'Made of?' Mihran asked.

'Stone with a metal core,' Crossley replied.

'And the gap between pillars?' Mihran asked.

'The same all the way through.'

Too narrow for a Lutamek to enter and, Mihran hoped, too small for a Brakari. The humans and Sorean would be safe inside the stone forest as long as they were protected from the inevitable bombardment.

'Anything else?' Mihran asked.

Crossley raised his eyebrows. 'Well, it's funny you ask. Hector here,' he pointed to a soldier Mihran didn't recognise, 'has found–'

'Wait.' Mihran held up a hand and dismounted his tocka. He didn't recognise the new soldiers: four men and one woman. 'Who are these people?'

'Soldiers who heard your call to arms and...'

One of the men stepped forward and held out his fist. 'I pledge my allegiance to your cause.'

Mihran stared at the broad-chested man and the newcomers. He ran their weapons and clothing through the list of soldiers Li had given him. The soldiers matched people missing from the inventory but Mihran had been fooled before. Behind them, the fastest foot soldiers were arriving: the Sorean and Olan were regrouping nearby having navigated the maze of trenches.

'Olan,' Mihran called out.

The large Viking sauntered over, panting heavily. 'Commander.'

'What do you see here?' Mihran gestured at the five new soldiers.

'More soldiers!' Olan forced a smile as he fought for breath.

'All human?'

'Yes.' Olan stared at the woman, who held his gaze, forcing him to look away.

It was enough for Mihran, who trusted Olan's chest plate. 'Good. You are welcome in our army.' He pointed at the oncoming enemy, who were forming a wide shadow across the horizon. 'Your timing couldn't be better.' Mihran stared into Hector's eyes. 'Have you had any… changes?'

'I…' the man looked down at his feet.

'Just tell him,' Crossley said. 'All of you – we haven't got time for this!'

The big man gave Crossley a look similar to the one Lavalle saved for him, then turned to Mihran. 'I can push arrows away with my thoughts.'

Mihran's eyebrows raised. 'Good.' He'd last longer than most when it comes to hand-to-hand combat, he thought.

The other four listed their adaptations, none of which were game-changers, but Mihran added them to his model. 'Crossley, I need the archers in position. Direct them as they arrive. All other troops are to be scattered throughout the fort.'

'Yes, Commander. I know the perfect spot,' Crossley replied.

Mihran closed his eyes to thought-cast the same message to his captains.

Nearly there, Samas replied.

And then we fight, Gal-qadan replied but Mihran didn't respond. He wanted Gal-qadan's tocka hidden deep inside the fortress.

Looks like I might be waylaid, Commander, Bowman replied and shared an image of a group of Brakari who had his group surrounded. Ethan and Euryleia were with him.

Lavalle, Mihran thought-cast. *Help Bowman.*

There would be fewer archers at the fort than Mihran had planned for. He adjusted his models. They were running out of time.

Mihran led his tocka into the fort, calming it with soft words as they passed in between pillars and into the darkness. This sanctuary would have to suffice, he told himself and, after a quick saunter around, he sought Crossley, who was giving directions.

'...up that stairwell then jump over and you've got a perfect view. Hey, Commander, our spot is over here.' He led Mihran and his tocka up a slope to a metal platform that gave them a clear view through the diagonal gaps between the pillars and a view of the ground straight ahead.

'Perfect. And what about our other plans?'

'Pretty perfect too.' The American smiled.

A flash of light on the open plain caused them to turn and cover their eyes.

Mihran blinked to get rid of the black and white lines. *Report,* he thought-cast.

We've lost Ethan, Bowman replied. *Several injured.*

Get to safety, Mihran ordered. *Lavalle is coming to your aid.*

'Well that screwed up my eyes.' Crossley blinked and stared into the dark centre of the fort.

'Leave me, I need to think,' Mihran said. 'Get the army in as quickly as possible.'

'Yes, Commander.'

Mihran stood beside his tocka on the platform with a hundred questions circling his mind. He stroked his dyed beard, took a deep breath and started bringing order to the chaos. He visualised his thoughts as birds in a clear sky and herded them into groups. Thoughts about the origins of the fort; Gal-qadan's alien weapon; injured soldiers; the new titans; Belsang. Categorised and prioritised, he pushed away the frivolous questions and concentrated on the immediate problems.

Regroup. Assess. Attack.

Words Li had told him came to mind: 'In war, numbers are not an issue – concentrate your strength, assess your enemy and win the confidence of your soldiers.'

It was time for his wildcards: the unpredictable weapons and abilities. He couldn't calculate their effect but they needed something to catch Belsang off guard.

First they needed to set the trap.

Billy, Mihran thought-cast the Scottish warrior, *Sing me a song.*

Aye, Commander.

Mihran saw Gal-qadan's tocka winding through Crossley's trenches and minefields.

Come straight through, Mihran ordered him and spoke when he came into earshot. 'Send your troops deep, to our right flank. Then we must talk.'

Gal-qadan gave his orders then brought his tocka to the base of the ramp.

'You have a choice, Gal-qadan,' Mihran said. 'Give your weapon to the infantry and lead your men, or dismount and fight here with your weapon.'

Gal-qadan snorted and looked away. Mihran took it as a sign he was weighing up his options. He was well aware he was forcing Gal-qadan to give up what the Mongol regarded as half his power.

'It is borrowed anyway.' Gal-qadan cut a strap holding the large gun on the back of his tocka, sending it crashing to the ground, and rode off without looking at Mihran.

'Keep on the flank,' Mihran said. 'I'll need you soon.'

'Crossley,' Mihran called out, 'I have a new toy for you.'

Mihran scanned the army. If he pushed his mind out, he could feel where the archers and foot soldiers had been stationed. He could also feel the mass of Brakari and slave soldiers pressing down on them. He opened his eyes and listened to the Scottish lament that came and went with the breeze. Then he saw the first ghost warrior, standing by one of the front pillars, another shimmering into existence next to it.

The way of war, he thought, is a way of deception.

Now to prepare the attack.

John scanned the bodies on the valley floor and assumed the army had been taken into slavery by the Brakari, but the blinding flash over the horizon told him the fighting was still going on.

Millok pulled the cart to John and he clambered in. His friends needed him. How could he look them in the eye after all this and tell them he hadn't tried to help?

Millok pulled away and, as they passed bodies and trails, John built a picture of his army's last actions. The storage boxes lay empty where John had last seen them next to the bodies of the Lutamek, and a stream of abandoned weapons, bags and dead soldiers led back in the direction the army had walked that morning. John saw the hazy silhouette of a thousand smokestacks in the distance and it became clear.

'It's a retreat!' he shouted to Millok. 'A tactical retreat!'

'How do… if it is… best?' Millok's words were cut off as she ran.

'It is,' John replied, guessing what Millok had said.

They had no time to stop and talk.

He pictured Crossley by the tall stacks of the ruined fort and smiled at what his friend would have in store for the Brakari. It was all part of Mihran's plan! He must have known this would happen all along. The wind rushed past John's ears and tousled his hair. It felt good. But as they passed more bodies, John's good humour faded. Clusters of burnt human and Sorean bodies lay smouldering. A few Brakari carcases could be seen seeping dark blood into the grassland, but only a few.

John's army was being hunted down and slaughtered.

Millok slowed down when the rearguard of the Brakari army came into view. From this distance, the haze of Brakari and their slave army looked endless and he didn't recognise the huge lumbering beasts on the right wing.

He spotted the silhouette of a Lutamek.

'I'll turn the box on,' he said to Millok, who unhitched herself and came round to inspect the Lutamek gadget.

'Do you know what to do?' she asked.

John stared at the twinkling lights and coloured buttons and swallowed. 'I thought it would be obvious when the time came.'

'How about this one?' Millok used a leg blade to tap a square shape.

Nothing happened.

John rotated the cube, searching for a sign. A glass panel covered rows of tiny coloured lights and beneath each light he could see rows of dots, which matched the patterns he had seen on the Lutamek. He scanned them until he found one he recognised.

'Here, Ten-ten.' The light next to the rows of dots was red, while others flickered blue and many showed no light at all. 'What does it mean?'

'I assume the empty boxes are dead Lutamek.'

John scanned the empty lights until he found a set of dots he recognised. 'Two-zero-three.' He remembered the leader's deep tones and stern manner. 'He must have died when the Brakari set them against each another,' John said. 'What would the survivors do without a leader?'

'Don't worry about that, it's the flashing lights we need to concentrate on – they must be the enslaved Lutamek,' Millok replied.

John pressed one of the flashing lights and it turned red. He looked up and stared across the prairie, expecting one of the huge robots to jump into the air. But nothing happened. When he looked back it was flashing blue again.

Crossley would know what to do, John thought. Or Mihran or Althorn. But they were on the other side of the enormous enemy army. John started to feel hot. He didn't want to make a decision like this, he just wanted to go home and leave all this behind.

'Oh, bloody hell!' he cursed and pressed all the flashing blue lights. They all changed to red, but a second later they were winking blue again.

'Maybe we need to get closer?' Millok suggested.

'Closer?' John knew they had to fight but what use were two soldiers against an entire army? Maybe distracting some Brakari would buy the army some time? He grabbed the tin soldier under his shirt. 'Okay, let's do it.'

Millok set off, skirting a wide arc to the Brakari's left flank and John pressed the buttons. He looked for other signs on the box but, as they drew closer, his attention drifted.

'What's that?' John pointed to two huddles of shapes off the left flank. Light flickered between them as though they were inside a tiny lightning storm.

Millok headed for it and John realised it was a separate melee.

'They're rounding up the stragglers!' John shouted and his gun-arm clicked.

As they neared, John made out a group of twenty humans and Sorean hiding behind rocks, while several well-armed Brakari tried to surround them and blast the cover away. One of the Brakari ventured wide to get around the open side of the defenders but was sent scuttling back by a laser shot that ripped off a forearm.

John recognised Li's rifle.

'We need to distract them!' John shouted and started spinning shapes in his gun's chamber.

His stomach tightened and he retched. This was it. Into battle. Time to fight.

A shape to the right came into John's view and he turned to see a swathe of tocka rushing with it across the plain at a speed greater than Millok could manage. Lavalle rode at the head, splendid in his black armour, sword raised and visor pushed up. As their speeding paths closed, John could see Lavalle's eyes were lit with anger and his tocka bared a mouth bursting with razor-sharp teeth. A memory of his grandfather came to John: his red face and foaming mouth as he recounted a cavalry charge. Now John was really doing it!

He couldn't help himself. 'Charge!' he shouted, willing Millok on.

Millok sped up and John braced his gun-arm on the cart side. His heart was racing as they neared the Brakari, who were turning to face them. John started spinning bullets: long and pointed to fly far and produce less heat, he hoped. He held his breath as Lavalle's tocka met the first Brakari. Lavalle hung on as his steed weaved and leapt at the Brakari with the prowess of a lioness. It took a slash on a hind leg but was too quick for the lumbering Brakari and was on its back in a flash. Lavalle was slashing his heavy broadsword, cleaving limbs from sockets and parrying blade-legs from below but, as John and Millok passed, the Brakari rolled over, sending Lavalle and his tocka flying.

John couldn't look back. Millok was heading straight for another Brakari, who flashed green like Doctor Cynigar. John aimed and fired a stream of bullets. It was harder than firing the old gun because he had to build the bullets as fast as he fired them, but he soon caught the knack and threw in a few corkscrew shells to tear at the Brakari's thick shell. It wasn't working though.

The Brakari fired back, releasing a ball of light, the cart exploded with a flash and everything stopped. The ground and sky sped past, one after the other and, when he stopped rolling, roaring sounds and flashes filled John's mind as he struggled to pick himself off the ground. Apart from his dazed head, he was uninjured. Millok was nowhere to be seen and the battle raged around him. Tocka dashed past. The blue shells of the Brakari were near, as were the rocks where the soldiers had hidden, who were out now, attacking.

He saw a woman – was it Euryleia? It looked like her but John's head was spinning and something seemed wrong with her body. He blinked and turned to see Millok fighting. It was the first time he had seen her in her element. Released from the cart, she was nearly as fast as Althorn. It was obvious she was on the allies' side and her grey colour set her apart, but John still worried someone might fire at her by mistake.

John dug his metal foot into the dirt and pushed off his gun-arm to stand. Now he could see the fight more clearly. Lavalle's tocka had regrouped and were charging three Brakari who had created a defensive position against the rocks, while a party of Sorean were spinning and dancing around a cornered Brakari as they fought in their energetic way. A laser shot flashed as it pierced a Brakari head shell, frying its brain. John followed the beam back to Li's rifle and was surprised to see someone else holding it.

'Bowman?'

The fight was nearly over and, for a reason John couldn't understand, he felt sad. He felt left out. He hadn't done anything to help this group effort and he felt like he had to be part of the group. He headed towards the three Brakari and pictured corkscrews spinning in the gun chamber. He added barbs and fine points and found himself running as the group of tocka attacked the Brakari. Two tocka were brought down, sliced to pieces by the Brakari blades, and John saw an unsaddled rider hammered into the ground with a rock-like claw, yet John ran faster. One of the Brakari saw John and ran at him: claws raised and mouth blades slashing. It let out a screech as it charged.

John didn't think about what to do next because it came naturally. He slowed, planted his feet, raised his gun-arm and fired an infinity shape, crossing over at the Brakari's head.

But the Brakari still charged.

Puffs of dust were exploding behind the Brakari, who sped up.

Thirty paces away; twenty-five.

Had he missed? John created and fired new bullets. More tiny explosions ripped the ground behind the Brakari.

Twenty paces.

He fired more.

Fifteen paces.

He noticed a change. The rhythm of the Brakari's pace became disjointed as one leg stopped moving in time with the rest. Then another leg. It didn't slow down, but its legs were dropping limp one by one. John fired more as the huge blue-shelled beast closed in on him, shaking the ground. Then a front leg fell, tripping the next, sending the Brakari into a stumble and roll. With a piercing scream and wildly slashing claws, it rolled past John.

Only when the Brakari stopped did the dark blood spout from the myriad holes created by John's bullets. He stood in silence, staring at the dead soldier. Had he done that? He looked around. The rest of the Brakari were dead.

A scuttling sound behind him made John turn and raise his gun.

'Well done, John.' It was Millok. Her sides flashed blue and her spiracles gasped for air.

'I–' John panted for breath as well.

'You can lower your weapon now,' she said. 'The fight's over.'

'Oh.' John let his gun-arm swing down. 'Sorry, I just…'

Lavalle arrived with a clatter of tocka feet. 'Your weapon is working now, John?'

'Yeah.' John smiled at Euryleia, who sat behind Lavalle.

'And the box? Did you get it?' the knight asked.

'Well, yes.' John gestured back at the cart. 'I tried working it but nothing's happened.'

'I'll let Mihran know,' Lavalle said and closed his eyes to thought-cast their commander.

While he waited, John watched Bowman help injured Sorean onto the cart and coaxed a tocka over. Euryleia was bending a bow and stringing its tight cord. Didn't she already have a bow during the fight? John thought.

Lavalle opened his eyes. 'John, join Bowman on the cart and hold back with…' he cast a glance at Millok.

'Millok,' John said.

'Millok, yes. Then follow us.' He turned the tocka in the direction of the main Brakari army.

'What are you doing?' John asked.

'We're attacking of course!' Lavalle's eyes glinted and he kicked the tocka into a gallop. 'With me!' he shouted to his cavalry.

As they paced away, John had a clear view of Euryleia on the back of Lavalle's tocka. She had two quivers strapped across her back and held two primed bows. John blinked and looked again.

She held two bows in her four arms.

Why didn't Belsang just finish these weaklings off? Panzicosta's plates snapped in annoyance as he galloped across the grassland. Everything was in Belsang's favour: a weak, unprepared enemy; a battlefield of his choosing; the power to bring back the first army; even a platoon of unexpected allies for Brak's sake. With all this, Belsang still let the humans crawl away undefeated. Victory was there for the taking, so why didn't he grab it and be done with it? Did he want the 'perfect victory'? That kind of talk got you killed in Panzicosta's day. War was ruthless and unforgiving. You won or lost.

'Get out of my way!' Panzicosta bellowed at a pair of young Brakari who veered into his path.

He might not be manoeuvrable or slim like other Brakari, but when he got moving nothing could stop him.

'General.' They submitted and parted.

Up ahead a stack of broken towers loomed: a safe haven for the humans. The dull sun was still high, so they had time, but what if darkness fell before a victory was established? Would they still win? And why did Belsang insist on sacrificing the one-eyed human in front of the enemy? There were far better ways to intimidate them.

Ahead, a group of Brakari captains were feasting on slaughtered humans and Panzicosta felt his hunger rise as he watched them rip into their abdomens and gorge themselves on the foetid bowels within.

It gave him an idea.

'Cease!' he ordered and, with great effort, slowed his hulk of a body to a trot and curved a path round to face them. 'Cease your feeding.'

The Brakari officers looked up.

'You are welcome to your portion, General.' A sleek Brakari captain pushed a corpse forward.

Panzicosta closed his spiracles and fought the urge to dig in. 'No, I have a better use for these.'

One of the officers, his mind fogged by bloodthirst, stood to his full height and approached Panzicosta with both claws raised.

'We are in battle, Sergeant,' Panzicosta roared, 'hand the corpse to me or face instant punishment!'

The sergeant snapped its shells without slowing its stride. Its mouth-pieces gnashed rhythmically against each other, forming a foam of human blood, which dripped from his mouth.

'You risk death over a meal?' Panzicosta was almost bemused by the behaviour and flexed a back leg. 'So be it.'

Panzicosta clicked a button with a foreleg and a silver tube emerged from his undercarriage and sprayed the advancing Brakari with white gas. The sergeant froze instantly. Panzicosta walked over with no rush, tapped the Brakari on its head plate and, with a sound like breaking glass, the large arthropod's shell shattered and collapsed to the floor, followed by his warm innards.

'Now.' Panzicosta faced the other officers. 'Load the bodies up and take them to the catapult.'

'Yes, General. Victorio Brakarius!' they chanted.

Panzicosta flexed his plates and stretched his legs. 'Yes, Victorio Brakarius.'

He stalked away without looking back and cast a glance to where Belsang floated on his lumbering Vaalori, surrounded by guards and dragging the human sacrifice behind on a broken Lutamek. Around them, other sparking, collared Lutamek peppered the host of slave soldiers, hemmed in by Brakari guards. Light-blue clones mostly. Which reminded Panzicosta – where was that dried-up Skrift turd, Cynigar?

General!

Panzicosta reeled back as Belsang's mental icicle drilled into his head. *Yes, Dominus.*

Cease killing my officers.

Dominus, his insolence needed reprimanding, Panzicosta replied.

So will yours if you disobey me. The sharp pain pressed deeper into his head, then disappeared. Panzicosta swayed and opened every set of eyes as he fought a wave of nausea. He breathed deeply and caught sight of a troop of slave species carrying large metal canisters. These were the energy potions Doctor Cynigar brewed for Belsang. An idea formed and Panzicosta smiled, but a sudden flash of light made him turn with a gasp.

'Brakarius!' he groaned.

Two sets of eyes were temporarily blinded but others compensated and focused. He could see a host of dead soldiers: the fastest Brakari and their last few Skrift had been destroyed by whatever weapon had released the light. Some humans and Sorean had been injured too.

'Report!' Panzicosta shouted at one of the nearest Brakari officers.

'General?'

'The explosion – what happened?' Panzicosta asked.

'A human detonation, General.'

'It sacrificed *itself*?'

'It's not clear, General, but–'

Panzicosta held up a front claw to silence the officer, who cowered, waiting to be relieved. The General ignored it and stared at the tall towers in the distance: the humans' refuge. They must be getting desperate if they were sacrificing soldiers. Was that Belsang's plan? To force them to use up their hidden weapons until they were broken and could fight no more?

Panzicosta set off, striking the officer with a tail blade as he passed.

The tocka pulled the cart faster than Millok had been able to and, despite the fear tightening John's stomach as they closed in on the Brakari army, he felt exhilarated. The two Sorean clinging to the tocka's back looked wide-eyed and happy too, with their fur flowing in the wind. A hundred paces ahead, Lavalle and the other knights were veering to the right.

'What's this then?' Bowman strained his neck to get a better look from where he sat next to John.

Their tocka followed its instinct and stayed with the herd.

John peered back, past the injured Sorean who shared his cart, to see Millok keeping up with them.

'That's where we're heading!' Bowman pointed at the huge beasts.

From this distance it was hard to make out individual Brakari soldiers but Belsang's huge steed was plain to see at its core, as were the large creatures on the right flank. John squinted as a shape rose off the catapult on the back of one giant, lifted high into the air and smashed into the ruined fort with a hollow echo.

'We have to help,' John said.

A whip-crack signalled a new bombardment, followed by another soon after.

Bowman shrugged his broad shoulders. 'Lavalle said hold back.' He smiled and patted Li's rifle. 'But this should make easy work of them, eh?'

John nodded and stared at the flashing lights on the gun, which were as much of a mystery to him as the Lutamek box. 'How did you get it?' he asked. 'What happened to Li?'

'They picked her off,' Bowman replied. 'Then Ethan had the rifle… amazing shot he was.'

'What happened to him?' John wondered who in their army was still alive.

'We were caught back there.' Bowman nodded back to the plain. 'Whole bunch of us. You know how his skin was turning grey?'

John nodded. He'd heard Dakaniha tell Mihran it was a skin disease.

'Well he must have been absorbing light, that's my guess. God knows how in this bloody cloudy land but, anyway, we were surrounded and defending ourselves. Lavalle and his lot were off chasing Brakari and Gal-qadan's tocka were long gone.'

John took another look at where they were headed while Bowman talked. More catapults were firing and he could see the red worms massing together to load more boulders.

'He waited till they were near enough then he exploded.'

John turned back. 'A flash of light?'

'Yep. Then he was gone.' Bowman shrugged.

It was the flash he and Millok had seen from the first battlefield.

'He took out most of the Brakari and we finished off the rest,' Bowman continued as the cart bobbled and jolted beneath them. 'A few of us were caught in the blast though.' He looked over to where Lavalle rode at the head of the pack.

'Is that how they were injured?' John nodded at the burnt cat-like soldiers who looked like children with their hair burnt off.

'Yep,' Bowman replied.

'And Euryleia?' John asked.

Bowman's eyes widened. 'Yes, strange thing. Should be used to it now but, well, she was in a bad way and then these new arms grew.' He stopped with a shake of the head.

They were getting close and John saw more detail in the Brakari army: individual slave soldiers; Belsang on his beast; the enslaved Lutamek. John picked up the metal cube and handed it to Bowman. 'If you can work Li's gun you might know what to do with this.'

Bowman frowned. 'Just a load of flashing lights to me.' He played one-handed with the lights on the panel John had found, pressing them in a random order. Then he laughed. 'Funny how you turn them off and they turn on again like someone's playing a game.'

'Well it's not a ga–' John stopped mid-sentence. 'Maybe someone *is* switching them back on again.' John stared across the enemy army and spotted a green mass of thrashing vines. 'Look, there's Mata!'

The Maori was in full battle mode on the edge of the army: covered in skin of a hard bark core, trapping anything in his path with thorn-ribbed tendrils as he stalked the prairie. He reminded John of the sea creatures they'd seen in the lake, as Mata reeled in his prey on tentacles and pulled the tough Brakari apart like Cromer crabs.

'Looks like it's our turn now.' Bowman nodded to where Lavalle led his knights on the right wing.

Bowman handed the Lutamek box back to John and got on his knees. 'Ready for some target practice?'

John looked at the box and saw a new section where Bowman had slid a panel back, revealing three new buttons. He didn't know why but he held them all down with his thumb, then ran the muzzle of his gun over the lights. This time they stayed red.

'John!' Bowman shouted. 'We're getting close!'

He saw the worms wriggling across the backs of the giant catapult holders, less than fifty paces away.

'Okay, let's do it!' John shoved the box in his satchel and started spinning long-range bullets.

Bowman attracted the attention of the Sorean on the tocka's back and explained what they wanted to do: circle in, fire and speed off before the enemy could retaliate.

John looked back at Millok and hoped she would understand what they were doing.

'Fire at will!' he shouted, pointing in the direction of the lumbering beasts, and the cart dashed in for their first attack.

'Aim high,' Bowman shouted over the noise of the wheels, 'we've got a wind coming in from the right.'

John felt the spinning air-bullets line up and aimed at the red worms on the nearest beast.

'Bet I hit more!' Bowman's eyes were wide with excitement.

'Let's see.' John gritted his teeth as they fired in unison.

The flash from Li's rifle startled John, sending his first burst of bullets to the right, knocking off one of the catapult loaders.

'Yes!' John shouted.

As they closed in, John fired flat-nosed bullets that punched the worms off their platforms. One of the Sorean on the tocka's back was firing a crossbow, while the other steered the tocka around the back of the enemy beast. John kept firing in bursts, trying to keep the temperature of his gun-arm down. He'd lost count of how many enemy he'd hit. One had been thrown backwards by his shot and tangled up in the catapult mechanism which fired prematurely, sending its lump of rock spinning into the Brakari army.

'Nice shot!' Bowman shouted.

'Cheers,' John replied.

'Bring us around!' Bowman shouted to the Sorean jockey and they wheeled away.

Looking ahead, John saw a group of Lavalle's tocka had leapt on a fallen behemoth, while another stomped about blindly with one of Euryleia's arrows protruding from an eye. Behind them, John caught a glimpse of Millok disappearing into the throng of catapult giants only to appear on one's back, flashing electric blue and flitting about quicker than John's eye could keep up with. A second later, the platform dropped from the beast's back, smashing into the ground.

John's tocka swung towards the group on the far right. Bowman took a long shot, trying to hamstring the nearest beast, but its tough armoured skin absorbed the energy pulse.

'It isn't enough,' John shouted to Bowman.

Dozens of catapults still threw their devastating loads and the nearest battalion of Brakari had turned to defend them.

'Aim for the straps,' John shouted and Bowman nodded.

The tocka sped up again and they aimed low. Bowman's pulse caught a side strap and melted the lacquered hide but it didn't split. John tried to finish off the job but just peppered the strap with holes. They cut left and swerved back to the next beast where Bowman's second shot had more luck, cutting through a major strap, jolting the catapult. The weight shift pulled the beast into the next behemoth and it fell to the ground with a deep bellow.

The tocka wheeled away as a wave of Brakari rushed through, firing energy pulses and spinning missiles at them.

'Watch out!' John shouted as a devilish snake-like torpedo whipped through the air and blasted the archer Sorean off the tocka's back.

John turned and fired at the Brakari. Bowman had given up on the rifle and fired his trusty longbow now, sending Marodeen's bird arrows into the sky, followed by some of Crossley's explosive mini-spears. Together they bought enough time to retreat and regroup.

'We need to get to Lavalle or back to Mihran,' Bowman said when the tocka slowed for a rest. 'I'll thought-cast for orders.' He closed his eyes.

'Right,' John said and slumped to a sitting position but only had to wait a few seconds.

'Shit!' Bowman's eyes snapped open. 'We need to get out of here. Quick, pull them around!' he shouted at the Sorean jockey. 'Everyone, this way!' Bowman beckoned the group of tocka away from the Brakari army.

John was looking around in panic as the cart sped away. Something was about to happen, but what?

Then he heard a deep rumbling sound.

Chapter 21

Olan was daydreaming when the lump of entrails smashed into a tower and showered him with some unfortunate soul's partially digested last meal. Four new shapes tumbled through the sky. Were they limbs? Or bodies? The shapes increased in size and crashed into the men around him before many could raise a shield. Screams could be heard where bones and armour injured the unprepared. Most just wrinkled their noses and started picturing what they would do to the Brakari who had disrespected their dead friends.

On a distant hill, Olan caught a glimpse of a familiar silhouette: the tall shape of Peronicus-Rax. Then he saw movement on the left wing: the titanic catapult bearers had started firing. Warning shouts came through, but there was little they could do as the first white boulder hit a grey tower and splintered into knife-sharp shards of white and grey stone that stabbed at the army below, dodging and sheltering where they could. Another boom signalled a new boulder, followed by another, and soon everyone felt the rain of stone. And so the music of war began: deep echoes, splintering destruction and yells of pain.

Olan looked back to the raised platform where Mihran sat on his tocka. He had finished with his captains, who walked down to their respective troops. The Commander's head turned from left to right and back again in the rhythmic motion Olan had seen on the first battlefield. When would they charge? Sitting here was going to be suicide.

'They're approaching.' Dakaniha pointed to the Brakari army.

'Good!' Kastor replied. 'We need to meet them on the field!'

'Are you ready?' Samas shouted as he pushed through to the front, wearing his gleaming armour.

'Yes!' the warriors replied as a new shower of stones pattered against shields and helmets.

'Have the enemy learnt their lesson?' Samas stepped up onto a broken boulder and faced the bulk of the foot soldiers, who craned their necks to see him.

'No!' they answered in unison.

'They come back for more!' Samas gestured at the army of giant blue-shelled arthropods and alien slave warriors, just two hundred paces away now, with Crossley's trenches and yellow markers sitting halfway between them.

'We need to teach them again!' a soldier cried out.

'Yes.' Samas smiled. Olan relaxed as he watched him and felt eager to fight. 'They learn slowly these Brakari… and the best way to learn is through practice.'

'Yes!'

'They've lost once before, so let's show them how to lose again!' Samas shouted.

'Yes!' The army surged forward a step.

'But first,' Samas held up a palm for quiet, 'first we need to let others have their moment.'

Samas was stalling, Olan realised.

'Not the archers again?' Kastor said and the men around him laughed.

'No, not the archers.' Samas turned to face the Brakari horde who were close but, Olan could see, had stopped a distance from the trenches, which looked different from this angle. Samas cast a glance back to Mihran on the platform and gave a quick nod. 'This time!' Samas raised his great stone fist. 'There will be no retreat. No defeat. Victory will be ours!'

As Samas finished, a deep cracking sound erupted and Olan felt vibrations through his feet. Moments later, far away on the battlefield, a mountain of dust blasted out of the ground, but not between the armies, as it had done at the first battle. This time the explosions ripped a line behind the Brakari army, encircling them.

'Now we have the bastards trapped!' Samas shouted over the roar of the army, which mingled with the echoes of the vast explosion. 'Let's kill them all!'

Olan was pushed forward with the army as they ran to fight. He stared wide-eyed as the Brakari army surged forward to meet them, moving away from what he imagined was a semicircle cut at their backs.

'Attack!' Samas shouted and led them full speed towards the trenches. 'Fear nothing!'

The Babylonian didn't slow down. Was he going to leap over the trenches? Olan slowed his pace, as did others around him, but watched as Samas ran straight across the open holes, his sandalled feet throwing up dust as he crossed the dark lines.

'It's paint!' Kastor shouted.

Another trick. And one Olan's chest plate was powerless to reveal.

Olan kicked on, gripped his battleaxe tight and looked for his first target. Pushed by their panicking rear lines, the Brakari had spread out. The front line must have assumed the humans would jump into the safety of the trenches, so were standing in casual stances.

'Bring them down!' Samas shouted.

New explosions ripped the ground apart around Olan, scooping holes out of the battlefield. Then came the erratic energy beams and wild missiles Olan remembered from the battle a few hours earlier and he recognised their smell. He kept focused and picked out a large, dark-blue Brakari with an orange claw and long, scorpion-like tail. No puppets now and no diggers – these were the real warriors. Olan raised his axe high and dodged right as the armoured beast stabbed with its tail. Olan swung low and swiped it as he passed, but the tail spike hadn't been aimed at him: Osayimwese was right behind him and parried the blow with his shield. On the other side, Kastor had leapt high and struck his long spear into the soft section between the leg and body shells, sending the Brakari leaping back with a roar.

'You'll pay for that, human!' it shouted.

Olan skidded and ran back, determined to slice off the tail. Dakaniha was there as well, with all four eyes open, firing arrows at weaknesses in the shell that only he could see. Olan was about to rush in when Dakaniha fired an arrow straight past his head. Olan threw a glance back and saw the arrow bounce off a huge, hammer-clawed Brakari covered in arm-length spikes. It was distracted long enough for Olan to roll away as the hammer crashed into the ground and he was back on his feet in a second. Olan didn't think now: he fought. Down came his axe, biting into the nearest claw arm, and out, followed by a turn and a burst of pace, then another powerful swing at a leg. He saw Osayimwese at the broad beast's tail, stabbing with his spear. With a violent flick of its thick tail, Osayimwese was sent flying back, and behind him a hammer-claw swung low to take out an armoured swordsman who had joined the fight. The beast rounded on Olan, foaming at the mouth, shuddering and twitching, reminding Olan of the real, drugged berserkers he had fought alongside.

'Kill all humans!' it screamed. 'Victorio Brakarius!'

Olan sidestepped into a crater, but the Brakari was faster than it looked and reared up to more than three times his height, ready to pummel him with its many, heavy-headed claws. Olan tensed, ready to dodge and run, but the huge creature paused. Olan heard a deep crunch, followed by a crack and the Brakari's forelegs scratched at its belly. Another crack and a bulge pushed out of its chest. Another crunch and the front shell splintered with a shower of blue liquid and Samas stepped through with his rock-arm glowing orange.

'Thanks,' Olan said. 'I owe you one.'

Out of breath, Samas simply nodded.

Olan ran back to the scorpion Brakari whose tail had been sheared off. Dakaniha and Osayimwese were either side of it and Kastor had returned from another kill. Dakaniha leapt in with a spear and skidded away to avoid a bladed arm.

Then something strange happened.

The Brakari flinched for no apparent reason and slowly raised off the ground. It rocked back and forth in the air, swiping at its side while Dakaniha kneeled beneath, staring in confusion. Then it fell limp.

Kastor walked forward, patted Dakaniha on the shoulder and pointed to three holes in the dead Brakari's body. 'Good fighting, Sakarbaal,' he said and smiled.

'Sakarbaal?' Dakaniha stood up slowly.

Olan caught a glimpse of a grin beneath the Brakari and dark blood poured from the holes to form the shape of a trident. The Brakari body fell onto the grass and the trident disappeared with a laugh, lost in the sounds of battle.

Kastor jogged away, swinging his spear and searching for his next opponent.

'Come on!' he shouted back with his typical smile. 'The next one's mine!'

As he turned around though, a large Brakari covered in spiked armour rose from a deep crater and leapt at him with frightening speed. Kastor stood no chance, and Olan could only watch as the Spartan was sliced in half with one powerful blow.

Panzicosta released a wild roar that shook his armour and sent the scrawny humans around him into panic. He picked up the top half of the soldier he had killed and pushed its torn guts into his mouth. It tasted better than Sorean. Panzicosta's enjoyment was short-lived though, as the creature attacked his face; before he could rip its head off, it had sliced one of Panzicosta's main eyes and disabled a mouth pincer. Still, a new eye would grow back, he thought, as he cast the human's remains aside.

The other humans attacked him: blunting their spears and wasting their flimsy arrows on his armour. They tried to surround him: one with four eyes, another with armour that shone with odd light frequencies and the last with an orange appendage Panzicosta didn't trust. With the crater just behind him, Panzicosta had to make some room to fight.

'I'm going to tear you apart!' he shouted at the four-eyed human and slashed with his longest fore-blade.

The human was nimble and rolled away, giving Panzicosta's blade nothing but thin air.

'And then I'll eat you headfirst, you little shit!' Panzicosta slammed a hammer-claw down but it met dry ground.

A sharp pain in his right side made him turn and lash out, striking the human who had been stupid enough to come close. He took a step forward and felt the pain again. A quick feel with a lower leg revealed the issue – his side armour had been dented and was cutting into his carapace. He knew he couldn't trust that human's fist. What material could dent Brakari cold armour? Panzicosta turned as another warrior joined them, armed with a spear and a short, white blade. He needed to kill before he was completely surrounded, so he charged up the pulse rifle embedded in his thick belly armour: an old weapon but useful in a scrape like this.

Now the human with the shining armour attacked, hacking at his legs, and here came another spear thrust, and where was the human with the fist? Panzicosta turned and swiped with his longest hammer-claw, cursing his armour for restricting his movement. Still, he had knocked two humans down. A quick lunge sent another one scuttling back and he had his moment: he blasted three energy bolts into the ground, sending dirt flying, then ran as fast as his large bulk could take him through the opening.

But he didn't make it far. Something was stopping him – a green tendril coiled around one of his hammer-claws.

'No!' He turned to see a writhing green shape on the other side of the crater throwing more barbed vines at him.

Panzicosta slashed at the thick tendrils as they wrapped around his limbs. He had seen the creature in action and knew what it was capable of. The creepers were coming too quick. There was only one option if he was going to survive. He strained against the vines, hit a red button on his armour and shouted, 'Brakarius armis redux!' His spiked armour released instantly and General Panzicosta leapt out, smashing through the nearest humans and away to open ground.

Once he was clear, Panzicosta turned a pair of eyes back, saw the humans' despair and released a bitter laugh. He had lost his armour but he was alive. Now he needed a victory he could brag about if he was to replace Belsang as leader.

He paused in an open space to take stock of the battle around him. The Brakari army was trapped. Well played, humans. But in their haste they had trapped themselves and, for all their tactical gambles and victories, the human–Sorean alliance was still outnumbered by the Brakari's slave army. Victory was still possible despite Belsang's ineptitude.

Panzicosta scanned the nearest enemy troops and focused on a pack of tocka attacking the left wing. He had witnessed them tear apart some of his finest officers, so wanted to avoid those bloodthirsty creatures. He turned to the broken fort and there, alone on his tocka with his red robes waving in the prairie breeze, Panzicosta spied his prize.

Delta-Six flew fast from the silver gates, keeping to an altitude below the lightning strikes, and took a second to study the battle valley when he passed. The evidence, combined with his min-sat's data, gave him all the detail he needed.

By the time he reached the live battle, he knew he had to concentrate on the enemy leader, so set his suit to camouflage and weaved through the slave soldiers and Lutamek. The instant he saw the Brakari leader he fired a trio of tiny missiles from his wrist launcher and hovered to watch them explode impotently against a white shield bubble.

Numbers flashed up in Delta-Six's vision and he prepared a new volley of missiles, designed to disrupt the wavelengths of the shield. He fired two, but he didn't get to see if they had worked. An explosion to his right sent him crashing to the ground, where he drew the attention of a large Brakari with smouldering claws.

'You're a long way from your army, human,' it growled and leapt in to attack.

Althorn retched and spat out what little liquid had come up from his stomach. He lay on his side, dribbling onto the compacted earth and willing himself to sit up.

Several hairy creatures with short limbs were mixing a cocktail of chemicals twenty paces away and the gaseous products were wafting in Althorn's direction. Was this how he would die? he thought. Were they preparing his sacrifice? The lack of food and water was making him delirious and images of dead kings and his sister washed through his mind. Her eyes had smiled at him as she died, he was sure.

A wind cleared the air and his head. He had to escape. Break free of this trap. He felt his wrists: no ropes. Had they left him untied?

A sound behind him made him freeze. Something was near. Althorn felt a tug on his hair, yanking his head back, and a tiny hand popped something in his mouth.

'Swallow,' said a familiar voice.

Althorn tried to shake his head. A bottle appeared and he drank.

'That'll fix the lungs and shield your mind. Brother, the other one.'

Althorn saw the soft brown scales of the creatures who had untied him in the cart.

The hand brought a new pill. 'This is for energy.'

Althorn swallowed it and asked for more water. His head felt clearer already. The giant legs of Belsang's creature were near and, beyond it, he saw the blue shells of the Brakari. He raised his head and saw a cracked white sphere around Belsang.

'Good, One-eye.' Both creatures moved into his line of vision.

'Thank you,' Althorn's voice was husky. He coughed.

'It is our pleasure.' One of the scaled creatures nodded. 'Now you can complete your mission.'

'Mission?' Althorn said.

'To kill the enemy commander.' The other brother gestured at Belsang. 'Good luck.'

Althorn nodded and his tiny helpers scuttled off on all fours. He blinked and stared around. He felt good now – really good! What was in those pills? Colours were more vivid and his leg muscles itched. He stretched and stood up. Humans, Sorean and Brakari were everywhere, fighting tooth and claw. He heard the shriek of tocka in the distance and swore he saw a Lutamek fighting. Deep in the centre, Althorn recognised Mata. The Maori's natural defences had been kicking in and he had turned into a mass of rough bark and barbed thorns.

A line of red light erupted from Althorn's left and he looked up in time to see the laser blast catch Belsang on his shoulder. He was weakening, he thought. If he was going to kill him he would have to do something different to last time. But what? He ignored the spiked armour on the Vaalori and thought about how to get Belsang off the giant.

His answer came when the brothers returned. The two armadillo-like mammals had popped up directly in front of the Vaalori.

'Dominus!' they called out in unison. 'We want to say how much we enjoyed your battle, but it's time for us to move on now. You gave it a good try – better than the last time but–'

Althorn saw Belsang's blue colour glow a little brighter but he stayed silent.

'Oh.' One of the brothers tilted his head to one side. 'No, your mental abilities won't work on us and, to be honest, I'm finding this body a bit cramped.' He looked at his brother. 'Shall we?'

'Yes, please!' the other replied.

'Whatever you are planning will fail.' Belsang's deep voice made Althorn step back. 'I'm aware of the human's recovery and your aid, but you will fail, he *will* be sacrificed and we will be victorious.'

Althorn felt a cold shiver run down his neck. Had he wasted the chance to get to Belsang? The brothers' distraction had been his last chance and he was just standing here, watching.

'No, sorry,' one of the brothers replied, 'this really is the end.'

A blue bolt of lightning leapt from Belsang's arm and smashed into the brother on the right, throwing him back twenty paces. His brother watched casually then turned to Belsang with his arms wide open. 'I really have enjoyed every–'

A second flash of electricity cracked and sent him flying back in a shower of sparks. This was Althorn's moment! He dashed forward as fast as he could, picked up the two prostrate animals and sped away. He was fast again – and getting faster! The thrill was back. His one eye was wide open as he dodged and jumped a wide circle around Belsang.

'What are you doing?' One of the brothers looked up.

'Throw us,' said the other.

'Throw you?' Althorn was weaving in and out of craters and avoiding the fighting soldiers. 'Where?'

'At Belsang!' they cried.

Althorn could see they were serious. He cut back and lobbed them through the air towards Belsang's Vaalori.

Then, and not for the first time in this land, Althorn was amazed. He skidded to a halt and watched as the small mammals ballooned in size in mid-air. Legs popped out, arms swelled and their heads mushroomed. By the time they hit the ground, they had transformed into two thickset, brown-scaled giants, bigger than any Lutamek. They barged into Belsang's five-legged steed with a double, shoulder-barging attack.

Belsang floated higher, seemingly unaffected by the charge, and zapped the brothers with more energy. But the power was weaker this time and they barely flinched. One leapt up and grabbed Belsang.

'Come here!' he shouted, as though playing a game. He squeezed the wriggling Brakari and breathed a red gas over him. 'Here you go, One-eye!' He threw Belsang at Althorn as though feeding a dog.

'Quick, One-eye!' the other brother shouted.

Althorn snapped to attention. He ran to where Belsang had landed and drew his knife. He could feel Belsang trying to slow him down with his mind but whatever the brothers had given him created a barrier. With Belsang's energy drained and no mental powers, Althorn could fight Belsang hand to hand, so he stabbed with his blade.

A blue claw slashed out, cutting Althorn's arm, but he sped up, circling and stabbing. Each turn, attack and parry took less than a split second as the Celt and Brakari fought at a speed few witnesses could follow. All Althorn could do was get nearer and go faster. A series of fists struck out at him, thumping him in the head or body, but Althorn's momentum was too great. Lightning flashes blinded him but he carried on spinning round, getting closer like a comet drawn to a star. All he saw was the blur of Belsang's blue body and his eyes. Althorn felt the pain in his empty eye socket and lunged with his blade: in and out. Tightening the circle and slicing fast.

It felt like he had cut Belsang a hundred new wounds but had no way to tell.

Then a burning flash took his energy and Althorn spun away in pain.

Mihran felt the draw of victory. His feet twitched as he resisted the urge to spur the tocka into action. No. He had to control his mind and keep calm. He had moved out of the ruined fort and onto the open grass for a clearer view of the battle, but needed to direct the troops to where they were most effective. The models had swung in their favour but the Brakari still outnumbered them and who knew what tricks they still held up their sleeves?

Speed is the essence of war, he thought. Take an unexpected route.

He had followed Li's advice and turned the tables on the Brakari: trapping them and quickly coming out to fight when Belsang had expected them to cower in the ruined fort. Now, the mass of human and Sorean soldiers fought hand to claw, while the archers and riflemen grouped in clumps as he had ordered, covering the foot soldiers. The British contingent of redcoats held their own on the left wing, combining their forces with Jakan-tar's fleet-footed fighters. Mata was rooted to the spot, attacking any Brakari who dared approach him, and Lavalle's cavalry had regrouped after driving into the wing of the army. Gal-qadan's tocka were doing the same on the other side. Which reminded Mihran of Gal-qadan's weapon. He looked for Crossley. Shoot fast and move, he had said, or risk sharing Li's fate. But he had yet to see the lightning snake across the battlefield.

Crossley, Mihran thought-cast. *Have you fired the weapon?*

Either the goddam thing's broke or it's a phoney, Crossley replied.

High-pitched shrieks drew Mihran's attention to the right where Gal-qadan's tocka leapt into action again: teeth bared and claws unleashed. Had Gal-qadan tricked him? He only had to wait a second to find out as an oscillating wave of energy ripped into the Brakari army, frying and splintering the soldiers in its path.

Gal-qadan was never going to give up his power.

Abandon it, Mihran ordered Crossley. *Use whatever weapon you find.*

Mihran ignored Crossley's swearing thought-cast response, which had been sent to all captains, and focused on his primary model: they could force a victory.

Commander. Samas' voice entered Mihran's head. *Gas attack!*

Mihran picked out Samas and saw a yellow mist flowing from a swarm of hairy beasts near Belsang. Movement in the sky caught Mihran's attention and a huge rock smashed next to a group of spearmen, sending them flying. He looked to the left flank – the surviving titans were still crawling with red worms which worked the last few catapults. Everyone was desperate for victory.

Push left, Mihran ordered Samas.

The yellow gas would divide the army if he wasn't careful. Why had he allowed himself to think about victory?

Come on! He willed Samas and his men to move faster.

Gal-qadan, Mihran thought-cast, *cut through and hold your side.*

If Gal-qadan's cavalry could push from the right, they could reverse the effect of the gas and corral the Brakari into a tight circle.

Commander, I see the Draytor. Olan's comment surprised Mihran.

Where? Mihran replied.

Near Samas' troops, Olan thought-cast. *In disguise but I see its true form.*

Mihran scanned the mass of human soldiers pushing away from the gas. Samas led his troops across a barren patch of grassland to join Sorean and the redcoats, while injured soldiers limped at the rear, away from the Brakari, who advanced with the mist, unaffected by the gas.

Where were Gal-qadan and the tocka? They needed to drive in before the foot soldiers were surrounded. Mihran saw one Brakari slashing and stomping at thin air. It winced as though struck and lashed out again. It had to be Sakarbaal, and there was Samas, ready to fight with his rock-fist and spear. How did he get there so fast?

Samas, Mihran thought-cast Olan. *The Draytor is Samas.*

Nobody will know which is which, Olan replied. *I will attack the Draytor.*

Good luck.

Mihran glanced at the second Samas but he had gone. On the ground he saw Sakarbaal's discarded trident next to his broken body. Mihran altered his model accordingly. The Carthaginian had been tricked and now the Draytor had disappeared.

More movement caught Mihran's eye – laser fire this time. Was that Bowman with Li's rifle or… Delta-Six? Had he returned or was it the shape-shifter? Nearby, three shapes were attacking a Brakari: taking it apart with sharp, speedy movements. The three ghost samurai Gal-qadan had bragged about. Here came Gal-qadan now with his tocka. Had the Draytor changed into a riderless tocka? Mihran rubbed his brow. He couldn't answer every question – he had to concentrate on the big picture.

Commander, a new voice thought-cast.

Mihran recognised it but immediately threw up a mental shield. That was the voice Belsang had used when he had given false information: Althorn's voice.

Mission accomplished.

The voice was followed by an image of a powder-blue body on the ground with a fixed look of shock on its face. Was this more trickery? Mihran looked to the centre of the battlefield and saw two monstrous, brown beasts pushing the giant Vaalori to one another like boys bullying a sheep. In front of them, Mihran could make out a short figure with a brown hood standing beside a tiny blue body.

Is it true? Mihran asked Althorn.

'I'm the Brakari leader now.' A deep voice made Mihran turn and miss Althorn's reply.

Mihran recognised the large, dark-blue Brakari from John's description. 'General Panzicosta,' Mihran said and remained motionless on his tocka.

'Dominus Panzicosta now, Commander.' His reply was accompanied by a snapping sound. 'Who will be your replacement after you die?'

Mihran's models shifted to accept the death of Belsang. 'When I die?' Mihran smiled as the thought sunk in. All the pieces he had meticulously positioned and manoeuvred like in a game of chess had played their part but one piece had been missing: himself. 'Many could replace me.' He knew it. All the men and women of his army had qualities he had never credited them for until he took the time to understand each individual.

Now it was his turn to fight.

'But tell me,' Mihran stared at his enemy, 'how did your leader die so easily?'

'Pah! Belsang?' Panzicosta moved forward slowly. 'He was a strong warrior once but came from an age of martial weakness. His doctor plied him with chemicals… once they had been removed and his mind tricks neutralised, he was running out of time. When he used the last of his energy he was little more than seven pairs of eyes stuck on a bag of shit.'

Mihran raised his eyebrows but shouldn't have been shocked by such contempt. He had assumed the Brakari army had underperformed because so many were enslaved, but now he could see the other half had followed through fear.

'And so he died, like so many others,' Mihran said.

He heard the snapping sound again and Panzicosta reared up on his back legs, causing Mihran's tocka to stir. 'Enough of your delays, human. It's time for you to die and for the victory I deserve.' He scuttled forward and raised his front claws.

Mihran's tocka pawed at the ground and its back muscles rippled, ready to pounce.

'No,' Mihran whispered. 'You need to sit this fight out, my friend.'

Mihran dismounted and released his long, maroon cloak to reveal his sabre. 'So be it.' He whispered a prayer to the clouds as he unsheathed the blade and took up a defensive pose.

As the huge shape of Panzicosta loomed closer with his large fore-claws raised, Mihran pushed his mind out to feel his thoughts. He winced, feeling their strength: fuelled by bitterness. Once he filtered the emotion away, Mihran could read Panzicosta's intentions.

Panzicosta leapt forward and smashed with both fore-claws, but they only met dry ground: Mihran had been quick and now stood to his side. His sword flashed and drew a white line across the Brakari's shell. Reading the next move, Mihran ran in the opposite direction, then rolled and sliced again, this time clipping one of Panzicosta's trailing legs.

The fight carried on with Mihran closing his mind off to his army and the battle around them. He focused on Panzicosta and avoided every blow, but his sword only scratched his enemy's shell. The Brakari didn't seem to be losing energy either, Mihran thought, as he paused to catch his breath. The next move was quicker than he anticipated and he took a glancing blow from Panzicosta's hammer-claw, bruising his side.

He had to concentrate and find a weak spot.

The tocka were clear of the explosions when the ground ripped apart. The rift was so large John had to take Lavalle's word that it cut around the ruined fort from flank to flank.

'I didn't know Crossley was capable of such endeavours.' Lavalle shook his head as they let their tocka rest.

'Well, he said he knew explosives,' John replied with a smile.

'Better than the first lot anyway,' Bowman added. 'At least these went off at the right time.'

'The only question is,' Euryleia jumped off the tocka to stretch her legs, 'how do we get over the trench to fight the Brakari?'

John had always found it hard not to stare at Euryleia, but now her four arms made it impossible.

'We'll use the bridges,' Lavalle replied. 'They left three bridges in the design – wide enough for the tocka, but too narrow for Brakari.'

'Do we have to go back in?' John asked. 'Can't we just fire at them from this side?'

Lavalle shook his head. 'They're too far away.'

He was right. Even from here, John could see the few titans that hadn't fallen in the chasm were fifty paces in and the rest of the Brakari army had pushed even closer to the fort. John's bullets would be useless from the edge of Crossley's rift.

'Do we spilt up or cross as one?' Euryleia asked as she stroked a riderless tocka. 'What?' she said when Lavalle stared at her.

'Is there something wrong with my tocka?' he asked.

Euryleia shrugged. 'Apart from its metal skin? No, but I can ride *and* shoot now.' She raised her arms and smiled. 'So do we split up or are we one army?'

'One.' Lavalle tore his gaze away. 'We'll take the central bridge and–' he stopped and closed his eyes.

Everyone waited while he thought-cast.

John checked the Lutamek cube and noticed some of the lights had changed.

'New orders.' Lavalle was back with them. 'We take the right bridge. Gal-qadan's horsemen will take the left bridge.' He pointed to the left flank, where John saw a host of tocka coming from the fort.

'And the central bridge?' John asked.

Lavalle gave a half smile. 'Let's just call that Crossley's bridge.'

'Oh.' John looked away and nodded.

Lavalle turned his tocka a full circle. 'Every soldier take a tocka. There are plenty. If you can't ride, sit behind a rider. Leave the injured here – we don't have time to get them to safety.' Euryleia shot Lavalle a look but the knight shook his head. 'This is a battle we have to win and time is running out.'

'Right then,' John unhitched the cart and spoke to the Sorean who had been riding it, 'looks like I'm with you. I might need a hand though.'

The Sorean pointed to its throat and offered him a hand. Must be a mute, John thought. The Sorean was stronger than he had expected and pulled him up with ease.

'It's quite comfortable,' John said and remembered Jess, his old carthorse. The others were following suit, with Bowman sitting nervously behind another Sorean as they headed off.

The bridge was only two paces wide and John kept his eyes to the sky as they crossed: one slip and they would fall into the rift, but the tocka was more nimble than John had realised and, by the time he opened his eyes, they were on the battlefield, approaching the enemy from the rear once again.

'Arrow formation!' Lavalle bellowed from the front. 'Drive in a wedge and split their forces!'

John looked to the left flank, where Gal-qadan's larger force was forming a similar triangular shape, and gripped the tocka with his knees. He started forming bullets in his gun-arm. What he really wanted to do was ride a wide curve and shoot from a distance like before.

'Aim for the light-blue enemy,' Lavalle shouted as the herd sped up in unison. 'They have softer shells!'

To John's right, a group of light-blue Brakari were retreating. John squinted and caught a glimpse of Millok's orange flashes. Were they her children? John felt a sensation of calm wash over him as he watched her retreat to safety. She would be happy, he thought, and smiled.

'Weapons raised!' Lavalle's voice rose above the rushing wind, shaking John.

The thrill of the speed sent waves of adrenaline through John's body. This was amazing! It reminded him of his grandfather's stories and John was a part of the action now. The tocka's muscles tightened like steel rope as it sped up and John imagined it baring its hideous teeth.

'Attack!' Lavalle shouted, and a barrage of fire was unleashed by the riders. The flash of Li's rifle in Bowman's hands lit the air and John fired, keeping the bullets coming. It was just like breathing now: he could do it without thinking. In and out. Build and fire.

The ground was uneven and scattered with deep holes from Crossley's explosions but, without the cart, John's tocka was fast and nimble and soon had a Brakari in its sights. John stopped firing and leant forward to grip the Sorean, who was hanging on the tocka's neck. Maybe this wasn't such a good idea after all, John thought, with his eyes clenched tight. He felt the tocka leap and release a wild shriek. Teeth gnashed and claws snapped and John felt his grip loosen. He saw the tocka bite the Brakari. He saw blue shell, green sky and burnt earth, teeth and claws. Then he was falling.

Time slowed as John spun through the air and manoeuvred to land on his back. The ground loomed up and past him… he was still falling. Swallowed by the earth.

Down.

Darker.

Until he hit the ground.

John rubbed his head with his good hand. His back had absorbed the fall but he was still dazed. He looked up to see the sky framed by a ring of broken earth.

'A crater?'

John sat up slowly. His head felt woozy but, if he strained his neck, he could see over the crater's edge. It was just like the crater from his war. His heart started racing. Wherever he looked he saw Brakari. They must have swarmed back to defend the rear lines and he was surrounded. He lay down and rolled to the safety of the crater's edge. Explosions sent tremors through the ground and the earth smelt of faeces. He heard a scratching sound and kicked his feet.

'Bloody rats.'

He clenched his eyes shut but all he could see were the eyes coming for him – always getting closer. Was he really here again? Mud had formed a crust on his gun-arm, which clicked nervously. What was he going to do?

'Get a grip, boy!' His grandfather's voice sent a chill through him.

John's eyes snapped open. All he saw was death. Broken bodies lay everywhere. Soldiers were pushing their bodies to their physical limits: straining every muscle and shell; twisting; stabbing; leaping; smashing.

Unpredictable, animal power.

John was panting, close to hyperventilating. The sound of his own rasping lungs was lost in the barrage of war surrounding him. The sound distorted and he mistook it for giggling. He turned, looking for the source of the noise.

'Joe?'

The giggling continued.

Was it another trick? Were the Frarex here to make a fool of him again?

'Silly…'

John turned. 'Who said that?'

The crater was empty.

'Silly Daddy.'

It was Joe's voice.

'Joe?' John closed his eyes and felt tears run down his cheeks.

The sounds around him faded away and he pictured his son running up to him with his beaming smile and his arms outstretched for a hug. Rosie was kneeling behind, smiling.

'Gotcha!' John caught Joe and picked him up in a bear hug.

Joe looked straight into his eyes. 'Daddy?'

'Yes, Joe?'

'It's time to fight now, isn't it?'

'Yes.' John took a second. If he couldn't be honest with his son, when could he? 'The trouble is I don't want to.'

'Silly Daddy!' Joe giggled. 'If I can do it, you can do it.'

'What?'

Joe climbed off John's lap and ran away. The sounds of battle came back as the vision faded.

'It's time to fight, Daddy!' Joe voice echoed away.

A pulsing vibration by John's arm distracted him. He opened his eyes. Explosions rocked his senses and he could see a yellow haze spreading across the battlefield. Gas mask! In a well-drilled manoeuvre, John swung his satchel round, grabbed his cloth gas mask and pulled it over his head. He looked up as a large silhouette stomped out of the yellow mist and fired a bolt of energy at an unseen enemy.

The Lutamek were free.

Mihran lay broken and bleeding into the grass. His breathing was laboured and pain flashed across his body when he moved. Beside him lay a severed claw. His last view of Panzicosta had been watching him limp away.

He looked up at the immense towers of the ruined fort pointing to the sky like giant fingers. His tocka had left to join its herd so he was alone. Mihran pushed his mind out one last time: less than half the humans survived but they still had a chance.

The Lutamek are free. A voice came to him. He didn't know who.

Mihran smiled. His job was complete. Belsang was dead and the Lutamek would fight on their side. The Brakari would lose. Victory was theirs. He didn't need a model to tell him that. He had served his purpose. If he had been part of someone else's plan then he had done well.

God is great, he thought, and closed his eyes.

Chapter 22

John didn't get a response from Mihran.

The Lutamek are free, he thought-cast again. *Commander?*

He couldn't explain it but it felt different now. Maybe the gas mask was interfering with his message? He tried someone else. *Lavalle, have you seen Mihran? The Lutamek are free.*

No response.

Crossley?

Anyone?

He was just saying the words in his mind now, he realised, as normal thoughts.

He stumbled forward. All he could see through his gas mask and the yellow mist were silhouettes and the tops of the fort towers. Shapes came and went in the deadly fog and John heard muffled screams and explosions. A gust of wind cleared the view and he saw three swordsmen he didn't recognise fighting a heavily armoured Brakari. Then the mist moved to reveal Olan in his gleaming, golden chest plate. Was that Panzicosta he was fighting? John's gun-arm clicked and he formed thick, armour-piercing bullets. Olan was swinging his axe low and aiming for the legs, but the gas drifted back.

John ran forward, jumping over a dying Brakari, and nodded up and down to see through the mask's glass eye holes. There! The gas thinned and Olan came back into view but now he was fighting Crossley.

Olan, John thought-cast, then shouted, 'Olan! What are you doing?'

The large Viking was too busy charging at Crossley, who was far quicker than John had given him credit for. The mist drifted in and, when the view came back again, Olan was fighting Mihran. A thin cloud of yellow passed between them and Olan was fighting John. He stopped and watched in confusion. There he was: dressed in khaki; his machine gun stuck on his arm; both legs back to normal.

Then it made sense: Olan was fighting the Draytor.

A large shadow to John's right made him turn as a Lutamek stepped out of the gas and said, 'Come with me, human.'

'But what about–' John pointed at Olan.

'You are needed elsewhere, the battle is over,' the Lutamek replied.

John saw the yellow mist drawing into vents on the robot's legs.

'If you're sure,' John said and followed it across the scarred grassland with the gas thinning about them. Slowly, the battlefield was coming back into view and he saw more Lutamek silhouettes, gathered in a circle.

'Here he is.'

A thin robot, a shade shorter than the rest and covered in red stripes, stepped forward. 'John Greene, I am Nine-five, the original Lutamek leader. I believe you have our Lombetulat unit?'

John looked from side to side, unsure how to reply. 'Is it safe to take off my mask now?'

'Yes,' Nine-five replied, 'we have neutralised the chemicals.'

John pulled the canvas bag off his head and felt the breeze cool his sweaty forehead. 'That's better. So, this combobulater?'

'The cube, John Greene, please hand me the cube you retrieved from Abzicrutia.'

'Oh, yes.' John swung his satchel round and pulled out the cube. 'They're all red now.' He pointed at the panel as he placed it in Nine-five's enormous metal hand.

'Thank you.'

John felt his cheeks redden. 'I'm glad you're free.'

The gas had dissipated now and, apart from a distant melee, the fighting had stopped.

'What now?' John asked.

Nine-five gestured to a patch of ground near the ruined fort and John felt rumbling through his good foot. He stared as the ground rose and cracked, sending clods of soil rolling away from its epicentre. Then the white obelisk John and his companions had longed to see pushed up through the earth like a new tooth. John was drawn to it along with scores of other soldiers, including Crossley, who had managed to pilfer a cigarette and was coughing between puffs.

'Hi,' John said but Crossley held up a hand as he produced another round of rapid, gurgling coughs.

He left the American to his own amusement and read the black words on the pristine white stone:

Here the allied forces of the humans, Sorean and Lutamek defeated the Brakari and Comglo pact.

'So those red worms were the Comglo?' Crossley said when he stopped coughing.

'I guess so,' John replied.

Crossley looked over to where the titans and their drivers lay dead under the weight of their catapults. 'Bad choice, Comglo!'

John looked around, taking it all in. 'So that's it then? The fighting's over?'

Other soldiers had been drawn to the obelisk, reminding John of what they had looked like when they first arrived: battle-weary and wearing confused looks. Delta-Six was among them, scanning the obelisk, just as he had done with the first.

'There are still a few mean-looking Brakari out there,' Crossley pointed to where a platoon of the blue-shelled arthropods had regrouped, 'but the Lutamek will take care of them.'

Nine-five and his band of emancipated soldiers were fanning out to create a barrier across the burnt battlefield between the Brakari and the humans and Sorean. The other slave soldiers had abandoned the field, fleeing across the prairie or taking shelter in the ruined fort.

'Who did we lose?' John asked.

Crossley's shoulders dropped as he listed the names. 'Li, Tode, Sakarbaal…'

John raised his eyebrows but didn't say anything.

'…and Kastor.'

'And Mihran?' John asked, feeling he knew the answer already.

Crossley nodded. 'His tocka led Lavalle to his body.' He nodded towards the fort. 'Some big Brakari bastard killed him apparently.'

John pictured Panzicosta and forced the thought away – it could have been any Brakari.

'We should pay our respects.'

Crossley looked John in the eye but said nothing.

'He gave us our victory and–' John said.

'I know,' Crossley cut him off. 'I just want to check a few things here first.'

'Okay, but keep an eye out for Euryleia – you have to see what happened to her.'

John patted Crossley on the shoulder and headed for the fort. He could hear Crossley coughing for several steps before his thoughts took him away. Who would be in charge now? One of the captains, John guessed. Samas probably. Bowman was too new to the post. Lavalle? The Black Sword had redeemed himself and the army's opinion of him must have changed. And what about Gal-qadan? Did his soldiers still follow him? They made up a good proportion of the survivors. John shook his head and peered up at the green clouds: there was plenty of light left but they were tired. Better to rest during the night and walk the following day, he thought.

'John Greene.' A deep voice made John jump and his head shot up from his daydreaming.

'Panzicosta?' John stumbled back.

He looked around for help but he'd wandered far from his army.

'You recognise me?' Panzicosta's voice was as demonic as John remembered. 'I worried you would forget me and we would have to be reacquainted.'

The large Brakari stalked slowly forward.

John backed up towards his army. There was no way he could outrun such a large beast and his bullets wouldn't stop Panzicosta if he charged. Still, he spun a few bullets in his gun-arm's chamber just in case.

'You know, I could bring those memories back for you.' Panzicosta was walking at an angle, trying to guide John into the shadows of the fort beyond.

'I remember enough.' John tried to hide his nervousness and anger.

'The memories Krotank and Millok took from you?' Panzicosta replied. 'Such cherished memories…'

John held his tongue. There was no point talking to this mad creature who was only here to feed his bloodthirst. Any sign of weakness or defiance fuelled his fun.

'I remember it all,' Panzicosta continued and John carried on stepping backwards. 'How easily your leg detached at the knee… once I stemmed the blood flow, it was only a matter of a few snips and it came away easily.'

John fought the urge to look at his metal leg. He could feel the anger burning in his stomach again – the need for vengeance for being taken from Joe and for his injuries. But he knew when he was outgunned.

'I could show you again, would you like that?' Panzicosta stopped walking.

John saw tocka swinging over from the right. Were they looking for Mihran's body? Bowman was there, with Lavalle and Euryleia. Would they see him in time?

A sharp snapping sound made John turn as Panzicosta clacked his shells.

'Answer me, human!' He lunged forward and swiped at John, who fell back and rolled over.

John scrambled away, keeping his eyes on the Brakari.

'I could make your death quick – like I did with your commander.'

'You killed Mihran?'

Saying it out loud made it real. Another reason for vengeance.

Panzicosta advanced. 'He put up a good fight.' He raised a blue arm stump where one of his main claws had once snapped menacingly. 'This will grow back. Your commander will not.'

John saw the tocka approaching behind Panzicosta, suggesting they had seen him. If he could keep Panzicosta talking, he would be in with a chance.

'You've lost!' John shouted. 'So just give up… leave me alone.'

'Why?' Panzicosta's head twisted at an odd angle. 'We were having such fun before, and our time is limited. I need something to take the pain away – the pain of loss.'

'The pain of loss?' John shouted and couldn't control his emotions any more. 'I'll tell you about loss – losing my wife, losing my son, my friends and my whole bloody world!'

'I don't give a Vaalorian shit about your losses, you little soft-bellied worm.' Panzicosta's mouth-pieces sharpened against each other and two of his smaller bladed arms unfurled. 'This is war! Fight me if you want, but either way you are going to die!' He flew forward and slashed at John, who ducked and rolled. A blade scraped against John's back and he fired his gun as soon as he saw the black mass above him, then scrambled away as a club-claw came crashing down.

As quickly as he could, John was on his feet and running towards the tocka. Panzicosta gave a howling roar and John did not dare look back.

'Bowman!' John shouted. 'Three! Use three!'

It was useless, they couldn't hear him.

Feeling the ground shake behind him, John dropped and rolled into a small pit. Black blades and claws came crashing down around him, but John had escaped. He crawled away, avoiding another swipe, and ran as fast as he could. He looked back to see Panzicosta hadn't followed him. He had seen that the incoming tocka had turned to face them: twenty of them bearing down on him.

'Bowman!' John shouted. 'Use number three!' He held up three fingers.

Panzicosta stretched tall on his legs and was making an odd, low sound. Then segments of his shell fell off. Was he dying? No, it had to be the enhancement Millok had mentioned – something Panzicosta didn't want to use. Lumps of dark shell fell away, revealing a pure white body beneath with tiny electric-blue ripples running over it. Then, out of his back plates, four large wings unfolded and pumped full of blood.

The tocka were still out of firing range but closing by the second.

'Bowman!' John held up three fingers. 'Three!'

Panzicosta's transformation had been quick and he stood like a huge brilliant-white dragonfly. With little effort, Panzicosta's wings flapped and he lifted off the ground. He opened his jaws and spat electric-blue fireballs at the tocka, sending riders spinning into the grass and setting the tocka ablaze.

John snapped into action and fired his gun. Long, thin bullets ripped through the air and tore into Panzicosta's tail and wings. Panzicosta spun around in response and released a fireball at John. It exploded near his feet, sending John stumbling backwards.

Panzicosta opened his mouth to fire again but paused mid-air as a bright burst of light shot from the tocka. The energy bolt hit Panzicosta in the back and he spent a motionless second in the air before crashing to the ground like a stone.

John scrambled to his feet and ran to get to Panzicosta before the tocka tore him apart. He held his arm up at the riders. 'That's enough! You've got him!' He waved Lavalle's cavalry down.

'Setting three?' Bowman asked, as he pulled up to John.

'It's the one Li used on Millok. It froze him.' John was still catching his breath. 'When it wears off he won't be able to walk for hours.'

Lavalle and the other tocka pulled up alongside Bowman.

'You want to kill him yourself?' Lavalle asked, with a sideways glance at Euryleia.

John looked at Panzicosta. His mouthparts were the same, if frozen, but his body was the opposite of before: white and soft. John placed the barrel of his gun-arm on the centre of Panzicosta's forehead. He remembered letting the Draytor go and remembered the carnage it had caused on the battlefield. Doing something or doing nothing seemed to have an effect later on, so what should he do now? The battle was won. John had his victory, so he could leave through the silver gates, wherever they led. That was the only reason he had fought, so would killing Panzicosta make a difference?

Joe was dead and there was no going home.

John formed a long, spiked bullet and stared into Panzicosta's numerous eyes. Panzicosta's face twitched and, for a second, John felt sorry for him. He knew he could still see and hear him, just as John had when he'd been tortured, and John felt a wave of power. One bullet and Panzicosta was gone, forever. No more threat. The memory and the fear would disappear and John would be one step closer to getting revenge on those who had brought him here.

Or would he?

Panzicosta had been brought here too, against his will.

John took his gun-arm off and spoke to Panzicosta. 'You're not my real enemy.'

'Good choice, John,' Euryleia said.

John looked to Lavalle. 'If we move fast we can get to the silver gates before sundown.'

'Are you our new leader now?' Crossley stepped forward and put an arm around him, ''cos God knows we need one,' he cast a glance at Lavalle, 'and I'm not sure who can fill Mihran's shoes.'

'Samas will lead us,' Lavalle replied to Crossley's barbed comment. 'He will lead us to the silver gates and complete our journey.'

The alliance of humans, Sorean and Lutamek wound its way off the battlefield, bound for the silver gates, led by Samas, who talked with Nine-five and Jakan-tar. Lutamek scouts were chasing the surviving Brakari back to Abzicrutia, giving the army a clear path ahead, while other Lutamek had constructed carts to transport the entire army to the gates before sundown. Althorn lay prostrate on a cart next to a burnt-out tree stump, which John assumed was Mata, Dakaniha was on a tocka with Gal-qadan's cavalry, which he kept separate from Lavalle's, and Osayimwese was walking with Olan.

Delta-Six walked with them and soon picked John out. 'John Greene!' he said and joined him.

The athletic man looked different; his skin had a metallic shine and he seemed more relaxed.

'Delta-Six,' John replied and put his good hand in his pocket. It was the electric shock that had caused his arm to melt into his gun after all.

Delta-Six pointed at his gun-arm. 'I'm told it works?'

John nodded. 'It can do some damage,' he said. 'How about your changes?'

'Let's just say they're interesting…' Delta-Six smiled.

It was the first time John had seen him smile and he relaxed a little. 'You must be looking forward to getting back to your war now?'

Delta-Six stared at John for a second, as though holding something back, then said, 'Actually, no. I'm not sure where I want to go now.'

'But you wanted to fight.'

'I was needed and I had a duty but…' Delta-Six shook his head.

'We all had to fight in the end,' John said. 'This land made soldiers of us.'

'Made?' Delta-Six asked. 'I was born to be a soldier.' John could see pain in his eyes. 'If we weren't born to fight, why are there so many warriors here? It must be in our nature.'

'But that means we don't have a choice,' John replied. 'That we have to fight… but we always have a choice.'

Delta-Six nodded.

'Delta-Six!' Samas shouted. 'There's someone here you need to meet.'

'It was good to talk,' Delta-Six said.

'Yeah, bye,' John said, and watched him join Samas and the Lutamek.

John scanned the rest of the army. There were some faces he didn't recognise: two enormous, brown-scaled creatures and an Asian swordsman.

'Who's that?' John caught up with Crossley and asked him.

'Oh, that's Isao.'

John didn't recognise the name.

'The samurai,' Crossley explained. 'He was one of the spirit warriors Dakaniha told me about.'

'Oh.' John remembered seeing the ghostly swordsmen through his gas mask. 'And the two big brown…?'

'Armadillos?' Crossley laughed and shook his head. 'Dunno, Althorn brought them along. Hey, did you hear about what that swindler Gal-qadan did?'

John shook his head.

'He gave me a duff weapon and kept the real thing, you know, the one he found. Then five minutes ago I saw him giving it to that one-eyed giant.'

'Peronicus-Rax?' John asked. 'He's here too?'

'Yeah, the watcher. So I just walked over, cool as anything, and gave him the dud weapon too. Even Gal-qadan couldn't…'

Crossley's words faded as John watched the people walking with them, sharing stories and showing off trophies, talking of lost comrades and heroic events. They passed three Lutamek pulling a cart loaded with large metal eggs, each one nearly as big as him.

By the time the silver gates came into view, some hours later, the green clouds were tinged peach as the sun started to set. They descended a long hill past a squalid encampment teeming with more bizarre alien soldiers, surrounded by a wall of mist. In the distance, John saw the shadow of Abzicrutia and realised how close he'd been to the gates.

'Jeez, look at that!' Crossley pointed to where a wind had pulled back the mist to reveal the gleaming silver gates.

John had never seen anything so large or beautiful.

'They're set in glass walls,' Crossley said, when the cart slowed down.

John peered up at the walls, which disappeared into the clouds above and the mist, which ran as far as he could see on either side. 'Will they open?' he asked, as they joined the queue Lavalle was organising.

Crossley shrugged. 'Who knows.'

'Stop!' A shout rang out, followed by a wild roar of a hundred warriors baying for blood.

'Oh, hell.' Crossley peered past the Lutamek. 'Looks like we've got trouble.'

John squinted. Ahead of the line, Samas talked to a small army carrying an array of lethal-looking alien weaponry.

'I will deal with them.' Peronicus-Rax lumbered past with his cascade of weapons clattering with each step.

Crossley gave John a look. 'He's probably in cahoots with them, you know, wants to take a cut of whatever we pay.'

John shook his head. 'No, he may be selfish but he wouldn't do that.'

'Really?' Crossley raised his eyebrows.

'Look.' John pointed to where Peronicus-Rax stood with the aggressors. He unclipped one of the long, silver weapons and handed it over.

'He's done that before.' Crossley stood with his hands on his hips.

'Who cares?' Lavalle had overheard. 'He's bought us safe passage.'

'Whatever,' Crossley replied, and the army walked past the grinning alien soldiers, tinkering with their new toy. Crossley turned to John. 'That was *my* weapon – he sold them a dud,' he chuckled, but the sound of power coursing through the glinting rifle made Crossley frown. 'Ah, goddamit.'

'Don't worry,' John said. 'We're leaving now.' He pointed at the enormous silver gates. 'You won't need it anyway.'

'Why? What do you think's through there? The land of milk and honey?'

'No, I…' John had suppressed his true wishes since Li had told him about Joe's full life. There was no way of going home, but there was always a chance, wasn't there? 'I don't know.'

'I don't either but it won't be pretty.'

'What do you mean?'

'Well, Althorn said his mates, the two huge armadillos, come in and out when they feel like a fight,' Crossley said.

'They come back in?' John didn't understand. 'Why would they want to come back into this hellhole?'

'Exactly!' Crossley replied.

John saw the two huge brothers at the front of the file. They were enormous, even bigger than the Lutamek.

'Do you think they have to win a battle every time they want to leave?' John asked.

'Maybe,' Crossley replied. 'I haven't seen Peronicus-Rax doing much fighting though and it looks like he's joining us.'

A motley group of malnourished soldiers of various shapes and forms watched on with envy as the victory parade passed through the encampment.

'Poor bastards,' Crossley said.

These were the losers, John thought, and tried in vain to remember some of the names of the armies who had lost. Some were lone warriors, others huddled with their comrades. Was this what would become of the Brakari? John wondered. And Panzicosta?

An explosion made him turn to see a cloud of smoke where the guerrillas had been standing. Bodies lay in piles around a small crater and the nearest alien soldiers were rushing in to pilfer from the dead gangster clan.

'Hurry up!' Lavalle beckoned them over and John and Crossley jogged through the camp to where their leaders stood at the seam of the two silver gates.

'Their prices were getting too high,' John overheard Peronicus-Rax explaining to Nine-five.

'So, what now?' Crossley shouted.

'Now we pass through.' Peronicus-Rax gestured to Samas, Jakantar and Nine-five, who pressed their hands against the metal of the seam.

A low rumble shook the air and John took a step back as a dark line ran down the seam and released steam. Beside John, Crossley was coughing. Deep clicks resonated from the wall above as the two enormous doors slid apart, sweeping up into the walls on either side. John craned his neck, trying to get a view through, but all he could see was mist. He gave up and ran his metal toes through the ash on the ground, which reminded him of the soldier with the red armband Delta-Six had zapped on the first day.

'And now we walk through,' Peronicus-Rax said and the three leaders walked with him into the mist.

The nearest soldiers followed and the host of Lutamek, Sorean and humans slowly disappeared.

John cast a glance back at the land that had been their home for the last fourteen days. The green clouds turned a shade of purple and Abzicrutia shimmered orange in the distance.

'Here goes then.' Crossley gave John a wink and they stepped through together.

The mist was cool and refreshing. John turned to Crossley but couldn't see him. Was this it? Am I going home now? he thought. Will I walk through the mist and find myself back in Flanders? Back to the mud, the rats and the bombs? John's gun-arm clicked.

You are strong, he told himself. You're ready for anything now.

Five steps later, a new world opened up before John. He blinked and cupped his eyes with his good hand. The light was intense after so many days under a clouded sky and, after a few more steps, the immense landscape became clear. On the horizon a blood-red sun set the sky aflame with vibrant oranges and pinks.

'Jeez!' Crossley was next to him. 'I need my shades.'

John rubbed the tears from his eyes. Silhouettes of the leaders and other soldiers were ahead of him and the vast landscape took shape as his eyes grew accustomed to the light. It was larger than any view he'd ever seen and seemed to go on forever. Hills and ravines flowed away from their position. Everything was blurred in the distance and the colour of the setting sun, which sat minutes from the horizon, didn't help, turning everything orange.

John walked to where the leaders talked with Peronicus-Rax.

'...only as far as the second ridge. At least three days to that point.'

'And the domes?' Lavalle asked.

'What domes?' John focused on the distant hills. They were symmetrical and glowed as though reflecting the sun's rays. Were they domes?

'They look like huge greenhouses if you ask me,' Crossley said, shading his eyes like John was.

'As far as I can tell they're the same size as our dome,' Peronicus-Rax said, 'but I've never ventured that far.'

'Our dome?' John asked.

He felt his neck crawl. Slowly, he turned back to look at the silver gates, which were hard to see through the mist, but the surrounding walls were clear: curving away to the left, the right and straight up.

They had just walked out of an immense dome.

A blue bolt of electricity caught John's eye as it leapt out of the left gate and turned a silhouette into a pile of ash.

'Coward,' a voice said.

John looked up to see one of Althorn's giant armadillo allies. 'He didn't fight,' he explained.

John nodded.

Crossley said, 'So the rules about the land were true? Fight or die.'

'And all of that land was inside a huge dome?' John asked, and shook his head.

'Looks like it.' Crossley was staring up, open-mouthed. 'I'd guessed something was up from what I saw underground, but I never expected it to be this big. Jeez!'

John's eyes followed the glass wall up and, scattered across the dusky sky, he saw what looked like dozens of small moons. 'What is this place?' he asked nobody.

A hissing sound signalled the closing of the silver gates and John turned back to the long view. He could see everything clearly now. The distant horizon was an undulating line of curved domes. Too many to count.

Nine-five's voice caught John's attention. 'You're saying the entire planet is covered with these domes and the orbiting spheres could be related?'

'Yes, it's possible,' Peronicus-Rax said, and pointed at one of the nearest domes. 'Look – another species is coming in.'

A dark shape descended from the orange sky. If the size of the dome was anything to go by, this aircraft was immense. The whole army watched as it gently landed on a flat landing platform on top of a distant dome.

'That's all we'll be able to see from here,' Peronicus-Rax said. 'Everything else happens inside.'

Questions were coming thick and fast from everyone now, but the leaders had priority. What happened now? Why were there no obelisks? Where should they go? How could they get food? Were they allowed back into the dome?

Peronicus-Rax and the armadillo brothers answered where they could.

'Stop!' Peronicus-Rax eventually yelled, and held up his huge hands. 'All I know is we were brought here to fight.'

'But we've fought already and won!' Samas said. 'Who brought us here and what do they plan for us next?'

'I don't have all the answers,' Peronicus-Rax replied. 'Everyone brought here is of a warrior-class species and has to fight. However, I have heard of the Ascent.'

'The Ascent?' John repeated. 'Is that who brought us here?'

Peronicus-Rax blinked his solitary eye. 'I don't know.'

'So this place was just some bloody gladiator's arena?' Crossley asked, pointing at the dome.

Nobody replied. The truth was sinking in for everyone. They were soldiers. They had to fight.

Just like when they had crowded around the first obelisk, Althorn stepped forward, now wearing a cloth eye patch. 'I believe everything within the dome – our enhancements, our battles, our alliance – has simply been our training.'

'Our training?' Crossley almost screeched.

'Training for what?' John asked.

'To get used to your new abilities,' Peronicus-Rax replied.

John squinted at the gigantic domes beyond. 'And to get ready for the next battle.'

THE END

Read on for an exclusive extract of the next book in the Origin Trilogy, *Survival*.

Extract from *Survival*

Find out what happens next by reading this extract from *Survival* (Book Two of the Origin Trilogy)

John was desperate for answers but couldn't make sense of the diagrams and numbers on the screen in front of him. Delta-Six had been able to read them and had pressed the buttons on the desk to change the symbols on the screen but he'd disappeared to search for more information.

'We haven't got long until the Synchronisers come back,' Osayimwese hissed.

'I know!' Crossley replied before John could. 'I'm still searching… Delta-Six said telomere latency, right?'

'Yeah,' John replied, vaguely remembering the conversation, and Osayimwese nodded.

They had found records for other species brought into the dome but they needed to find details on humans, Lutamek or Sorean and then transfer everything to the thin sliver of metal Ten-ten had given them. Just thinking about it gave John a headache: his reading skills had never been great and, after he'd left school, he hadn't had much need for them delivering veg or defending his trench.

'It would be quicker if Delta-Six was here,' Osayimwese said.

'Sure it would,' Crossley replied, 'but he's off on one of his missions, so…'

John looked around the curved room for any telltale shadows. Rarkin, the Sorean, was outside, tending to the young Lutamek that had brought them to the top of the dome using the helium-filled sac on its back, so any shadow would belong to Delta-Six or one of the robotic Synchronisers who ran the dome cap.

The building was bigger than any he had seen before – an immense doughnut-shaped structure that capped the dome top and matched the locking connectors they had seen on the transportation ships. The hole in the centre gave them access to the dome to deposit the new soldiers.

John stared through the rectangular window above the computer screen at the locked-in ship. He was still amazed at the thought that he and his friends had gone through the same process these squid-like creatures had endured when woken from stasis. They were still being processed by the look of things, which bought them more time.

'Ah, what's this?' Crossley said and John leaned over to see a list of names, which he guessed he could read thanks to the translator fungus in his brain.

'Looks like us,' John said with a smile and tried to find his name.

'Just save it to that… piece of metal,' Osayimwese said.

'Already on it,' Crossley replied and slipped the grey sheet into the slot as Delta-Six had shown them. 'Just move that there… and some more files here… Lutamek, Sorean, the new guys are the Tathon apparently… and here's the Brakari.' He gave John a wink. 'Might as well have them too, eh?'

John looked away and wondered what had happened to Millok and General Panzicosta? He moved to a new screen that showed images of life inside the dome, beneath the haze of cloud that obscured the Synchronisers' base.

A sound made him turn.

'Do you hear that?'

'Yes.' Osayimwese was already in a defensive position, holding his spear and eggshell dagger. 'Someone is running this way.'

'What do we do?' John asked. 'That's the way back out.'

'I'm still saving the information,' Crossley said.

An elongated shadow appeared on the distant curved wall as the rapid footsteps came nearer, followed by a distant shout.

'Retreat!'

'That's Delta-Six,' John said and looked at Crossley. 'Come on, something's up.'

'Alright, alright!' Crossley replied and pulled the metal sheet out of the computer.

Delta-Six rushed into view and sped up to them. 'Come on, we're running out of time!'

Crossley handed him the metal and ran his hand over it.

'Is it the Synchronisers?' Osayimwese asked.

'No,' Delta-Six replied, 'I... there's been a malfunction and I need to communicate with Command.'

A flashing light on one of the screens caught John's eye and he saw an image of the new hilltop in the dome, now covered with the octopus-like creatures from the ship. They were all shaking and writhing in a way that reminded John of Doctor Cynigar, the Brakari who had mutated.

'What happened?' Crossley asked.

Delta-Six looked away as he spoke. 'I... attempted an interface with the sequencing technology to understand how the rejuvenation process may have stimulated our mutations, only...' He looked at each of the men. 'I inadvertently increased the parameters and...'

'You boosted the power?' Crossley asked.

Delta-Six nodded. 'We have to get out of here before the Synchronisers work out what's happened.'

On the screen, John saw the results of the boost as the tentacled, large-eyed creatures' bodies warped in size and shape as their mutated DNA struggled to assert itself.

Acknowledgements

A huge thank you to the pledgers listed in this book. *Darwin's Soldiers* only exists as a result of your generous patronage, for which I am humbled and eternally grateful.

Those who deserve special mention include the *Darwin's* cheerleaders, Tracy, Mike, Claire and Wayne, and all my friends and colleagues at The Book Service and at Penguin Random House who championed the book and tiptoed around my desk during my writing sessions.

I am indebted to the team at Unbound who made bringing *Darwin's Soldiers* to print an incredibly smooth process. Thank you for believing in me and, Kwaku, thanks for being there for my frequent Friday questions. My gratitude to my structural editor, Hal Duncan, who pulled the novel up by its bootstraps and knocked it into shape, and to my copy editor, Derek Collett, for ironing out the grammatical creases.

To my fellow authors in the Unbound Facebook group and at Suffolk New College – your honesty, creativity and humour have been a boost on many occasions. Thank you for your advice and for sharing your knowledge.

And for the three most special people in my life, who entertain and inspire me on a daily basis. To my gorgeous wife, Cath, thank you for listening and giving me the space to create. And our sons, Harry and Oscar, may your curiosity always remain limitless!

Bonus material

Thirteen Sevens

Michael Hunt

They call me Seven. It's a throwback to the recent Genera wars. Four hundred thousand troops engaged in a tragic waste of human life, and only thirteen survivors, not all from the same side.

As a captain I had several companies under my command throughout that short but bloody fiasco. I lost every man. Initially, I was seen as a lucky charm but I became a figure of fear: drafts to my units meant certain death.

My aptitude for survival and close-combat instincts marked me out as a mascot. Conversely, my men were never so fortunate. Even the best of them fell. Then the rumours started. They said I was shielding myself with my team for my own survival; called me Captain to my face but coward behind my back.

It really wasn't like that. I had a kind of sixth sense; a way to know what my opponents would do next and how not to be on the end of a knife or bayonet. Even with high velocity projectile weapons; pistols, rifles and, in the latter stages, lasers. I could dodge anything.

Snipers couldn't take me out. It's not that I could tune into their minds – nothing so complex – but my senses picked up the vibrations in the air around me. My mind translated those agitations as acceptable or life threatening. In the early days I took a few wounds as this nascent ability developed. The distances to which I could detect became greater until I maxed out at around one klick. Inevitably, the fear among the troops grew: I was doing the impossible.

It all felt so natural; I just moved out of the way of anything that was a corporal threat. Curious about the rumours, I jacked into a video feed which exposed the reason I was shunned. It was as if I was displacing myself from one place to another in a split second; almost zapping from point to point in feats of innate self-preservation. No deft dodging movements, just a blurring between two positions, the threat passing by or through me but rendered ineffective. I was considered inhuman.

After the carnage, thirteen of us remained, marked out by our factional colours. I was alone for our side but there were twos and threes in other armies. Five factions, thirteen individuals and we couldn't kill each other.

The Battlemaster Generals brought the combat to an end, and the politicians divided the perceived spoils. War is nonsensical to grunts on the ground; we just have the necessary incentives and the will to execute orders. However, it seems that they got what they wanted: an elite squad of enhanced-ability soldiers. Something in our modified DNA allowed us to perform miracles. The whole war had been a smokescreen and a sifting process, a cull in order to reveal the results of their joint, covert experiments.

We are Darwin's theory taken to another level, beyond the talismanic sixth sense; we are Sevens, every one of us. We want to know why.

The Rage Machine

Kerensa Jennings

Her eyes had started to rearrange themselves on her face, puffy and swollen.

I have known rage. I have felt hate. I have faced the black.

She was murmuring under her breath, busying herself through foggy tears.

The lab was gleaming with chrome reflections bouncing light off every surface. Small, neat silver bottles lined up on shelves, their classifications documented in codified sequences.

A wall chart, breathtaking in complexity, showed concentric circles plotted with DNA helixes and twisted correlations of data criss-crossing like lacework.

Dr Harlow worked swiftly and efficiently, unblinded by the relentlessness of her crying eyes. Pipettes were administered, Petri dishes prepared, test tubes labelled.

She glanced from time to time at the photographs on the wall. Each and every one a moment in history, an emblem of the darker side of humanity. There was a picture of a sole, valiant protester, standing in front of a line of tanks at Tiananmen Square. A photo of a young girl running in Vietnam, scarred with the effects of napalm. One showing Jackie Kennedy's face the moment her husband was shot. The bassist from the band The Clash, thrashing his guitar onto a stage.

Defiance. Fear. Horror. Rage.

Each and every photograph painted a story. Each and every photograph encapsulated an emotion.

To an untrained eye, the dissonance – the incongruity – of these pictures hanging in a sterilised white laboratory was striking.

To anyone educated in art history, or professional photography, the images told a different story. In every case, the photos on the wall were the very first manifestations of each image, produced in person by the photographer, developed straight from the roll. What at first glance looked like poster art were carefully preserved, lab-sealed, forensically prepared originals.

It turns out cellulose acetate has a secret attribute which can only be accessed through a rare and complex process. Dr Harlow had discovered that using holographic extraction, quantum atomic transmitters and laser telemetry, subatomic particles of subject DNA can be accessed to release the biometric data of emotions. This happens because of a chemical mirroring that takes place at the moment of photography, meaning minute indicators can be scraped, preserved and distilled, like the essence of a perfume. Each one encapsulating the core emotion of the subject at the moment of photography.

Dr Harlow had perfected the technique, having stumbled upon it quite by accident while analysing the chemical structure of a photograph one empty Tuesday afternoon. She had been struck by a luminosity it appeared to have.

Like it's alive… she thought.

Today she followed the routine she had established, extracting the essence of emotion, growing it in a culture, then gently injecting it into the pupae of butterflies.

On closer inspection, rows and rows of clustered brown pouches were breathing, softly, hanging behind temperature-controlled glass.

Dr Harlow was breeding a new species of killer butterfly, intoxicated with defiance, fear, horror and rage.

She christened the pupae incubator The Rage Machine.

Any day now, the first specimens would emerge to start wreaking hate into the world. Well, it was what the world deserved. No-one understood. No-one but her. The weight of responsibility for what she had to do anchored an ache in her heart. She had to save the planet, and the only way to do that was to exterminate humankind.

She had visions of a black, vibrating cloud, spiralling into the sky to take its revenge. In the twist of a DNA helix, she had captured the nexus of man's hate.

The butterflies would fly. And rage would perfume the air.

Follow the Light

Andrew Checker

Torin's consciousness returned slowly. His head throbbed and it took several minutes for lucid thought to be called forth. He knew he was dead and yet he felt euphoric.

He could feel the reassuring hardness of his sword hilt in his hand and he smiled. Valhalla! He had made it to the blessed land. He could not remember how, or where, he had died but he was sure it would have been in glorious battle. He would not be here otherwise, with a wonderful eternity of fighting, feasting and drinking until Ragnorak, the end of days, was finally upon him. His brothers and his father Leif would be here too. He would find them.

Torin sat upright and opened his eyes to take in the landscape around him. All was alien and the half-light seemed strange, as if it would persist, never becoming lighter or darker. He seemed to be alone. There were hills, plains and some patches of vegetation but none seemed familiar. Still, no one ever said that Valhalla had to look like home or any other place for that matter. As long as there were warriors to challenge him and a warm hearth with plenty of mead for after the day's slaughter, it would do.

The throbbing in his head started to subside but the lights that had played on the inside of his eyelids would not stop making strange patterns whenever he blinked. He decided to close his eyes again for a few moments and try to let the lights clear.

But the lights would not clear. Instead they began to move and form vague, disconcerting shapes. They formed hideous figures wearing ghoulish masks of different designs; some had human faces yet many had unnatural misshapen underworld heads. He opened his eyes. The lights did not stop but faded slightly, allowing his normal vision to prevail.

The lights flashed again violently and took over his vision once more, drawing his attention to a point behind him. Torin avoided the killing thrust aimed at his middle by quickly twisting and guiding the slender blade past his body with the hilt of his sword. Using the momentum of his assailant to trip him down to the ground was simple; his enemy was not an accomplished combatant. Torin pushed the point of his sword into the prone body before him until it stopped moving. A twist of his blade made sure. His first victory in Valhalla! He bent over to inspect his kill. It was one of the ghoulish figures from his light visions. The one with the insect eyes and cone-shaped cheeks. His weapon was some kind of half-sword strapped to a wooden shaft, inlaid with fine metals. A clumsy weapon.

Crouching down into some thick foliage, he closed his eyes again and this time embraced the patterns of light, inviting them to show him more. With a little practice he could cast out into the half-light and locate the presence of other beings in the alien landscape. He already knew that the lights were watching over him to alert against any assassin closing in from behind. Valhalla was full of surprises. With this new sense he would be able to defeat all enemies of any form and become a legend amongst his kinsmen! It seemed that death was granting him more than life ever did. The afterlife was going to suit him well.

Patrons

Peter Abbott
Eli Allison
Ricardo Alves
John Auckland
Casey Berson
Lizzie Bibby
Jane Carrell
Kaval Chadha
Victoria Chaplin
Siobhan Clark
Jason Cook
Amanda Dack
Jonathan Davison
Penguin Random House Distribution
Chris Dobbie
Grant Doole
Neil Farley
Ruth Fitzgerald
Polly Foster
James Franklin
Raymond Hamilton
Derek Hartwig
Richard Irving
Nick Jarrold
Vaughan Knight
Carol Limer
Costas Louca
Jemma Maddams
Carlo Navato
Ian Orchard
Kevin Osborne
Emma Page

Matteo Palacios
Peter Ross
Steve Routledge
Malcolm Sharp
Harry & Oscar Sharp
Annette Smith
Gary T Smith
Rashi Soni
Daniel Spencer
Rupal Sumaria
Heidi Woodgett